To Laura,

Enjoy the history + mystery

Islands of Vengeance

The fall of the Pequot Nation

By Robert E. Keating

"For we must consider that we shall be a city upon a hill.
The eyes of all people are upon us…"

Governor John Winthrop
Massachusetts Bay Colony – 1630's

"We shall *all* be starved."

Miantonomo – Grand Sachem of the Narragansett Nation

For Brianne and Kelly

PROLOGUE

The Song of the Sorceress

*   *   *

Circe's brilliant, silvery-green eyes eagerly scanned the briny sea that stretched out for miles before her. Alone on her island of solitude, she was prepared for battle. She knew the winds and the tides of Long Island Sound as well as the English captains, and what direction they would come - if they had the courage to come at all.

The sun beat down on her sandy beach reflecting light in blinding veils of shimmering silver. The tide, in waves of blue and pale green, rolled toward her. White foam hissed all around like whispers of a thousand ghosts. The fragrance of the ocean filled the air as the Sorceress of Fisher Island stood out in all her glory. Her toned muscles, bronzed skin, powerful hands, and long amber hair added to the enigma she had become.

Circe watched and waited. She wanted just one more tall ship to appear, but none would come on this clear beautiful afternoon. And that meant no one would die at her hands on this day. She glanced down at her weapons concealed in the sand. Too hard to spot by those coming in from the sea yet close enough for her to snatch up and wreak havoc. She was pleased with her vigilance and preparedness.

Circe wet her lips.

"Where are you, my love?"

These words came from a longing in her heart for a man that she loved. They dangled in the thick, salty air and rose to where seagulls soared in playful circles. The birds seemed to understand, as they had heard these very words many times before.

Circe turned her attention to the sky for a sign. As clear as the sea, it was a profound statement of Mother Earth's magnificence. And where the sky met the ocean, a dark pencil-thin line marked the very edge of the earth. When her question failed to bring an answer, her disappointment turned to anger.

"Where are you, my nemesis?" she asked, this time with a hatred emerging from a dark corner of her mind.

"Will this be the day?"

An unexpected cool breeze washed over Circe's face and bare shoulders, it was a sign that evening would soon arrive. She closed her eyes. Turning her face into the ocean air she inhaled deeply. There was no scent of a ship. Nothing.

Stepping back into the shade of the trees, she reflected on all that had happened to her. It was safe to think about it now. After all, this was her island, her place - a place where no man would come unarmed. She had made it so.

And it was her mother who filled her heart now—the fair Running-bird, the Seer of Block Island, who loved all and tried so hard to keep the peace. She was the one who saved Peter Wallace from oblivion, making his life meaningful. He was the closest thing to a father Circe never had. She loved Peter too, without measure.

"I will go to the mainland tomorrow," she said to the island. "I will seek out the Mohegan who ruined my life. I will kill his children first, then cut him up a little at a time and make him suffer as I have. It will be done."

Circe, Little-grey-feather, and all the other names she was called by smiled warmly, contentedly, as another cool breeze swirled around her. Her plan was set. And, as before, with any clandestine excursion to the mainland, she would make love to the sea first.

She raised her arms and spread her legs a bit wider, letting the air currents play on her inner thighs. Closing her eyes again, she felt her lover once more. He was there, tender in his touch, as his love was forever embedded in her soul. Then she saw his face. He was walking toward her. She could see where he was at that very moment. He smiled at her, knowing she was watching. He was well. And he was keeping their little secret protected.

From the green canopy above her, a songbird chirped out a melodious tune. It broke her vision of her lover. She felt an urge rise within her heart to answer the bird, and she did by letting her voice join in and flow uninhibitedly. It was a song her Indian mother had taught her. Throwing her head back, and shaking her hair to and fro, she reached around to her side and found the single wooden fastener that held her silk wrap in place. With a flip of her finger, she undid the clasp and set herself free from the colorful garment. She stepped forward, naked in the sunlight, and strolled toward the shoreline with her arms and fingers extended to the side. She sang joyfully. He was all over her now; his breath was in the wind, his scent was in the salty air, his body heat rose from the sand. She could hear his voice speaking as soft as a whisper. He was close to her ear, as he was so many times before in their moments of triumph. She scampered to the water's edge and kicked her feet in the foam. It was wonderful. It was bittersweet. It was of love ... and of love lost.

As she stepped deeper into the surf, her sun-darkened body swayed to the rhythms of her song. Her spirit floated above the beach and then out over the island like an angel with soft cottony wings. Her lean figure and full breasts easily revealed how she had enchanted so many. She was one with nature ... she was nature ... she was...

PART I

1634

CHAPTER 1 – The Appointment

* * *

Peter Wallace stood at the front door of Reverend John Cotton's church with the brash confidence of a young man in his prime. Nothing would stop him now from officially receiving the appointment for which he had been so carefully groomed. The crisp June summer morning in the thriving Boston Colony added to his exhilaration.

As he was about to lift the metal knocker affixed to the center of the huge oaken door, a willful horsefly buzzed by his ear and landed on the door latch. A sparkle of sunlight off its back magnified its size to a point where he could almost smell the thing. Annoyed by its sudden presence, he watched as its black-green body twisted itself round and round. Peter wrinkled his nose. The tiny beast then proceeded to take a few nippy licks of the tasty metal handle.

The young Puritan was dressed in his finest woolen breeches. He wore a white linen shirt that he had washed and pressed just that morning. Over it, a heavy navy blue doublet with six silver buttons aligned in two columns three to either side. The contrast of darks and lights matched his black hair and his fair skin. His navy-blue felt hat, ankle gathers, and black leather shoes rounded out his uniform. And no insect would ruffle it – no, not even one thread of it.

A glint of youthful pride raced through Peter. He raised his hand and flicked it sharply at the insect. His knuckles collided with the metal latch much harder than he had planned. Grimacing in pain, the church door opened with a loud clang.

"Is that you, young Wallace?" a firm, but aging voice inquired. A shapeless figure emerged, barely recognizable as human, but for a pair of squinting red eyes.

"Yes, Reverend," Peter said, straightening himself. "It is."

The Reverend's pale, wrinkled face was accentuated by his black robe and the dark interior behind him. He poked his head out briefly into the light of day. He looked up and down, and around, and lastly behind Peter, and then gave a quick frown to something tiny he thought he saw flying away. Finally, he looked into Peter's eyes.

"Do come in," he said. His words flowed decisively from his thin lips.

Peter stepped into the cavernous wooden structure as he had done many times before. He followed the old man down the center aisle to the pulpit area. He could smell the ever-present mustiness of the place. He speculated, as he often did, as to whether it was coming from the wooden floors or from the Reverend himself. In the end, he concluded it was from both. The church had become part of the Reverend, and the Reverend part of it.

Before the Reverend opened the door, before the horsefly appeared on the latch, Peter found himself walking on the beaten path toward the front of the church. He was in his moment of doubt. He was observing everything: the sunlight that washed the open field that surrounded the worn path, the amber and gold colors sparkling on the tall grass, the houses in the distance, and the tiny specks of people down at the river scurrying about their business. Peter reflected on his appointment and his past. He recalled his arrival four years earlier and the sickness that consumed the colony. He recalled losing his best friend to the disease. He knew it would be easy just to stay in Boston and work down at the docks. He knew he could sail on occasion with his mentor, John Gallop. He would be safe from warlike Indians; he would have a good life in Boston, one that his dying mother had begged him to have when he left London. There was no need to take this appointment.

Inhaling deeply, Peter knew that staying in town simply wouldn't do. It just wasn't enough. The thing that had being tugging at him and his subconscious propelled him forward. With a lively step, he raced toward the door that he thought would open his life.

The interior of the church now filled Peter's vision. His dark brown eyes adjusted to the dim light and he readily observed three men sitting at a table near the pulpit. He recognized them as prominent leaders of the Massachusetts Bay Colony. One was a judge and another was a shipping master, the third man he knew only vaguely. He graciously removed his hat and offered a nod in their direction.

The Reverend thrust out his right hand, pointing to a seat in the front pew. Peter understood immediately and positioned himself directly in front of it. He waited until the Reverend took his position alongside the other men before taking his seat. No one spoke for what seemed like an eternity. Peter sat nervously while his hands were busy rotating his hat, his brow now damp with sweat. Finally, Reverend Cotton broke the silence.

"There has been a slight change in plans."

Peter's eyes widened as he steadied himself. His hands stopped fiddling with his hat. He held his breath and now expected that they had changed their minds about the appointment. Frustration swept through him. Silence filled the church and the ever present dankness became magnified. After an endless passage of time, the judge leaned forward and spoke.

"There has been a murder."

Peter looked at the judge - his long bony face was surrounded by an overly full white wig, a horse face with noble lineage, his voice in high pitch and overly English – a London English that the judge did not want anyone to forget. It was his mark on reminding his people of their roots, even though they were separatists. Peter's gaze sharpened on the judge, as he knew he should at this revelation.

"A fellow Englishman," the judge continued, "and one who we had relied on to keep the peace with the Pequots. He was brutally murdered near his home on the Thames."

"I see," Peter said, letting the air out of his lungs. *My appointment is intact!*

"His name was Jonathan Miller," the judge continued, "stabbed through the heart apparently without a struggle. He leaves a wife and two daughters."

"How tragic," Peter said – his words were the last spoken for over several interminable minutes. The unwelcomed silence filled the dim room. The stuffiness weighed heavy on all present. Peter's thoughts turned to the few times he had witnessed violent acts among men and tried to configure how this act, presented to him so unexpectedly, had played out in real time. He thought best to respond quickly, as he needlessly assumed he should. "May the Lord protect them."

"Indeed!" the Reverend exclaimed. "Miller's daughter witnessed the atrocity."

Peter's eyes froze on the Reverend's. The Reverend's gaze remained steadfast, yet a hint of sadness began to show through his stern countenance. Peter glanced over at the judge with a dozen questions forming in his head, but the judge spoke before he could organize his thoughts.

"His daughter said it was an Indian who killed her father."

"Was the Indian apprehended?" Peter asked, firmly.

"No. He remains at large."

Peter looked at each man in turn. He could read their minds by the expressions on their faces. He knew what was coming.

"As our new Sheriff of the Connecticut colony on the Thames," the Reverend said, "it must be clear what is expected of you. Our plans were for you to work with those at the outpost and build supply lines to Fort Saybrook. There is much to coordinate in this task."

"Yes," Peter said. "I understand."

"Peter," the judge interjected, "we will need you to look into the murder as well."

Peter looked at the judge, not knowing what to say. The inclusion of a murder investigation was an unwelcome surprise.

"We did not want such a difficult start to your appointment," the judge said, "but this task is imperative. We will provide you with whatever support we can."

Reverend Cotton chimed in. "A great responsibility has been assigned to you and we do not want you to get hurt in the process. You must proceed with caution. You will be in the heart of Pequot territory."

The Reverend raised his hand just as Peter was about to respond.

"We have chosen you because of your devotion to God, your strength, and your youth. What we are now asking you to do is … to take the place of Jonathan Miller."

Peter's eyebrows rose for an instant, as if inquiring without words, as to what this all meant. *How could they expect me to fill a role that would take years, he thought?*

Peter shifted his weight in the chair. "Reverend, I … I…"

The Reverend raised his hand.

"You have been briefed by Governor Winthrop about the Pequots. They have been known to be the most belligerent of all the Connecticut tribes. Do you have any questions about them? Do you have any concerns about your mission?"

"No, Reverend," Peter said, a bit dazed.

"No to what?" Reverend Cotton said, raising his bushy eyebrows.

"Your pardon, Reverend. I …I'm just a little confused, I suppose."

The Reverend raised his hand again.

"As one of the authorities in Connecticut, you must be firm in answering questions and in decision-making. Think about what needs to be said before it is said. Pause for a moment when indecision arises, and ask for God's help." The Reverend raised his head and closed his eyes. Seconds passed, then he dropped his head back down and flashed his eyes wide open. "Respond with conviction, Peter Wallace!"

Slowly, the Reverend lifted his hand to Peter, palm open.

"I see, Reverend," Peter replied. "Then … I have no concerns, just a few questions."

"We are happy you have no concerns."

"I can do what you ask."

"Good!"

Peter nodded, then added, "I shall not fail."

"Good. Now we shall hear your questions."

Peter was lost at where to begin. At lightning speed he sorted through the myriad of questions roaming his mind and sorted out the pertinent ones from the rest. *The Indians, the murder, he thought.* Peter caught his breath. He asked a few more questions about his role in conjunction with his religion. Finally he asked about his mission – the mechanics of it. In rapid fire he asked: Who will I sail with? What provisions and tools will I be supplied with? What provisions will I be bringing for others? Will I have maps? Who shall I seek out when I arrive? He spoke proudly and confidently. A slight smile crossed his face when he was done. The answers came quickly, many of which he had heard before and were appreciated nonetheless, if for nothing else but reassurance.

Reverend Cotton was pleased. He knew he had prepared the young man properly. He suggested to all that the meeting was at a close. Looking at Peter as a father would, he said, "Now, go forth to the outpost on the Thames River and establish yourself. Find a home, a base of operations, and build a supply line. Plan a visit to see the Millers. Seek out the advice of William Smith who runs the trading post. Others will be coming to support you in seven days' time. Make the way ready."

"Yes, Reverend," Peter said, solemnly. "I am looking forward to the challenge. It is what I was born to do. I can feel it in my heart."

"And Peter, by the grace of God we *will* survive in this land."

*   *   *

One sleepless night had passed for the young sheriff. It was from anticipation more than anything else. He was ready, and would deal with people and problems as they came. He rose early and set about packing his few things for his trip. Whatever else he needed would be waiting for him at the trading post on the Thames River.

Later in the morning, Peter found himself walking at such a lively pace through the thriving streets of Boston that he inadvertently bumped a few passersby. Apologizing sincerely each time, he would tip his hat for added emphasis. He was heading toward the Charles River where the wharves, houses, and shipping structures were doubling in size every year. So much was changing so fast, he knew that if he ever left town for a period of time and then returned, things would most likely not look the same. But, his mind was filled with exhilaration and a longing to get the journey to Connecticut going as soon as possible.

As he approached the bustling harbor, he stopped at the top of the hill overlooking piers. Several hard-packed roads had taken shape over the last two years and were now dotted with many houses and storage facilities. Just then, a familiar figure caught his eye.

"Ah, there he is!" Peter said softly to himself. Then he called out, "Captain Gallop!"

A festively dressed man with a sweeping hat and high boots stood next to a mountain of crates and barrels at the water's edge. With one foot perched on a small wooden box, it was all that the Captain needed to show his pedigree and flair for the dramatics. Had the box not been there, he would have found something else to rest his foot upon. It was his signature pose and acknowledged by many. He was fifteen years Peter's senior and his maritime mentor. Gallop considered Peter his own son as Peter's parents were deceased.

Gallop heard his name called and spied Peter directly. He waved vigorously with his large hat that was adorned with a colorful feather fastened to one side. Peter smiled in acknowledgement then crossed the street which was lined with carts and wagons being loaded and unloaded at a frantic pace. As he skirted past one wagon atop a steep incline, he noticed the workers carelessly tossing barrels in, causing the wagon to sway and buckle. A single wooden block held a wheel in place.

"Take care there!" Peter called out. The men ignored him.

Captain John Gallop turned his attention to supervising the movement of cargo from one ship to another smaller one. Then he heard a desperate shout. Looking up he watched a wagon break loose from its block and plummet down the road unattended. A worker rushed after it, lunged to grab on, but fell short.

Peter was a fair distance away, but stepped quickly aside to avoid it. As he did, he noticed an Indian woman turn a corner with two young children, one in each of her hands. Distracted by them, she was not paying attention to the commotion up the hill. Finally, she turned her head and saw that she was in the path of the careening wagon. She responded by pulling her children to one side. But the two-year-old boy broke free from her and stumbled back into the path of the onrushing wagon.

Peter ran down the hill, his legs responding to a calling he had felt many years prior, a calling that put him in service to others, a calling he let consume him naturally. Racing alongside the wagon, he managed to outpace it. He crossed in front of the rolling monstrosity with a burst of speed from his strong, nimble legs. He reached down and snatched up the Indian boy just as the wagon closed in. He leaped as far as he could to the side, turning his body so that he landed on his back with the boy safely tucked into his chest. The wagon raced by them and exploded into the side of a nearby building spewing large pieces of wood and debris in all directions. Several people rushed forward including the shamefaced workers who caused the problem.

The Indian woman reached out and grabbed her son. She gave him a hard shake and spoke forcefully to him in her native tongue. After she regained control, she looked briefly at Peter who was still sitting on the ground. She frowned, then turned and left quickly. Captain Gallop stepped forward, extending a hand to help Peter up.

"It seems you are a hero, Peter."

Gallop pulled him off the ground. Peter stood, brushing his clothes. "I think not," he said, somewhat embarrassed.

"Perhaps a fool then?" The Captain asked, with a chuckle.

Peter smiled and lowered his head momentarily. Gallop grabbed both forearms of his young protégée and looked him over. "Not a scratch. You look fine, young man."

"Thank you, Sir." Peter acknowledged. He looked up at the Captain's huge hat with its dreadful, overly adorned feather. "Is that new?"

"Yes, from France. Do you like it?"

"Well, I must say, it does fit you."

"Ah! And I assume you are not speaking of my hat size," Gallop exclaimed. Before Peter could respond, the Captain pulled it off his head and proceeded to give Peter a demonstration of his new sweeping bow, with his hat flowing through the air and feather billowing behind it as though it was still alive in flight.

"I've missed you," Gallop said, and followed his words with a very fatherly embrace.

Peter gathered himself. He looked down at the busy harbor that was filled with a dozen ships of all shapes and sizes and purposes. "How are things on the high seas?" Peter asked.

Gallop fixed his huge hat smartly back upon his head. His playful countenance disappeared. He knew Peter had important matters on his young mind that needed attention - matters that would change the course of the young man's life forever. Without delay he spoke.

"We lost another good sailor off the Connecticut coast," Gallop said. "Captain Stone ... and his crew of six."

"I do not know him," Peter replied. "The Indians again?"

"We believe so," Gallop said. "We will take more arms and powder with us now as a precaution. Come, let us walk."

They proceeded to the docks. When they stood in front of Gallop's ship, Peter looked about the busy harbor. Many ships were being loaded with goods and supplies while others were being unloaded. It was clear to both men that it was a sign of how important the Boston harbor had become.

"Looks like you have much to do," Peter said.

"Busy, as you can see," Gallop swept his hand across the landing, indicating the length and breadth of his responsibility. "I am happy you will be sailing with me."

"May I lend a hand?"

"I welcome it. It must be done before the tide changes. Half of what you see here is going directly onto my ship." He pointed to the smaller pinnace.

"To the Thames?"

"Yes, and then beyond to the Connecticut River. The Indians call it the Quonitocutt, so become familiar with that name." The Captain smiled broadly and extended a hand. "Forgive me. I must congratulate you on your appointment."

"I thank you, Sir," Peter said, shaking firmly and then tipped his hat. "However, it seems I will have more on my hands then I originally thought."

"How so?"

"A settler was recently murdered on the Thames."

"Yes, Jonathan Miller. Heard the news yesterday."

"You knew him?"

"Not very well. Met him twice at the outpost. Quality man."

"His daughter claims it was an Indian."

"Indeed. I have also met Anne. She is a beautiful and willful young woman, and I pray this will not ruin her."

On Gallop's words, Peter tried to visualize what this Anne was like. What she had lived through and what she may be feeling at this very moment. He wondered if he would be able to speak to her and gain any worthwhile information. He wondered if she would break down and cry at the suggestion of an interview about the murder. And, he wondered if he was even going to be allowed to talk to her at all.

"Would you have any idea which Indians may have done this?" Peter asked.

"There are a number of troublesome Pequots in that location. After all, it was their land until they sold much of it. Even though they were paid handsomely, they still hold a grudge."

"The Pequots. Any names?"

"The grand sachem is called, Tatobem. He is a fair man, but rules with an iron fist. Several of his lieutenants are not as easy to deal with. Be wary of his son, Sassacus. It is said he has ambitions of expanding his domain. I do not know much more than that; they keep to themselves."

"Could it be possible that it was an Indian from another tribe?"

"Well, the Mohegans are also active in that area. The fishing and trapping are splendid along the Thames. Other tribal Indians do drift through from time to time."

Peter extended his hands in a gesture seeking support. "You are not making my job any easier."

"I wasn't intending to," Gallop said with a faint smile. "Speak to William Smith at the outpost. He has the most knowledge of the locals."

"Fair enough."

"Jolly good! Come meet the others that will be sailing with us; they are a young couple and their son, along with three of my best sailors"

Gallop found them all and made the proper introductions. They then quickly split up to do final preparations. Several sailors took up the chore of carting the heavy cases down a pier and up another to where Gallop's pinnace was docked. When they were finished the Captain found Peter again.

"I am sailing the pinnace down to the Thames," Gallop said. "It is better in the shallow rivers of Connecticut. There are many hidden rocks along the Connecticut coastline and I fear I would ruin a bark. Most of the rivers are estuary, so the tidal peaks and troughs are important to know. If you miss one, you will never get in … or out."

"I submit to your knowledge," Peter said.

"Do not be surprised if you see a number of Indians at the outpost when we arrive. Most simply are there to trade."

"I will be on my guard," Peter said tapping his sword.

Gallop waved off his reply saying, "That might not be enough. If you do get the chance to meet Tatobem, bring a tribute, gifts and the like, but not wampum. That would be considered an insult."

"Point taken, Captain."

"Bloody good."

Peter opened his mind and filled it with the tasks that he must accomplish and endure, along with the certain disappointments that were sure to be attached. When in this world, he felt the best way to cope was to think about the sea and waters he would ride upon - the deep blue and green waters that took all men away from their troubles. And he wondered why men do not feel as open on the land as they are on the sea. As his mind envisioned the waters and the land he would explore for the first time in his life, he tried to picture what the grand island would be like, Block's Island, the one at the turn to the west into the great sound, the guardian of all points in that direction.

"We will be sailing past Block's Island," The Captain said.

Startled, Peter said, "You read my mind."

"I did!"

"Yes. The Manisseans, what should I know about them?"

"Ah yes, the inhabitants of the Island-of-little-god. That's what they call it and a strange lot they are. I do not understand why anyone would want to live out there. It is very isolated from the rest of the world. I suspect that is why. But, I have been there on several occasions. Resilient people, yet by and large, peaceful. There is a seer on the island. A woman no less!"

"A woman seer?"

"Yes, a young woman barely twenty."

"Interesting."

"She is hard to find, likes to spend time alone in the back hills of the island. They call her Running-bird. It is a name given to her by her half-breed husband. He forbids anyone to use her Indian name."

"Running-bird," Peter repeated.

"Indeed. And very pretty. Her husband is called Samuel. His father was Dutch, and sailed with Adrian Block."

"Will they welcome me then?" Peter asked.

"Yes, I believe they will. They are not hostile towards white men. Their natural enemies are the Mohegans."

Peter looked away then up at the sky. A dozen seagulls began to descend on them, looking for scraps of food as they always have and would, for centuries to come. Peter closed his eyes and filled his lung with the salt air. Once content, he eyed the seagulls as they landed near Gallop's provisions.

"The gulls will have your food," Peter said.

"Never mind them. Come now and let us prepare for our voyage. Your life is about to change."

*   *   *

Peter had one more person to see before he embarked. He raced back into town looking for Governor Winthrop and in short order came to the place where they were to meet. John Winthrop was a man a large girth and simple dress – a sign of little physical activity but a man who worked tirelessly at building a strong Puritan society, albeit from behind a desk.

Peter suddenly heard men arguing in the square from a distance away. Several women who were walking ahead of him heard the commotion as well and turned away, heading off down a side street at a quicker pace. As he drew closer, he could easily identify the Reverend and the Governor, but had not seen the third man before. This man wore garments of a sailor, but more refined; *perhaps he was a sea captain, Peter thought.*

The sailor was gesticulating wildly, clearly showing his frustration with the others. There were two soldiers standing just behind the Governor, and another sailor stood off to the side of the Reverend.

"You cannot tell me what I can and cannot do," Captain John Oldham said, finger-pointing the Reverend.

"Do not raise your voice to Reverend Cotton," the Governor interjected.

"I do as I please," Captain Oldham said.

"You can argue with me in this tone, no one else."

"He is the one who is making it difficult for me."

"No, it is I. It is my law," the Governor said, patting his chest.

Oldham hesitated, shook his head. "I know the Reverend and his conniving influence is behind my banishment."

"You blasphemous fool!" the Governor cursed, "Your words will send you to hell. You are to leave Boston at once."

Captain Oldham's hand moved onto the hilt of his sword. His sailor did likewise, backing him up. The two soldiers snapped to attention and took to either side of the Governor.

"Let me speak," Reverend Cotton said, raising his hands. But it was at that moment he saw Peter approach. The Reverend's pale face turned into the sun and looked at Peter. His blood shot eyes fluttered in the bright light; he struggled hard to keep them open, but he managed a quick smile at Peter and gave him a nod of approval. Peter stepped forward and stood near the Reverend.

"Captain Oldham," the Reverend said, "We appreciate the service that you have provided us. And we understand that the many years at sea have taken you far from the Puritan way of life …"

"Hogwash!" Oldham blurted out. "I'm in no mood for a lecture." He turned sharply away, nodded to the sailor and tilted his head toward the harbor.

"Wait!" Reverend Cotton exclaimed.

Oldham stopped, turned around. "I am tired of waiting. I am tired to your laws. I care not for the Puritan way of life since it does not serve me. I have goods to deliver, and I will do it when and where I choose."

"Let me speak," The Reverend demanded.

"There is nothing more to say," Oldham said firmly. He stepped forward toward the Reverend in an aggressive manner. Peter reached out to impede his progress. Oldham shoved Peter back but Peter had braced himself and stood fast.

"What trouble is this?" Peter asked, placing his hand on the hilt of his sword.

Oldham squared up to Peter. "Touch me again and I will take your hand off."

Peter's eyes deepened, he pulled the Reverend behind him. Finally the Governor cried out, "Stand apart you two!" His soldiers encircled Oldham and his shipmate. Oldham realizing he was outnumbered spat on the ground in defiance, then turned his back to them and walked sharply down the hill toward the harbor. The others held their ground and watched the two fade away.

"Not a pleasant fellow," Peter declared.

"No, he is not," the Governor said. "Be cautious of him. As if it is not enough for us to be concerned with the Indians, now we must watch out for our own."

Peter secured his sword and fixed his ruffled sleeve, his pride a bit bruised.

"He is arming our enemies," the Governor continued.

Peter frowned. It was always disconcerting to him to hear this sort of thing but he had met others like Oldham – transients, men who were out for profit only. He had no use for this type of person and always kept his distance in the past. But now, it occurred to him, he was going to have to get involved as it would be part of his new position. He offered, "Can you not appeal to his English heritage before he leaves?"

"He is not English anymore. He is selling gun powder, muskets, and hatchets to the tribes just south of us – to where we are sending you!"

Peter took a long look at the angry man who were now almost out of sight. He made a note to himself of his size and color and put him first on his list of persons to keep watch of, especially when he gets to Connecticut.

"He has broken away from the Puritan way of life," the Governor continued. "He has decided to make his own rules about religion."

"He has God to deal with as well, then."

"Yes, I wish never to see him and his family again. Come now Peter, walk with me."

As they left the scene, Peter could see that the Governor was in deep thought. Finally, he said, "Let us have a talk about Connecticut. It will be a difficult beginning for you."

"Nothing is easy. But I will prevail."

"Well put, young Wallace. I hear the Reverend in you."

"Thank you, Sir."

"I will not keep you but five minutes. We would not want Gallop to miss the tide."

* * *

He was filled with a euphoria that was as strong and pure as his body and his heart. He was invincible, indestructible, on the verge of greatness, and ready to take on the world and all that it would throw at him. Regard for life and limb was a non-sequitur. In his mind his task was simple; he would do all he could to maintain peace with the Naturals and to help his exiled countrymen survive.

It was at times like these that he remembered his mother who had died in London when he was ten-years-old, her words of encouragement and adventure thrilled him to the bone. She told him many stories of the New World and all the opportunity that was open to him there. It was a land of freedom of prosecution of their Puritan faith and a place where new laws could be born and nurtured. She had worked hard at securing passage for them but died before she could fulfill her dream. Peter had no sisters or brothers, at least none that he knew of – a testament to his father's recalcitrant nature as philandering seaman. He had few friends including a Scottish boy who had vowed to be his business partner in the New World. The two befriended a fearless sea captain, John Gallop, who took them under his charge. And when Peter reached twenty years, the Captain took them across the great ocean on his magnificent bark.

At last they were out on the sea with the waters of the Atlantic Ocean rushing all around them. And as evening came they turned west and headed into the great sound. He had sailed with Gallop all around the Cape and to parts north but this would be his first time entering the Devil's Belt – a great body of water that other's called the Long Island Sound. Peter looked out across its blue hues, with all its shimmering flakes of silver, and saw that it was different. He couldn't pinpoint it, but it was indeed brighter, filled with colors of the rainbow. His thoughts drifted to his goal of being successful and building a name for himself, not just any name, but a name that would be associated with honesty, fairness, and with brotherhood, regardless of race or nationality. It was the New World, the New Land and *he* was part of it. He was to be the harbinger of good things to come for his people, and with a little luck, good things to come for the Naturals of this wonderful, untamed land.

With a firm grip on the rigging at the bow of Captain Gallop's pinnace, Peter leaned out over the water rushing beneath him and scanned the horizon. As the dawn rose over their backs, the rainbow colors illuminated a land mass to the port side. Then he saw it – *the island.* Block Island.

As they drew closer he felt its radiant golden warmth. But just as quickly as it appeared, it faded as his ship swung to the west. He wondered about the people who lived there. He wondered if the seer woman was as beautiful as the Captain had said, and if she knew he was out on the water this day. He wondered how long it would be before he made a voyage there. But the ship raced with the wind farther and farther away from the beautiful gold and green land mass in the middle of the vast sea. There was no stopping him from making his mark, no turning back. And he vowed he would visit Block Island on another day.

CHAPTER 2 – On The Thames

* * *

Running-bird stood on a high windy hill at the north end of her sacred island. It was covered in green dune grass, golden sand, and large sculptured stones as only a superior being could arrange. With keen eyes she scanned the waters of the straights of the Devil's Belt, drawn there by a premonition that consumed her just one hour earlier. She cradled her newborn daughter in her arms but felt no strain from the infant's weight or from the ordeal of the difficult delivery just ten days ago. In fact, the child was light as a feather in her arms and was as alert and playful as the day was glorious. The sky was cloudless and cerulean blue; the sea, a deeper shade of ultramarine and flaked with sprays of white mist.

"I know it is there," Running-bird said softly.

Within seconds of her plaintive words, a white speck appeared far out to sea standing out in glory in front of the distant muted dark colors of the mainland behind it.

"Ah! You see my daughter, I knew it was there."

The infant suddenly grew still, seemingly in acknowledgement of her mother's words. Running-bird shielded her eyes from the sun and looked further out across the waters of the great Sound. She lifted her daughter so that the child faced in the same direction she was looking.

"You see it? Do you see that small white cloud on the water? See how its sails are filled with the warm air. Filled more than any we have seen before. That ship brings hope. I know it. I can feel it."

The infant turned her little head to her mother's face. Running-bird looked down at her and carefully moved her back into the cradled position. The infant never lost eye contact.

"Hope has come to this land at last," the young mother said. "Hope has come."

* * *

Captain Gallop's pinnace turned sharply northward and left Long Island Sound behind him. He was now heading toward the mouth of the Thames River. In short order the sails lost the wind and the Captain ordered them down. Once done, the men pulled out the oars from under the planking and took positions on either side. They were fitted carefully in their mounts and the oarsmen fell into a well-paced rhythm lapping their oars against the strong current. The Captain turned to Peter who was at one of the oars.

"I saw a Dutch ship in the east just as we entered the river."

"I saw the ship as well," Peter responded, as he pulled his oar in cadence with the others.

"I didn't want to alarm anyone," the Captain said. "But I want you to know that it was there."

"I see."

Gallop gave Peter a stern look, then nodded.

"But they have no settlements here," Peter said.

"That is not the case. Even though they have moved west and north, they still claim that all the fertile river valleys are theirs. We need the land around the Thames and the Connecticut to place the thousands of our countrymen who are arriving every year."

"There is plenty of land for all in this country from what I see," Peter said.

"Yes, there should be."

The Captain then explained how the Dutch Director-General of New Netherlands had send a commander on a mission many miles up the Connecticut River, this to establish an outpost near Massachusetts. The Dutch built a fort there and called it Huys de Hoop. "They claimed it was simply a trading post," Captain Gallop explained, "but the placed twenty soldiers there."

"They were driven off. Were they not?" Pater asked.

"Not completely."

Peter looked away then back at the Captain. "And what do you suggest I do?"

The Captain paused and considered the question then he slowly shook his head. "Do what you think best. I know you will say and do the right thing when the time comes. I just want you to be diligent and help me build a solid chain of communication between here and Hartford."

"I will, Captain," Peter said with a smile. "You can count on me."

"I know I can."

* * *

As they rowed up river they finally came upon the small English outpost. A single dock jutted out just forty feet from the shore. But it was enough to allow the pinnace to tie up and stay afloat without having to beach it. No one was about and the few wooden structures up the path seemed empty. They secured the ship to the dock and prepared to disembark. Gallop's sailors proceeded to unload supplies for the outpost. Peter gathered his belongings and placed them on the pier. When done, Peter turned to Gallop.

"As I calculate," Peter said, "we are ahead of schedule."

"The benefit of sailing through the night," Gallop said, smartly, "and having the wind in our favor."

"Doesn't appear to be anyone here," Peter said.

"You'll find them soon enough."

Captain Gallop shook Peter's hand and wished him good fortune. The Captain knew the waters around New England and the advantage of having the small, fast, and maneuverable pinnace. These boats performed exceptionally well in the many estuary rivers of the coastline. And he knew he had to leave fast to catch the tide.

Peter gave the vessel a shove to help it separate from the dock. Looking up, he locked eyes with the Captain. He then scanned the deck and smiled at the other passengers who were bound for other settlements.

"Thank you, my friends," he shouted, as he watched the three-man crew hoist the square-rigged sails. "May you find the seas favorable," he added with a wave of his hand. His big brown eyes smiled as brightly as those of his Irish mother had once done.

A young couple and their five-year-old son were the only passengers left on board. They were heading to a new outpost up the Connecticut River. The woman and child expressed a sudden look of loss in their faces. They had felt a sense of security with him around. Peter waved, and gave a smart wink to the boy. The father held his son's hand reassuringly and smiled. They both waved in unison.

"Fair thee well," Peter shouted. "I will come see you soon, up on the Connecticut River."

"God be with you, Peter Wallace," the husband called back.

"And to you, brother."

Peter noticed the unsettling look in the woman's face. He wondered if something he said or wore was out of place. He looked himself over and found nothing. She continued to gape at him. *But why would this woman do that?* It didn't take long for him to realize that perhaps he could be desirable, even to married women. He let the thought leave him before any sin festered. Then he heard the Captain call out his standing orders, as he always did when he headed out to into open sea.

"A stiff wind is coming, men." Captain Gallop called out, "Time to hoist the sail."

Peter watched from the tiny dock as the wind filled each sail of Captain Gallop's two-masted pinnace. As the boat faded from view, Peter's heart sank to a level it had not been to in a long, long time. He looked beyond the ship and could see the Sound. He turned and looked up river. He then pictured what it must have been like on the night Jonathan Miller was killed. It was said by Miller's daughter that the Indians came by the river, this river, on a dark and rainy night.

With his short sword at his side and a satchel of clothes and provisions slung over his shoulder, Peter felt abandoned for the first time. He surmised that if he were to fail in his mission or die from whatever cause, he promised himself at least he would have given it his best effort. As he looked up the road at the half-dozen wooden structures that made up the outpost, he drew upon the words that the Reverend imparted to him:

"Every evil deed is the work of the devil!" the Reverend had bellowed. *"Constant watch must be kept in order to keep the demon at bay."*

He looked back down river one more time. Then he scanned the sky before turning his attention to the building he would walk over to.

"It is time," he said aloud. "My first step."

As he walked forward, his thoughts turned to the sum total of his short life. Reverend John Cotton's words of hell fire and brimstone echoed in Peter's ears as he approached the tiny village. He knew he would have to draw on all his strength to succeed. And, he knew he would need to use all his cunning and temperance when dealing with the hostiles. It wasn't long ago that his foster parents had set him free. They had passed on to him their faith and knowledge of survival when he was just ten. And now, he was ready to apply all of what the Reverend had taught him.

He looked over the rustic cottages and shacks, and suddenly felt something strange. *Is this place deserted?* It was curious that no one had come out to greet him. *Perhaps the harbor master didn't see the ship coming*, he thought.

Peter understood that the Reverend and the Governor had big plans for a free Puritan society in the New World. The Puritan dogma would restore faith to the people in the colony who had lost their way with God. And they would bring it to the Naturals of the land for their salvation as well. It was to be so, and was to be outside the influence of their ungrateful King. Peter was given the Pequot history, a history learned from the Dutch and from the Wampanoags of Massachusetts. He was informed that they had come down from the north many decades ago, and violently took over the smaller tribes that stood in their way. He also knew that they were concentrated between the Thames and the Connecticut rivers, a place where the soil was good and the fishing plentiful. These rivers also made safe havens for sailing ships and were crucial to the survival of the Puritans in the new world.

Peter recalled that this trading post had been established many years ago by an Englishman who had no ties to the Puritans. It was located not far from the mouth of the Thames River, and was also frequented by many Indians. *But why is so quiet today?* Peter was told that the Narragansetts from the eastern regions went there regularly to trade. They brought fish, clams, and other shellfish to trade for pelts, linens, and cooking items. They were friendly with the English and the Dutch, but kept their distance from the Pequots. To the west of the Connecticut River, was the Mohegan territory, and beyond that, the French territory. They, too, were generally friendly with the Dutch and English, but had great issues with the Pequots just like everyone else in the colony.

As he approached the structures, he wondered whether he would find enough support from the settlers, both English and Dutch, and from the friendly inhabitants to help him with his mission. Surely, he wasn't going to be able to do it alone. And above all, he knew he had to find the killer of Jonathan Miller. It was the devil's work and it had to be undone.

The first building Peter came to was the largest - the main trading house. He heard voices of men from the inside and felt relieved. The windows were few and small, and through them he could not see any human form. Peter stepped up to the large front door and observed its rough design. He winced at the lack of artistry in it and then proceeded to place his travel bags on the ground. Examining the latch, he remembered the horsefly on the Reverend's door. He smiled. As he lifted the latch the door didn't move. He gave it a good shove and as it swung inward he instantly heard a voice call out.

"Yah back again?"

Peter took several steps inside and then stopped. Backlit by the brilliant summer sun, he figured the people inside would need a moment to identify his silhouette as a friendly one. From his viewpoint he could easily make out the vast room filled with various goods. He could see two openings to one side indicating several other rooms. It had a high roof and wide fireplace. Several ladders led up to storage areas.

"What's this!" a gravelly voice exclaimed.

"I am Peter Wallace ... from the Massachusetts Bay Colony." His statement was followed by an unsettling quiet that should have lasted for only a few seconds – but did not. He could see four men standing deep in the recesses of the dim room. One, the oldest one, was behind a huge table piled with furs and hides; the other three men stood in front of it. All of their eyes were upon Peter in anticipation of his next move. A bottle of rum, so cherished in the colonies, was carefully placed on the table before them. But at that moment, it was uncharacteristically ignored. All around the room were barrels, wooden boxes, metal cooking items, straw, and other containers filled with supplies. Hanging from every wall were various tools and materials for building houses and repairing ships. No one would argue that it was not a well-stocked outpost.

"Peter Wallace; I heard that name before," one of the men said.

"The Governor has sent me," Peter responded.

Peter stepped forward, showing his full form and color. The men he faced looked tired and worn. Three were dressed in buckskins and linen, much like the way the Indians had dressed. The man behind the table was grey-haired, his face was weather-checked, his shoulders slouched. He was dressed in a round Puritan hat like Peter's, but his clothes looked foreign.

"I am looking for William Smith," Peter said, in a manner as casual as if these men had been his friends for a long time.

"What's he done?" the old man asked.

Peter stood silent for a moment looking for a convivial response - his eyes scanning the room and the men.

"A hard man to find, I'll bet." one of the trappers said, with obvious sarcasm.

"I was appointed as Sheriff...," Peter blurted out, "...of the Connecticut colony." The men instantly chuckled.

Peter looked around the room again. He drew in a deep breath. "I am looking for William Smith. Do any of you know of him?"

The men in the room ignored him. One grabbed the jug of rum and took a long pull. Peter stepped closer. He continued, "I also am here to investigate Jonathan Miller's murder."

The jug of rum hit the table hard. "Did you bring the Almighty with yah?" the drinking man in buckskins asked. The other men laughed harder this time.

"I see no humor in mocking the Lord," Peter said sharply. He placed his hand on the hilt of his short sword. The laughter in the room instantly diminished. The men in buckskins turned and faced him.

"Well, you just missed a half-dozen Pequots," one said, reaching for his knife. "You could have asked them." And then the trapper forced another disingenuous snicker.

Peter held his tongue and released his grip on his sword.

"Alright yah hounds," the grey-haired man finally interjected. "Ya've had yah fun. Now, go on about yah business."

The old man made his way around the table; the trappers withdrew and took to conversing and drinking amongst themselves.

"My apologies, Peter Wallace," he said, extending a hand. "We just haven't seen anyone so well dressed in a while. The boys here like to make fun of strangers."

"No matter," Peter said. "Were Pequots here?"

"Yes, they were."

Peter looked at the man carefully. "I see," he said. "No trouble?"

"None... this time."

Peter paused. He thought about the words of the Reverend. He looked around the room, straining to find the right follow-up.

"Did they bring that?" Peter asked, pointing to a number of sacks and baskets of food near the door.

"That's right." They both looked down at the baskets of corn, squash, fish, and other food. "It's just what we needed. Running low."

Peter regarded the bounty. "Are they not considered our enemy?"

"Look, young man," the old man said. "Is this yah first time out of Massachusetts?"

Peter fumbled with the hilt of his sword. He breathed in slowly, looked the old man in the eyes, and simply nodded in the affirmative.

"Well, what yah hear up in Massachusetts isn't always what really happens down here. We all trade to stay alive … we fight only when we absolutely have to."

Peter took a moment before continuing. He scanned the room once more then gathered his thoughts.

"Sir, will you help me find William Smith?"

The old man looked up and smiled at him. "I got word the Gov' would be sending someone," he said. "Just didn't expect someone so … young."

He lumbered towards the front door, signaling for Peter to follow. His shoulder rolled in an obtuse pattern. Peter wondered what his life must have been like. From the nicks and scar on his face and hands he figured this person had been through some tough times.

"You know my mission?" Peter asked, breaking the silence.

"Yes, I usually know everything that goes on in these parts. It's pretty easy when yah have an active trading post."

Peter sized up the old man. His rugged, hard edge made of for his pour appearance. Peter asked, "Can I count on your support?"

"Come outside with me," he said, extending his hand in that direction.

Peter followed. They stepped outside. The old man looked down the lane to the pier.

"I could help yah," he said, "for a price."

"That can be arranged."

"Good!"

They looked at each other and smiled.

"Apologies again," the old man continued, "I didn't see yer boat come in. I must be slipping in my old age."

There was a tall post planted in the ground near the front door with no apparent function until old man pressed his back up against it. Peter said. "The Captain was in a hurry to catch the wind."

The old man grunted and began rubbing his back hard against the pole. Finally his eyes closed. "Ahhhh." He stepped away from it and instantly seemed to have grown several inches taller. "I usually go out and greet the incoming ships. Who brought yah here?"

"Captain John Gallop," Peter said, as he raised his chin. The old man noticed it and smiled.

"Ah, a good seaman… and a gentleman."

"He was my mentor. He taught me how to sail."

The old man seemed to ignore Peter and pressed his back against the pole again.

"He was very skilled at navigating his way in here," Peter continued. "For a moment I thought we might run aground in the muck, but he has sharp eyes and found deeper water. He could not stay. He was sailing west to the Connecticut with settlers and supplies."

The old man stepped away from the pole. He looked at Peter smartly. "He's always on the move."

"What is your name, Sir?" Peter asked.

The old man chuckled. "There I go, forgetting my manners. I'm William Smith," he said, smiling, from a tooth-deprived mouth.

"You!" Peter exclaimed then offered a slight bow. "Pleased to meet you."

"The same here. My wife and I live here," Smith said. "Is them yur bags?"

"Why, yes."

"Put 'em inside for now. I want to show yah something."

Peter did as he suggested. As he was putting his things in a spot that Smith had pointed out, he asked, "So where is everyone else?"

"Catching fish, trappin', wood gathering and the like. They'll be twenty-five or so here by evening. Come back outside with me." They stepped out into the brilliant June sunshine. Smith then turned and pointed up the lane.

"The Pequots usually come from that direction."

He turned slowly back toward the water.

"The Narragansetts and Niantics from the sea." he added, pointing.

Peter looked in both directions to acknowledge the man's acumen. But before he knew it, Smith had already turned away and was heading up the lane at a pace quicker than Peter thought possible. Peter watched as the old man's shoulders rolled with each step, as if a machine was working deep within his body – he hurried to catch up.

As they walked to the north end of the village, Peter could make out the faintest hint of a trailhead far beyond the last house that stood at the edge of the wood. Smith became quiet and appeared to be having some trouble breathing. Peter slowed his pace and came to a stop. Smith halted as well and drew in a deep breath.

"What can you tell me about the Pequots?" Peter asked.

Smith smiled. He placed his hand on Peter's shoulder.

"They trouble yah, huh?"

Peter looked at the man intently. Smith waited for a reply then realized he wasn't going to get one.

"Well then," Smith said. "The Pequots were once part of the Mohegan tribe, but they separated over thirty years ago after the killing of a princess. The name Pequot means destroyer." Smith paused to observe Peter's reaction. It was met with the expected surprise. Smith explained further that Pequot villages were usually walled fortresses and, unlike the other tribes, were well organized with a central authority and a tribal council. "And a grand sachem with complete power," he concluded with a frown.

Peter grimaced. "Why don't you have a stockade here?"

"It's better that we're in the open," Smith said, smartly. "It shows we have no ill intentions."

Peter inquired about the other settlers along the Thames River, and William volunteered that further up river was a stockade with forty-five English settlers, and a few from other countries. The sparse region held a dozen or so homes and farms of various sizes, a smattering of domesticity budding up in a land rich in natural resources. "By the way," William asked as they continued walking, "how long have yah been in the colonies?"

This caught Peter a bit off guard.

"Why do you ask?"

"No reason; just wondering."

"I arrived over four years ago," Peter said.

"Seventeen ships that summer. Were yah in that group?"

"Yes."

"Ah! So yah were here during the last outbreak."

Peter's face saddened. Recollections of his arrival in Boston rose within him to a place he had hoped he would long forget. The town was sick and reeling with misery. He remembered helping as many as best he could. Several children and the weak died first, the older settlers next, and finally one of his friends succumbed to the disease who had worked hard at bringing comfort to the sick – a red-headed Scottish boy of eighteen, much like Peter in age and determination, but unlike Peter in that the lad was on the run from English law. They bonded in London and made a pact to become business partners in whatever enterprise they could drum up. After he was buried, Peter kept his distance from the Boston inhabitance for many months thereafter.

Peter squeezed his eyes shut for the moment. Then opening them, he replied, "Forgive me, I saw many die. We lost over forty."

Smith reached up to Peter's shoulder and gave him a quick double-pat. "Don't feel so bad, the Pequots lost nearly half their number during that outbreak – over two hundred."

Peter looked at Smith grimly, his thoughts trying to comprehend the numbers.

"Yes, it was nasty. But I'm not sorry for 'em," the old man said.

"And, why is that? I was taught to both fear and respect them. Are they not God's people too?"

"Not likely. Some are driven by the devil and they seem to have more devils then the other tribes."

"I hope to change that," Peter said with conviction.

"That's right," Smith said with a half-smile, "it's your mission." He gave Peter another pat on the shoulder.

Peter hesitated. He frowned at the old man's sarcastic gesture. Then he wondered if the Smith had any religion left in him or if he had any at all to begin with. Indications were that he had none. Peter passed it off to the difficult frontier life.

"So, you've been here since 1619?" Peter asked.

"Longer."

"How much longer?"

"I've been here since the Captain Adrian Block sailed these waters. It was in early 1616 when I started my trading operations."

"Extraordinary!" Peter exclaimed, stopping in his tracks momentarily.

"Just lucky, young man."

As they walked further, Peter inquired more about the past. Smith explained that the Dutch outposts along the coast had welcomed a number of English fishermen like himself. But they eventually moved west leaving the settlements empty. Smith said that is when he took up residence along the Thames. Many of the Dutch had died in the first winter, and many from an illness they attributed to the Indians. Smith also told him he went to Plymouth after the first winter when the Pilgrims arrived. He and several men from the outpost had gotten word of their plight and went to deliver food.

"They were happy to see my white face," He explained to the attentive Peter. "When spring finally came, only three women of the original seventeen survived. Many men perished as well. They were afraid to bury them during the day for fear the Indians would see their dwindling numbers." the old man said, clearing his throat. "So, I have no sympathy for the savages when it comes to disease."

"It was a difficult time," Peter said. "You must understand the Indians had little control over this."

The old man stopped, faced Peter, and shook his head. "Young man, I like yah," he said, "but, don't defend these savages to me. It's not in my blood to love them anymore then I have to. I just trade with 'em, nothing more."

Peter tried to understand Smith's attitude about the Indians. He thought best to let it ride. He understood that Smith has chosen his way of life for some reason or another and that, in time, he would learn more about this engaging man.

"Enough of this," Smith said. "Let's walk."

They walked on for a while in dismal silence. Peter felt the man was in great pain with each rounded-shouldered hump step. But it clearly did not seem to deter him; he plowed ahead like it was nothing. Finally Peter felt it was time to get down to business.

"Where can I find the Millers'?" Peter asked.

"Ah…the Miller killing!"

"I need to speak to his wife."

"Widow."

"Yes, sorry. Widow."

Smith nodded then pointed to the north. "Indeed, I will show yah where they live. It is not far. Just a little more than an hour's walk."

"I feel I have a long way to go," Peter said with a sigh. "That is, before I can find the murderer."

"Well, it might not be as hard as yah think."

This caught Peter's attention. A wave of comfort filled him – this William Smith was proving to be a solid source of information and finding him so soon after his arrival gave Peter the sense that he just may be able to solve the crime sooner than later. "Why is that he asked?"

Smith continued, "Most of the savages are proud of their kills. They usually carry trophies of the slain."

"Oh yes, of course," Peter said. "I forgot…"

Peter stopped himself. The Reverend was in his ear again.

"Start there," Smith said. "With their gossip of a kill."

The trail closed on them as the woods became thicker. The grade of the land rose under their feet. Smith began to show some signs of fatigue. Peter asked him if he would like to rest for a bit. Smith turned his slumping head and gaped into Peter's sympathetic brown eyes with a look of determination and disappointment. Peter didn't need to ask again. They pressed ahead. The trail made a turn to the west and the trees thinned. Peter could see flashes of white light, reflections of the summer sun bouncing off the river below. It was the Thames, and drew Peter back to his needs.

"I must find a place to stay."

"I'll see to that," Smith replied in between heavy breaths.

Peter nodded in acceptance.

The two men continued walking in a northerly direction. The grade in the land rose steadily through a wooded area and eventually leveled off at the crest of the hill. The path led straight towards the edge of an eighty foot cliff that overlooked the entire area. The view was spectacular. A wide, glistening river meandered to their right, running as far north as they could see. Peter stopped and gazed outward.

The vista was like no other that the young man had ever seen. The colors and hues of greens and blues filled his eyes and all of his senses. The warm air of summer and the heat from deep within his body became one. Peter inhaled slowly and deeply. And, after a moment, he let it all out in a puff of acceptance.

The young sheriff slowly drew himself back to his task at hand. He wondered what lay out there before him. And, whatever it was, would he meet the challenge and perform as worthy in the eyes of God. Ah, yes! He felt his God was with him now, at the edge of that cliff, on a beaten path to nowhere.

"It is lovely country." Peter said.

"That it is," Smith said, smiling. "Are yah good with your sword?"

"Yes, fairly well. I would say."

"Good. I figured yah had to be for the Gov' to send yah."

"This view is spectacular! Makes one forget … about home."

"England? Nah!," Smith exclaimed, smiling warmly. "I…" He suddenly stopped himself. Grabbing Peter's wrist, he pointed far off to the northeast. "Look!"

In the distance, over a half mile out ahead of them and down below, Smith waved his finger at a clearing in the forest. In it, human figures appeared. A troupe of Indians entered an open meadow in single file like a line of ants with a clear purpose.

"That's them," Smith said.

"Peqouts?"

"Yes, the ones that came to trade today."

The two men watched silently. The Indians crossed the field carrying the items they had just traded for. They walked close together, one behind the other, with a single scout off to the left of the column. When it appeared that the last Pequot had crossed, another suddenly appeared way behind the others. He was set apart; there was something different about his posture and his nature. His cadence was free of burden and not following the rhythms of line of ants that preceded him. It appeared as if he were dancing.

The two Englishmen looked on amused. Eventually, Smith smiled and gave a forced laugh when he realized who the Indian was. He grabbed Peter's wrist again and pointed sharply at the last man in the line.

"That's him," Smith said. "The strange one."

"How strange?"

"His name is Dekanawida - a powwaw. Crazy as a madcap."

CHAPTER 3 – Dekanawida

* * *

The ant-line of warrior-traders left the open meadow and walked carefully into the wooded dell on the far side. They all felt good to be back under the canopy of safety. The last man, however, was immersed in deeper thoughts and stayed out in the open, singing:

Fresh, the air today. Clear and clean.
Sweet is your fragrance, oh Mother Earth.
I will hold my head high to you in this late morning sun.
And you must kiss me with your soft summer breeze.
I extend my arms, throw my head back, and close my eyes.
I spin, whirl, tumble, bumble, and laugh.
Your tall silver trees and rich green leaves fill my head.
I trust you will keep me from falling completely.
I laugh ever louder, how wonderful to be alive.
My friends mock me; think I am silly.
But I know Mother that I am from you and a part of you.
I will always be one with you, and you one with me.

Look, the others laugh at me because my arms are extended.
They think I've gone mad. They think I am hexed.
They do not know our secret.
You cure me, you fill me, and you lift me.
I will be shaman some day.
I will owe it all to you.
I love life.

Dekanawida suddenly snapped out of his euphoria. It was the harsh cracking sound of a bullwhip that brought him around. Regaining his bearings, he gapped in anger at the man holding it.

"That wasn't necessary," Dekanawida cried out.

"Powwaw, keep up with the rest," a tall, powerfully built Pequot said. He was holding the whip out for Dekanawida to see.

"I was communing with Mother Earth," Dekanawida said. "It is part of my training."

"That is not my concern," Sassacus said. "We will not wait for you if you fall behind again. My job is to get these provisions back to our village without delay."

"You almost struck me!"

"Next time, I will not miss."

Dekanawida eyed the whip in Sassacus' hands and frowned. "I cannot believe you traded your furs for that thing."

Sassacus sneered at Dekanawida. Then he turned and waved for the others to continue their march. The powwaw stepped up and was now face-to-face with his leader.

"Am I to believe that we all will need to watch our backs when you are near?"

Sassacus raised his head and looked down into the face the young man.

"The English use this for livestock and for obedience. I intend to do the same."

"It should not be *our* way," Dekanawida said loud enough for the others to hear.

"Our way has long gone," Sassacus said, mockingly. "The white men will keep coming until we do something about it. We will use their weapons against them."

Dekanawida suddenly felt a sharp pain. He reached for his neck. It was an old wound that haunted him, one his fellow tribesmen would never let him forget it because the scars still showed. The scars consisted of a series of white streaks running along his neck, a constant reminder.

Dekanawida knew he would become a full-fledged powwaw one day, a true medicine man -- a vocation he chose because of his need to be different, to be a leader, to show that there was another way instead of revenge. He was the oldest of three brothers, but his shame from a whipping by a white man five years earlier would be his mark of irrelevancy unless he rose above it all.

Sassacus turned away and signaled the others to resume their march in quiet. Dekanawida suddenly felt a sensation that he was being watched. Turning quickly, he scanned the woods to his right and left. Then he turned his gaze towards the hills that rolled toward the west. He stepped out into the open field. There, at the top of the nearest hill, where the path broke into a small clearing, he saw two men.

"William Smith and …?" Dekanawida said aloud. He did not recognize the second man as any who were at the trading post. No, this was a new visitor. A sudden flash from a shiny button on the stranger's dark jacket caught Dekanawida's eye.

A Soldier? He wondered.

Letting out a short yelp, a subtle cry of warning, Dekanawida alerted the others. Some of the Pequots turned and followed Dekanawida's line of sight. A reply signal was given by Sassacus, and they all disappeared into the woods.

More trouble, Dekanawida wondered. *These English just keep coming. There must be a way to live in peace.*

The powwaw felt the pain in his neck once again. It felt like a tight pull as if his flesh was tearing. He had received the wound when he was fourteen years old. He recalled how his father and others had organized a major trading event at a neutral site not far from their Pequot village at Missituck. The English, Dutch, the Narragansetts, and some of the Manessians from the Island-of-little-god, were all invited. Fur was the cash commodity for that day, as well as wampum. The day had started out on the right foot and the many had felt they had done well. Dekanawida remembered how excited he was but also how quickly it was dashed by an error in judgment that would haunt him for many years.

He had inadvertently picked up a jewel encrusted fencing sword he thought some nobleman had left behind. It was, in fact, on display for trade by an English brigand, named John Oldham. A commotion ensued with two English boys, and one young girl, the daughter of an English merchant. They accused Dekanawida of trying to steal the thing. John Oldham, looking for notoriety, jumped to the rescue and lashed his whip across Dekanawida's chest and neck. Oldham laughed when Dekanawida fell to the ground. Dekanawida had never felt such pain, and he was shocked to see his blood flow all over him.

The English and Pequots drew sides, until a level headed Nobleman fired his pistol in the air. Carefully, and with great skill at offering some trinkets, he appeased

Dekanawida's people and averted a disaster. The trading event slowly ended for the day, and the Pequots left with a bitter taste in their mouths.

Dekanawida never forgot that day, nor the man who whipped him, but he knew sacrifices would have to be made on each side for them to survive.

As he left the meadow, he wondered about the soldier he saw on the hill. Would he be as dangerous as John Oldham or friendly like William Smith? The fact that this man was with Smith gave Dekanawida some level of comfort.

"I must meet this newcomer!" he exclaimed aloud to no one, and then smiled.

* * *

Dekanawida and the trading party entered their Pequot village at Missituck with the expected fanfare. Young boys ran out wanting to see firsthand what treasures they brought back from the English trading post.

Dekanawida was the last to enter the village. He wanted to see how his people would receive the return of the trading party. He carefully watched as the items were displayed and accepted as value, or rejected as worthless. Copper pots thrilled the women, and iron hatchets intrigued the men.

All in all, the village took on an air of exuberance that afternoon. Even the grand sachem, Tatobem, let a rare, simple smile cross his face. However, Dekanawida was still troubled by the man he saw on the hill. That man looked so different from most of the English he had seen before. His dress and posture were a mystery. In any event, he felt that the strange man standing alongside William Smith must have been someone important.

Several single women, all carrying flat baskets filled with berries and nuts, saw him and smiled. Dekanawida was considered one of the handsomest men in the tribe, in spite of his scars. As the women approached him, a number of the older children surrounded them and took away the baskets. One young squaw separated herself from the rest and called out to him.

"Dakanawida, what treasures have you brought us today?"

"Come see," he said, smiling.

She drew near. "I do not see anything?"

"Sometimes nice things come in small sizes."

"Oh please," she said, and took another step closer. "Show me."

He looked into her eyes with the passion he had always felt for her. She, too, could not take her eyes away from his. She smiled so tenderly her face filled with light. "Show me," she asked again, this time with softness in her voice that revealed a torrent of passion. She reached out and held his hand.

"Very well." He opened a small pouch tied to his belt and extracted a fine necklace made with a center stone of deep glistening blue and fastened to a long polished leather cord.

"This is beautiful!" The young squaw exclaimed, with her eyes lighting up like candles.

"And it is for you," he said.

"For me!"

"Indeed, for you."

"But I cannot take it … it is far too valuable."

He smiled at her, and she at him. He undid the clasp and placed it around her neck. Once set, she turned and faced him. "I cannot…"

"There, you are a princess now."

"Oh, but you cannot…"

"Hush, my sweet."

"It must have cost you a fortune."

"It was all I could think about," Dekanawida said. "I wanted you to have it. I…wanted to see your expression."

Sassacus had been watching this exchange from a safe distance. Finally, he couldn't take it any longer. He walked over to them and grabbed the squaw by the arm.

"What is the meaning of this?" he growled.

"The meaning is between us," Dekanawida said, reaching out taking her other hand.

Sassacus pulled her away from him.

"Be silent, Powwaw."

"She does not belong to you!"

"Be silent ... I swear ..."

Dekanawida knew his adversary had seniority over him and that the parents of the squaw had plans for her to marry the sachem's son. But Dekanawida was persistent in his efforts to transform the old ways of his tribe, including allowing women to choose their husbands. He knew the tribe would have to adapt in order to survive the changing times.

Sassacus led the young squaw away. Dekanawida let him do it, but vowed to speak to Tatobem about his love for the woman. The grand sachem would know how to handle this. It will be done correctly.

In the morning, when Dekanawida awoke, he found the necklace on the ground next to his cot.

CHAPTER 4 – A Walk in the Woods

* * *

As Peter Wallace rounded a bend in the wooded path, he noticed a clearing off to his right. He had left the company of old man Smith over an hour earlier, and had traveled in peace and solitude. He had prayed to God for guidance and protection. Taking careful precaution to avoid contact with the Pequots he had seen earlier, he followed Smith's advice on where to go to find the Miller home.

As the clearing became brighter and took shape, he said in a low whisper, "That must be it." It was an innate response to the long quiet walk he had just endured. But his own words startled him, as if it was an inquiry from another person. Yet it was not another, it was his voice and it was his essence that was all around him - it was not the words of the Reverend or the Governor, nor would it ever be again.

My words echo in this soft wood.

It was all up to him now. Peter shook his head and proceeded forward. The dark trail lightened further. With each step he took, he saw more of the glistening fields of amber, gold, and viridian that he thought must be the Miller's farm. He saw small fields of corn, wheat, and other vegetables arrayed in carefully planned rows and separate plots. It was enough bounty to feed three families through a long winter. The house was a well-built, a one-story colonial with a loft, and showed no signs of loose timber or decay. The front faced the south and was filled with the light of the summer sun. Two windows with wooden shutters graced a full sized door placed in the center.

"What have we here?" he asked aloud.

The path intersected with an ample roadway. Many tree stumps had been removed and tossed aside to allow wagons to pass easily. Peter stopped at this junction and looked down the road in each direction. Far down on either side, he could make out several other clearings. *Other settlers*, he thought. *Maybe they can help me with my mission.*

Without hesitation, he crossed the road and headed toward what he assumed to be the Millers' home. As he drew near, he suddenly noticed the figure of a young woman standing near a covered well. She was pulling on a rope threaded through a pulley drawing up water.

Peter was struck by the grace of her movements. She wore a light summer dress that clung tightly to her mid-section. Her traditional Puritan bonnet was draped over her back, revealing her long flowing amber-gold hair. Her laced shoes did not appear to hold any mud nor did a single scuff show on them. She wore all this without burden; her garments one with her, and she, one with them. Peter's midsection instinctively tightened, and his broad shoulders rolled back. He stepped lively towards her.

"Hello!" he called out, with a beaming smile.

The girl was instantly startled and let out a tight, shrill cry. But, as soon as she saw Peter's European outline she quickly regained her composure.

"Forgive me, Madam," Peter said.

He stepped closer, and his expectations of her beauty were not dashed. "I come in peace," he added.

"Shame on you, Sir!" The young woman blurted out with an edge. "How dare you sneak up on me?"

"I assure you, I had no inten…" He was moving quickly toward her when she lashed out, "Stop where you are! Don't come any closer."

Peter froze, held his hands out, open palms revealing no ill intent.

"I am from the Boston colony, Madam. I was sent…"

The young woman raised her hand, waving him off. "I am not a Madam. Can't you tell a married woman from one not?"

"I am sorry… Miss, I…"

"Your apology is fine. Now, who are you and what do you want?"

Peter took a step closer to her.

"Well, I am Peter Wallace, and I am pleased to meet your acquaintance. I have come in search of the Miller …"

"On whose instruction?" She asked, interrupting him again with the sharpness of a knife.

Peter hesitated. He was puzzled at how such a young beautiful woman could be so direct.

"I am the Sheriff of the Connecticut colony, Miss," he said, hoping that was enough.

"Sheriff?"

"Indeed," Peter said. "I was appointed by Governor John Winthrop."

"I see," she said, softening her tone. As she did so, her face lit up. Peter was struck by the sudden change. Her face was a perfect oval, her eyes deep and curious. But it was her full moist lips that intrigued him the most. He had not seen such total beauty in a single woman before.

"I…I arrived today."

"Have you found the Millers?" She asked, quizzically.

"I was told they live here," Peter said. "I received a description of the property from William Smith. I thought this was it."

To his surprise, she giggled at his response. She had transformed herself instantly into a schoolgirl. She dipped her head and looked into Peter's eyes with a salacious gaze. She parted her lips and Peter suddenly felt that the air all around him was being drawn into her body.

"I…I was told…" Peter couldn't speak, his throat was as dry as sand.

"Don't you want to know who I am?" She asked.

"Why…yes, of course," Peter said. "Who are you?" He silently cursed his naivety.

She laughed at him, a light-hearted romp of a laugh.

At that instant the door to the house opened. A woman in full Puritan dress stepped out into the sunlight. She wore a broad rimmed felt hat, shading her eyes just enough to add a hint of mystery. She called out:

"Anne, who is that with you?"

The young woman looked sharply at Peter, knowing her game was up.

"So there," she said to him. "I am Anne, Anne Miller, and that is my mother. You have found us."

Peter turned and gave a nod to the woman at the door. Anne suddenly darted by him and headed toward the house. Peter followed slowly and carefully.

As he drew near he said, "My name is Peter Wallace, Madam." He removed his hat and bowed gracefully.

"So, you have met my headstrong daughter."

"Why…yes, I suppose I have."

"I am Elizabeth Miller."

"Pleased to make your acquaintance," Peter said.

"You came on foot?"

"Yes, I walked from the outpost down on the Thames."

"You must be thirsty, then."

"Yes, thank you…I am," Peter said, smiling for the first time.

Elizabeth turned to her daughter, "Anne, fetch Mister Wallace some water."

Anne walked back to the well and retrieved a large wooden bucket that she had been filling. She returned quickly and stepped up to Peter and extracted a long metal ladle from the bucket.

"Thank you, Anne," Peter said.

Peter reached out to take the ladle from Anne, but she held it firmly, not giving it away freely. As he wrapped his fingers around the handle, several came in contact with Anne's hand. The sensation of her cool skin raced throughout his entire body, then the exchange transformed into radiant warmth like nothing he had felt before. She noted his reaction and leaned in closer to him. There was barely a foot of distance was between them and Peter could not take his eyes off her.

"Mister Wallace," Elizabeth said, breaking the tension. "Are you here to seek knowledge of my husband's death?"

Peter snapped out of his trance and turned to her. He apologized and offered his condolences. For several minutes he filled Elizabeth in on his assignment and his meeting with William Smith. She listened carefully, without expression, until he was done. Anne stood quietly beside her mother, cradling the ladle in both hands, listening intently.

"I grieve over the loss of my husband," she said. "However, he was a difficult man at times. He would not listen to reason and now he's gone, leaving me and my daughters here in a vile land."

"My condolences again to you, Madam," Peter said.

"So you say," Elizabeth said. "We buried him there." She pointed to a small fenced-in plot far off towards the tree line. "He is there with his brother and his brother's wife."

"I see," Peter said. "What happened to them?"

"An illness. It killed them two winters ago. We do not know what it was. It looked like the pox. They suffered but somehow we were spared from it. Between the savages and the sickness, I cannot stand this country anymore."

"I am sorry, Madam," Peter said.

"She wants to leave," Anne chimed in bitterly.

"Mind your tongue, daughter," Elizabeth said.

"We are making every effort to colonize this land properly," Peter said, firmly. "Our duty to God and country will not go without rewards." He was reciting words he recalled from Reverend Cotton. He had done this before, and every time it felt awkward to recite.

"Rewards!" Elizabeth Miller exclaimed. "We've been on our own for nearly a week, living in fear. Where are my rewards? All I have to show is a dead husband and a mountain of work ahead of me."

"Trust in the words of the Bible."

"I am out here in the evil woods with Satan lurking everywhere," Elizabeth said. "At night, we can hear his evil creeping about." She paused as if to allow the evil to pass. "I want to return to England. I am finished with this savage land."

"Mrs. Miller," Peter said, softening his tone. "I want to help you. I intend on bringing the person who killed your husband to justice. Without justice there is no law."

Elizabeth was losing her composure. She hung her head, the corner of her eyes dampened. "Oh, why...." she started to say.

"Can we sit down and discuss this?" Peter asked.

"Sorry," Elizabeth said, "Forgive me. Do come in."

They stepped inside the house, and Elizabeth instructed Anne to bring some bread and cheese to the table. Hilary emerged from a back room and was introduced to Peter. After they exchanged pleasantries, Elizabeth motioned for Hilary to sit at the table. Anne sat down with them opposite Peter.

"Please, Mister Wallace, have something to eat," Elizabeth said.

Peter thanked her and took a piece of bread and a small lump of cheese. He asked if she would join him, but she politely refused.

"I see you have neighbors," Peter began.

"Yes, there are three other families down the road from us," Elizabeth said. "Trappers and farmers mostly. One family has been here for a long time and has a good relationship with the Pequots. It is what has kept us alive...until now. We were trying to clear the land between us and build a bigger farm. But we cannot get the help."

"Did they see what happened to your husband?"

"Why, no," Elizabeth said, startled. "Did the Governor not tell you?"

"I have little information. I understand one of your daughters saw..."

Elizabeth raised her hand to him, then moved it to cover her mouth. Her eyes saddened, dampened, then after a moment, she placed her hand back on the table. "It was Anne who saw it happen," she said, with a quiver in her voice. She glanced briefly at Hilary then back to Anne.

Following Elizabeth's movements, Peter turned his attention to Anne. She was expressionless.

"Yes," Elizabeth said. "Fine thing for a daughter to witness."

Peter said to Anne. "I am deeply sorry you had to see that." He considered how to continue the conversation but everything he wanted to say seemed inappropriate. Anne, however, appeared unfazed and did not seem upset, so he asked her, "Do you think you can discuss this now?"

Anne sat quietly for about a minute, just staring off towards the door at times then back to the others. Peter thought to ask his question again, but assumed the young girl needed some time to collect her thoughts. Finally, she flashed her eyes at Peter along with an inkling of a bemused smile.

"I saw them," she said, sharply.

"Them?" Peter asked.

"Yes, there were two of them."

"Indians?"

"Yes, *savages*. I hid behind a tree so they wouldn't see me."

"And, you saw your father with them?"

"Yes, he had gone out to secure our boat to the dock. I had run out into the storm to help him, as mother had directed."

Anne's eyes flashed at her mother. Peter noted the continuing level of friction between them. Elizabeth stared back, a frown forming on her brow. Just as she was about to speak, Hilary started to fidget and became noticeably upset.

"My young daughter has taken this hard…"

Hilary's hands were on the table tapping out her anxiety when suddenly she bumped one of the candles. It fell over into the cheese plate.

"Hilary, to your room," Elizabeth commanded.

As Hilary got up to leave, Anne set her deep eyes back on Peter. He felt them before he returned the look. Turning slowly to meet her gaze, the room suddenly grew very quiet. As he faced her and locked eyes with her, he felt as if she was pulling him right inside her head. Peter could not turn away. Anne parted her lips - the lower one was as moist as an apple's flesh. Her tongue played on her lower lip; her eyes narrowed but did not lose contact with Peter's. She smiled. Peter lost his train of thought and struggled for something to say, but no words came. He straightened in his chair and forced himself to break away from Anne's vise-like stare. He turned to Elizabeth and raised his eyebrows.

"The storm was terrible," Elizabeth said, breaking the brash silence.

"Yes…yes, I had heard that," Peter said. He looked over to the window in an effort to divert his eyes from Anne, but directed his speech toward her nonetheless. "It must have been awful," he said.

Anne didn't respond. Peter waited a moment; then looked directly at her. A slight inclining of a smile began to show on her face again.

"I understand it was at night?" Peter continued. He wanted to get her to talk in the worst way. And he wondered…*is she indeed, flirting with me? If so, it would be a despicable thing. Anathema! Yes, she has the devil within her, perhaps. Yet, she is so lovely. A thing, a feeling, and an experience I cannot comprehend.*

"Yes," Anne said abruptly, "but I saw him clearly." As she said this, her countenance returned to normal, as if no hidden agenda was being proffered.

"Have you seen this individual before?"

"No, but I can tell you, I will never forget him."

"Yes … of course."

"No, I mean it!" Anne exclaimed.

Elizabeth raised her hand in a gesture for Anne to hold her tone. Anne gave her mother a harsh look.

"Anne claims she saw my husband murdered," Elizabeth said. "The actual act." Elizabeth's body shuttered for a moment, images of that night filled her mind in half-truths, as if she had been there by the riverbank. She had been filling in the gaps with what she wanted to believe, needed to believe.

Peter said. "I will not question your daughter any further."

"No! I want to tell you." Anne shouted. "I saw him!"

"*Anne!*" Elizabeth exclaimed.

"It is quite all right," Peter said, holding his hand up. "I believe you, Anne."

"I can see the savage clearly," Anne said, angrily.

Elizabeth stirred, and was about to lash out again at Anne but something held her back. Peter saw this and waited a moment until he felt she was at ease.

"This can be of assistance to me, Mrs. Miller," He said. It took a few seconds for her to respond but she eventually did, in the affirmative.

He turned to Anne. "If it is not too painful, can you describe the Indian for me?"

Without so much as a glance at her mother, Anne said, "Yes, I can."

Anne proceeded to give Peter a description of the Indian. She was focused, detailed, and angry.

"Did you see the other Indian clearly?" Peter asked.

Anne looked surprised at the question. Her attention suddenly seemed lost.

Peter pressed the issue. "Was the Indian … who killed your father alone?"

Anne's eyes darted back and forth for a minute. She looked away, gathered herself and continued.

"No."

"There were only two then?"

"Several more … no, two. I'm not sure. Wait! There were others. I remember now."

"Can you describe one of the other Indians?"

Anne looked down. "No, nothing… well maybe."

"Anne," Elizabeth said, interrupting her daughter, "we have been through this before. You cannot possibly know what you saw. It was dark and rainy, and if you accuse the wrong tribe we could be…"

"Mother, I know what I saw!"

Elizabeth raised her hand to her daughter again. Elizabeth turned to Peter. "She is obstinate. When we found her that night she was in shock. I do not understand this insistence of hers. I myself was unable to go down to the river. Others went for me to … retrieve my husband's body."

"Well, she sounds willing to give solid testimony."

"Very well," Elizabeth said. "Go ahead, Anne."

Anne proceeded to tell Peter the details of what she saw. She included a full description of the events that night, including the argument between her father and one of the Indians. Not once did she flinch or show any sign of remorse. Her temperament was filled with anger and frustration, though she highlighted a big wound running along the murderer's neck.

"A wound?" Peter asked. "So there was a struggle."

"No, there was no struggle. My father simply gave up."

"Did it look like an old wound?"

"No, it looked fresh. It was ugly… and red."

"Do you know what tribe they were from?"

"No…well, I say they were Pequots."

"Pequots?"

"Yes, they are all bad."

"Are you sure?" Peter asked, cautiously. "I am told the Mohegans travel through these parts as well."

"Yes, they do," Elizabeth chimed in, "as do the Narragansetts."

"I can tell the difference," Anne blurted out.

"You must be certain, Anne," Peter advised.

"I am." Her face was glowing. She was flushed with pride.

Peter watched her carefully, looking for anything that might resemble the manipulating, flirtatious look he received earlier. He needed to know if her insistence on the Pequots was real or contrived. But there was nothing insincere now.

Peter asked, "Was the murder weapon found?"

Both Anne and Elizabeth looked puzzled by the question. Finally, they both shook their heads.

"Well then," Peter said, "when I go to the Pequot village, I will take careful note of whom I see. If there is a warrior that matches your description, I will do everything in my power to bring him to justice."

"Surely you will not go to Missituck alone?" Elizabeth asked.

"No. I will return to the outpost and gather up some men to support me - men who know the sachem. I believe I would be a fool to go there alone. I will find a way to provide advance notice of my intentions. It will be of maintaining peace but seeking justice at the same time."

"Your intentions are noble," Elizabeth said, "but your expectations are unrealistic. The savages will not confide in you."

"We shall see. However unrealistic I must do my duty. Perhaps, Mrs. Miller, you can tell me about that night. Everything. What you saw and heard from Anne's recollection. What you heard from the people who brought your husband's body back from the river. As much detail as you can recall. Any small item you mention may help me in my investigation."

Elizabeth looked down and away - a bittersweet sigh running from her lungs and heart. Finally, she raised her head and gazed into Peter's eyes.

"Mister Wallace, I will not stay in the country. I do not care if you find the murdering savage. I simply cannot stand it here any longer. I am planning to return to England once I can secure passage."

"No! You can't." Anne lashed out.

"Anne!" Elizabeth fired back. "Leave us. Go outside and return to your chores."

"Mother, no! I am not going back to England with you."

Elizabeth rose. Anne did likewise, her fists slamming into the table. Peter stood quietly.

"Now, you go outside and resume your chores," Elizabeth said, sternly. "I do not want to discipline you like a child. You are too old for that, Anne. Act like a lady and leave this house with grace."

Anne hesitated. She looked at Peter, was about to reply to her Mother, but something changed. She straightened herself, gave Peter a subtle smile, turned from the table, and walked out as graciously as her mother had just suggested.

"You see," Elizabeth said, with anger still in her voice, "she has lost everything by growing up in this savage land. She is disrespectful and even speaks in the slang of the New Land. I am certain you have noticed how she does not speak in the King's English. I have lost her ... but I tell you, I will not lose Hilary. Elizabeth slapped her fist into an open palm – a gesture that Peter saw coming. She then bit her lower lip. "I blame my husband for this; his idealistic dream - a dream that has become a nightmare for me. I will take them home with me to England. If Anne fights me along the way ... well..."

Elizabeth was breathing heavily. She told Peter things that she would have never told anyone even in her wildest dreams. She was open now, a torrent of confession. Peter stood tall in front of her, his comments reassuring, his posture defending her position. He gave her a nod in agreement.

"You appear to me to be a fine young, devout Puritan," she said, as she slowly sat back down at the table.

"I strive to be," Peter said, sitting down as well.

"I do need to return to England. It is the only way I can save my children. So, what else can I tell you? Please let me know so that I can get on with my life."

"Yes, indeed. I would like you to start from the beginning."

"If that will help you, of course," She replied. "What little I know, is what Anne told me when she returned. But, I must tell you, the Anne that returned that night was not the Anne who went out into the storm."

"Let us start with Jonathan," Peter suggested. "Why was it so important for your husband to go out in the storm?"

CHAPTER 5 – Jonathan Miller

* * *

Jonathan Miller looked into his wife's eyes and knew immediately what her answer would be. His inalienable love for her would not permit him to take one step closer to the door until she responded. Regardless of her reply, he would do what he *had* to do, but he would wait for her response nonetheless.

The rain had been coming down in heavy sheets of fury for several hours, with no signs of letting up. The wind howled around the corners of their humble dwelling, adding to the racket. Their nerves were at the breaking point as they prayed quietly to themselves.

Elizabeth Miller flashed her eyes toward one of the boarded up windows and simply said, "No."

"Elizabeth," Jonathan said, firmly, "I *must* get down to the river and secure the boat."

"Jon, just listen to that wind. It is far too dangerous."

She was the only one who called him 'Jon' and she did so for emphasis when she wanted to get her point across. He was strong she knew but he was showing his age as his hair was now half-grey, and face filled with many more lines than just one year ago. As he made a gesture to continue the argument, Elizabeth raised her hand stopping him cold.

Elizabeth turned her attention to their two daughters who were sitting at a large oak table in the center of the main room. She needed some way to show that she was the authority figure. Never would she let her husband be such. Three candles with reflective holders flashed an amber glow on the tender faces of the young girls. Across the room, a freshly stoked fireplace warmed the interior.

"Anne, Hilary, clear the dinner dishes," Elizabeth ordered, "and then I want you to prepare for bed," she added.

Elizabeth turned her eyes to her husband. He looked at her, and she would not let him look away.

"But, mother …" Anne began.

"Be still," Elizabeth Miller said, waving her hand at her. "Do as you are told."

The two girls got up from the table and started their chores. Hilary, who had just turned twelve, was just like her mother, a true aristocratic Britton while Anne was the opposite. Anne obeyed, of course, and went about her chores but grumbled under her breath. For the two girls, hearing their parents argue was nothing new.

"Elizabeth!" Jonathan said. "I simply cannot afford to lose that boat."

He was speaking loud enough for all to hear.

"Nonsense!" Elizabeth exclaimed.

"But, darling … it is our livelihood that is at stake," he said, his hands outstretched.

"If we lose the boat," she argued, "you can always barter for another one."

"Impossible, Dear."

"Why is that?"

"You know I don't have the means to purchase another. Need I remind you how poorly our crops have done, and how bad trapping has been?"

"Since we do not have coin … or wampum… what do we have?"

"Elizabeth, we …" He looked away.

"It is your fault for not securing the boat properly."

His head jerked back, his face burned with rage.

"I did secure it, but I never expected a storm like this!"

"You can build a new one."

"I have not the time for this!" Jonathan yelled out.

Hilary gasped at her father's words and intensity in his volume. She nervously dropped a small stack of plates, the bottom one shattering on the floor.

"Hilary!" Elizabeth cried out. "What did you do?"

Hilary started to cry.

Elizabeth got up and pulled Hilary away from the mess. She called for Anne to help clean up, and the two of them carefully picked up the broken pieces. Jonathan quietly escorted Hilary into the girl's bedroom.

"Sweet Hilary," Jonathan said, softly, as he sat her down on her cot. "It is not your fault. You are a good child and this trouble will soon pass."

Hilary stopped crying, but was still noticeably upset. She worshipped her father. He was tall and strong and brave, everything a young girl would want in a father. Hilary remembered the time he had saved a cow when it had gotten stuck in deep mud. They all thought the poor bovine would die there. But, he devised a series of ropes around an old pulley, and with all his strength, he got their only cow out of its predicament.

"Father," Hilary said, meekly, "Are you going out into the storm?"

"I must, sweet Hilary. I need to make sure we do not lose our boat."

"What about what mother said?"

"Please, trust me. I need to save this boat. It will not take much, and I will be back straight-away."

She looked up into his eyes. His heart soared. He knew he had to get down to the river before it rose any higher. He knew the boat would provide a faster means of transporting his bounty to the trading posts and a means to give his family all that they needed. He envisioned the new clothes and gifts he could bring to his girls and to his wife. And he knew they couldn't afford to lose the boat just now, in the height of trapping season.

"I will be home directly, dear child," he said, and hugged her for a long, lasting moment.

He rose and told her to prepare for bed. As he was leaving the room she said, "God be with you, Father." He smiled and blew her a kiss.

Elizabeth stood by the front door of the house blocking his exit. Her heart was pounding with animosity and disappointment. She could not look her husband in the eye.

"Wife!" Jonathan said, sternly, "I am going now. Speak not another word of this. If you do, it will be the devil's work. I swear to you... it will be the devil's work. And... and he is not welcomed here."

Elizabeth's eyes swelled with fury, but she dare not say another word. She knew the consequences she would face with her maker...and with the Reverend...if she continued to fight with her husband. Her eyes turned watery and red.

"Fare thee well, husband," she finally said. It took all her strength to say it.

Jonathan Miller looked deeply into his wife's eyes again. He did not smile, nor frown; he simply acknowledged her role and her respect for his role.

"I shall return as soon as I can," he said. He wrapped his cloak around his shoulders and pulled his broad hat down tight over his brow.

As she stepped away from the door, he looked once more over his shoulder and saw his wife's eyes glaring at him. His heart momentarily warmed, she was a beautiful woman and she had his heart, and knowing all that she had been through in this new world, he suddenly wavered.

"Elizabeth, when I return I will consider your request to return to England. Perhaps there is merit in it after all."

Anne, looking on from across the room, suddenly stomped her foot. "No!" She cried out.

Jonathan Miller spun around to face her. His eyes darkened.

"*Daughter, be silent!*" His words stung all ears in the room.

Anne shook her head. Jonathan turned, unwilling to continue the debate any longer, and walked out into the maelstrom pulling shut the door behind him.

Elizabeth stood frozen in time. She knew she had lost this battle. It was the first time for her in many years. She usually had her way with him, ever since he convinced her to come to the new world. Now, she felt hurt and discouraged - and loathed her existence. But, underneath it all knew she still needed him. She closed her eyes. The exterior world faded as she shut it out. Her breathing grew heavy: long had she wanted to return to her England and her homeland; long had she hated the new land, and long had she regretted her commitment to a man who never understood her.

Anne called out to her. "Mother!"

"Silence!" Elizabeth screamed.

Anne shook at her mother's outbreak. After a moment she regained her composure and thought best to return to her chores.

Elizabeth watched her daughter go about gathering up the leftovers, wrapping them in cloth, and then preparing to take them to the storage bunker. She knew her daughter would have to go outside briefly to fetch water but she also knew her daughter was strong. Anne was so unlike Hilary, who was just too fragile for this new world.

As Elizabeth watched Anne scurry about, something stirred deep within her. It began as a small bubble rising from the bottom of her heart. Curious it was at first, she thought, and tried to pass it off as nothing. But it welled up again, and this time she let it develop further. It grew as a flame grows from a simple spark. It rose higher and higher within her body. It warmed her. Then it settled momentarily in her throat. An abrupt cough cleared it all out. She stood.

"*Jon!*"

Anne stopped in her tracks and gaped at her mother.

"What have I done?" Elizabeth said to no one. She was shaking violently.

"He went out, Mother," Anne said, puzzled by her mother's sudden confusion.

"Yes…yes. I can't believe he went. And, he went in anger…the worst way of all."

"But mother."

"You must go…"

"What?"

"You must go after him."

"But mother," Anne said, "you said it was too awful a night to go out."

"My…my husband is in danger!" Elizabeth said, trembling. Moisture was forming in the corners of her eyes.

"But he…"

"Silence, daughter."

Anne frowned at her.

"Anne," Elizabeth said, snapping out of her trance, "please…put on your cloak and go after him."

"Mother!" Anne exclaimed. "Let Hilary go. She knows the way."

Elizabeth was still trembling. She was squeezing her hands as she gaped at her daughter. Her eyes were damp and red. Anne looked away.

"Nonsense, Anne."

"Mother."

"You are the strong one. You must go."

For a moment Anne hung her head. Then she looked up and saw the fear in her mother's eyes. Anne knew she had to go; it was the only way to stop the madness.

"Fine," she groaned. "I will go."

Anne went into her bedroom and retrieved her warm woolen cloak with a hood sewn into it. It was summer, but the rain from this storm was cold and biting. She had been in and out several times doing chores and knew what she would be up against. She hated being subservient and could not wait to get out on her own. Unlike her mother, she had visions of grandeur in this new world. All Anne needed was just the right opportunity to set herself free.

"You know where to find him?" Elizabeth asked, knowing there was no need to ask.

"Of course, mother. He went down to the boat."

"Yes, yes, go directly there. Do not hesitate."

"Yes mother," Anne said, pulling the hood over her head.

Anne Miller opened the door – instantly, rain flew into the house. It dampened her clothes and wet her face. The wind howled and momentarily startled her. Drawing on her courage and strength, she stepped outside.

Anne closed the heavy door behind her, but the damp, cool wind found its way inside and made Hilary shiver. The young girl was still in the back room, but gave a whimper when she heard the wind. Elizabeth ran to her and held her tightly, praying to God for the safety of her husband and her headstrong daughter.

Outside, in the blackness, Anne had a moment of doubt. The driving rain pelted her face, making it almost impossible to see. Her instincts led her across the yard and she found the beaten path that began at the edge of the woods. She would have to travel a few hundred yards, up over a hill, and then out into a narrow cornfield. On the other side of that, would be another small wooded area, and shortly beyond that, the Thames River. Throwing all caution to the wind, she figured she could catch up to her father in short order if she ran fast. But she didn't. Instead she took her time, occasionally seeking shelter under a tall oak tree.

Jonathan Miller discovered that he was right in his decision. Standing over the dock that he had built the previous year with the help of several neighbors, he was glad he arrived when he did. One of the lines holding the boat to the dock was loose. The second line was frayed from rubbing on a post, and it was on the verge of separating. The far end of the dock was missing. The river had risen about three feet over the normal high tide, and he could see that the storm surge was still coming in. The wind was increasing in intensity.

Racing over to the boat, his hat blew off wildly into the air landing in the muck behind him. He ignored any need to retrieve it. Grabbing hold of the remaining line, he pulled it toward him. Reaching down, he found the second line and pulled it out of the water. Relentless rain pelted down, waves splashing heavily against the dock. The water line was mere inches below the dock, and Miller knew it was just a matter of time before the river would tear it to pieces. With his feet in constant battle with the sucking mud, he pressed on. The boat was tossed about hither and yon, making it even more difficult for him to pull it in. He stepped onto the dock and managed to bring the two lines together and hoisted them up over his shoulder.

Just as he started to pull the boat towards the shoreline, he saw something that shocked him. Without letting go of the lines, he turned to the river and squinted to clear his eyes. The rain slowed dramatically making it much easier to see. A few yards from the shoreline out on the river an Indian canoe appeared. On either end, the shapes of two humans loomed. They paddled slowly, as if they were in slow motion. Jonathan craned his neck for a better look.

"Ahoy there!" he called out.

His words cut through the night carried by the wind. His familiar voice reached Anne who was still a distance away. She heard him clearly, as though he was standing right in front of her. She slowed her pace and proceeded cautiously through the wet and muddy terrain.

"Ahoy there!" Miller called out again.

There was no response from the ghostly figures.

Miller gave a tug on the lines. His boat cleared the dock and came to rest on the muddy embankment. He raced off the dock but in doing so, he promptly slipped and fell. He rose quickly. Not letting the line go, he dug his stout legs into the oily embankment. Driving his body away from the river, he pulled harder on the lines. Again and again he pulled with all his strength. All the while, he kept an eye on the long canoe which was now turning towards shore.

"Who is there?" Miller called out to the shadowy aberrations.

"Owanux!" a voice from the long canoe fired back.

Miller recognized the word as that to mean 'Englishman'. He felt that was a good sign in that the Indians may have recognized him and might lend a hand. The canoe turned immediately towards where he was securing his boat. As the Indians approached, the rain started to ease. Miller stood, covered in mud. His boat was halfway out of the water and shifting about in the muddy embankment.

"Ahoy there, friends." Miller said.

At that moment, Anne reached the last line of trees where the terrain fell away to the river bank. She heard the Indian voices and she slid behind a stout tree, just as they stepped out of the canoe. She caught her breathe and fell to the ground instinctively.

Knowing his boat was finally safe, Miller wrapped the lines around the base of a nearby tree. Cakes of wet mud fell off of him. The Indians approached him slowly stretching their legs in the process. Harsh words flew from the mouth of the smaller Indian. He spoke in anger and in his native tongue. Miller tried his best to follow the source of his irritation but to no avail. The night air filled with a tension as nasty as the storm.

Up on the embankment, Anne looked on terrified. She clung desperately to the base of the tree. She could hear the heated words in the voice of one Indian and felt the tension in the voice. Instinctively, she thought to run to the house and get a weapon for her father. But this seemed impractical, as she calculated how long that would take. Something told her to stay. She felt powerless, unable to do anything but pray.

The rain stopped completely. Far overhead the storm's heat lightning persisted. Flashes illuminated the shoreline, making the figures look larger than life. Anne covered her eyes in an effort to clear the twisted surreal images. She tried to pray with every ounce of faith she could muster, but the words of prayer would not come to her. Another brilliant flash forced her to look up sharply the quickly down to where the men stood. She could see her father was still arguing with the smaller Indian. Suddenly, she heard the Indian scream a war cry.

Anne straightened and saw the warrior swing his knife high over his head. Its nasty blade flashed brightly for a second from an unknown light source. She did not know why her father didn't try to move away. He seemed to just stand there and take the blade full into his chest. As Jonathan Miller crumbled to the ground, Anne's body went limp and she dropped to the base of the tree. A shiver ran through her; her stomach heaved and turned itself inside-out. She tried to cry out, but couldn't. In her mind, she saw the scene clearly. It would not go away: the stabbing, the face of the Indian, her father sinking into the mud. All she could do was hug the earth, burying her face deeper into wet ground.

A new series of lightning bolts filled the air around her. A nerve shattering crash of thunder followed, pulling Anne away from the earth. She lost her sense of being and of where she was. Then she heard the voices again from down at the riverbank. She looked out but her eyes could not focus. All was a blur. She saw what looked like several warriors pushing and shoving each other. Shouts came and went. The Indians seemed to be everywhere.

Anne ducked down again behind the tree. She felt the Indians were all around her now. Minutes flew by but they felt like hours to her. She dug her fingers into the bark of the tree she hid behind. She did not feel the pain of her gripping so tightly, nor see the blood rolling out from under her fingernails.

"Where are you Lord God!" She whispered angrily.

More minutes of desperate confusion slid by, it was interminable. Anne rolled away from it, away from reality, and drew back behind the solid walls of her relentless desires. It was stable there, calm, controlled. Secure in her new surroundings, Anne saw that she was no longer in the Connecticut colony…no longer a member of any family, or country, or race. In her delirium, she saw herself as a single ray of light floating over a drab landscape. Then, suddenly, she started to move. Faster and faster she flew -- a green landscape gave way to a dark void – a place where nothing was, nor ever was. No humans, no animals, no trees, rivers, or sky. She flew like a bird over dark emptiness, and she flew for what seemed like an eternity. She flew at a maddening pace until she finally saw a dim light off in the far distance. Racing towards it, she realized they were the stars in the sky -- millions and millions of stars. Clear, twinkling, shining so bright they made her laugh. Anne laughed louder and louder until all was wonderful again. She smiled and hugged herself in sheer delight. In a flash, a face appeared. It was the young Indian; his beaded head-band, face and body paint, so well defined as the lines in the palms of her hands. And there, on his neck, was something else - a deep, long gash running along the side of his neck. The warrior laughed at her, mocking her with muddied hands raised.

A sudden cold cutting sensation disrupted her dream. She opened her eyes and a drop of rain hit her in the face. The shock of where she was caused her to catch her breath.

"Where am I?"

Anne rose to her knees. She looked out toward the dock.

"Father?!"

Her own cry startled her. It hurt for just a moment. It was a strange pain, the like of which she had never experienced. As it slowly eased, she felt light and euphoric. She closed her eyes and tried to shake it free. She lost consciousness, and felt hard to the wet earth.

A swirling vortex of color and noise made her limp body twitch. She saw herself holding her ears and screaming so loud that the trees began to fall all around her. She heard her father's words over and over again; '*I will consider your request to return to England. Perhaps there is merit in it after all.*' Anger and hatred replaced her fear. '*I will consider your request to return to England. Perhaps there is merit in it after all… perhaps there is merit in it after all … perhaps there is merit in it after all.*'

As the anger festered the vortex evaporated, and a sense of calm and bitterness swept over her. Hours of wonder in this new world consumed her. And then, she saw a young, handsome man appear in the middle of it all. He smiled at her. Before she could smile back, the image was gone. At that moment she regained consciousness.

Anne lifted herself to her feet. All was quiet. The Indians were gone. She looked around and saw her father lying in the mud directly in front of her. She could not remember walking down the embankment. That did not matter now, for she felt nothing about anything. The storm evaporated but for a few scattered raindrops popping here and there - the wind down to nothing. Now, for the first time, she heard the lapping of the river against the shoreline. She looked at the body lying in the mud. It was all that was in focus now. She closed her eyes briefly. When she opened them, she found that she was still on earth and still alive. She was in control of her life; it hadn't fallen apart. She was stronger now and she felt it, and it felt good. All was going to be fine.

Through her clouded vision she realized that her father's boat was missing. She smiled. "So, it was a wasted endeavor," she said aloud.

Her body and mind were now at ease. She knelt down next to his body and checked for a pulse. She then checked for a breath. There was nothing. She lifted his arms and placed them carefully on his chest. Content that she had done all she could, she rose to her feet.

"There is no God," she said, her words rolling off her lips with ease.

She looked into his face, but couldn't discern any of her father's unique features. It was simply a person, a muddied person, any sleeping person or dead person. Eventually, she convinced herself that, perhaps, it wasn't her father at all.

Anne thought she heard someone coming, but she quickly realized it was nothing more than her own anxiety. She saw images of the events just moments earlier. The chill of the young warrior's scar and his muddied hands were all she could think about. She knew it was time to leave. For a moment she thought she forgot something. Looking back at the body, she frowned.

"Who are you?" she asked.

Anne waited several minutes for an answer. None came. She felt warm and content that she had completed her chores, and now it was time to head home. And then, gradually, she walked away. She no longer felt an attachment toward the lifeless man lying in the muck. He was gone, and all her feelings about her father and the life she had before were lost along with his ridiculous boat.

CHAPTER 6 – A Clue

* * *

When Elizabeth Miller finished recanting her recollection of the night of the murder, she looked as if her soul had left her. Her eyes were damp, cheeks gaunt, and posture misshapen. Peter knew she had reached deep down within herself to pull out everything she should tell him, and things she should not have. To his disappointment, however, he had gained a little more than he knew already. It was clear now that the answers would have to come from Anne.

It was time to leave. Peter rose from the table, excused himself, and promised to provide her with reports on his progress, though he knew his words fell on deaf ears. As he walked out into the daylight he saw Anne in the distance. She stopped what she was doing and waved to him vigorously. He could see her smiling and knew not why she was so happy in light of the circumstances. As he turned away and headed back down the path he had come by, he suddenly knew why. A smile crossed his face. And, without thinking twice, he vowed he would return as soon as possible.

* * *

When Peter returned to the outpost it was getting near evening. He found a number of people moving about doing different things in the bustle of a growing outpost. The place was alive now with some semblance of normal village activity in preparation for dinner and securing their homes and livelihood for the coming of the night. The familiar smell of freshly caught fish greeted him. He soon entered William Smith's place to find him with an older woman engaged in a lively conversation.

"Ah Peter! Come meet my wife."

A round, cheeky woman of fifty walked quickly toward Peter. Her full dress was draped with a soiled apron. Introductions were exchanged and Mrs. Smith offered Peter some tea while William proceeded to show him a room where he could stay. It was a simple boxy room with two bunk beds, no windows, and a series of wall hooks for hanging clothing, weapons, and tools.

"There's no one else using this room," Smith said. "So it's all yours for now. The room next to yah is larger with four bunk beds but we have two trappers in there now and we felt yah might not like the smell of 'em."

Peter laughed. "Thank you," he said.

"There ain't no door as you can see, but yah can hang some of them hides over the front if yah like some privacy. Someday I'll put doors in."

"I can help you with that," Peter said. He stepped into the room and considered it carefully. "It will do fine, Mister Smith."

"Will, call me Will."

Peter nodded.

A voice from the main room rang out. It was Mrs. Smith calling them back into the main room where she was pouring the tea. To Peter's surprise she had brought out biscuits, some dried slivers of smoked venison, and a bowl of apples, all of it placed on the dining table they used for themselves and their guests. Three small plates accompanied the tea cups and they looked to Peter like they were imported from Europe.

"Here we are, a little dinner," she said.

"I will be glad to pay for mine," Peter said.

"That won't be necessary," She said. "First night is free."

The three sat down and ate and drank with a lively flare. Peter felt his mind and body slowly unwind and become filled with a state of comfort he had not felt for days. He felt a home, at last. He let his excitement about being in Connecticut known to them as well as his appointment as sheriff. He asked a hundred questions about a hundred things but did take care to avoid any conversation about his trip to the Millers. He knew such talk would sour the moment. Before too long the food and tea were gone and Mrs. Smith rose and picked up a plate.

Peter rose also. "May I help you clear the table?"

Mrs. Smith looked at him and smiled. She turned to William. "Do you see this?"

"Huh!" The old man grunted.

"Mister Wallace, it is a pleasure to know that good English manners are still in practice. It has been a long time since anyone has offered to help this woman with kitchen chores. "

"It would be my pleasure to help you, Madam."

"Well, I thank you but no.," she said, and added Peter's plate beneath her own. "It is a refreshing change to have you here. Please sit. I'm certain you and Will need to discuss more important things.

"Good words, woman," Will said. "Now, bring us the rum."

Mrs. Smith stood over him and made a face. She would not budge.

Finally, Will rose as gracefully as he could. "Please."

She smiled, went off and deposited the plates, then she stepped into the back storage area and emerged a few minutes later carrying a large bottle of rum and two pewter mugs. She poured them a heaping amount and left. The two men tapped their mugs together then took a long swig. On the swallow, Smith squeezed his eyes tightly and gave a wistful sigh. Peter watched him in sheer delight and smiled.

"So, yah met Anne?" Smith asked.

"Interesting you should bring her up first."

"She's a willful young lady."

"So, I've seen."

"You're a handsome lad. Did she flirt with yah?"

"Mr. Smith!" Peter exclaimed, incredulous. "She is the daughter of a fine…"

Smith raised a hand, shook his head and said, "No need…no need to explain."

Peter looked at him from the corner of his eyes. "But, you are correct," he admitted. "She is willful."

William examined his mug as if it held great value. "She comes here often, unlike her mother who we never see. Most times it was with her father. He kept her on a tight leash. But other times she came alone, walking all that way through Indian Territory. I could never understand it. And when she got here, she lost interest in what she was sent here to gather and would wait down at the pier for any sea captain or other adventurer to arrive."

"I see."

"She took a fancy to one sailor who came here often. They would disappear at times. Now, I'm not suggesting nothing but … well, she *is* ambitious."

"Well that would be hard to believe from what I saw."

"And…," Smith said in a leading way. He took another long swig of the rum, closed his eyes as before and loosed another sigh.

Peter became challenged. "And what, Sir?"

"Will."

"And what, Will?"

"And beautiful?"

"I …," Peter started to say. "I do not want to talk about Anne. I want you to tell me about that night. What can you recall?"

"Ah! Back to business I see. Yah can talk to me about Anne another day young man - any time."

"So noted."

"Right. And now, what I must tell yah must stay between us," the old man said with a sobering change in his demeanor. "Never tell anyone what I am about to say. I need yah word on this."

Peter leaned forward. Smith did likewise – their faces illuminated by a single candle. Peter's focus was complete, his words in low volume. "Will, you have my word."

"If what I tell yah gets back to me, my entrails and my wife's will be wrapped around that pole out there. That's what the Pequots do when they get mad."

"I understand. Not on my dying breath will I reveal my source."

"Well then, that night was destined to be something special, errr …dare I say, something ominous. We could smell it in the air just hours before sunset. It was a warm day to begin with, a true early summer day, nothing special just a good day to fish or trap or to build a home. Then, just a few hours before sunset, the dark purple clouds rolled in from the south as fast as any I have ever seen in my entire life. Our dogs and livestock became agitated. We went down to the river and looked out over the Sound. We could see it engulf the outlying islands. The lightening was intense, the wind and rain a torrent of energy and hell. Some here prayed for anyone who was out on those islands or the water." Smith was visibly strained and paused to catch his breath. He took another sip of rum.

"Did you see any Pequots that evening?"

"Yes," Smith said clearing his throat. "And this is what yah need to keep quiet."

"As I said, not a word to anyone."

"Well, at first we had some Mohegans and a few Niantics at our village just before the storm arrived. They were here to trade. It was simple and then done. They came in their canoes, but they were long gone before the storm hit us. As I was going about securing things I happen to see a Pequot canoe coming up river. Two of 'em in it. I recognized one as the grand sachem's son. His name is Sassacus. In spite of my better judgment, I walked out to the river bank to see if they were comin' in for shelter. I called out to 'em. Sassacus turned to me and gave me a look. It was one I had not seen before from him. If looks could kill, if yah know what I mean."

"From what I've learned," Peter said, "the murder happened sometime just after the main part of the storm had passed through."

"Yes, now here's more," Smith said, then took another long sip of rum. He savored this one.

Peter grew inpatient. "Yes, please go on."

"Well, Sasscaus gave me this ugly look and simply proceeded upriver as if driven by the devil. He was angry and up to something."

"And do you think he killed Jonathan Miller?"

"Well, here's the point. I don't know if he did, but later, much later, after the storm had past I was out again to assess the damage. It was dark as pitch still; suddenly I see an Indian coming out of the woods. He looked stunned and disoriented."

"Who was it?" Peter exclaimed, his eyes bright.

"It was Dekanawida."

"The Powwaw you pointed out to me today?"

"Yes."

"What was he up to?"

"Well, he was dazed, yah see. I called out to him. He walked toward me and didn't stop. We nearly collided so I reached out and grabbed his wrist to stop him. It worked. He turned and faced me. When I released him I noticed my hand was covered in mud. I looked at it and it was that greenish kind. Yah know, the kind you find along the riverbank. Both of his hands and wrists were covered in that stuff. I called out his name and he suddenly snapped out of his trance. Then he apologized to me."

"Apologized?"

"Yeah, he may be crazy as a madcap, but he has always been polite to us. All of us at the outpost respect him."

"And the mud? Miller was killed at the riverbank."

"Which I didn't know until the next day. But I did ask him about the mud on his hands. He said he was communing with mother earth. I know the powwaws have strange training methods. And one is that they go off on their own into the forest or, as in this case, to a river, lake, or near the Sound, and bury their hands in the soil. Then they sit there and drift off into some kind of a trance. They say that over time they can feel the earth talking to them. The earth tells of her sorrow and pain, or her joys and whispers, and sometimes of impending doom."

"I see."

"Yeah, so I didn't think anything of it until I heard of Miller's killin'."

"It sounds suspicious."

"Yep! But he's not the type that kills."

Peter cradled his mug in his hands. "You have told me he is crazy as a madcap a number of times now. Could he have been that crazy to kill a man?"

William paused and thought on this a moment. "I recon' he could-a."

"And Sassacus? Maybe he was out on the river to find Dekanawida."

"Yeah, it's possible. But that look. If anyone was out for a killin' that night I'd say it was Sassacus."

Peter looked uneasy but managed to say, "I do want to speak to them."

Smith laughed.

Peter smiled at the old man. He admitted that he needed to be careful with his approach to Sassacus—if he managed a meeting at all. Any discussion of the night of the murder would be tricky—and probably awkward—especially so given that Sassacus was the son of the grand sachem. Nevertheless, Peter knew he had to try.

"And yah not mentioning my name, right?" William asked with a lift of his mug.

Peter met William's mug with his own. "I will find another way to broach the subject with them."

"Yah can't go there alone either."

Peter nodded and set his mug back on the table. "I know. The Governor is sending more men here in six days' time. Several will work with me as deputies. I will put together a small group with a guide and translator then approach them. I was told I can bring some gifts to Tatobem as a sign of good intentions of my arrival and my purpose here."

The news of more men arriving seemed to encourage Smith, and he wiped his mouth with the back of his hand. "That should work. Just don't discuss the Miller murder on yah first visit."

The two men talked for another hour before Peter got up and excused himself. He told the Smiths he was retiring and thanked them for their hospitality.

In his small room he hung a large animal skin over the doorway for privacy, but the two nails gave way and the skin crumpled to the floor. So Peter fetched a hammer and rammed the nails hard into new spots above the doorway. A voice from the next room rang out, one of the trappers in the four-bunk room shouted for quiet. Peter muttered something about the smell of trappers, re-hung the animal skin, added a second skin to buffer the wafting stench, and crawled into bed.

*   *   *

Over the days that followed, Peter went about making a name for himself in the little village of New London. Though it wasn't officially called that yet, there were suggestions that it should be named such. Most of the traders simply called it the 'The Pequot Outpost'. Peter had visited most of the homes in the area and let the settlers know that he was there for them and that the Governor would continue to support the new Connecticut colony. Peter also would not rest until he asked everyone about the Miller murder. But in spite of his efforts, there were no new clues.

Peter studied the land: its rivers, mountains, shoreline, forests and swampland, and there was plenty of it. Some of what he found was not on their maps. He wrote down and drew up much of what he observed on parchment paper provided by the Smiths'. He often thought of Anne Miller. She was so beautiful and had been through so much. It amazed him how well she recovered from seeing her father murdered. He surmised that she had a strong constitution and was truly a frontier woman, the kind of woman that would make someone a fine wife. He had hoped she would have come to the outpost since his arrival, but she had not. Or, at least if she had, he had not seen her. Finally, he determined that after his deputies got to the outpost, he would go and visit her.

On a crystal clear morning, Peter found himself walking down river following a school of fish that had been churning up the water all morning. It was nothing like he had ever seen. The fish frolicked happily flashing their silvery bellies in the sun. *Clearly a mating ritual*, Peter thought. He took note of the day, season, sun and weather. *Perhaps it would happen again under the right conditions.*

A flock of birds suddenly flew out from a large tree. At that instant he turned and spied two Indians on the opposite side of the river. They were heading south, in the same direction he had been walking. They were carrying a small bark-canoe filled with fishing gear and nets. Peter waited along the shoreline and followed their process. They had seen him as well and decided to launch the canoe. But instead of going about their task, they paddled straight toward him.

Peter had a lump in his throat as they approached. But, as they drew near, he saw the calm in their faces and realized they had no ill intentions.

"Greetings, English!" The younger Indian called out.

Peter raised his hand in acknowledgement. He felt a sudden weakness in his knees, but it was just for a fleeting moment. He swallowed hard. They wore only a simple cloth around their waists, moccasins, and their bodies were painted. They beached their canoe with ease and quickly brought it ashore. They flipped it over to drain the water that had collected, all the while keeping an eye on Peter. He stepped up to meet them.

"I am Peter Wallace. Greetings to you."

The young one looked a bit puzzled. Then he smiled. "I have seen you," he said, extending his hand to clasp with Peter's. "I remember your jacket and hat.'

"And I have seen you." Peter said, returning the smile.

"I am Dekanawida, powwaw of the Pequot's of Missituck."

The other Indian was much older with a fair amount of grey hair showing, but sporting the powerful arms of a man much younger. He wore beads on his head, indicating a symbol of his authority and stood three inches taller than Peter. He stepped up alongside of Dekanawida.

"This is our sachem, Tatobem." Dekanawida said, his tone one of respect.

"An honor to meet you, Sir," Peter said, extending his hand.

"He does not speak much English."

"You speak it very well."

"Yes, my father brought me to the White villages many times when I was young. He had me stay with a family until I learned your language. I will translate."

Dekanawida exchanged words with his leader. They spoke in their native tongue for a period longer than Peter would have liked.

"I told him I saw you on the hill a few days ago. You were with William Smith. This makes you a friend."

Peter nodded. "Yes, that was me. I saw you too. I wish to be a friend to you and the Sachem."

"We seek this."

"As well, I do," Peter said.

The Indian pointed out over the water. "You were following the fish?"

Peter looked downriver and saw fish teeming on the surface again. "Yes, I've not seen that behavior before."

Dekanawida followed Peter's stare towards the fish. "This is a good time to catch."

"So it seems."

"But I am a spiritual man first, one who heals and drives away illness. We came also to find you. My Sachem wants to know if you are a soldier."

"Tell him I am not a soldier," Peter said carefully. "My job is that of... Well, a man of the law."

"Man of law!"

"Yes, we call that position a sheriff: one who executes the law of the land."

"The land cannot have laws," Dekanawida said flatly.

"Well, not the land... what I mean is ... the people of the land need laws, rules to live their lives by; the righteous and just way."

"And you watch over them."

"Well, yes," Peter said realizing, for the first time, his position in a different light. "That is what I have been changed with." A subtle frustration was becoming apparent to the both of them.

"Just one man?" Dekanawida asked.

Peter hesitated. He though that should these Indians learn his deputies were coming soon they might turn away from him. For a moment he struggled with being honest or not. Taking a deep breath he said, "I will have help soon."

"You sound like a soldier," Dekanawida said, pointing to Peter's short sword fastened to his wide belt.

Peter looked at the Indian carefully. He could tell his own words were falling into half-truths. Peter shook his head.

"Dekanawida," Peter said, with a smile that cleared the frustration from his face. "I would like to have an open dialogue with your people - a way to communicate without fear of reprisals. I want you and your Sachem to know I can be trusted."

"I am sure you know that that sort of thing takes time."

"Yes, of course."

"I will discuss this with my Sachem after we have fished."

"Yes, yes that would be fine. It will be at your convenience."

"Peter Wallace, perhaps we can talk again on another day."

"Yes, I would welcome that," Peter said.

Peter's mind was racing. *Was it time to mention the Miller murder?* He thought.

Dekanawida sensed Peter had more on his mind. They walked a bit further then Dekanawida asked, "Our people want to know how many more English will come?"

Peter looked down. He realized the Indian probably already knew the answer. Without another wasted second he said, "There will be more. How many, I cannot say. My plan is the same as yours. And I do want to meet with you again. You can convey to your people what I am here for and what my intentions are. You and I can work at keeping the peace."

"I welcome that."

"This is a good start."

"Yes. However, I see you are still troubled," Dekanawida said.

"You are very astute. I, indeed, must ask you something. And we can keep this between us. Did you know an English settler named Jonathan Miller?"

Dekanawida's eyes darkened. "I have heard of his death. He was a good man – an honest one. We trusted him. But it is not a good time to discuss this. White men are accusing us."

The Sachem grabbed Dekanawida's arm and spoke to him in a whisper. Peter realized that while he did not know much English he probably understood what Peter was discussing once he mentioned Miller's name. Peter waited patiently until they were done conversing.

Dekanawida turned to Peter. "My Sachem feels it is time to go. He invites you to walk with us for a while. We can talk a little more today, but we will need to leave you soon. We have to fish."

Peter motioned for the two to go first. "I will follow."

They walked along the shoreline for some time and then returned to where the canoe was placed. When they departed, Dekanawida planned to meet with Peter again in two days' time at that same place by the river.

As Peter returned to New London, he was thrilled at his progress. His happiness suddenly made him think about Anne Miller. He could not get her off his mind. She was so beautiful, and that inadvertent touch of her hand still lingered on his skin. But it was her lips that haunted him most of all. He wanted to taste them so, and he prayed to God that she was as interested in him as he was in her.

CHAPTER 7 – Running-bird

* * *

The last few days June had slipped away like water through fingers. Peter was so busy helping the settlers and writing letters to Boston that he nearly lost track of time. July rolled in and with it the salty, sticky humidity that would build slowly during the day and then drop itself on New England like a lead veil. Peter could no longer wear his navy doublet and his white linen shirt was soaked with sweat by days end. The Smith's tried to get him to wear the more confortable moccasins but he was not quite ready to abandon his black leather shoes. Still, he realized that eventually he would need to have something else that fit the environment.

Dekanawida was true to his word and arrived at New London two days to the hour after his first meeting with Peter. There was a sense of urgency in his step and after gathering up Peter he led him to the far south end of the river where a rocky bluff rose high and offered a wide view of the great Sound. When they reached the crest of the bluff, Dekanawida pointed out over the water to the southeast.

"That is where she lives. You cannot see the Island-of-little-god from here but once you are out on the open water it will come into view quickly. She is the seer. This is the time for you to go to her if you want answers to your questions."

"I have heard of this ... seer."

"She has helped others, but guarantees nothing."

"She is the squaw called Running-bird?"

"Yes, she only goes by that name. Her half-breed husband said it was good for her to have an English name now that your people are in this land to stay. It is a way for her to be recognized among all peoples as someone important."

"I see," Peter said. "But does her tribe accept this?"

"The Sachem of the Manisseans often uses an English name as well, as does his wife. They support Running-bird and look upon her as a gifted treasure. He is called Grey-feather, his wife, White-fox."

"I will remember these names should I encounter them."

"It is a long journey from here over the salt water. But Running-bird only needs to feel a person's voice and to hear his words and she will know the truth."

Peter turned his keen eyes out over the great sea. He tightened them in an effort to see further, that done, his vision would lengthen more so than any ordinary man. He was capable of seeing things on the water that others could not, but no island came to his view. "Will she come here, to the Thames?' he asked.

"No. We received word from our neighbors, the Niantics, that there was trouble on her island the night of the great storm."

"Trouble?"

"Yes. A Mohegan scouting party was there. A fight took place."

"How can she help me?"

"The Jonathan Miller murder. It was the same night. The Niantics say she has knowledge of the evil on that night."

Having heard the word, 'evil', Peter juxtaposed the evil Elizabeth had described with what Running-bird must have experienced. The resulting image was so incomprehensible that he had no reply for his new friend.

"Peter Wallace, you must go to Running-bird before she loses this knowledge. She does not hold it forever it is said."

The harsh imagery was now injected with a sense of urgency, and Peter managed to blurt, "I will … I will, Dekanawida. I thank you."

Dekanawida motioned for them to go. They walked down the bluff and into the thinly wooded area along the river and headed north. Dekanawida hesitated once then proceeded unevenly, his gait not the free cadence Peter was used to seeing. Finally, it came out. "And Peter," the Indian said, with a firm tone, "I know you know that Sassacus and I were on the river that night."

Peter stopped abruptly, Dekanawida likewise. They faced each other. Peter looked into his eyes and waited.

"It does not matter," Dekanawida continued. "It is simply that I know what you have learned. And it is true - we were on the river that night. But now I will tell you this, and you cannot be in doubt of this, I will tell you that neither I, nor Sassacus killed Jonathan Miller."

*   *   *

On the afternoon of the great storm, Running-bird had been out on the southeast corner collecting shells, down at the rocky cove she loved so dearly. The cove was a place she enjoyed going to for solace and discovery: each benevolent tide presented her with fresh shells, and every new wave brought a renewed sense of adventure. The shells arrived in all shapes, colors, and sizes. The sea birds helped contribute to the shelly graveyard by devouring the leftover flesh inside, leaving a clean trinket behind. She would make tools out of them or polish smaller ones to make wampum and jewelry. Her handcrafted items were desired by many, and were used as barter with the mainland tribes.

But now she was in a hurry to leave. A sudden, foreboding wind brought with it purple-dark clouds filled with anger. There had been little warning as the once brilliant day quickly vanished like a frightened deer.

Fair Running-bird was nine-months pregnant, and the southeast corner was a good three miles from the Manissean village. She could only waddle as she desperately tried to reach the crest of a high dune. She was in great discomfort with her unborn child and normally would not have been concerned about the impending rain. However, this was different. She knew she had to get back to the village post haste; there was danger in this tempest and her baby meant everything to her.

She rambled over a series of large rocks and then up over some low sandy dunes as fast as she could. Finally, free of the shoreline, she raced out across a grassy open meadow. The storm followed on her heels. Her youth was in her favor; she was just nineteen, but old enough to have her first child as many of the women in her tribe had by that age. Beautiful indeed, and with the warmest, light-brown eyes that anyone had seen the likes of before. She was the prize of the island.

When the village finally came within sight, she breathed a sigh. But the ominous clouds now loomed overhead, making the land nearly as black as a moonless night. Running-bird looked skyward, and at that moment she felt warm water run down her legs.

"*Samuel!*" she cried out for her husband as loud as she could. He was always easy to spot, being the tallest man in the tribe. But this time, he was nowhere to be found.

"Husband! Where are you?" she cried out again above the strengthening wind.

Several of the village women heard her and rushed to her assistance.

"You should not be running," one said with a frown. "What if you fall?"

Running-bird was too sure-footed for that to happen. Blessed with balance and speed, she could scurry down the sandy cliffs even faster than any man. Ignoring their concern, she pleaded with them:

"Have any of you *seen* my husband?" she cried out.

"I saw him just before the sun disappeared behind the clouds," the oldest woman of the group said. "He had returned with the hunting party."

Confusion and pain raced through Running-bird. She reached out to the woman for support. Her body trembled.

"He may still be with the other men," the old woman said.

"Oh find him, please," Running-bird said.

"Do not worry about him. You know men are not allowed at a birthing."

Running-bird looked around frantically.

"We will take care of you," the old woman said. "Please, come now."

Running-bird suddenly stopped, and reached down.

"My baby is pushing me. Help me!"

The old woman lifted Running-bird's arm and placed it across her back. She signaled another woman to take her other arm. They made haste toward one of the wigwams.

Finally, a young girl said, "I saw Samuel return. But then he went out again ... alone."

Running-bird drove her feet into the ground, forcing all to stop. She looked over to the north where several trails led into the dark wood. Suddenly, raindrops the size of small stones crashed down all around them. Running-bird threw her gaze at the young girl.

"The men said he went back to look for something," the girl said with a quiver in her voice. "But they know not what."

The older woman glanced at her in disgust. She frowned at the girl and shook her head.

"He is in trouble!" Running-bird blurted out, in between waves of pain.

"Nonsense, he is our mightiest warrior," the old woman said.

Running-bird's eyes danced about from woman to woman. Her body was shaking out of her control. She clung tightly to the others.

A brilliant flash suddenly lit up the dark sky. It was followed immediately by a booming thunderclap.

"*Samuel!*" Running-bird screamed, and then collapsed.

The women carefully lifted her and carried her off to her wigwam. They had thought to take her to the sweathouse where women usually went when they had their monthly cycles, but the sachem's wife insisted they take Running-bird to her own wigwam. They arrived in seconds. The women helped her to the ground in a sitting position and braced her back with a wooden structure. They prepared her for the birth.

The old woman dismissed the others. She was the sachem's wife and was named White-fox. This name was given to her when a fox as colorless as a ghost was seen shortly after her birth. Everyone in her tribe revered her. She was second only to the sachem.

With the comforting hand and soft words of White-fox, Running-bird slowly regained her bearings.

"Do you not see him?" White-fox asked.

Running-bird looked into the old woman's eyes. Minutes passed. Her breathing quickened.

"No."

"You are distracted," White-fox said in a comforting tone.

"No, there's something in the way."

"What is it, my child?"

"I … I … nothing like this before…it's just … empty."

"Then clear your mind. There are more important things to concentrate on."

Frightened, Running-bird reached out and held onto White-fox.

"Reach into your past. To happy times," White-fox advised.

Obediently, Running-bird searched for all the good things she and her husband had done. She hoped she would find enough to quantify that the sum total of her life was worthy and honorable. Suddenly, there around the edges of fond memories, she remembered the day she met Samuel. She let the joyous moments of her love for him flow to the front of her mind. She felt no pain now; she bathed in those euphoric days of adolescent infatuation and discovery. And, she remembered that magic day when they were married -- a day all her fellow tribesmen would long remember.

In her relaxed state, she knew it was time to concentrate on delivering her child. But just as she thought she'd get through this ordeal, her contractions intensified. Running-bird's moment of joy ended abruptly with a pain so severe she thought it would be the end of her.

She screamed out above the rattle of the rain.

Three squaws suddenly entered the wigwam, soaking wet. The oldest of them whispered something to White-fox.

Running-bird knew that her husband was in trouble by their long faces. A grey vision suddenly materialized deep within her mind, and she sensed that there was a struggle.

Her visions were a curse and a blessing. They ranged from images of joy, to those of great fear. Faces appeared and disappeared amidst the colors of her delusions. It was a gift she had come to accept after many years of denying it. She used only the good visions to help her people, and never spoke of the bad ones. But this new vision had colors of red and purple, unlike any visions that she had ever seen or felt before.

"*Husband!*"

"Running-bird, hear me." White-fox said softly, "He has not returned." She reached out and held her arms. "The Sachem has sent some of our men to find him."

"He...he...he must come back," Running-bird said, pushing and grunting. "He must."

"He will. And he will see your beautiful child."

"*No...I...*" Running-bird struggled to get the words out. A flash of red crossed her vision. "*Ahhhhhhh!*" She screamed out.

"Princess!" White-fox shouted above her. "Concentrate. Help your baby."

White-fox's demeanor quickly changed to one of great concern. She examined Running-bird's body. She turned to the other women in the wigwam. Her face darkened with despair.

"Is something wrong?" someone asked.

"Fetch the birthing oils," White-fox ordered. She told the squaw to also find the powwaw, the tribe's medicine man, and bring him. She instructed another to bring some cloth and medical instruments that was used for difficult deliveries.

"*Hurry!*" she added.

There was only one young squaw left behind with White-fox.

"Tell me what's wrong?" the young woman asked. "Running-bird cannot hear us now. Just look at her."

Running-bird was sweating profusely. Her eyes closed and her cries diminished into a distant gurgle.

"This baby is larger than any I have seen," White-fox said, as she spread her fingers over Running-bird's extended belly. "You must fetch the Sachem."

"The Sachem?"

"Yes, I know it is forbidden," the old woman said, carefully. "But Running-bird may die if we do not."

"But, I ..."

"Quiet! Bring him to me. Now, do as I say."

The young squaw hesitated for a moment and then said, "Yes ... I will get him."

* * *

Samuel knew that he could find it again. He had seen a strange flowering plant on the return trip from the hunt, but was too pre-occupied with carrying the slain prey to fetch it. He had memorized its location and had ideas of returning to dig it up as a gift for his wife. It would be a wonderful surprise for his loving Running-bird.

He was much older than she was, but Running-bird showed great maturity for a woman her age and the two had become one. And when he married her, he wanted the best for her, and that included a private wigwam not to be shared with any other. It was built with great zeal, and she filled it with her colorful shells and fragrant flowers.

So tall and strong he was, yet fair in skin - fairer than all the men of their tribe, and his eyes were as silver and green as the full moon. The two were very different from the rest and some in the tribe tended to avoid them. Running-bird adored Samuel. She saw deep into his heart and knew it was true.

Many years earlier, Samuel had come from the mainland aboard a great Dutch ship on a warm summer day. It was a day designated for peace and for trading, for all men. Samuel's father was a Dutch mariner, who sailed with Captain Adrian Block. It was this Dutch Captain that brought Samuel to the Island-of-little-god for the first time.

Samuel's mother was a native Narragansett, land of the parent tribe of Running-bird's people. His mother had told young Samuel many stories of the beauty of the island where their ancestors had lived, and he yearned for the day he could see it.

Captain Block had visited the island on several occasions, and traded in peace with the Manisseans. When Samuel's father had died, Captain Block had taken him under his wing and treated him like a son. It was this captain that brought him to the island of beauty. On a sunny June day when young Samuel's feet first touched the shores of the island, he knew that he wanted to stay. And indeed, he did. No one could persuade him otherwise. Everything on the island had seemed brighter and cleaner than places on the mainland. Fish and game were plentiful; the sky bluer, and the water clearer. And, when he saw the young girl they called Running-bird come flying down sandy dunes, he knew his destiny was sealed. Young Samuel begged Captain Block to let him stay on, and the wise Captain agreed. He knew the young man was ready to make his own decisions.

And now, with their first child on the way, Samuel was the happiest man in the universe.

Samuel ran fast through the forest, gobbling up the trail with his long stride. He knew he would have to hurry when he heard the rumbling thunder approach. Deeper and deeper into the forest he ran, heading toward the north end of the island.

There were many trails in this section of the forest. Some very narrow where a hunting party would have to go in single file; other trails opened up very wide and would melt away into clearings. Here and there, views of the great sea could be seen. One trail cut out from the forest and edged a high sandy cliff overlooking the straight. On a clear day, the mainland was visible. Occasionally, a storm would wipe out the footpath, and other times, the trail would just fall out from under foot. Samuel knew of two men who were killed this way several years back, having fallen from a great height, their bodies crushed by boulders that were torn away from the cliff wall.

After several more miles, the forest suddenly grew strangely still. The air turned dark and gloomy, and a grey mist rose around his feet from a place deep within the earth. He stopped for a moment to listen.

Where is the usual clatter of the colorful warblers and singing thrushes? He thought. He recalled that the birds usually panicked before a storm. Perhaps they were already in hiding.

Looking up, he found a small opening in the canopy of thick leaves. He could see the rushing of the grey clouds, slung low in the sky, but he heard no wind. His confusion evaporated by the popping sound of rain on broad leaves. And, at last, the wind's voice returned and filled the air, rustling the leaves on high.

Samuel got his bearings and sprinted even faster toward the location of the prized flower. His senses told him that Running-bird needed him, and that he should hurry. He crossed over a log bridge that covered a low muddy area and then scaled up an embankment. He stopped again to listen. Unnerved by the sounds of nature and the need to get back home, he ran faster.

The trail dropped down into a narrow ravine that channeled a small stream at its center. The path grew faint here, as a thorny thicket consumed most of it. Samuel had to slow his gait so as not to tear his ankles to shreds. As he did so, he felt the strange quiet return. The pitter-patter of the rain drops had subsided. He knew something was wrong. His thoughts turned to Running-bird and his soon-to-be first child. Above all, he knew he must return safely.

Suddenly, he heard a branch snap behind him. Reaching for his knife, he turned sharply only to see the flash of an arrow fly at him. He tried to dodge it, but was an instant too late. The arrow cut through his flesh at his midriff, just as a hook does as it is torn from a fish's mouth. Samuel saw his own skin open and blood erupt from his side.

"*Mohegans!*" Samuel shouted in pain, as he spied his attackers. Instinctively, he clenched the loose flesh at his side and held it firm.

Samuel dropped to the ground. The air was split by a war cry from a location behind him, and then another in front of him. Playing dead, he let the first warrior come down on him. At the last instant, Samuel sprang to his full length and faced the man head on. The young Mohegan was immediately startled by Samuel's size and tried to stop himself. Samuel lunged with his knife and sliced the young buck's neck, not far from his jugular vein. The attacker stumbled sideways trying desperately to maintain his balance. Samuel reached out and grabbed him before he fell and threw him to the ground even harder. Not wasting a second, he jumped on the young warrior and slammed his enemy's face into the ground.

The second Mohegan was on him within seconds. This attacker was older and stronger. He swung a tomahawk high over his head as he closed in. The two men collided while Samuel was still kneeling. The warriors rolled backwards and separated, one clasping a tomahawk, and the other, a long bloodied hunting knife.

"Mohegan vermin," Samuel said, amidst the growing pain in his side.

"Die, Manissean dog," the Mohegan said.

"*Leave us* ...." Samuel struggled to say.

"Not until you have paid for our fathers."

"*Leave us in peace.*"

The Mohegan charged again; their weapons locked as Samuel fell on his back. The warrior suddenly noticed Samuel's eyes. They were a color he had seen only in the Europeans, but none like this color.

In a flash, another figure emerged from the woods. Samuel had to act quickly. A twist and a kick with his powerful legs caught the Mohegan on top of him by surprise. He freed his weapon and slammed it into his opponent's side. Blood sprayed over the two of them, and Samuel rolled free.

The third Mohegan quickly noted the size and strength of his enemy and pulled up a safe distance away. He had never confronted an adversary as tall as this one. He hesitated momentarily, and then locked eyes with the bloodied Manissean before him. A stark realization swept over the Mohegan – the silvery eyes of the tall Manissean were giving him away.

"You will die, now," Samuel said. He was breathing heavily, but still felt he could fight on. He squeezed his eyes shut to clear the sweat rolling down from his brow. Then, realizing who he was now facing, he braced himself. *This one is going to be difficult,* Samuel thought.

The Mohegan warrior was armed with a tomahawk and knife, and the gaze of the devil. He showed an air of confidence that was unnerving. He was known as Quick-blade. It was the English translation of his Indian name that he preferred to be called by. He had wanted it so to make it clear to all white men what his talents were, and to his Indian enemies, a name that inferred he had English ties.

"*You die!*" Quick-blade fired back. Raising his knife, he flipped it in the air in front of him. Then, grabbing it in mid-tumble by the blade, he hurled the knife at Samuel. Not wasting a second, he charged down on him with his tomahawk and a war cry that echoed through the forest. In the seconds that followed the forest grew strangely quiet. The sounds of the violent struggle became a distance echo.

*   *   *

The Mohegan who attacked first was covered with blood. He tried to sit up, but his head was still spinning. His companion, Quick-blade, came to his assistance. He extracted a piece of cloth and a leather string from his pouch and covered the gash along the young buck's neck. Quick-blade helped his friend to his feet.

"This...this tall Manissean...was strong," the bleeding warrior named Onasakenrat said. His body seethed in pain.

"He could have killed all of us," Quick-blade said, angrily.

The bleeding warrior winced in pain.

"He is a freak of nature," Quick-blade added.

"Yes, but did *you* kill him?" Young Onasakenrat asked.

"Look," Quick-blade said, pointing to his left.

The body of the giant lay sprawled out at the foot of a nearby tree.

"He was strong," the wounded buck said, struggling to walk.

"Yes, I know this warrior," Quick-blade said. "I saw his grey eyes. He is the one they call Samuel the Dutch."

"He was as strong and as fast as my father."

"Faster!" Quick-blade remarked, looking suddenly glum. "Your father lies dead, nearby."

Onasakenrat was stunned by these words. His father had been invincible. His name was Onerahtokha – a sachem of the Mohegans and sachems never die on scouting parties. *How could this be?*

The two warriors stood in silence for what seemed to be an eternity as they looked over the slain body of their mentor. Finally, the rain came again, and Onasakenrat dropped to his knees.

Onasakenrat cried out. "How? …Impossible!"

"I do not know," the Quick-blade said. "Your arrow did not hold true."

"I cannot explain it… I had him," Onasakenrat said. "My father wanted me to take him. I was certain my aim was true!"

"It is the forest. It is evil. It would not allow us to leave without losing one of our own. He had the eyes of the devil."

Onasakenrat reached out and held the body of his beloved father. The proud young buck was only nineteen and had never been humbled before, not like this. The feelings welling up inside of him were all new. His body shook, and now fears of losing control swept over him. He turned away from his friend.

Suddenly, a pain shot through his neck. He grabbed the bandage and held it firm. His neck burned and his insides burned even more so. He was back now, a son of a sachem, a warrior destined for greatness.

"Yes, I saw the devil's eyes, too," Onasakenrat said, gasping in anger, saliva spraying from his mouth.

Suddenly, a clamor arose in the near distance. Several small birds scattered among the tree limbs.

"We must go!" Quick-blade said.

Onasakenrat tried to calm himself and as he did his vision suddenly faded. "Help me, my eyes are failing. I cannot see."

"Close them," Quick-blade offered. He took out a soft cloth for his pouch and placed it in Onasakenrat's hand. "Let me wipe them clear."

Onasakenrat recovered a bit. He regained his vision and examined the area focusing on his father's body.

Quick-blade said, "We will leave your father."

"No, we will take him. I will bury him at home. The great Onerahtokha cannot be left like this."

"Your wound is severe. How can you..."

"Silence! I will carry him myself, if I have to."

"We cannot make it out of here with him."

"Watch me!"

Quick-blade understood it was no use arguing. He gave his friend a nod. With great effort, they lifted their dead leader. Young Onasakenrat's neck started to bleed again, but his anger drove him forward. His father was dead and this was never supposed to happen.

"Manissean dogs," he repeated over and over.

After a short while, they found their long canoe that had been left hidden in a small cove.

"Your father will be proud," the Quick-blade said, at last. "We came to scout this corner of the island and we have achieved that and more."

"*What more?*"

"We have killed a great warrior of the Manisseans."

"*It is not enough,*" Onasakenrat cried out, jeering at his friend. "I want vengeance. My father died on my account, and I *will* have vengeance."

They carefully placed the body of Onerahtokha in the center of the great canoe. Looking around to make sure they weren't seen, they launched the canoe into the Sound. They headed back over the dark waters toward the mainland and home.

*   *   *

Far off in the deep woods to the north, Samuel struggled to open his eyes. His lids felt so heavy and he was unable to move a single muscle in his body. Confused as to where he was and how he got there, his mind raced to find an answer.

He blinked. Something was taking shape. The world he saw was blurry and monochromatic. His heart ached for Running-bird. As it did, a short lived surge of strength filled him. Then it abandoned him just as quickly. He suddenly knew his life was draining from his veins. There was no stopping it. Unable to move his body, he squeezed his eyes shut and then opened them again. Color suddenly filled his view. Through the dark forest and heavy underbrush, he suddenly saw something that made him smile. At last he had found it.

Shades of gray encircled his vision. Yet, he remained focused on the flowering plant. So delicate, with streaks of white, purple, and blue, it was. He knew it would look perfect in Running-bird's garden. She would see it there and think of him when he was out on hunting parties. It would be a testament of his love for her. No one else in the village would have such a flower. It would be theirs and theirs alone.

He wanted to reach out and take it but his body didn't respond. The darkness swept over him quicker now. With his last ounce of strength, he lifted his eyelids one more time and took in the full light of the beautiful purple flower. That was all he could do. If he filled his mind with its beauty, he would know that somehow, Running-bird would see the same thing. He just knew it. It was his last reflection of life.

CHAPTER 8 - The Crossing

* * *

The great sachem of the island entered Running-bird's wigwam, looking as angry as the storm outside. He was drenched from head to toe, but after removing his deerskin cloak and examining the scene, his demeanor quickly changed. His gaze softened as an eddy of great pride enveloped him. He knew this birth was going to be a unique and important one, and yet, he also feared what it may bring.

He was called Grey-feather, and was the leader of all the Manisseans. The island he ruled along with the elders was the Island-of-little-god, a jewel set far out in the ocean. Occasionally, on a clear day, it was still visible from the mainland. Grey-feather ruled with a firm hand and a good heart. Now standing tall in Running-bird's wigwam, the heat from his fading anger was drying him off.

"Why did you call for me?" He asked his wife.

"We thought this would be normal birth," she replied sharply.

"You should have known better."

"But..."

"This is the child of Samuel. There is nothing normal here."

White-fox had assisted with difficult births before, but the outcome of this one was uncertain. She knew full well Samuel was a half-breed and his family lines might be an issue, but every indication from Running-bird was that she could manage the birth. Now, with her husband chastising her it was just one more distraction she did not need. However, out of respect for him she let him have his perfunctory words.

"Yes," she replied. "I should have called for you sooner."

The grand sachem looked over at Running-bird, ignoring his wife for the moment.

"Forgive me," she added.

Grey-feather crossed his arms. His wife dipped her head. She gave him the time he needed to quell his anger. Finally, she looked up.

"Sachem, what say you?"

He stepped closer and looked down at Running-bird. "Does she need to be cut?"

"Not yet. We will try one more thing."

Quietly, she asked him to kneel down behind the limp body of Running-bird. As he did so, two squaws entered the wigwam carrying linens and oils.

"Take Running-bird by the arms," the sachem's wife said calmly to her husband. "Hold her firm and pull her arms up."

As Grey-feather followed her instruction, his wife started to apply the oil around Running-bird's dilated vagina. Then, she carefully directed the other women to massage Running-bird's abdomen and legs. Slowly she directed them all into a rhythm of coordinated pushes.

"Good," she said. "The baby is coming now."

Applying oil to her hands, the sachem's wife stretched Running-bird wider. Within seconds she could see the baby. She grabbed onto its head, and gave a slight tug.

The baby arrived without a sound. For a moment, they all thought it might be dead. White-fox lifted the child carefully and wiped clean its face for all to see.

"It is a girl," she said, "and, she is breathing just fine."

At that moment, the baby opened its eyes wide enough for all to see. The infant stared at them at first and then, a moment later, cried out. White-fox observed the round shaped eyes and fair skin, and was not surprised. The others in the wigwam drew back in fear. Grey-feather looked upon his wife - she upon him with endearing eyes.

"Like her father!" White-fox exclaimed.

Grey-feather smiled. "Like her father, indeed. This is a great day for the Manisseans."

Running-bird had been in a catatonic state until she heard her baby cry. The young mother's eye opened wide and looked around, disorientated at first, but then smiled warmly. She reached out for her infant. "My baby," she said.

"Yes, and you have a daughter," White-fox said smiling broadly.

The women rejoiced as the baby cried out louder. Running-bird gathered some strength and lifted the infant resting her against her breast. The move worked as the baby stilled. The women took turns fawning over the infant, and little by little they could see that Running-bird appeared in good spirits.

After a while they all left the wigwam, leaving Running-bird alone with her child. She drew the baby's head up and carefully examined her.

"Like your father," Running-bird said in a murmur. "You will be as strong as he."

Two hours later the rain diminished and eventually stopped. White-fox returned with a goatskin filled with water and a handful of blackberries.

"What word of my husband?" Running-bird asked, excitedly.

"No word, princess," the sachem's wife said.

"You called me princess?"

"Yes, today, you are a princess. We have all agreed on this."

"That is kind ... but untrue."

"Your child is a gift from the great spirits, and she has made you royalty."

"No, we are like everyone else."

White-fox sat down on the edge of Running-birds cot being careful not to crowd the young mother. She reached down and stroked Running-bird's long, thick hair back behind her delicate face.

"We saw her skin color and her bright eyes," White-fox said. "This birth was special. Never has there been such a storm so severe during a Manissean birth, never have so many of us assembled before either. The spirits are speaking to us today. This makes you royal and your child has the signs of the great Dutch captain in her."

"No...no, she has the great Samuel in her."

The sachem's wife smiled. "Yes, of course."

Running-bird looked toward the door. "Do... do you think he is safe?"

White-fox gave her a puzzled look. "Well now, what do *you* see?" she asked, inquisitively.

"My gift fails me on this," Running-bird said.

White-fox gave her a moment. Finally, Running-bird shook her head in the negative.

"Samuel is a strong man," White-fox said. "And when he learns of this new child, he will be a very proud man."

"But, he needs a son."

"We need both sons *and* daughters to replenish our people."

Running-bird reflected for a moment.

"Can you sit up?" White-fox asked.

Running-bird shifted her weight and her pain returned. She winced but recovered quickly. She handed her baby to the sachem's wife.

"Drink this water," White-fox said, "and eat these berries. I will go out and see if there is word about your husband."

"Thank you … my queen."

White-fox smiled warmly at her words, then rose and left the wigwam.

Moments later the dark sky started to lift. Slivers of light cut into the horizon like the long knives of warriors.

White-fox stepped outside to witness a glorious sunset of warm colors and misty sunbeams. She was very happy for Running-bird, and for her people. All the nations had lost so many of their people over the last winter and the feelings of sadness and melancholy had held its grip on them for many months. The Manisseans, like her cousins, the Narragansetts, were still in a catatonic state of disbelief. Over half of them had perished from a disease that swept the tribes during the previous winter. They had been lucky many years earlier and escaped loss when the first epidemic broke out. So many were gone now - so many of the innocent, and so many of the good ones. White-fox had prayed hard for their survival on this earth, and now, with the birth of Little-grey-feather, perhaps there was hope after all.

White-fox moved quickly throughout the village, gathering what information she could about Samuel. She met with her husband briefly and then returned to Running-bird's hut.

"The Great Sachem says your child can have his name," she said, with a sparkle in her voice.

"Grey-feather?"

"Well, Little-grey-feather for now," she said, as she took the baby and lifted her high above her head. "We'll see what she becomes later."

"But my husband had…"

"There is no greater honor," White-fox said interrupting her. She lowered the infant and rocked her for a spell.

Running-bird hesitated. She knew the sachem's wife was right.

"Yes, Little-grey-feather, it will be."

The baby was handed back to Running-bird. The instant she touched her, Running-bird's countenance darkened. She sat up and looked again at the doorway.

"What is it?" the old woman asked.

Running-bird did not respond.

"What do you see?"

Running-bird lifted her head higher. Except for a rain drop or two tapping on her roof, all fell silent. The quiet was deafening.

Then, Running-bird spun around and looked directly into the eyes and heart of her mentor. The young mother's face was filled with fear. Her lips quivered. Tears formed in the corners of her almond shaped eyes. Without a word, the old woman knew she had seen an unthinkable terror.

The sachem's wife sat down next to Running-bird and held her tightly. The baby stirred but did not cry. It was this new life that kept the two of them from going insane over what they knew had happened to Samuel.

*   *   *

The body of Samuel was found the day after the great storm. When news of this was brought to Running-bird her worst fears and premonitions were brought to bear. The sum total of all that she had learned about love and life in her brief time on earth fell into mass confusion. The loss consumed her; the fear of being alone sent her into a panic like none she had ever felt.

Running-bird struggled to get up from her birthing cot not realizing she was clinging tightly to her baby. She managed to lift herself off the cot but didn't get very far. The baby twisted in her unfeeling arms and finally gave out a cry. The sound and length of her voice was so stark and similar to Running-bird's own. The young mother snapped back to reality. She gazed upon her daughter. The child cried out again. Running-bird gasped. She pulled the baby up and kissed her forehead. Cradling her now, Running-bird started to sing. As she sang, she drew from deep within her mind and called upon her gift to see the light. But the light was only a dim collection of vague images of Samuel with nothing for an answer.

The women who had brought the heartbreaking news to Running-bird returned and entered her wigwam. They tried to comfort her but it wasn't until White-fox arrived that things were put in perspective. Dismissing them graciously, White-fox was left alone with Running-bird. Running-bird was sitting on her cot with her baby cradled in her arms, both in a relative calm.

"Has your child suckled?"

Running-bird seemed to not hear.

"Princess, has the child eaten?"

Running-bird turned to her, a pale blankness on her face.

"Ah yes, you grieve," the old woman said. "This is good. You must know that all Manisseans grieve today."

"My husband will never know his child," Running-bird finally said.

"I disagree. Through your gift and through your eyes, I know that he will. And he will smile."

"Thank you, my queen. My baby suckled just a short while ago."

White-fox took the baby and examined her. "Does she have a good appetite?" the sachem's wife asked.

"Yes, indeed. And she sleeps very well."

The sachem's wife stepped over to the edge of the cot and knelt down. She slowly placed her hand on Running-bird's forehead and held it there until she was satisfied with her temperature. Then, with the tenderness only a mother would know, she stroked the young girl's long hair and spoke softly to her.

Running-bird reflected for a moment on her words as her body and mind slowly found peace.

"And what of Samuel?" Running-bird asked.

"Your husband's body has been taken to the burial grounds," the old woman began. "He was our greatest warrior. And now, his spirit is on the long journey to the final resting ground."

"His life was too short."

The old woman dipped her head. Running-bird's breathing quickened.

"You must remember never to mention his name," the old woman said. "At least, not for one year, as is our tradition."

Running-bird nodded. She felt her strength returning.

White-fox looked at her with endearing eyes. She waited until she felt Running-bird was at ease. She said, "He was a devoted husband."

"Yes, I love him so. I miss him …" Running-bird couldn't finish.

"His spirit is on the long journey to the southwest," the old woman continued, trying to divert Running-bird's sorrow. "Should he hear you call his name, you may delay his progress, or worse, confuse him to the point of losing his way."

"Yes. I will respect his name."

"And remember to tell the young ones in the village, too. No one should speak his name until your child is one year of age."

"I will, my queen."

"And when my husband dies," White-fox said, warmly, "you must change Little-grey-feather's name to another."

"But…but Grey-feather will never die!"

"Someday he will, my child."

"I cannot see this," Running-bird said, raising her hand to her forehead. "Oh Spirits, I have never seen it."

"Your powers are great, sweet princess, but we all must pass on to the other world when our time is called."

"Why have I not seen this?" Running-bird suddenly felt frightened. "I have never thought to look on his passing, not ever. Now, I see nothing!"

"Please, do not upset yourself. Your grief blinds you. It is normal."

"But…does this mean … I could die before him."

"Hush now, sweet princess. You will find the answer in due time. And you will certainly out live my husband."

Running-bird looked down at her baby. The child's face was bright and content; she had finished nursing. Running-bird handed her over to White-fox as she rose to her feet. The old woman wrapped the baby in some fine linen cloth she had received in trade with the English and sang softly to her. Running-bird sat up.

"I am ready to stand," she said in a determined voice.

"Let me get someone to help you."

"No, just lend me your arm."

White-fox hesitated, but then knew this strong-legged independent woman would prefer to do it on her own. She extended her free arm to Running-bird.

The young woman reached out and held on, then rose to her feet. Running-bird took several careful steps.

"Do you have any bleeding?" White-fox asked.

Running-bird checked herself.

"No, not severe my queen."

"This is a good sign."

"I think I will go outside. I need to see where my husband rests."

"You are too weak. Please rest."

"All I need is some water. Would you get me some?"

The sachem's wife nodded and handed the baby back to Running-bird. She stepped over to a corner of the room and extracted a skin filled with fresh water. Then she took some ears of corn that were hanging from a support beam. Reaching down to a covered hole in the floor, she extracted several root vegetables.

"I will prepare these for you in my wigwam and bring them right back," White-fox said. "Rest now, Running-bird, your baby needs you to be strong.

* * *

Onasakenrat and his comrade, Quick-blade, had just left Block Island and found they were in another fight for their lives. They paddled hard with their sturdy oars putting distance between them and the cursed island. All the while, the wounded Mohegan continued to grumble, "Manissean dogs! I loathe them."

The waves were now twice as high as they had been when they first came over to the island. The sky was dark as pitch. They could see very little and welcomed the occasional flash of lightning to give them bearings.

"It will catch us," Quick-blade said in disgust. "The storm will swallow us, and no one will learn of our triumph today."

"Ha! What triumph?" Onasakenrat said. He spat on the water.

"I *am* certain the warrior I killed was the one they called 'Samuel'," Quick-blade said. "Surely, you could see that we have achieved a great victory?"

"*Fool!*" Onasakenrat cried out. "He killed my father, and now we are dead."

Quick-blade, paddling in the front of the canoe, turned and glared at his friend. To his shock and awe, Onasakenrat indeed looked like a picture of death – his eyes were as black as the night, his face was white as a ghost.

Suddenly, a wave crashed over the bow and smacked him in the side of his head. He managed to hold on for dear life and then turned back to the dark sea, driving his oar into the briny blackness.

Onasakenrat cried out, "My father, the great Onerahtokha, sachem of all the Mohegans east of the Quonitocutt River, lies dead in front of me. And you … you, my friend and brother in war, you say we have achieved a great victory?"

Onasakenrat would have continued, but his wound opened slightly and a trickle of blood flowed out. He clutched at the bandage and secured it tighter.

Quick-blade remained silent. He could see white caps and foamy spray ahead. He knew it would get worse and would require all their strength to pull the oars through the rough water. His keen eyes, however, kept them on a true heading.

"Yes, my friend," Onasakenrat said, more softly now, looking at his friend's back, "row … row until you die. Until we die. No one will know."

The waves suddenly shifted and rolled against them. The canoe was built from a solid piece of maple nearly twenty feet long. Hollowed out and charred on the inside to make it water tight. It was designed to withstand the rough waters of the straits between the island and the mainland. Both Mohegans had been in rough waters before, but now they were pushed to their limits.

They started to pitch-poll, but Quick-blade was swift to respond. He shifted his weight and steered the long canoe into the waves. Then a series of high waves crashed over the bow, punishing them severely.

A disheartened Onasakenrat wondered what his father would do in a situation like this. *Return to the island until it blows over*, he thought. That would not work; they were half-way across to the mainland already. Though the storm and sea were worsening, he thought it best to press on. Little by little, his strength faltered and his will diminished.

The body of his father was nearly floating in the water that had filled the wooden canoe. All Onasakenrat could do was watch its grotesque form float lazily like a jellyfish, as if it had come back to life.

Another huge wave crashed over the bow slamming Quick-blade in the face sending him reeling backwards. He found himself next to the body of their dead leader. The face of the corpse brandished a sardonic grim that startled Quick-blade.

"*I can't pull it alone!*" Quick-blade screamed. "*The canoe is too heavy.*"

Onasakenrat just looked at him. He tried to stand in the stern of the canoe, but fell back. Water sloshed and sprayed all around him.

"*Help me!*" Quick-blade cried out.

Onasakenrat rolled onto his side and sneered at his friend. "But it was you who killed the great Samuel of the Manisseans," he growled. "Was it not? Was it not you?"

The wind howled above his words with just a few of them landing on Quick-blades ears. But in spite of nature's buffering, he understood what his friend was after.

"Yes, I killed him… No… We both killed him," Quick-blade said, as sheets of water sprayed across his face. "Now, *help me!*"

Onasakenrat lifted himself out of the mess he lay in. He gaped down at his father's body.

"We?… Yes, *we* killed him!"

"Yes, that is it," Quick-blade said. "You attacked first."

"My arrow brought him down."

"Yes…"

Another wave crashed over them.

"*Help me take the water out!*" Quick-blade screamed. He gave his friend a threatening gaze. "Bail or we die!"

Onasakenrat did nothing. He sat up and just smiled in his false glory.

Quick-blade crawled carefully through the salt water and over the body. Grabbing Onasakenrat by the shoulders, he shook him violently.

"We must get your father's body out of this boat," he screamed above the wind and waves. *"We must survive this!"*

The jolt from his friend and his incomprehensible words snapped the young brave out of his trance.

"What are you saying?"

"We need to remove the water *and* the body. We can't control the canoe," Quick-blade said, frantically.

Onasakenrat looked up. A flash of lightning illuminated the violent sea all around them. He shielded his eyes. His feelings of sorrow and grandeur faded. At that moment, Quick-blade grabbed his oar and slammed it on the side of the canoe within inches of his friend.

"We are sinking!"

As his friend's words reverberated through the empty canyons of Onasakenrat's pity, something changed. All around them the sea instantly became silent like nothing they had ever felt or seen before. The wind diminished and died out; the waves calmed to an even smoothness. The two men looked around. Then Quick-blade started to tremble.

"It is an omen," Onasakenrat said, regaining his senses. "I can see the storm ahead of us. It has not gone away ... It is the sea. The sea wants my father."

"The sea ... yes, the sea," Quick-blade said.

"Never mind," Onasakenrat said. "Come, help me with my father. You are right, my friend."

Without a word the two young bucks carefully lifted the slain warrior chief. They slid his body into the dark purple sea. Onasakenrat watched his beloved father float away from the long canoe. It was as if something under the water was pulling him. When the body was nearly out of sight, the waves started to rise again. The wind suddenly whipped up, and white frothy wisps of salt water filled the air all around them. Quick-blade resumed bailing and removed as much water from the great canoe as he could.

"Row!" Onasakenrat now screamed. "Row, you devil! Row or I will kill you. I will gut you and toss your entails out over the sea. I will feed you to the fish."

Onasakenrat slammed his oar into the purple-dark sea and drove the tormented canoe forward. It rose and crashed down over each wave more violently with each stroke forward. The young buck found the hidden strength and will he was born with. Quick-blade slipped and fell on his back. He was tossed about, but grabbed onto the side with both hands and regained control. Still, he was hard pressed to keep from being thrown overboard.

"*Row!*" Onasakenrat screamed again.

Quick-blade rose in the bow, found his oar, and struck the water hard with it.

"Row harder."

"*I am with you!*" Quick-blade screamed back.

"Someone will die for this! Someone will pay for my father," Onasakenrat said. But the anger was short lived as fatigue set in.

"Someone will pay...." He said, weakly.

*   *   *

A day after his fight with Samuel, Onasakenrat awoke in great pain. He looked around and realized he was back in his home village, not fully recalling how he got there. The wound along the side of his head and neck throbbed like nothing he had ever felt. Swiftly the events of the day and night before came back to him in detail. And the loss of his father - coupled the anger in his heart - provided a welcome distraction from his physical pain.

The village was in turmoil over the loss of the grand sachem, Onerahtokha. The Mohegan elders held a meeting and debated on how they would retaliate against the Manisseans, and they discussed who should be their next sachem. The debate lasted for days. Tempers flared. Bodies were shoved about and some vying for dominance had to be restrained by cooler heads. Eventually, Uncas, the great one's brother, was named the new grand sachem of the Mohegans.

When Onasakenrat heard of this, he demanded to know why he was not selected. The elders pointed to his age. So he withdrew from them and sought medical treatment for his wound which was becoming infected. Gradually, over several days, the long gash closed and healed. He strolled around in the sun, often with his arms folded. He held his head high and acted like he should be the heir to the title. And, indeed, many felt he was.

"Tell us how the great one died?" they would ask him.

Onasakenrat told of his father's heroics and of the many Manisseans he slew, and of how he held off three of the enemy while he and Quick-blade escaped. But Quick-blade looked on from a distance and spoke just a few words about their ordeal. Quick-blade simply would not be part of it. He let his friend run on with his stories. He knew Onasakenrat's stubbornness and anger were just too much for one man to challenge. Plus, it would not have looked good had the tribe members found out the truth; how the great one's body was dumped into the ink-black sea in an effort to save their own skins.

And as for Onasakenrat, he was planning greater things for his people and greater revenge on the Manisseans, including the elimination of the remainder of Samuel's family and all that stood in his way.

CHAPTER 9 - The Will of a Woman

* * *

Peter would not wait until his deputies arrived before securing passage to Block Island. He found two fishermen with an eighteen foot skiff and a mast just as long who would take him there as part of their normal work day. He paid them well and they set out early the day after Delanawida advised him to go. He was assured that the Manisseans were friendly toward the English and that some knew the language well enough to communicate with him.

They left the Thames behind and headed out into the great Sound. Being out on the water again filled the young sheriff with a renewed sense of adventure. The water was an open highway without forest or river to impede his progress. He could go anywhere.

As they drew closer and the island took form, he could see the gold cliffs rise high on the southeastern side, nearly nine-hundred feet it was estimated. Toward the north end the terrain was low but filled with green forests, and at the center the main Manissean village stood adjacent to a large open meadow.

Peter looked into the depths of the water and could see it was taking on a brighter blue-green color indicating the bottom would soon rise to meet them. The fishermen executed a tack to the starboard and pulled down the sail. The boat drifted quietly toward the sandy beach in a slightly parallel course.

"Right!" the older seaman said. "You're off now. You have one hour and then we'll be back for you. If you're not at this spot, we'll have to leave you behind."

"I understand," Peter said. He unfastened his belt and sword and dropped it in the boat. He removed his shoes and stockings as well. The boat slowed further and he jumped over. His feet didn't hit bottom until he was chest deep. The water was cold but not icy cold. The boat nearly rolled over his head but he managed to use the hull to push himself aside. The fishermen dropped in their oars and steered the boat back out to deeper water.

Peter pulled himself forward through the water being careful to keep his hat dry. The rest of his clothes would have to stay wet on him. Looking toward the beach, he suddenly noticed two braves standing at the shoreline in his line of approach. Emerging from the water, he walked slowly to where they were standing.

"Good day to you," Peter said cautiously. "I am English."

One of the Indians replied in what Peter knew to be a positive greeting. They wore no war-paint but each held a bow, with a quiver of arrows slung across their backs, and long knives secure in leather sheaths'.

"I am here to see Running-bird."

The Indians looked at each other then back at Peter - their matter-of-fact countenances changing to a tinge of anger.

"I am here in peace," Peter quickly offered. "I wish to speak to Running-bird."

With that, one of the Indians turned and ran off up the dunes toward the village. The second one held his hand out indicating he wanted Peter to stay put. After a while Peter tried to strike a conversation with the Indian but he simply remained mute with his eyes constantly glued on him. Seeing it was hopeless, Peter proceeded to take his shirt off and wring it out. Once he was satisfied that he extracted as much water as possible he put it back on and smiled at his watchman. The Indian shrugged.

Moments later, a diminutive Indian woman appeared at the top of the dune, the Indian he had met earlier right behind her. Running-bird appeared to Peter as a mere girl, small with a slight figure. Not what he had imagined at all. He fully expected an older woman with a strong build. She approached him slowly with a very confident gait; he noticed she was carrying an infant.

"I am Running-bird," she said raising her eyes to Peter.

He saw the beauty in her instantly. Her almond shaped eyes lit up as she spoke, her face full of energy.

"I am Peter Wallace, from the Pequot outpost on the Thames … we call it New London."

"I know this place."

"Good. I'm happy you speak English."

"I know English, Dutch, and many Indian dialects. And, you are all wet!"

"I …" Peter looked down at himself, hands extending to the side. He gave her an awkward, embarrassed smile.

She laughed at him but quickly put her hand to her mouth. "I am sorry, you look funny, all wet except for your hat, but you have a nice face. A face I can trust. Let us walk. I think better when I walk, don't you?"

"Yes…yes, indeed."

She led him up the dunes and out into an open grassy field. The hill rose and they climbed higher, the two Indian guards followed a safe distance behind. Near the crest, Peter caught a majestic view of the coastline and the water beyond. Peter could see where the sound ended and where the ocean consumed it. Huge, round waves in long deep-blue undulations rolled in from the southeast smothering any influence from the sound's tides and moods.

Still looking outward, Peter's heart was pounding. He said to her, "Your Island is lovely."

Running-bird turned and stood alongside him. They looked out and as far over the deep blue waters as possible. Without turning to face him, she said, "It is. We try to protect it. Many wish to rule this island. If it weren't for our allies we would have been gone a long time ago."

Turning to her, Peter saw the light from the sea fill her striking face. Her huge almond shaped eyes sparkled in joy. He understood easily how she could captivate anyone's attention. Running-bird's locked eyes with his, her chest filled with air as she understood what he was thinking. Her child stirred upon her chest breaking the silent. She looked upon the infant and murmured something in her native tongue. Peter relished the moment but finally managed to regain his bearing.

"I wish to speak to you about the night of the recent great storm."

"That was the night I lost my husband," Running-bird said sharply.

Her unsettling words struck Peter; he was at a loss for an appropriate reply. Running-bird suddenly turned and began to walk back in the direction they had come. He followed, but could still feel her gaze digging into his mind and soul, and that nothing he thought going forward was without her knowledge. She turned and looked at him, expressionless, as if she was reading his mind.

He found words: "I am sorry. They tell me you have the vision to see things deeper and farther than others. Do you know who killed your husband?"

"Not completely. I have a vision but it is cloudy, and I cannot disclose it at this time. I must be certain before I do, else the innocent will suffer."

"I see. How does your vision work?"

"It just comes to me at times." She reached out and held his wrist. They stopped walking and she turned and faced him.

"You are here to learn from me what you can about the White settler's murder." Peter's eyes widened. "As I look at you," she continued, "I see many things. I can see your heart aches for a woman, and I can see you have the burden of a leader of your people. But there is no magic in seeing this. You wear it clearly on your face."

Peter tried to respond, his mouth opened but nothing came to him directly. After a moment, however, he simply said. "You are quite observant."

"It's nothing really. I just pay attention to detail. You can do it if you try."

"What do I look for?"

"If you want to know if someone is lying to you watch the corners of their mouth, is there a quiver? Observe how they stand: are they standing square to you or is one foot behind the other, or are they moving unnaturally? Are their hands nervously twitching, not knowing where they should be? Are their words forthcoming or in fragments? There, you see, it is easy."

Peter looked down, taking the time to absorb what she had just said. It was clear to him now that she would be able to help him in his task. Looking up at her, he offered, "I will look for that."

Running-bird's child suddenly stirred and made a noise of distress. The young mother shifted the infant and placed her against her chest. This seemed to calm the child.

"I cannot tell you much about the murder of the settler," Running-bird said. "But I know he was killed at the riverbank. So, find out who was on the river that night. Look them in the eyes when you question them, see how they react. And speak again to the daughter who saw it happen. Be firm with her. Have her take you to the location of the murder and see if anything new comes to her."

He considered her advice and nodded in the affirmative. "That sounds prudent. I will go to her."

"May I touch your cheek?" She asked carefully.

Peter looked at her and frowned. Her hand extended toward his face. Their eyes locked and everything around him suddenly vanished. There was no green hill, no blue ocean, no sky. He could only see her warm, liquid, brown eyes grow large and fill his vision. A quiet moment passed. Then his cheek became electric. He felt someone inside his mind, learning his thoughts and desires. Peter recoiled. Still locked in her eyes, he watched hers slowly fall away, back into her face. The absent sky filled in, the hills and ocean returned.

"What happened?" he asked.

Running-bird's face suddenly darkened. Her lips opened and rolled in an effort to form words. Her infant child stirred and let out a cry. Running-bird's posture faltered. The two Indians guards move quickly to her side, pushing Peter aside.

"What is it, Running-bird?" Peter asked. "Did I say something to offend you?"

Running-bird looked up at him, dampness filled her eyes.

"Be careful with her," she said, then lowered her head and walked off with her people.

"Who?" Peter cried out after her. But no answer came.

* * *

Upon his arrival at the Miller farm, Peter found Anne all alone tending to the vegetable garden. She rose when she saw him, smiled warmly, brushed the dirt off her hands and straightened her clothing. She placed her Puritan hat back upon her head and told him that Elizabeth and Hilary had just left by boat to go down to the outpost to sell personal belongings. She said her mother was making every effort to raise money for their passage back to England. Peter had mixed feelings at what he was hearing. But now, overriding this, he felt awkward being at the Miller home alone with Anne. With a warm smile, she invited him inside the house.

Once inside, she had him sit at the main table while she brought out some water and bread. When satisfied that he was comfortable, she sat at the table opposite him. Peter could not take his eyes off her. He tried to remember what Running-bird had told him, but his anxiety to do everything right in front of the woman his passion was screaming for, clouded his thinking. He had watched her carefully as she sat down with all the movements of a lady in the King's court, a woman well groomed and of quality stock. Her posture and grace changed from that of a young girl to that of a woman. It seemed as though he had known her for a long time. It was as if she had chosen that moment to transform her strangeness into the warmth of a lady or of a tender wife. Peter smiled at her and she returned a sweet one. A long quiet moment passed, and Peter felt his body stiffen, his rational mind was leaving him. He took a drink to ease his nerves. Finally, she spoke. She spoke smartly and with exuberance. Peter was then able to relax, as she spoke with the sweetness of a song bird. He listened to her talk excitedly about her dreams and was amused by her animated gestures. She talked exuberantly of her goals and of the future of New London. She spoke of transforming the little village into a main hub of commerce. She told him of her role in all of it. Finally, after many minutes of her excited, rapid conversation, she paused to catch her breath.

Peter was amazed at her energy and offered, "So you have grand aspirations. Do you believe this will happen quickly?"

"Yes! There is great promise here," Anne said. Her eyes were wide open and her breathing began to accelerate again.

"But certainly," Peter said, "you will go back to England with your mother?"

Anne jumped to her feet. "She doesn't want me!" She spun around showing her back to him. A startled Peter watched her, then she turned back around – her face red with rage. "As you will see, Mr. Wallace, she and I are at odds."

Peter leaned back on the bench and watched her carefully as she began to pace about the room. The grace and maturity she demonstrated before the outburst had all but disappeared in a flash. *She is still a young girl, too young to get serious with*, he thought.

"I am old enough to be on my own," Anne said forcefully, alarming Peter (as though she had just read his mind). "I will be eighteen next month."

Peter gapped at her. Finally, he managed, "I see."

Anne caught the doubt in his tone. She stopped pacing, looked down at the floor pretending to be embarrassed. Looking up quickly, she gazed right into his eyes. She straightened her dress without blinking. "Forgive me, Mr. Wallace."

Walking slowly back over to the table, she took position opposite him. She sat down with the grace and poise he had seen earlier.

Peter expected her to speak directly but nothing came. She smiled at him, her face began to glow full and warm. Her beauty was impossible for him to think around. Her chest filled with air and her ample bosom rose and fell with each breath.

Peter blinked and offered, "How will you support yourself? Where will you live?"

"I see you are a practical man, Mr. Wallace. I like that."

"Well, I … I am just concerned that…"

"Fear not, Sir," she said quickly, "I told my mother she could sell the land to the neighbors. They want it. I can stay at William Smith's place temporarily. His wife has already agreed to it."

"Oh!"

"Yes, Mr. Wallace, I have it all planned out."

Peter paused. He was thrilled at the prospect of her being in New London, not far from the new lodging he was to move to. He couldn't understand why he hadn't heard of this from Smith. But, another side of him was anguished at her apparent disdain for her mother.

"Very well, Anne." It was all he could muster.

"Mr. Wallace, have you found the savage that killed my father?"

Peter was puzzled for an instant. He gathered himself. Her eyes narrowed, her head dipped, her arms folded across her chest.

"Why… No."

"He should be easy to find," she said, sharply, "He has that ugly wound I told you about."

"I am sorry to say, I have had no luck, Miss. And, please, call me Peter."

"Peter!" She exclaimed, turning her head slightly aside, eyes strained to their corners facing him.

"Yes," he said, hand moving to the back of his left ear, then rubbing his neck, "you may call me by my first name."

"Very well; so what have you been doing?" Her eyes were square to his now.

Peter shifted uneasily on the bench. "Well, I have made good contact with some of the Pequots."

"Those savages!"

"Do not be so judgmental, Miss. The few I have met are very friendly. But I should find out more soon. I promise you."

"Promise me, Mister Wallace?" There was an immediate shift in her demeanor to that of sincerity. So natural, not contrived, her face looked even more beautiful now to him.

"Peter," he said, correcting her, smiling.

"Peter... Hmmm... I think I would like to call you 'Peter'."

Anne leaned forward, resting her arms and breasts on the table. She looked at him warmly, her eyes lighting up. She pulled her lower lip in and wet it with her tongue. "Peter, indeed," she said.

"Yes, Peter is fine." He said, but didn't hear his own words – he was lost in her. Her face softened even further, a radiant glow all around her now.

"How old are you, Peter?"

"Well, I am ...twenty-four."

"You have nice eyes."

He blushed and dipped his head slightly. He put the mug of water aside and placed his hands on the table seeking to steady himself.

The room fell into a heavy quiet. Slowly, she extended her hands toward his. They looked as soft as cotton, yet with the strength of a good worker. Peter looked to the side. Anne moved her hands closer still, to within inches of his. He looked up nervously, and uncertain on what to do. *Does she want me to take her hands, he wondered.* Flustered, he pulled his hands back and dropped them to his side. She gave him a coy smile.

"I thank you," he said nervous.

"You are indeed a handsome man...Peter Wallace."

"You should not say things..."

She rose from the table before he could finish. He couldn't speak. A lump developed in his throat. She was smiling at him, the richness of her youthful beauty on display. She walked slowly around to his side of the table. Peter's heart raced with excitement. It was like nothing he had ever felt before. It took all his strength and concentration to keep from showing his anxiety.

"Peter Wallace... Hmmm... That, too, is a handsome name."

Peter slid his chair back and attempted to stand. She blocked him.

"Miss... I want to talk to you about the Indian."

"Peter," she said with a grin, "I think you came to see me."

"Nonsense."

"No, it's true; you have come to see me. Haven't you?"

"No, Miss... I..."

Anne slid into the space between him and the table and stood just inches in front of him. She reached out and placed her hand on his shoulder. She pushed him back on the bench. He reached down and held onto it. Peter immediately felt her warmth; her scent filled his head. It was a soft, powdery scent with a hint of apple. His body tingled.

"What's wrong, Peter?" she asked, smiling salaciously. "Why can't you speak?"

She leaned forward and came face to face with him. Her breasts swelled from the gravity change, lifting up so that he could see their fullness. His ears went numb. With a simple flick of one hand she removed a ribbon holding her hair back and let it fall around her face and into his. He opened his mouth in an attempt to speak but she cut him off. She placed her finger on his chin and pushed it up, closing his mouth. Then she kissed him.

CHAPTER 10 – The Capture of Tatobem

*   *   *

It was a dreary morning on the waters of Long Island Sound, when Captain Cornelius Bol embarked from New Amsterdam on his long journey east along the coastline. There was enough wind, however, to keep them moving at a good clip. By the end of the day, he was carefully navigating his bark through a thick mist as he entered the mouth of the Thames River. Headstrong and determined, he thought he was on the Connecticut River and refused to turn around. Finally, when his men began to question his ability, he realized it was time to admit to his error.

"Full about!" he called to the helmsman.

His expedition of twenty heavily armed soldiers and a crew of five had left early that morning and had encountered a heavy fog all along the coast. A summer heat wave ravaged the area for several days, but a cooling front had come in during the night. The resulting fog caused them to sail right past the mouth of the Connecticut; their haste had gotten the better of them.

The Dutch governor had sent them out to punish the Indians responsible for recent hostilities to the people living along the Connecticut River. Three Dutchmen had died over the last month, and when they heard of Jonathan Miller's death, that was their excuse to enter English territory. While Miller was English, he was well liked by the Dutch. Miller and his family had helped several Dutch families get their farms started in the region. The Millers had traded regularly with them.

Fingers were being pointed at Onerahtokha, the grand sachem of the Mohegans, who had indeed been stirring things up. The Dutch and the English settlements were expanding along the Connecticut, but this was Mohegan land. To set things straight, Onerahtokha was conducting raids along the river and in Pequot territory. What the Dutch didn't know was that Onerahtokha was also out on Block Island, causing mischief there, too. Nor did they know that his lifeless body had floated far out to sea.

As they came about, Captain Bol spied a series of buildings on the western shore of the Thames.

"Make towards land," he said.

They dropped anchor a safe distance from the shore. The sun was setting quickly so the Captain ordered a small landing boat to be lowered. He and six of his men rowed toward the lone pier. The outpost loomed ahead and appeared eerily macabre as the weather shrouded everything in grey. An odor of dead fish filled the air. As they secured the boat to the pier, they stepped out and observed what looked like a deserted village.

"They are here," a sailor of rank said. "I can feel it."

"They should be," another said. "With the way the Captain's fuming, I would run for cover, too."

"Might be a trap!" the first replied, looking as nervous as a caged tiger.

Captain Bol raised his hand, indicating he wanted silence. Nothing stirred in the village. He ordered his men to move forward. They quick marched over to the largest building.

"*English!*" Captain Bol shouted at the wooden structure.

Slowly, the door opened.

William Smith emerged, weaponless. Peter stepped out from behind him.

Smith saw the armed men approach his outpost from a side window and knew he didn't stand a chance in a fight. Even with Peter Wallace and a few other able bodied men in town, it was simply not worth it.

"Yes," Smith replied, showing his empty hands.

"What place is this?" Captain Bol ordered, in broken English. He carefully examined the younger man who was armed with a short sword. It dangled menacingly at the young man's side. The Captain spoke to one of his men to keep an eye on him.

"Well…" Smith began with a little hesitation. "I call it Smith's Outpost, which is my name, you see. But my Gov'ner wants to call this place 'New London'."

"New London!" the Captain repeated in a mocking tone.

Smith, still cautious, realized he needed to make clear his neutrality.

"A name isn't important to me," he said. "I deal in trade. I trade with anyone who will trade with me. I have little allegiance to anything else."

The Captain laughed. His men didn't understand at first, but after a quick translation, they too chuckled at the old man's words.

116

"That is typical of you English," Captain Bol said, with a disingenuous smile. "You are always out for yourselves."

"So, what brings you here?" Smith asked, cutting to the chase.

"This infernal fog sent us off course, but now we know where we are. This is the land where Jonathan Miller lives, isn't it?"

"Why yes," Smith said. Peter Wallace's interest was piqued and was about to speak when the Captain cut him off.

"We are here to find a sachem responsible for the murder of our settlers and of Jonathan Miller."

"Is that so?" Smith said, rubbing his chin.

Before they could utter another word, two Indians emerged from the woods just a short distance from them. One was adorned with intricate body paint, finely cut leather pants, moccasins laced with colorful beads, and carrying a neatly tied bundle of eagle feathers.

"Tatobem!" Smith exclaimed.

Cornelius Bol looked briefly at Smith and then back at the approaching Indians.

"I have heard this name," the Captain said, sharply.

"He is…"

"*Sieze them!*" Bol ordered.

At that, the company of Dutch soldiers made haste toward the approaching Indians and surrounded them. Tatobem held his ground as swords and muskets were thrust out at him.

Tatobem and his comrade unsheathed their hunting knives and braced themselves. In his haste, a single eagle feather he wore on his belt fell to the ground.

Peter Wallace could not stand it any longer. It was time to act.

"Captain!" Peter exclaimed, wrapping his hand around the hilt of his sword. "Restrain your men."

Captain Bol spun around and glared at Wallace. "Who are you to speak to me this way?"

"I am Peter Wallace, sheriff of the Connecticut colony."

Captain Bol chuckled once again, translated to his men who laughed along and then replied by repeating: "…The Connecticut colony!"

"You heard me," Peter declared, sharply.

"Regardless," Bol said. "I want this savage."

"He cannot be the one you seek."

The Indians attempted to move away, but the Dutchmen kept them at bay. Tatobem looked a Peter and frowned.

"I accuse this man," Bol continued, pointing to Tatobem, "of insurrection."

"This is an outrage!" Smith exclaimed.

"He is responsible for the death of Jonathan Miller and of my people."

"Impossible!" Peter exclaimed, lifting the hilt of his sword.

"Consider the killer found. We knew him to be a sachem and by the looks of this fellow we have found him."

"How could you possibly …"

Peter's words were cut short as the two Indians made a move to escape the Dutch soldiers. Tatobem's comrade lunged at one of them, and cut the man's forearm sending a spray of blood over the man's tunic. A soldier with a long pike thrust it at the Indian, who dodged out of the way, but fell sideways to the ground. Before he could get up, a second pike pierced his side; the Indian crumbled to the ground in agony.

Tatobem tried to assist his fallen friend, but a sharp blade stung his back, while a second one appeared from nowhere right under his chin. Slowly, Tatobem yielded, dropping his knife in the process.

At the same time, Captain Bol's sword was drawn and was placed just one inch from Peter's chest. Peter made a slight move to back off, but the Captain stepped toward him, waving a finger in the process.

"Stay where you are, sheriff," he said.

"I must protest!" Peter cried out.

"Take the savage to the ship," Captain Bol ordered, signaling his men.

Peter took a threatening step toward him, when suddenly a blunt object struck him on the back of his head. He dropped to the ground like a sack of potatoes.

* * *

Dekanawida had acquired a white linen shirt from William Smith's trading post just over a week ago and had not yet put it on. He felt that by wearing it today, he would be able to set himself apart and focus on the spiritual needs of his people. However, deep down, his plan was to continue to be the link between his people and the Europeans. It was morning and he knew he had an important day ahead of him.

The high walled village at Missituck had given his people a sense of security and power. The Pequots had felled many a stout tree and hewn them into smooth poles that were raised in a wide circle to fend off man or beast. The village had grown to over four hundred people, and they had been living in relative calm since the winter. There were thirteen Pequot villages between the Thames and the Pawcatuck Rivers but this one at Missituck was the largest.

Dekanawida, dressed in his new shirt, stepped out of the wigwam he shared with three other young men. He held his head high as he faced the new day.

Looking up to the sky, he raised his hands and asked the great creator for guidance. His role as powwaw had grown, and he was destined to succeed his mentor who was ailing.

"Today, I begin my new quest," Dekanawida began. "Today, I will devote my life to bring peace and prosperity to my people. Today, and every day for the rest of my life, I shall change the perception our white brothers have of us. When it is done, we shall no longer be known as the destroyers."

"You are a dreamer!" Knoton said, startling the powwaw.

Dekanawida spun around, lowering his hands. "Knoton!"

"And you look ridiculous," Knoton added.

Dekanawida examined his friend up and down, trying to read his body language. It was part of his training.

"It is a symbol..." Dekanawida said "...a symbol of hope."

"It is a foreign one."

"We use their tools, their weapons, and cooking things. They buy our food and use our wampum. We trade with them, do we not?"

"And soon, we will become them?" Knoton asked.

Knoton was five years older than Dekanawida and a hardened fighter. Yet, he cherished his friendship with the young powwaw and feared the direction in which he was heading.

"The Europeans are here to stay," Dekanawida said. It was a tone that was heartfelt, one that drew many to him to hear him speak. "We know that; especially you, Knoton. We have seen more and more of them come each year. They have been a part of this land going back many decades."

Knoton shifted his weight, raised his finger to his friend and said, "My sister and mother died because of them!"

"I know this. The white man's disease has killed many of our people. But, it was a disease, nothing intentional. And, don't forget we have returned the favor. Many of them have died from our sicknesses."

"Not enough of them have died as far as I am concerned. I have killed one white man in my time and will kill again if need be."

"Killing is not the answer. You are the wind, as your name indicates. Be the messenger and scout that you are, and not a killer. "

Knoton raised his head high at the mention of his namesake. He breathed in deeply, held the air in his lungs for a moment then let it out firmly. He knew he was the fastest man in the village. Running messages and warnings across great distances was his calling and his joy in life. Often he felt he was not recognized for this, but now hearing it from his dear friend perhaps his prowess was getting noticed. Both men remained silent for a full minute. Finally, Knoton added, "What is the answer, then?"

Dekanawida looked into the eyes of his comrade. He smiled.

"That is why I wear this shirt, my friend," Dekanawida said, in his musical tone. "It may help me find the answer one day."

"Bah! You make no sense."

"Someday it will, my friend."

"It may be too late by then."

"Will you trust me to do my work?"

Knoton hesitated. Dekanawida's soft, clear tones filled his heart. For a fleeting instant, he wondered if the young powwaw knew something he didn't.

"I will try," Knoton finally said. "But if another Pequot dies at the hands of the white men, I will kill again."

"And I will not let that happen," Dekanawida said, extending his hand. Their arms clasped.

"Dekanawida, you are a good friend. Go ... do your work."

"I will, friend."

Late in the day a great commotion stirred the entire village. Word spread that the grand sachem, Tatobem, had been taken prisoner. Sassacus, the sachem's son, raced through the village gathering warriors. He was seething with anger, and when his eyes locked with Dekanawida he stopped in his tracks.

"It was your white friends," Sassacus growled. "Nothing will save them now."

Sassacus did not wait for an answer – he turned and disappeared in a gathering crowd of warriors. A cry for war rose throughout the walled village. Warriors collected their weapons and raced out through the gates.

Dekanawida followed slowly at first and then broke into a run. Within minutes, over two dozen warriors were across the open field and into the woods. They made haste to reach the long canoes. They ran carrying weapons, oars, and a few sacks filled with provisions.

The Pequots moved quickly through the wooded trails and down toward the Thames River. As soon as they reached the riverbank they launched four long canoes, eight men per vessel. They rowed hard down the river until they saw the Dutch bark. They were in luck, as the bark was grounded in the muck of low tide.

The Dutch had prepared themselves ahead of time, knowing full well what to expect now that they were sitting ducks. The ship was equipped with two small cannons mounted on the stern and capable of swiveling in any direction. Six loaded muskets were mounted on stands to steady the aim of the marksmen.

Captain Bol was furious with his helmsman for incorrectly navigating the river. The poor sailor was thrown down in a makeshift brig next to Tatobem. The bark was tilting on its keel, making it difficult to maneuver the cannon, but somehow the Dutch managed to make them effective.

Sassacus sat in the front of the lead canoe, while Knoton sat in another one directly behind him. The two other canoes were heading across the river in an attempt to see if they could get around on the shallow side. Dekanawida was with this group.

Several of the Pequots launched some arrows at the boat to test the distance. Once they did, the Dutch opened up with all cannon and muskets firing in unison. The clamor was deafening as the air was still heavy with the morning moisture. Only one Pequot was hit in the shoulder with a piece of lead which was enough to knock him overboard. Sassacus signaled his men to back off and retrieve their fallen comrade.

On the far side of the Dutch ship, the two other canoes were closing in. The Dutch scurried about on the deck, mindful of their footing, and aimed their weapons as best they could. All the Pequots stopped rowing in unison and raised their bows. A wave of arrows fell into the ship, hitting two of the Dutchmen, one in the leg, the other in his chest. The Dutch returned cannon fire and managed to hit the back of one canoe, killing one of the Pequots. Immediately the Indians backed off again.

The four canoes regrouped outside of the range of the guns. Sassacus reorganized them, sending the damaged canoe back to shore with the dead and wounded. Dekanawida stayed with the wounded.

Minutes later on the eastern shore, Dekanawida watched the sachem's son mount several more attacks on the grounded bark. None of these were successful. On the last attempt, one of the canoes was split in two by a direct hit from one of the cannons, sending his brethren into the river. Dekanawida raised his hands and whispered a prayer.

Finally, several hours later, Sassacus called off the attack. He returned with a quarter of his men missing.

Furious, Sassacus walked up to Dekanawida with a gaze as hateful as the one he gave him back in the village.

"And you still want to make peace with these devils?" Sassacus asked.

"You can see what war brings," Dekanawida said.

"Powwaw, you amaze me."

"Let me speak to them alone."

"And accomplish what?" Sassacus demanded.

Dekanawida held his ground. He let a moment pass until his leader's words subsided in the echoing air. "A truce," Dekanawida offered.

"A *truce*! The word has no meaning with these white men."

"It is worth a try. I am heartbroken at the loss of my brethren. I cannot stand here and watch more die."

"Tatobem is everything. We must save him."

"Then let me try my way."

Before they could continue, a commotion erupted from woodlands behind them. Minutes later, Peter Wallace, William Smith, and two other white men were brought forward with their hands bound in course twine. They were thrown down at the feet of Sassacus. Venom flew from Sassacus's mouth as the sachem cursed them. As he raised his war club with full intent of crushing the English skulls, a hand suddenly reached out. Dekanawida's eyes locked on his leader. Heated words and accusations erupted between the two until cooler heads prevailed. Then, they all sat. A swift sinister silence filled the air around them, but nothing was said for another hour. Dekanawida finally rose and stood in front of Sassacus.

"My plan was to pay for Tatobem's freedom," Dekanawida said.

"I will not allow it," Sassacus demanded.

"I will take Smith and Wallace with me, no others."

"They will cut you down."

"I think not."

Peter stood. "Listen, to him. I can negotiate with them. They know I am the authority here."

"You," Sassacus said, "you are nothing."

Smith struggled to his feet. "Sassacus, son of the grand sachem, I agree with yah. They'll not listen to Wallace. But Dekanawida's plan can save the lives of your warriors. I can provide you the wampum to free your father so the cost to the Pequots is nothing. In return, I just ask for our freedom."

Sassacus glared at him. He stepped away and walked over to the river's edge. Looking out at Dutch ship, he saw that they were positioning more muskets on the deck. He returned quickly to face Smith and the others.

"Hurry then," he said. "The tide is rising and they will escape."

Part II

1635 - 1656

CHAPTER 11 – A Day to Trade

* * *

One year passed over the land and many more Europeans arrived with alarming regularity. The native inhabitants had long accepted this fact and knew that the trend was irreversible. The key to survival was to build alliances among themselves and with the newcomers.

It took some time to put the Tatobem incident out of Peter's memory but it left its mark on him nonetheless. The Dutch would not negotiate with the Pequots and hung Tatobem in spite of efforts to free him. Peter counted his blessings for making it through his first year alive. And now, he felt he had achieved some success, as relative peace was at hand between the Indians and the Europeans. This had to come months after the Pequots conducted raids on Dutch settlements in retaliation. The raids were not very successful and the Pequots had to return home empty of satisfaction. The Mohegans didn't make it any easier and fought with the intruders as the Pequots had to cross through their territory to get at the Dutch.

It was one year ago that he hand that saved Peter's life and the other white men on the shores of the Thames belonged to his new friend, Dekanawida. Both men worked hard for many months to make things right. After several more desperate Indian raids, the Dutch left the eastern end and promised never to return to Pequot territory. The irony, of course, was that it all started with the Dutch thinking the Pequots were Mohegans, and the Pequots thinking the Dutch were the English.

The murder of Jonathan Miller became old news. Peter was denied an audience with Sassacus and was forbidden to visit their village. His only suspects were the Pequot leader and the Mohegans who were alleged to be on the river that night. The Mohegan villages were many and spread from the western shores of the Thames all the way to the Connecticut River and north to Massachusetts making it a near impossible task to locate a single Mohegan to interrogate. Peter, however, was not deterred and continued to ask others what they knew of that night.

On the Island-of-little-god, or what was becoming the more common reference; Block Island, many still remembered the storm that brought Little-grey-feather to

Running-bird - the same night she lost her husband. The child was already standing and taking several steps. Her skin was fair and her legs very long. Her eye color was that of silver and green; like her father. Running-bird was proud of her child, but became cautious when she realized that she was developing the gift that she herself possessed. But more, it was her likeness to Samuel that Running-bird knew would bring the most trouble. Knowing this, she would have to keep her from contact with the outside world and teach her child how to survive on her own.

By June 1635, trade had become vibrant among all peoples, and the villages and colonies prospered. Block Island was visited during the summer more than ever before. Traders of both races and many nationalities came there to barter their goods. The island was considered neutral ground and its beauty mitigated any hostilities.

On the mainland, Peter watched as the village of New London doubled in size. There were now over fifty permanent residents and dozens of transients could be found there on any given day. In all, nearly a thousand new Puritans came to Connecticut during the spring and early summer. Half of these settled along the Thames River, and the rest to the Connecticut River and points west. Three large settlements took shape: Fort Saybrook, at the mouth of the Connecticut River, and further up river at Wethersfield another grew, and at New Hartford, which was geographically appealing as it was halfway between Boston and Fort Saybrook. Peter was instrumental in moving people to these places.

The Dutch had interest in taking control of Fort Saybrook, and several small skirmishes erupted there in the spring. Eventually, the English built a larger, formidable stockade and were able to keep control of it. The Dutch eventually gave up all desire to control the Connecticut territory and focused on New Amsterdam and developing colonies along the Hudson River.

Peter was now living in New London in a small four-bedroom home, built for government employees and transient sea captains. It had a fireplace where they were able to cook their own food. Peter knew it was going to be temporary for him and spent as little time there as possible. During the year, he had made several visits back to the Millers' farm. It was Anne that he wanted to see the most. He just couldn't get her out of his mind and his heart. He had approached Anne's mother appropriately, as a gentleman would, when courting a lady. And, Anne indeed had become a lady that summer. She was eighteen and filled out with fine proportions as befitting a hard working woman. Anne had taken on many of the chores her father had done, but needed help from the neighbors from time to time. Her sister, Hilary, was only thirteen and could only do so much. Peter lent a hand as well, spending long hours and afternoons at the Millers'. It didn't take long for Elizabeth to see what his intentions were, and she was pleased.

On Peter's next visit, he chose a blustery summer afternoon when no one cared to work very hard. It was a free and easy day. As he turned the familiar corner in the path to the Miller farm he saw Elizabeth near the front door to her home. He approached her smartly.

"Mr. Wallace," Elizabeth said, smiling. "It is a pleasure to see you again."

"Good day, Madam," Peter said, lifting his hat.

"I presume you came to see Anne."

"I cannot deny that, but first I must ask if there is anything I can do for you today?"

Elizabeth looked out across the yard in front of her modest home and then over to the fields beyond. It was past the time for cultivating the land and getting too late for planting seeds. Only a fraction of the fields had been prepared. But, she didn't care anymore. A pile of garden scraps and stale bread lay near a stool where she had been peeling and cutting.

"Well ...no, it is...well, there is nothing urgent. I simply do not want to spend any more time or money on this farm. I do plan to leave soon."

"Please do let me know if you think of anything."

"Very well, Peter."

They stood there for a moment in silence until a whiff of soil and germination filled the air. The sun was bright and heavy on the land -   various bird species were chirping wildly at each other competing for what Elizabeth had left on the ground. Peter saw the desperation in her eyes when she looked back at him.

"You will find Anne down by the river," she said.

"Thank you, Madam."

Peter stepped away and walked out into the field. There were just a few rows of green corn stalks showing and several other assorted vegetables. The livestock that once grazed in the fields were gone, as they had been sold for coin. As he looked around, he knew there would not be enough food to last through the next winter. He turned and headed toward the river.

Stepping sharply onto the trail he had traveled many times before, it suddenly brought back the memory of the day he first came. He recalled how he saw Anne from a distance, pulling water from the well. He smiled. He thought about the first time she kissed him, and he smiled again; this time, broadly. And then he thought about all the other times, too. She had made it a habit to plant a kiss on him every time they were together. That is, when Elizabeth was not looking.

"Peter!"

It was Anne's voice. He looked up and saw her waving. She was wearing her signature summer dress that clung tightly to her thin waist. Her bonnet was draped behind her back, revealing her long amber hair. As always, it sparkled in the intermittent sunbeams that found their way through the thick green canopy. In one hand, she carried two fish suspended from a cord, and in the other, a fishing pole resting the length of it on her delicate yet strong shoulder.

"Anne!"

He waved and broke into a run. Anne dropped her catch, and they met in a warm embrace. He lifted her and spun her around as if she was light as a feather. They kissed in a sweet, sensual, single exchange of lips on lips – a place so private and delicate that only humans can relish in.

"Oh Anne, how wonderful to see you," he said.

"Oh my." It was all she could say.

"Anne."

"Peter, my love." She kissed him again.

"You know it is against Puritan law to kiss in public," he said with a disingenuous frown.

"There is no public here. Kiss me a hundred times. This is open land and no law exists here." She rose to his lips and planted a warm kiss, lingering just long enough to make him dizzy. "And I love you, Sheriff Peter Wallace," she added.

"We should be as one," he said, with what little breath he had left.

"Yes."

"Would you be my wife?" He asked awkwardly now.

"Of course."

"Oh, my love..." He hugged her even harder. "I ..."

"Would you provide for me?"

"There is no question," he vowed.

Anne pressed her warm body against his. Her breasts warmed his chest. Her left thigh pressed against his leg. "You could?" She asked, kissing him again. She could feel his manhood swell.

"Absolutely!"

"Then do it!"

"Will your mother approve?"

Anne pulled back and looked at him hard. "Forget my mother. She will not have anything to say about us."

Peter gaped at her. "We have discussed this."

"Peter, my mother is leaving soon."

"This does not bode well."

"Don't worry. *I* am staying."

"How can..."

"Hush, my darling. Leave this to me."

They talked for a while longer; then he accompanied her back home. He helped clean the fish she had caught while Hilary brought in some berries and vegetables in preparation of their dinner. His concern for their welfare grew as he observed their meager existence. Elizabeth invited him to stay, and while he did, he ate very little.

*   *   *

Peter's and Anne's love blossomed, and on one fine day, he proposed to her officially. To Peter's surprise, Elizabeth gave them her blessing. Deep down, she was relieved that Anne would not be part of her plans. Elizabeth took one last trip to Boston and was finally able to book passage back to England for herself and Hilary. At last, by the summer of 1635, she had achieved her goal.

"Peter Wallace," Elizabeth said, standing at the end of the dock in New London with one foot on the boarding plank, "please help me with my baggage."

"Yes, Madam," Peter said with unease.

"You will protect my daughter?"

"At all costs."

Peter reached down and lifted two large bags. Elizabeth watched him as he moved with ease up the boarding plank and onto the boat. A sailor came by and took the bags from him. Peter stepped up to Elizabeth. They stood face to face. Peter felt he should take her hand and kiss the back of it as a gentleman would. But Elizabeth's countenance was smug and indifferent. She noticed his frustration on what he was supposed to do in this current situation so she ended it by saying, "Peter, Anne will make a fine wife."

"We will … we will come to visit you in England."

"I trust you will and soon," Elizabeth said, not believing a word of it.

Peter looked at her with a tinge of sadness.

"Peter … I trust you will," she repeated in her duplicitous tone.

"We will write," Peter said.

"Do that."

Anne stepped up and stood behind Peter, clinging tightly to his hand. She had been unable to say anything to her mother for several weeks - only her words of 'thank you' had been proffered after her mother approved of her wedding. It was a rare moment when her mother's words for her happiness had been truly heartfelt. But deep down, Anne couldn't wait for her to leave. Only then could she take full control.

Reverend Cotton had arrived on the same ship that was to take Elizabeth and Hilary back to Massachusetts. A half dozen fully trained soldiers accompanied him and were intended to stay on in the new colony to help maintain law and order under the direction of Peter, and to assist any sea captain that might need their services. The

Reverend, however, would make Peter and Anne wait to take their vows however, until he was satisfied with the progress of the Connecticut colony. His attitude towards their pending nuptials was, *'A man should not start a family if he still has work to do in the field.'*

While Elizabeth struggled with Anne's attitude towards her, she still wanted to be at the wedding. Anne told her not to worry about it and that they would have a gathering in England the first chance they could get. William Smith and his wife agreed to take Anne in until the wedding day. Anne and Peter would return to the farm on an as-needed-basis. Elizabeth made Peter and Smith promise that Anne would never stay at the farm alone.

"You have found a great man, Anne," Elizabeth had said in her last words to her daughter. "Love, honor, and obey him."

Anne knew she had to make a statement, something to show Peter that she and her mother would be happy with the departure, and to make Peter not think about taking her to England in the future under any circumstances. Anne stepped around Peter and gave her mother a hug. Elizabeth held her arms away from her daughter for a moment then collapsed them around her. The two separated as quickly.

Elizabeth stepped onto the deck of the pinnace. Hilary followed. It would take them to the Cape where they would transfer to a larger vessel that was destined for England. Elizabeth motioned to Peter to bring aboard the last of her things. Peter turned to Anne hoping to see some sadness, but there was nothing in Anne's eyes - just a blank stare. He broke from her, lifted a trunk filled with clothing and carried it to the boat. Once it was secured, he bowed to Elizabeth, smiled at Hilary, and returned to Anne's side.

The pinnace sailed away with Hilary waving fanatically. Anne finally waved to her and to her only. Once they were out of sight, Anne turned to Peter and said, "We've got work to do."

*   *   *

With each new day of that summer, the sun seemed to rise higher and higher, angrily aching to reach its apex. Hot fiery air swept the land. The coastline from Cape Cod, all the way to New Amsterdam melted into watery images of brown and gold. Long

Island Sound boiled. No one slept. Humidity as thick as pea soup filled the evenings, leaving the inhabitants breathless. Dawn's dewy cool hours provided the only relief.

Out on the Island-of-little-god, the weather was somewhat more tolerable. Waves of blistering warm air mixed with cooler gusts blew in off the ocean and swept noiselessly up the beaches and into the Manissean village.

"*Little-grey-feather!*" Running-bird cried out.

The child had stood up by pulling on several blades of sea grass. She had taken steps toward the edge of the high dune when Running-bird finally noticed her. She ran to her daughter. Grabbing the child by the arm, Running-bid lifted her quickly out of harm's way.

"You are a clever one," Running-bird said, giving her child a big hug.

Little-grey-feature was still fussing. She made noises in phrases, as if to construct a sentence. Running-bird looked into her eyes with great pride.

"What, my child? Do you want to go for another swim?"

Little-grey-feather thrust her arm out over the purple and blue sea, her index finger slightly extended.

"What are you are pointing at, my little one!" Running-bird said, amazed at her child's awareness. "What do you see?"

Little-grey-feather kicked one foot and whimpered again. She pumped her cherubic little arm and finger toward the north.

"Very well, then. Let us see …"

Running-bird scanned the horizon. Nothing. The mainland was a vague ripple in the far distance. Suddenly, she saw it – a canvas-white sail in full bloom, heading east.

"Thank you, my child." Running-bird hugged her, and the child knew her sighting was acknowledged.

Troubled, Running-bird looked long and hard at the white dot moving across the water. Suddenly, a second one came into view, heading west, and then another. It was at that moment she knew the world would never be the same. But then, something flashed in her mind and filled her vision – a man on the far shore; he was searching for something. He was young, he carried a sword but he was not the threatening kind. She closed her eyes for a second and then saw him again, this time with an aura of hope floating around his being. He was English. He was Peter Wallace – the man who swam ashore to meet with her a year earlier. She then knew that he would be coming to the island again, she just didn't know when. But the harder she tried to see the time of this, the more the vision vanished.

Little-grey-feather suddenly smiled - she looked into her mother's eyes and appeared to want to say something. The child's lips parted but no words came.

"Perhaps…" Running-bird said aloud.

After a while, she collected herself and carried her child back home. There was trading to be done this day. *A good day of trade between all the peoples of the land meant that there could be hope for the future*, she thought. And if peaceful co-existence could be built from trade, then that is what she would work for.

As she approached the village, she crested a high bluff. From this vantage point, she could see a dozen or more long maple canoes resting in the protected cove just a half mile from the village. A few Indians from several nations stood guard over them. The Narragansett and Pequot tribes were present as well as a few white traders that tagged along with them. There were no sailing ships anchored off shore. At least, not yet, but Running-bird knew several would be along at any time. They had come in the past, and the Europeans would not miss out on a good trade.

She descended the bluff and entered the village. With the help of another squaw, they placed her shells, tools, jewelry and wampum, out on a blanket for all to see.

In short order, two Pequots approached her display. One was dressed in a white linen shirt, open at the neck.

"We understand you have the best tools in the village," Dekanawida said, in his soft but clear tone.

Running-bird looked up at him and held his gaze for several seconds before responding. She drew on her clairvoyance and searched deep inside this young man. He was so different. She knew he was a powwaw by his markings, but there was something else.

"I feel that I do," she said.

"We would like to trade with you. I am Dekanawida, Pequot from the Missituck village, and this is my friend, Knoton."

Running-bird gazed at the powwaw. *A pleasant face*, she thought, *and a wonderful smile, too.*

"You have a kind voice," she said. "We welcome…"

"We are as fierce as you should remember, squaw!" Knoton declared, interrupting her.

"Knoton, mind your tongue," Dekanawida said, raising his hand. "This is a day of peace."

"This squaw needs discipline."

"She is just being gracious."

"Brothers," Running-bird interjected. "May I show you my goods?"

"Please do," Dekanawida said.

They proceeded to discuss what each had to offer, with Dekanawida focusing on her tools. After a while, when the bartering was done, Dekanawida extended his hand to her. She backed away at first but finally extended her arm, and they clasped Indian style. The touch of his skin warmed her. She felt her body shutter ever so slightly. And when she looked up into his eyes, she felt ashamed. She had not touched a man since her husband was killed a year ago. She felt confused. *Was it time*, she thought?

Knoton grunted and wandered off when he realized he was the odd man out. Running-bird and Dekanawida stood in place, unaware of time, and spoke for long minutes. Their words and gazes lingered while traders moved all about them. Their tones harmonized as if they were singing. Running-bird bridged any difference in dialect with ease.

An ocean breeze suddenly swirled up and cooled them. They smiled in unison. Dekanawida knew he would never forget her eyes. The twin almond shapes curved at the ends in a happy sparkle. They parted when Running-bird got busy with new customers. Dekanawida promised he would come back and say good-bye to her before he left the island.

Several Mohegan long canoes arrived. They beached their boats a safe distance away from the others. A young warrior with a scar down the side of his face and neck led a group of men carrying furs. They made their way through the village peacefully and, without delay, proceeded to trade with others in a lively fashion.

Within short order, Onasakenrat spied Running-bird. He and several of his comrades approached her.

"I was not aware this island had such a beautiful princess," he said, grinning.

"Thank you, young prince," she said in a polite tone.

"Do you know me?"

"We have heard of a new, emerging leader in your tribe."

"And?"

"I sense it is you."

Onasakenrat started to slowly circle around her. He regarded her up and down. Stopping half-way through his saunter he said. "Perceptive squaw."

"It is a gift," she added with a smile.

"Are you the seer?"

"So, I am told. But I do not think I am any different."

"I say you are," Onasakenrat said.

"There, you see. You are perceptive as well."

"Do not mock me. I have the vision of a leader. That is all."

"Then perhaps you can mend the differences between our peoples?"

"Our differences, princess" he said, now showing some anger, "had to do with our fathers, not us!"

"Then, welcome. However, I am not a princess, though some of my people refer to me that way. I assume one of them told you."

"You are clever."

"When I need to be."

"Nevertheless, I too will call you princess. You are beautiful. And, I am indeed a prince. A prince looking for a fine wife."

"I am sure you will find one."

"I may have just found one!"

He was grinning even wider now. Running-bird looked away for a moment. She scanned the crowd, looking for Dekanawida, hoping he was nearby. He had stirred her so. She wished he would return and save her from the Mohegan's advances.

"Have you come to trade *or* to look for a wife?" Running-bird finally said.

"Ah, a shrewd business woman… This is very good."

"I appreciate your compliments, but please, it is too hot for anything but trade today."

"Very well, I…"

His words were cut short as Little-grey-feather rambled out of Running-bird's wigwam. A squaw who had been watching her, followed her out.

"There she is," Running-bird said, smiling.

"I am sorry," the squaw said, "she is just too fast for me."

Running-bird scooped her up, giving her a big hug and kiss in the process.

Onasakenrat gave a slight shrug and turned to his comrades with a smile. His men joined in the banter. Little-grey-feather made a sound, grabbing his attention. He stepped closer to the child, and just as he was about to speak, he suddenly recoiled.

"Her eyes…," he started to say. The other Mohegans took notice as well. They all became unsettled.

"Why, yes, she has silver and green eyes," Running-bird said. "She is a special child. A gifted one."

"Gifted!" Onasakenrat exclaimed, regaining his composure. Feeling a need to be alone with her, he signaled for his men to move on. Once they were out of range he took on a more demanding demeanor.

"Why do you think ill of my daughter?" She asked.

Startled, Onasakenrat began, "How do you know…"

"You thoughts are clear to me, prince."

"My thoughts are not for you."

"Well that is curious. It is the reverse of what I hear."

"You mock me once again, woman."

"No harm intended," she said, holding onto Little-grey-feather a little tighter.

Onasakenrat stepped closer, placing his face within inches of Running-bird's eyes. He pinched his eyelids together leaving just a thin slit trying to get a better look into her soul. Running-Bird stood her ground. Suddenly he heard words echo inside his head: *'Why do you think ill of my daughter?'* It repeated over and over, each time the volume growing louder than the last. He backed off, weakened. Turning from her, he raced off down the hill.

Running-bird whispered to her child: "We do not like him, do we?" More hugs and kisses. "That warrior is hiding something."

The child frowned and continued to gaze in Onasakenrat's direction. She frowned and pointed at him.

"It is easy to tell when someone is hiding something, my daughter," Running-bird said in a whisper. "The hard part is to know why."

Onasakenrat, who was now some distance away, spun around as if he had heard them. His gaze reeked with hate. He locked eyes with Running-bird and then with the child. Finally, he was satisfied with what he wanted to know and turned away.

A short time later, a commotion arose from the beach.

Dekanawida was first to notice the English ship approach. He calmed those near him who appeared agitated and then walked slowly down to the shoreline. A large bark carefully anchored in the cove, and a long rowboat was lowered into the water. Four white men descended into it, carefully lowering bundles of pelts, packages of fabric, and crates of other goods. They were lightly armed.

Dekanawida watched them row to shore. Then, suddenly, he saw a familiar face.

"Brother Wallace!" he called out.

Peter, who was rowing, turned and smiled.

"Brother Dekanawida," he replied with an energetic wave.

Within minutes, Peter and his company disembarked. A half dozen Indians swarmed around the row boat, eagerly examining their treasure.

Dekanawida and Peter clasped arms.

"Good to see you, my friend," Dekanawida said.

"And you, Powwaw."

Dekanawida outlined to Peter and the Captain of the bark which tribes were present and where certain goods could be found. After the boat was unloaded and the goods brought to dry ground, trading began with the English. Peter grabbed Dekanawida's arm, pulling him aside.

"And what is the disposition of the Pequots these days."

"Yes, my friend, we should discuss this," Dekanawida said with some sadness. "Even though we trade today, our people are still incensed over the death of Tatobem."

"But they must understand that it was the Dutch who were responsible."

"Yes, many of my people realize this, but they quickly forget and see all whites as the same."

"You and I worked hard to free him," Peter said in frustration. "I trust the Pequots know this, too."

"When we took you and the other white men at the river, we knew you were English. Otherwise, Sassacus may have had you killed on the spot. And even after you and I negotiated for Tatobem's release, there was still little trust from the sachem's son. Our people had another difficult winter, and this may have saved another outbreak of violence."

"I could come to your village," Peter said with renewed enthusiasm. "I can reassure your people of the English intentions."

"They see you as a threat."

"Why?"

"They know you are still looking for the murderer of Jonathan Miller."

"Indeed. But I fear now that I will never find him."

"Turn your passion to the living," Dekanawida said, placing his hand on Peter's shoulder. "This may gain you acceptance with our people."

Peter smiled. They turned and walked toward the shoreline. From the high ground overlooking the shore, Running-bird could see a white man taking to Dekanawida. The vision she had earlier returned and she was moved by it. She gathered up Little-grey-feather and walked down to them. The two men were still in conversation when they became distracted by her arrival.

"I see you are still here," she said with a smile, addressing Dekanawida.

Dekanawida felt the same elation he had just felt moments ago when he first met her.

"Yes, I am," he said, clumsily.

She looked over to Peter and smiled warmly at him. Returning her gaze to Dekanawida, she asked in Pequot tongue, "And you know this white man?"

"Yes, he is my friend. You two have met before. Have you forgotten?"

"No. He is not easy to forget."

Running-bird turned to Peter and switched to English, which she spoke with ease. "I am delighted to meet you again, Sir."

"And I, you," Peter said, removing his hat in the process. "I regret that we did not part well."

"It is I who feel sorry and should offer an apology."

"No need. I was concerned I had said something wrong."

"No, you didn't. My gift will sometimes cripple me and I lose my sense of place."

"I see."

"What concerns my people now is something that you can help us with," Running-bird said, with all the confidence of a leader. "We know more English settlers arrive every year and they need a place to live, hunt, and farm as we do. I was told the English are purchasing more land along the Thames from our brethren."

"Well... yes."

"Indeed, I hope someone is keeping track."

Peter felt a strange, sharp, biting tug at the edge of his consciousness. She had a valid point - was anyone keeping records? To date, the purchase of land was loosely define by geographic markings, brooks and streams, hills and forests, and stone walls that could easily be changed. Most of which was by word of mouth with little written down. He would add that task to his list. The woman had the charm and grace of nobility, yet she was as down to earth in her manner as Dekanawida was. Both intelligent beyond what he had been told about these people. For a moment he could not take his eyes away from her. He watched her move with confidence, and her face lit up as she spoke. He heard himself utter words in reply to her statement, but the content of which were strangely lost in his distracted mind.

Running-bird turned to Dekanawida and spoke in her native tongue to him. "He has kind eyes and a nice manner."

"Yes, he is all what you see and hear."

"He seems clear-headed. Will he protect our people from the English settlers?"

"I am certain. He has tried to help our people in the past."

"He is always welcomed, then. Has he found the person who murdered Jonathan Miller?"

"No. And he realizes that he may never."

She turned to Peter. He knew what she meant without translation when he heard Miller's name mentioned. No words needed to be exchanged between them - he returned a modest bow. Little-grey-feather suddenly broke from her mother's hand, took several steps then fell; her tiny voice filled the air.

"Is the child yours?" Dekanawida asked.

"Yes, she is."

"Your child is beautiful," he said, not really knowing what else to say. Dekanawida paused. Her words brought mixed feelings. Finally, he had to ask her a question that was burning in him. "We have heard your husband was slain the night your daughter was born. Is this true?"

"Yes, he was killed one year ago in an ambush."

"By White men?" Peter interjected.

"No," Dekanawida answered for her. "Nor my people."

"What they left behind," Running-bird confirmed, "did not indicate Pequot or White men."

"Who then?" Peter asked.

"We do not know who killed him," she said.

"I will pray for his soul," Peter said.

"I thank you, Sir. We feel he has reached his final resting place now. And I know he is happy there and awaits me."

She then reached out and turned Dekanawida away from the others. Peter took his leave and returned to where the trading was taking place. Running-bird and Dekanawida walked up the hills at the southeast corner. They spoke for a while in sweet surrender, unaware of all around them. Finally, Running-bird invited Dekanawida to take one last look at her goods, which he did. At the end of his review, she gave him a large, colorful shell as a gift. He was swept up in all this newfound passion he felt toward her. It was the last thing he had planned on, and the best thing about the entire trip. And when he left the island, he vowed that he would return and make her his wife.

The day waned, and the traders grew weary, knowing that the long journey across the strait still faced them. But most felt they had had a good day. One by one, they returned to their respective boats and left the island.

When Little-grey-feather took her nap, Running-bird saw it as an opportunity to return to her favorite place – a place where few had ever been. Leaving another squaw to look after her daughter, she raced across the meadow and out to woods on the southeast corner of the island. Not far on the other side of the forest, there was a place where she would find her answer.

Once there, she fell into deep solitude. The long hot day seemed to never end as her troubled mind wandered. All around her a new crop of shells were visible, a treasure offered up by the sea. But this time, she had no interest in the shells. Slowly, the colors of pink and purple appeared in the water, announcing the coming of night. An evening breeze arose and cooled her. She sat her tired body down on a large flat boulder, left by an ice sheet ages ago. Gazing out over the vast expanse of the sea, her thoughts came together.

My heart is an innocent prisoner. Buried deep inside my body, I forbid it to sway me - it has become a hostage without all hope of rescue. I have carried its yearning each day and have suppressed my true feelings as best I can. I will always love Samuel.

Once, my heart was a riot of joy and enchantment; a thrill and a terror all at the same time. It was fulfillment. It became emptiness. It was marvelous euphoria and maddening fury. Now my heart begs me; it pleads with me to re-consider.

My daughter came to me as a gift from the heavens ... when I least expected it. The beauty, grace, and the intelligence of her are all consuming. She deserves a father.

And so, I have let it all come undone with one moment of irrational madness, of love for another. Yet, I am. I feel. I yearn to be with him. I must be alive again. I am certain that Samuel has reached heaven. Farewell my husband. It is time for me to move on. I will always love you.

The night closes in. I will take another swallow of the ruby elixir of the evening air that brings me so near to Dekanawida - so near to where I once was. It tastes as sweet and as passionate as I know his kisses will be. Alas, he has taken my heart.

CHAPTER 12 - A Narragansett Threat

* * *

Anne Miller's promise to bring her father's murderer to justice had evaporated over the last year. She had bigger plans in mind now. When she first realized that her mother was, indeed, adamant about leaving the New World, she saw it as an opportunity to achieve her own goals. Wealth and fame would never come to her while under Elizabeth's yoke. And with a man of power like Peter Wallace at her side, it was just a matter of time and persuasion.

Anne was standing outside William Smith's trading post with the door wide open giving final instructions to several traders on a major business transaction. Peter was inside with a handful of wampum, waiting for Smith to return from the back storage area with an oil lamp he wanted to purchase.

"Will this do?" the old man said while wiping the dirty glass with his sleeve.

"It looks a bit worn," Peter said with a frown. Yet, he fully expected he wasn't going to get much better; considering the source.

Smith held the lamp high. "Ahh, it's as good as new."

"Looks like it has been at sea for a decade," Peter said.

"Well, yah getting it for next to nothing."

"Very well… done!"

Smith frowned as if expecting further complaint. "That was too easy, Peter."

"I just do not have the stomach for negotiating price."

"Aye, but yah bride-to-be does," Smith said with a wink, pointing towards the opened door. They both looked outside.

Anne had raised her voice to drive home a point to the traders. She looked so small compared to the two rugged men she was addressing. But when she spoke, she loomed larger than life.

Peter smiled and felt his love for her fill his heart. Anne's voice rose again but this time Peter's smile faded. She was everything he had always wanted: a beautiful woman with a warm touch – and one who was strong and worked tirelessly for hours on end. Peter admired her for that, but it was her short temper and lack of focus on the important things that he couldn't comprehend.

Anne's voice grew louder still. Her arms went up in a violent threatening manner. Peter's heart suddenly sank. *Surely she wasn't going to fight with them,* he thought. He headed toward the door.

"Never mind her," Smith bellowed out.

"She may strike a blow!"

"I've seen her like this before. She won't."

"But..." Peter stopped himself.

Smith peered over his shoulder. "She's a tempest when she wants to be."

Peter stared out at Anne, and seconds later he nodded in agreement. "It is a side of her I have seen as well."

"Peter, she's a fine, strong woman. I've known her for a long time. She has a hard way. She means nothing by it."

"Well, in the eyes of God this is not good behavior."

Smith retreated back into his store. "Then talk to her about it."

Peter felt a sadness run through him. It was a brief moment of doubt as to his ability to judge people. He wondered if he misjudged Anne, and her love for him. *What drives her*, he thought? After what she has been through, seeing her father murdered and all, he gave her the benefit of the doubt.

Suddenly, Anne turned from the men outside and stepped into the threshold of the door. Her angered face quickly changed to joy once she was able to focus on Peter.

"My love! Why the glum countenance?" she asked, as she stepped closer.

"Those men could have hurt you!"

"Nonsense!"

"You do not know that," he countered.

Anne stood her ground. "I was fine."

"You were shouting."

"We were negotiating."

He stepped closer to her, and she embraced him. Peter was caught off guard – doubly so when she kissed him right on the lips.

"This is inappropriate in front of others, Anne," Peter said. He turned around to see if Smith was watching. He was. And, Smith was smiling.

"Ahh, go on, kiss her back," Smith said with a chuckle. "This is the New World."

"Discretion is important," Peter said.

"Not here. The Puritan dogma doesn't rule here!"

"It is just not right, Will."

"So be it."

Peter turned to Anne. "And, you should not fight with men of that ilk," he said.

"I wasn't fighting, I said."

"I wasn't worried, Peter." Smith added.

"Well, I was," Peter said.

"I'm fine, darling," Anne said. "Now let us speak alone."

Peter finally offered a smile. He knew he would never win the argument. Peter and Anne left the building and bid farewell to Smith. Once outside Anne led Peter around the side of the structure to a nook in the wall where they would not be seen.

"Come here," she said, pressing him back into the wall.

He looked down into her eyes. There was a fire there, a yearning. She raised her lips to his. He leaned over and met hers with the same eagerness. Their lips flashed and sucked as the fire in their bodies raged out of control - each thinking it euphoric, each thinking it bliss, but each as naive as a child playing with a snake. But the kissing was filled with a subtle poison that would spread throughout each of them. Peter's eyes slowly opened, a thing he was unable to do before when she had him like this. To his surprise, Anne's persuasive eyes were wide open gaping into his. Peter pulled back, a shiver running through him.

"Let's go," Anne suddenly said. She took him by the hand and they were off in a flash.

* * *

Anne and Peter had plans to meet with a fifty-year-old widow who would be staying with Anne at the Miller house. The widow, Mrs. Hayes, had arrived in New London with her nineteen-year-old son, and they would stay on with Anne as hired hands and eventually, as a nanny after they were married. As they walked down the lane from the trading post, they could hear much hammering and commotion on the north end of town.

"You see, Peter, there is opportunity here," Anne said. "This town is growing fast, and we can be a big part of it."

"Yes, we can be," Peter said softly, feeling suddenly ill.

"I would like to move here after the wedding."

"But…what about the farm?"

"Leave it to Mrs. Hayes and her son," Anne said, with finality.

"She can't manage it alone."

Peter head was spinning. He pulled his hat off and rubbed his temples.

"We'll bring in a few hired hands," Anne said. "Then, over time, leave it to her…for a fair price, of course."

"I cannot help you with this. You know my job takes me away."

"I will manage it."

"I would not ask that of you."

"No need, my darling. I can manage it. We can get our own shoppe going here in New London a little at a time."

"What skills have we in running a shoppe?"

"None at the moment," Anne replied, "but if Will Smith can do it, so can we."

"Are you suggesting that we compete with him?"

"Well, not at first. We can work with him, learn the trade and then start our own business."

Peter remained silent after that, the poison that had filled him earlier was still flowing in his veins. Anne went on and on about how it would all work – the poison in her had dissipated. She was happy. Peter prayed for the two of them to come to common ground. Then, after a while, he just prayed for her.

* * *

Dekanawida was surprised to see Running-bird so soon after the trading day on the island. She had arrived with a dozen others from her tribe at the Pequot fortification in Missituck. Several of the men were high ranking elders. She was the only woman in the group.

Their arms clasped.

"When I heard your people were coming to Missituck," Dekanawida said, "I had no idea you'd be among them."

"It was my request. Grey-feather was against it at first, but I convinced him in the end."

"But, this is a political gathering."

"I know. I insisted." She turned and looked away, her body language clearly indicating that she belonged at this gathering of men.

Dekanawida reached out to her. She faced him, his gaze grim. He said, "The Narragansett sachem, Miantonomo, is threatening us again."

"Yes, and we consider the Narragansetts our parent tribe. But you Pequots are not without fault. Many blame your people for infringing on their hunting grounds. Miantonomo says his people will starve this winter if they don't expand their territory to the west. He says he cannot keep the English out as they come faster than he can count and with better weapons. The Narragansetts are trapped in a vice. Your people must move to the north, from whence you came."

"There is much to discuss," Dekanawida said, dejectedly.

As they conversed, their words were lost in the physical energy that flowed all about them. Running-bird was convinced it was a sign from the creator to move on. She knew that Samuel had arrived in heaven by now and was smiling upon her. In spite of the heated political debate, her heart soared in this young man's company.

Dekanawida fell silent. His mind and body longed for another touch of her velvet skin. He led her by the hand out of the fortified village and she gladly followed. They strolled out into the open field that was once a part of the forest. He explained to her the reason - to see an enemy coming. But, today the field was filled with life and color as the young lovers walked in peace.

* * *

Deep in the hills overlooking the mighty Quonitocutt River, Onasakenrat gathered several of his trusted comrades together.

"The woman on the island…" he began with great intent, "…the one with the child who has silver eyes. I know that she is the wife of the warrior that killed my father."

"Are you certain?" A brave asked.

"She is also a widow of one year."

"The child's eyes?" another asked.

Quick-blade spoke out. "Indeed, I saw those eyes, too. It had not occurred to me at first, but now I agree with Onasakenrat."

The warriors listened intently as the young prince and his friend described the battle they had out on the Island just one year prior. And they kept secret the untidy burial of Onerahtokha at sea. They lauded the sachem's acts as a great warrior and lamented that they had to leave his body behind because, they claimed, they were outnumbered.

One eager brave chimed in, "Then it is our duty to wipe out this family so their line is removed from this earth."

"Yes," Onasakenrat said. "The Manisseans need to be reminded of our power."

"When do we strike?"

"Their annual trading day implies they are important and strong. We will organize a raiding party on the next moon and complete the task we should have done a long time ago."

Many of the braves raised their voices, calling for war.

"*Once done,*" Onasakenrat cried out above the clamor, "we turn our attention to the Pequots."

More shouts and calls rose from his men. They eagerly worked themselves up into a frenzy of hate. The thought of eliminating the Peqouts from their territory and achieving their own dominance over the land east of the Thames River made their spirits soar to new levels.

Later, Onasakenrat had several of the squaws paint his body. He had learned that the Puritan sheriff was searching for an Indian with a scar. Whispers of this white man's relentless quest had reached the Mohegan village some time ago, but now it was getting louder. In an effort to camouflage his scar, Onasakenrat had the women cleverly paint in patterns that would mask its most distinguishing features.

CHAPTER 13 – Wedding Day

* * *

Peter was floating in jubilation. He was finally granted permission by Reverend Cotton to marry Anne. However, the wedding would have to wait for thirty days until the Reverend got his bearings on progress of the new colony at New London and elsewhere. This included a decision to take an expedition out into the Sound and up the Connecticut River to see how the settlements were doing there. Peter had to be part of this, of course, and he went with great disappointment.

The voyage took them up the Connecticut all the way to the outpost that was now simply called "Hartford". Across the river, at Huys de Hoop, the Dutch were vacating, and the Reverend, with orders from the Governor, wanted to make sure the transition of power went smoothly and in the eyes of God.

While there, Peter was fortunate to find the couple he met on his first voyage to the new colony. They were expecting a second child. All he could do was think about getting back to Anne and starting his own family. At age twenty-five, he was beginning to feel like an old man.

After what seemed like an eternity in Hartford, they finally set sail for New London and home. Once Peter was reunited with Anne, the Reverend gave them his blessing and instructed them to move forward with their wedding plans. Peter discovered that Anne had expanded her reputation in leaps and bounds. As he went about town with the preparations, so many people knew her by name and also about her plans for a new shoppe. It seemed she had become as popular, if not more so, as Peter. She had also stored away a fair amount of goods for her new enterprise in a shed provided by William Smith.

The Reverend was heavily involved with the wedding arrangements and ordered the ceremony to take place outside on the newly defined town green. A day in late August was picked and to everyone's delight the day turned out to be a glorious one.

The word was spread up the Thames River valley for all to come to the wedding. The weather was perfect and warm. Many people of various nations came to New London that afternoon.

Seven long tables were built and placed on the green just a short distance from William Smith's trading post. The tables were arranged in three rows, with the head table perpendicular to them all. This table was designated for the bride and groom, Reverend Cotton, and other important persons of the region, including Captain John Gallop who was rumored to be on his way. Peter was anxious to see his mentor again and prayed he would arrive in time.

A dozen men dressed in full military attire were on hand as honor guard for the bride and groom. Some Peter knew from the Boston colony and the others had just arrived in the New England for the first time. These men were assigned to Connecticut by the Governor to shore up his colonization efforts. All of this was flattering to Peter but all he could think about was being Anne's husband and consummating their marriage.

Decked out in new clothing, Peter walked in lively steps to Anne's lodging at the back of Smith's shoppe. He was not disappointed when she met him at the door. She looked stunningly beautiful.

"Anne!"

She hugged him but did not plant her usual kiss on his lips.

"My dreams have come true today," he said. "You look lovely."

"And my dreams have come true as well, my handsome husband-to-be."

"Are you ready?"

"I'm just waiting for the Smiths'," she said, her smile flirting with his own.

"Good."

"How big is the crowd?"

"Too big!" Peter exclaimed with a chuckle. "It is making me nervous."

"Have no fear, my darling, the more people the better."

"Still, I am not used to all the attention."

"That will change."

"Perhaps."

She stepped out and pulled the door closed behind her.

"Come," she said, "Let us find them."

Peter nodded.

"I have a few things to discuss with Will," she said, squeezing his hand.

"What things, my dear?"

"He has knowledge of a merchant coming from the Far East." The excitement in her voice was as grand as her initial greeting.

Peter fought back a sudden swell of disappointment. "My darling, today you should not be concerned with business."

"That may be. But just a few simple questions are all."

He did not care to probe any further and kept silent. *Why couldn't she simply delight in their precious day, their precious gift from God? Yes, I love this woman, and I know she is strong willed. I will deal with it.*

They found William Smith just around the other side of the building. For a moment he was difficult to recognize because he was dressed in clean clothes without holes and he must have bathed for he shed no odors, which was a rarity. His wife was primming, clearly indicating who had made him respectable. The four exchanged greetings and Anne went right to her questions about when, where, and what was being brought to Connecticut by the foreign merchants. Once satisfied, they walked to the green where the Reverend and crowd were patiently waiting.

As they approached the makeshift altar, more and more people drifted in to watch the proceedings. Some stayed along the main street and were just out for a quick look before returning to their busy lives. Others could not ignore the handsome couple and longed to have been in their shoes. There were nearly seventy people present, including a dozen curious Indians and several Dutch farmers from the Millers' old neighborhood. The soldiers formed two lines, and Peter and Anne walked alone down the center.

Peter noticed among those gathered was an Indian woman who he recognized to be Running-bird. She and her child were standing to one side, along with several other Manisseans. They exchanged warm and pleasant smiles.

Peter and Anne made their way silently to the main altar. They stood in front of the Reverend with the table between them. A fine silk cloth was placed at its center, and upon that were the Bible, a crucifix, and a few other religious items. The Reverend motioned for all to take a seat at the various tables. Most all of the whites did so, but only a few Indians joined them. The rest stood around the periphery. The soldiers stood at attention at the far end of the altar. The Reverend began the ceremony and Peter smiled with a renewed confidence.

William Smith was quick to look over his shoulder when he heard a commotion. Two Pequots had entered the town and approached the crowd in quickstep. Several of the women stirred. A shrill voice was heard exclaiming "Pequots!"

Smith smiled, "I know them!" he said out loud. "Friendly," he added. Dekanawida and Knoton slowed their pace when they saw Smith raise his hand in acknowledgement. The two young bucks smiled back at him. The crowd relaxed and turned their attention to the proceedings. Dekanawida scanned the crowd and saw Running-bird, whom he had heard would be on hand. He made his way to where she was standing. They clasped hands and smiled at each other for what could have been an eternity. Respectfully, they watched Peter and Anne at the altar.

Peter was fixated on Anne and what the Reverend was saying but could not help wonder what the commotion was about. Curiosity was killing him, however he dare not lose his concentration on his bride. He had hoped to see Dekanawida in the crowd before the ceremony started, but his friend wasn't there. Perhaps he had just arrived.

Anne had been looking at Peter with a gaze of absolute devotion. Her face was lit up with a slight smile, but she remained pious. Peter continued to look deep into her eyes. She stood there in front of him so close, so beautiful that any doubt he had on this day would not matter. Or, at least, he would let it fade in the presence of her beauty.

The Reverend spoke again, exhorting them with an instruction, and Anne turned toward him anticipating that vows were about to be exchanged. At this, Peter took the opportunity to glance back at the crowd. He found Dekanawida and smiled. Peter felt relieved. His Pequot friend was indeed trying to make a statement of friendship to all White men. Peter's aspirations for a peaceful future soared. He felt his hard work was coming to fruition.

Reverend Cotton spoke to Peter; then to Anne. Vows were exchanged, and they were pronounced man and wife. The crowd responded with excitement. Peter and Anne turned and faced them. Anne smiled broadly and gave a delicate wave. As they walked slowly between the rows of tables, the crowd stood and applauded.

Anne looked around, absorbed all the attention, and felt a sense of power unlike anything she had felt before. She was a married woman now, and would soon be a very important merchant of New London. She nodded to this one and to that. Then, she saw him.

Anne stopped in her tracks. Her smile faded - her once happy countenance was replaced with that of rage. She was gaping directly at Dekanawida, who had locked eyes with her. He was puzzled at her reaction and was completely unaware that his loosely fitted shirt revealed the full length of his old scars in the bright light of the August sun. These were the same scars inflicted by John Oldham many years ago.

"*That's him!*" Anne screamed.

Peter clutched her arm, and scanned the crowd, "Who, my darling?"

"*He is the one!*"

"Who!"

A dull clamor rose in the crowd.

"There!" She pointed.

"I know that Indian," Peter said, trying to clear her confusion.

"That is the savage who *killed* my father."

Peter shook his head. "No, it cannot be. I know this man. He would never do such a thing."

"Peter, do something!"

The gathering was abuzz and the clatter rose like a rogue wave toward a shore of innocence. Reverend Cotton approached quickly, followed by several soldiers. He asked, "Peter, what is going on?"

Peter looked confused. He scanned the crowd paying little attention to the Reverend. The Reverend stepped in front of him. With urgency Peter said, "Anne says she sees the Indian who killed her father."

"Where?"

Peter could not answer. Slowly, Anne extended her arm and with an accusing finger pointed it directly at Dekanawida.

"Well, arrest him!" Reverend Cotton exclaimed.

Peter remained silent. He looked to his right and locked eyes with Dekanawida. The young powwaw returned a stern, troubled look. Then his Indian friend turned and walked away with his head turned to the ground.

"Get Him!" Anne screamed.

*   *   *

As evening fell on their wedding day, Peter was breathing so heavily his chest felt like it was ready to explode. He and Anne had walked back to the Miller farm at such a rapid pace that it took his breath away. Anne managed far better but was exhausted nonetheless. In Peter's case there was more to it. After he was forced to arrest Dekanawida, all Peter could do was pray. His shock over Anne's determination on insisting that Dekanawida was the one who killed her father filled him with myriad emotions, some of which he had never before experienced.

And what of poor Running-bird? Peter remembered the initial restraint she showed, but then the anger and eventual break down that followed were understandable. She fought with those who tried to hold her back. It took several of the Indians to subdue her. His heart felt for her as much as for his friend.

Peter and Anne said very little to each other as they entered the bedroom. Much had already been said, and Anne's opinion had not changed. As she slowly undressed, Anne was content in what she had done. She was looking forward to consummating her marriage and having a child. Her child would grow to be wealthy like she would be. She would see to it, no matter the cost.

Peter watched his wife disrobe. Her full, firm youthful figure glowed ravenously in the candlelight. Her beauty could launch a thousand ships. Any man would have given an arm or a leg to be in his position. But, he could not feel one ounce of passion for her. Whatever he had felt before had left his body with each step on their long walk home. His disdain for what had happened to his Indian friend made him sick within every inch of his body.

Peter undressed and slipped into bed with Anne. She reached out and kissed him relentlessly. He took them one at a time, pondering what to do next. The hours of arguing over who was right and who was wrong were now behind him. Anne whispered in his ear nd then ran her hands down the length of his body. Peter closed his eyes and tried to magine her as he had on the first day he saw her. He prayed silently for her. Suddenly, he was touching his member at which point all rational thought left him. He opened his yes and saw the lust in hers. She was not the same person he had fallen in love with.

Rolling on top of her, he took command and returned the hard kissing in the same vay she had started. She fell back under his weight. He grew erect, more so than he had ver been. He felt invincible. Passion clouded his thinking and no one would get the »etter of him now.

He lifted himself and spread her legs apart with reckless abandon. He felt her lampness; and slide in effortlessly. There was no sign of her virginity and he did not :are. Her eyes closed and she moaned. Swiveling her hips to match his thrusts, she »ressed harder giving her body what it wanted. When he rolled his body to match her noves, she smiled. He grabbed her wrists and spread her hands out above her head. She ook it all in with gratitude. She showed no anguish, only great pleasure.

Peter slowed his pace momentarily disrupting her orgasm. She frowned across a sweaty brow.

"Come on!" She demanded.

He wrapped his hands around her back and proceeded to thrust as before. Slowly, ie felt the room disappear. Their heavy breathing, deafening. He lifted her off the bad ind pressed her body to his. They reached tumescence for several minutes, in total :uphoria. Seconds later, it was over. He released his grip on her and she dropped back lown on the bed; he rolled to one side. He heard her sigh and then something unexpected - she giggled.

"Wonderful, my darling," she softly said.

When their breathing returned to normal, the silence of the night took over. Anne felt victorious. She knew she would be able to explain away the lack of her virginity as an accident of nature. She knew she could convince him. She also knew she had her work cut out for her to convince her husband that the Indian she had accused was guilty. Nor would it matter if she was wrong, she needed closure on the problem. And problems needed to be eliminated in order for Anne Miller to prosper. No one would ever get the better of her or the Miller family name again. And, she would make Peter get over his insistence to the contrary. She needed him for other things. Anne closed her eyes and slept contently.

Peter lay in silence until he heard his wife wheeze in a gentle snore. He lifted himself up, and resting on his forearm, looked upon her in the dimness. There was enough light from a star filled sky entering the room that he could see her in detail. She was even more beautiful in sleep, so fragile now and incredibly harmless. He knew she was content and satisfied.

Anne stirred and crinkled her nose. Peter wanted to smile at the sight of her adorable face and that unrestrained response from some invisible particle of dust that tickled her nose. But he could not smile. He wanted to wake her and make love to her again, but could not. He wanted to look upon her for a long, long time, but could not. He lay back down and vowed that he would make her see her folly as quickly as possible.

CHAPTER 14 – Captain John Oldham

*   *   *

Peter stood on the deck of the Captain John Gallop's bark on a bright blue, sunny day of mid-summer. His heart was heavy when they had set out but there was something about being on the water that took his mind off things. There was a welcomed sense of freedom and joy in it that he could not find elsewhere. It was a place he owned and no one could take it away.

He mounted the gunnels of the port bow and clung to the rigging. There was much excitement in his heart now because the next destination was one he had been looking forward to for a long time. The waters of Long Island Sound were in relative calm and the air clear, but there was enough wind to keep them moving forward at a good tack. All around them the sun sprinkled its light in flickering flashes of silver. Sea gulls squawked as they soared behind the ship on its easterly course toward Block Island. It was July of 1636.

The crew consisted of five with a navigator and two teen-aged boys who were assigned to Gallop to learn the ways of sea. They were the sons of settlers from the Connecticut River. Captain Gallop and Peter had just delivered another seven people - along with their provisions - to a new settlement thirty miles north of Fort Saybrook, and were now heading east in pursuit of the outcast, John Oldham. They had learned that Oldham had been at Fort Saybrook with a cargo of goods he had brought up from the Virginia colony. But the magistrate seized his bark and confiscated the majority of his goods. Oldham was given a smaller pinnace and was allowed to keep just a fraction of his Virginia bounty before he was sent away.

Captain Gallop checked his course with the navigator. Once he was satisfied with his direction, Gallop handed the helm to one of the boys and walked over to the bow where Peter was standing.

"You will see him soon enough," John Gallop said, sharply.

"Uh, Captain! You startled me."

"Daydreaming?"

"Forgive me. I was thinking about the island."

"We have our bearing," Gallop said, "and you'll meet John Oldham within two hours."

"I hope so," Peter said, lamenting. "It has taken me so long to get to this point."

"Your Pequot friend is still alive; that's all that matters."

Peter looked out over the glistening water. He knew that Oldham was the man that had whipped Dekanawida leaving the scars his friend bore with dignity. Peter recanted his encounter with the same man in Boston to Dekanawida in an effort to solidify their need to be on guard against him. All Peter needed was for Oldham to mention the incident and identify Dekanawida as the Indian he inflicted the injury upon to help clear the false charge.

Gallop reached out and touched Peter's shoulder. Peter turned to him. Gallop said, "He will be there. He has a ship with unique cargo and knows the Indians of many nations will be assembled on the island. "

"But what if this Oldham doesn't remember the incident?"

"We cannot look that far ahead."

"I have to."

"The will of God is difficult to determine," the Captain said, looking skyward.

"The will of God?"

Gallop looked back down and into Peter's eyes. The tone of Peter's reply bordered on blasphemy. Peter knew he needed to clarify.

"Where was the will of God for the last year?" Peter asked. "All my hopes and dreams are in ruin. I have a wife who does not love me; a friend in jail for nothing, and my religion and career in doubt."

"Be careful how you speak, young man. Do not put yourself in league with the devil."

Peter reflected for a minute before responding. "Indeed. I do love the Lord. I just …"

Peter stopped himself. He knew the Captain understood full well. He turned his gaze to the sea again. Straining his eyes off the starboard beam, he scanned the horizon in search of the telltale cliffs of Block Island. Peter continued, "I have been tracking him for long time. His messages back to me said he would meet us at Fort Saybrook, and he did not."

"Do not worry," Gallop said. "I'm certain he is going to the island today to trade."

"If he sees us coming he may run."

"Why would he?"

"You saw what the magistrate did to him."

Gallop shook his head.

Peter said, "He knows what I want."

"Perhaps."

"He treats the Indians with contempt. He…"

"He is not alone in that," Gallop said, raising his voice. "As you well know."

Peter gaped at his mentor's outbreak. He said, carefully, "Yes, I know. And it is a sad reflection of our people."

Gallop looked off toward the east, hoping to see a sail aloft. But there was nothing visible to him. "Peter," he said, softening his tone, "We will catch him."

"I simply need to get him to tell us that he inflicted the wound on Dekanawida," Peter said, "even if I have to hold the point of my sword at his throat. With you as my witness to his confession; only then will I be happy."

"I will pray that he remembers then."

"He must."

"He may be an outcast but he is still English," Gallop said, with a hint of pride, "and I trust he will oblige you as one countryman to another."

"And I will pray for this as well."

* * *

Onasakenrat's plan for revenge of his father's death had taken a sudden turn. Much to his delight and expectation the grand sachem of all Mohegans, Uncas, officially granted him and his followers' freedom to branch out into new territory with him as their leader. They were to be known as the Wolf Clan, a frontier group of Mohegans. Among other tasks, they were to establish a new settlement closer to Pequot territory. The Wolf Clan would be the buffer between the Pequots and all tribes west of the Connecticut

River. Once done, Onasakenrat would actively resume his vendetta against the people on Block Island and any others that stood in his way.

While all this was forming, Onasakenrat decided it was time to marry. So, he found one of the most beautiful squaws and prepared for a family. He had turned twenty-three and was already considered late in getting started. However, his fear of the princess on Block Island and her evil-eyed daughter did not diminish. For now, his life had taken a turn for the better, but he vowed he would wipe these demons from the face of the earth. His father's death would only be avenged when the seed of Samuel was eradicated. All he needed was the right time and place, and the deed would be done.

* * *

Across the Sound and out on the island the annual July trading had begun. As usual, many of the Indians from the mainland were on hand, including Onasakenrat and several of his followers. Miantonomo, the Narragansett sachem, was also present, along with many of his braves. William Smith made a rare appearance when he arrived on a fishing boat filled with beaver pelts. Grey-feather had welcomed them all, but was disappointed that Running-bird was not on the island that day.

"I fear it will not be a good day to trade in Running-bird's absence," Grey-feather said to his wife. They stood on high ground overlooking the beach and fields where the traders were actively bargaining.

"Yes," White-fox replied, "her goods are always the main attraction." She was dressed in her finest clothing and adorned with beads fitting a sachem's wife.

"What word have you from her?" He asked.

"William Smith said she will remain on the mainland for several more days before returning home."

"Her Pequot has not been hanged?"

"No, she works as hard for his release as does the one called 'Peter Wallace'."

Grey-feather scanned the activities of the traders as they displayed their goods. He turned to his wife. He said, "I have met this Peter Wallace. He is a good man."

"He and Running-bird have become friends."

Grey-feather looked troubled for a moment. He scanned the horizon where the vaters met the sky. White-fox followed his gaze then continued.

"They have worked together for nearly a year," she said with a sigh. "And Running-bird loves the Pequot so. It could be a good sign that the English have not aanged him yet. They must not be certain of his guilt."

"Indeed," the great warrior said.

Grey-feather looked out over the cove where the long canoes of the visitors ested. Suddenly, to his left, out on the blue waters, a large white sail appeared.

"That must be Captain Oldham's ship," Grey-feather said, shielding his eyes.

"Yes, it is just the way William Smith described it."

"Maybe his goods will make this a good day to trade after all."

Within minutes, Oldham's ship entered the natural cove and dropped anchor. A ong boat was lowered and was quickly filled with goods. Four men arrived on the shore, and they were greeted by several of the Narragansetts who were eager to help unload and o get first look.

Trading was brisk, and Captain Oldham returned to his ship and filled the rowboat again with furs and kegs of gun powder and several muskets. After a third time back and forth, Oldham's goods were finally all gone. In exchange, he had taken mostly wampum but did purchase some fresh fish and Block Island spring water that was found to have aealth benefits.

"This Narragansett wampum is fine quality," one of Oldham's men said to him in confidence.

"Don't gloat over it," Oldham ordered. "We'll examine it later."

"I deserve my share. And I'd like it now."

"You'll get yours in due time."

The antsy sailor showed the Captain some of the finely polished shells braided together like nothing either of them had seen before. Oldham turned to the old salt, placed his hand on the hilt or his sword, and stepped up within a few inches of his face. "Prepare to leave!"

"We made out good with these, Capt'n."

"Put them away and do as I say. We will make for New London."

"New London! I though we was heading to New Amsterdam."

"No, New London."

"Ohhhh, I see. You wants to see that little tart again, don't yah?"

"Shut your infested mouth and prepare to leave, damn it!"

The old salt grinned and simple said, "Aye, aye, Capt'n."

Onasakenrat watched the white traders very carefully. He was still fuming over the fact that Running-bird and her evil-eyed child were not on the island. Over the course of the afternoon, he had planted the seeds of English conspiracy in the minds of the Narragansetts and to his fellow Mohegans. He suggested that the Manisseans were in league with the English and were providing them with information about the best places to fish and hunt, and that Narragansett land was ready for the taking.

Onasakenrat watched the Englishmen hoist the rowboat on board their ship and observed how the men scurried about a bit more urgently than necessary. He looked back to where the Narragansetts had placed the kegs of powder they had purchased. Then it occurred to him.

"Beware brother Narragansett," he called out to an Indian passing by him.

"Sachem, what is it?" the Narragansett replied.

"The White men make haste."

The Indian looked out across the water and took notice.

"Why is that?" Onasakenrat asked, knowing full well the answer.

"I know not."

"I do not like this."

"We traded our best wampum," The Narragansett said.

"Did you inspect the powder?"

Their shared glance was one of unease. Then they raced down the sloping terrain and out onto the beach. Other Indians followed, instinctively sensing the trouble.

A keg's lid was quickly ripped open. One look at the damp sludge was all they needed. A cry went up for the Narragansetts to gather. Sachem Miantonomo gave orders for ten of his warriors to launch their canoes and give pursuit. Within seconds of his command, two long canoes headed out into the sound.

Moments later, Miantonomo was joined by Grey-feather on a high bluff overlooking the cove. The Narragansett Sachem gave orders to his remaining countrymen to gather their goods and prepare to leave for home. Onasakenrat sought out the sachems and stood nearby so as to hear their every word.

"This is a bad omen," Grey-feather said.

"It will get worse for the English if they do not return our wampum."

"We must try for peace," Grey-feather said. "There are too many whites in our land."

"Miantonomo," Onasakenrat said, interrupting them, "you and Grey-feather are from the same fathers. You are right to seek justice."

"We do not seek the advice of the Wolf Clan," Grey-feather said.

Onasakenrat stood his ground. He squared off with Grey-feather and clenched his fist. "Miantonomo does not know what the English are capable of."

"Young Sachem," Miantonomo began, "I am indeed aware of English atrocities."

Onasakenrat backed off, "Forgive me."

"I will deal with these English as I wish."

"I am with you," Onasakenrat said.

Miantonomo gave Onasakenrat a stern look. "I have sent my men to deal with Captain Oldham in our own way," he said. "We will give him one chance to undo his thievery."

"He is dangerous," Onasakenrat added. "This Oldham is like all the other whites."

Grey-feather interjected, "Sachem, I must ask you to leave now."

"No need to, friend-of-the-English!"

"Leave my island!" Grey-feather demanded.

Onasakenrat would have loved nothing more than to throw down the old sachem and end his life. But, he knew he and his men were outnumbered. It would have to wait until another day. Besides, his true targets were not on hand anyway. He gazed into Grey-feather's eyes like a serpent eyeing a rodent. His hand clenched the hilt of his knife. Grey-feather and Miantonomo stood tall and squared off with him.

"Very well," Onasakenrat finally said, "the Wolf Clan leaves."

He turned and ran down the slope.

"Grey-feather, this warrior troubles me," Miantonomo said.

"And me."

"We should send word to Uncas."

"I fear Uncas cannot control him."

"I will notify the Mohegans when I return."

There was a pause in their conversation as they watched Onasakenrat and his Mohegans launch their boats in a quick and orderly fashion. All the Mohegan canoes headed west, except one that turned and headed east toward Oldham's ship. The sachems looked further out over the sea and saw that the Narragansett pursuit of Oldham's boat was coming to a close.

"It strikes me," Grey-feather began, "that this Onasakenrat has been on my island many times before, and in secret."

"How do you know?"

"It is what I feel."

"Do you believe he intends to settle an old score?"

"Perhaps. Two years ago, we lost our greatest warrior, Samuel, to an unseen enemy."

"Do you think Onasakenrat was behind it?"

"I fear he may have been," Grey-feather said.

"It is clear that he despises you."

"This does not bode well for any of us."

"Mohegan vengeance! For what?"

"Fifty years ago, the Mohegans suffered a great defeat at a battle on the southeastern cliffs," Grey-feather said as he pointed in that direction. "My father and the elders have told us the story many times so that we do not drop our guard. They invaded our island thinking they would not be seen by coming in from our blind side. A young girl saw them in the night and we prepared ourselves. As they were climbing up the bluffs, our warriors were waiting for them. We killed as many as we could and threw the rest down breaking their bones on the rocks below."

He paused again as he watched a small white puff of smoke discharge from)ldham's pinnace in the far distance. And then, several other puffs appeared. The sound ♦f the gun fire arrived several long seconds later.

"It has not gone well," Miantonomo said, straining his eyes.

"The Mohegan canoe has joined your warriors in battle," Grey-feather said, ♦ointing to the left of the pinnace.

"Yes, I have watched them."

"Onasakenrat, is with them."

"If he kills Oldham, he will use it to divide us."

The two sachems watched in silence for a moment as the fight on the sound ♦eveloped. Finally, Grey-feather said, "From this day forward, he is not to be trusted."

"I agree," Miantonomo said.

"I am glad you are with me, brother."

Without taking his eyes away from the action out on the water, Grey-feather ♦xtended a hand to Miantonomo. They clasped them Indian style. Out on the Sound, they ♦vatched their warriors climb onto Oldham's boat. Then a body was thrown overboard.

"What happens out there," Grey-feather said, without turning to look upon his 'riend, "may be the final breaking of the earth … and of our people."

CHAPTER 15 – Hell Bent

* * *

Running-bird stroked Dekanawida's hands the same way she did on each and every visit. She touched them delicately as he rested them between the bars in a small window of the door that separated them. Confined in a cell at the stockade of Fort Saybrook, she was all he had. She spoke to him sweetly, as she had so many times before. She stroked the back of his hands and in between his fingers; she made him forget his torment. She yearned for him, and encouraged him to keep his faith and courage. But over the last three months, she watched in vain, as his health deteriorated dramatically. Now, with Little-grey-feather standing beside her, Running-bird felt he was on the fragile edge of giving up.

"You must eat and drink everything they give you," she said. "You must keep your strength."

Dekanawida's sunken eyes peered out from the gloom. "I see no hope."

"Do not speak this way, my love. There is hope."

"I rot in here."

"Peter Wallace tells me he has found someone who can help."

"As much as I love Brother Peter, I fear he can do nothing."

"Peter is doing this for you while he carries his own burden. His wife that he has loved so dearly maintains her case against you. Peter struggles with his duty to her and his conscience every day. He could have done nothing, but instead..."

"Why does he waste his time?"

Dekanawida dropped his head; his weakness more evident now.

"Our creator gave us the gift of hope. We must seek it within us."

"Hope...again you say..."

He lifted his head with great effort. His checks were gaunt and creased. He looked years older than he should have. Running-bird fought hard to keep her despair from showing. Little-grey-feather began to fidget so she lifted her up.

"You know," she said, then paused. She looked away from him for a moment to ather herself, then continued. "He has found the man that gave you the wound. Peter is ut there trying to bring him here."

"Why would this man come here? For me? I think not."

"He will."

"The English will not wait much longer. They will find me guilty and they will ut me to death."

"But there are many braves with scars such as yours," Running-bird said, in an anxious tone. "We are all working hard to convince the English judge that it is a case of mistaken identity."

Dekanawida's eyes widened, a spark of youthful energy fighting back in his countenance. "Mistaken identity?"

"Yes!"

"That means nothing," he said.

"Of course it does!"

"This land is consumed with mistaken identity."

She looked deeply into his eyes, searching for a reply.

"It is the world we live in," he continued, as his body was sinking away from her, "I am but another victim."

"No, there is good …"

"No, my sweet, there is nothing." He released his hands from the window and drew back into the cell.

"Dekanawida!"

He fell into the rear wall, sliding down in the darkness.

"Dekanawida!"

A whisper of a man's voice replied. "My sweet, intelligent, woman and friend, please forget me."

"*Never will I…*" she cried so loud it startled Little-grey-feather. "Listen to me, my love. I remember a Mohegan who comes to my island every summer to trade. We do not like him; he has malicious intent. He was there two summers ago when I first met you and Peter. He has a long scar like yours. I felt his evil."

Dekanawida did not reply.

"He is our age and he is a sachem now," she continued, "and... and I am certain he wants to see us perish."

Dekanawida remained silent.

"I ... I..."

Running-bird looked away. A vision suddenly filled her mind of Dekanawida hanging from the gallows. She stepped away so that he could not see her face. Looking upon her daughter gave her an idea.

"Little-grey feather is here to see you," she offered. "She is two-years-old now and speaks very well."

Dekanawida slowly rose to his feet and moved closer to the barred window. Running-bird could see his hollow face more clearly now. She shivered quietly and blamed herself for not coming sooner. It was over five weeks since her last visit and over two months since she brought Little-grey-feather with her. She lifted her child so he could have a better look.

Little-grey-feather's bright faced filled his window. Dekanawida instinctively drew back, ashamed of his condition. But slowly, he regained his composure and looked upon her with great interest. The child showed no emotion, just a steady gaze as if she understood everything.

"I can see that she knows much," he said.

"Yes, many have said this."

Suddenly, Dekanawida's throat felt as dry as sand, he could not speak. The child caught his gaze and held him in a trance. She stripped away whatever it was he was about to say and seemed to read his mind as a mother would her child. He felt she could feel his pain, his anguish, and his love for Running-bird.

Little-grey-feather's mouth opened, words formed.

"Be brave," she said, in a child's pitch, but with a single clear tone.

Dekanawida, amazed, rolled his shoulders back and stood as tall as he could. He slowly let all the air out of his lungs. He stepped forward and raised his hand to the bars. The child raised her hand to meet his.

"You see," Running-bird said, "she knows, and she wants you to be strong."

She lowered Little-grey-feather to the floor.

A loud noise behind them indicated that the jailer was coming. Dekanawida caught his breath and pulled himself closer to the bars. He looked out at the beautiful mother and her daughter. Trembling, he knew that this would be the last time.

His hands came through the bars. She raised hers, and their fingers entangled.

"Whatever happens, Running-bird," he said, softly, "I will always love you."

*   *   *

Peter turned around sharply the instant he heard the gun fire.

"Captain!" he called out, pointing due east.

"Yes. I see it," John Gallop replied sharply. "*Load the cannons!*" He screamed to the boy nearest him.

On board the bark, were two small cannons mounted on either side of the stern. The young sailor was joined by the other and they moved quickly to bring powder and shot from storage to the deck. Peter and the navigator worked the sails as the Captain drove his ship hard toward Oldham's pinnace.

Gallop spun the helm port-side to find a tighter tack, within seconds he hit full sail, and the bark leaned into the water, rose and broke forward as fast as the wind could take them.

Peter took his position at the bow.

"Come on, come on," he growled under his breath.

Two Narragansett long canoes had closed in behind Oldham's pinnace. In panic, several of the sailors fired their muskets at them. The Indians returned a volley of arrows from two sides and littered the stern. One arrow struck the helmsman square in the back. He crumpled to the deck, still clenching the tiller. The ship jerked to the starboard, and several of the men fell. A third canoe appeared off the port beam. They launched their arrows, wounding two more of the sailors.

The sails of the pinnace went limp as the ship turned directly into the wind. Captain Oldham lost his advantage, and the Indians quickly closed in on his ship. Another round of gun fire missed their targets. But another round of arrows found theirs.

Oldham had ducked behind a mast, but when he looked around, four of his men lay prone on the deck. Only he and one other remained standing.

The Indians boarded, Onasakenrat along with them. Oldham's men--those that were still breathing--were slaughtered, and their bodies thrown overboard. Oldham dropped to his knees begging forgiveness.

"Bring the Captain to me," Onasakenrat demanded.

Oldham was dragged forward and thrown before the feet of Onasakenrat. The young sachem looked down at him in disgust. He drew out his long hunting knife and knelt next to the Englishman, who continued to plead for his life. Onasakenrat gave a signal for the Narragansetts to hold him down. With the precision and indifference of a butcher, he cut off one of Oldham's hands. Oldham screamed a blood curdling cry. Onasakenrat spoke in broken English.

"We cut off the hands of all who cheat us."

The Narragansetts rejoiced in war cries. They responded in turn by cutting off his other hand.

Blood flowed over the deck. Oldham rose and screamed in horror as he held his two handless arms up. Shock overcame him and he fell to the deck. The Indians laughed and then cried out again in triumph.

Suddenly, one of the Mohegan warriors called out to Onasakenrat and pointed to the approaching ship. Onasakenrat raced over to the side for a better look then signaled his men to leave immediately. The Narragansetts refused to give up their prized boat and scrambled to restore the main sail. Several of them dragged Oldham's bloody body below deck and hacked away at him with their long knives. Moments later they rejoined their comrades on deck as a war cry rang out for battle.

On Gallop's bark, the Captain had the boys load the cannons and several of the muskets. Peter was on the bow, still manning the sails, and he could see they were gaining on the pinnace.

"What can you see," Gallop called out to Peter.

"Two empty canoes have been tied to the stern. A third is far off to the port, heading to the mainland. The pinnace is heading east."

"Can you see Captain Oldham?"

"No, just the Indians. It looks like they are trying to sail the pinnace by themselves."

"Do you see any other Eng…"

Gallop's words were cut short. He clutched the helm tightly and looked carefully off the starboard side. His fears were confirmed: the body of a sailor floated by with ribbons of red flowing out of him. Gallop's blood boiled.

Peter saw it, too. He looked back at Gallop. He could see the hell bent look on his face. Of all things about Captain Gallop, he was an Englishman first and foremost. He would defend his countrymen when threatened by Indians, the Dutch, or any other foreigner. Peter had witnessed conflict before, but nothing like this. When he tried to free Tatobem from the Dutch, he did it under some modicum of control. He had raised a white flag and sought to negotiate. But this, this reckless attack on the waters of the sound drove terror and a thrill to his heart all at the same time.

Peter climbed out to the figurehead and grabbed a loose line while letting his body hang dangerously over the rushing deep blue water. He pulled on the line bringing more sail into play. The bark lifted a bit higher and flew out. Salty wind filled Peter's face. He took off his hat and tossed it behind him onto the deck. He let the wind run through his hair and let it make his eyes water. He felt a delight in all this. Uncertain of where the elation was coming from, he let it race through his body. He was there this time, not by the will of God, but by his own will - a will to solve a crime and save a dear friend.

The sun was behind them now, and Peter could see for miles ahead. All the details of the struggle became clear to him. He calculated how long it would take to reach the pinnace. He counted the heads of the Indians on board and then calculated his chances. All his work, all his dreams of peace, all his desires for love, filled him now in a riot of exhilaration. Peter looked back and spied the Captain. He waved in a motion for him to go faster.

"*I am at full sail,*" Gallop hollered back. He turned and gave instructions to the boys who were standing nearby steadying the guns. They dropped what they were doing and trimmed a sail, and then Gallop turned the helm slightly to starboard to try to find more wind.

The Narragansetts scrambled about the deck and tried everything they could to put distance between them and the fast approaching bark. They had given up on the sails and were now fumbling with the long oars. Then they realized that the canoes that were in tow had capsized and were creating a huge drag. They feverously cut both loose. The maneuver provided little relief, but then the large frame of the bark loomed near and crossed behind them.

Gallop ordered the boys to aim the cannons. They fired them upon his order and both lead balls hit the pinnace sending slivers of wood and metal all about. Some of the Indians grabbed their bows and launched arrows that fell far short. Captain Gallop handed the helm to the navigator and commanded him to tack back across the stern of the pinnace. On the second pass, both Gallop and Peter fired the cannons this time and scored two more hits. The Indians were persistent and continued to do all they could to navigate out of harm's way.

"Give me the helm," Gallop ordered. He brought his ship about, running it away from the pinnace.

"What are you doing?" Peter cried out. "We are sailing out of range."

"My ship weighs twenty tons," Gallop said. "I will ram the savages and send them below to their graves."

"*You cannot!*"

"Do you see any Englishmen?"

"*John!*" Peter cried out. "*Don't!*"

Gallop Spun the helm sharply around and the ship heaved with the wind to its side. Peter lost his footing and grabbed the side rail. The ship closed rapidly.

"Your eyes are better than mine," Gallop, said. "I only see savages aboard."

"We can't know for certain. We…"

He lunged for the helm but Gallop brought the wheel back and now his ship was just seconds from a full broadside. Peter knew he was too late and grabbed for the rail again. Gallop had used the wind masterfully. Six of the Indians saw their doom and jumped overboard. Two others lay dead already from the cannon fire, and the two that remained on board dropped to the deck and held on for dear life. The bark hissed as it closed, throwing waves of foam to either side of its bow.

"*Brace yourselves!*" Gallop cried out.

The bark slammed into Oldham's craft with a loud crunching, splintering sound. The timbers moaned as if they were alive and in great pain. The pinnace turned so far over that it nearly capsized. In spite of their efforts to maintain balance, Peter and the boys were thrown to the deck like ragdolls. Only Captain Gallop remained upright as he gripped the helm.

"To arms!" Gallop shouted, as his bark rolled back off the pinnace.

Peter and one of the boys grabbed muskets while the other boy threw a grappling hook onto Oldham's boat. Gallop helped him secure it. Peter now wielding a short sword as well as the musket, jumped onto the pinnace. The others quickly joined him.

Two Narragansett's were found on board: battered, bruised and frightened beyond reason. Gallop forced them to their knees and stood over one with his sword pointed at the Indian's throat. Peter stood nearby with a loaded musket trained on the other one.

John Gallop acted decisively and demanded to know what they did with Oldham. The Indians finally understood and pointed to the cabin. Gallop raced below and found Oldham's body, minus hands and feet and with his skull cloven in two. Incensed, Gallop raced back on deck. Pushing Peter aside, he lifted his sword and drove it right through one of the Narragansetts.

"*What are you doing!*" Peter cried out.

"They butchered Oldham!"

"But…"

"See for yourself."

Peter had already feared the worst – on all counts. He held a false glimmer that if Oldham was still breathing he could get a confession out of him about Dekanawida. But this was not to be. Peter went below and found Oldham just as Gallop had described. Oldham was dead but his body was still warm.

"So close," Peter murmured. He then searched the cabin for any records that Oldham may have had - anything to clear his friend of the crime he didn't commit. If there was just a note or something he wrote, a diary, a record…but there was nothing.

CHAPTER 16 - The Debate

* * *

As soon as Peter disembarked from Captain Gallop's ship, he heard his wife's voice. Her tone was that same harsh, penetrating crash of thunder that rang out on the day that sealed Dekanawida's fate.

"Peter! Peter Wallace!"

Anne was trying to run as best she could as she headed toward the pier. Her long dress and heavy shoes prevented her from doing it gracefully. Peter saw her, waved, then grabbed his travel bag. He turned one last time and nodded to Captain Gallop. Gallop raised his head and smiled at his protégée then he looked out at Anne struggling to reach them. He turned back to Peter and smiled one more time knowing the news he had to deliver, then went about his business.

Anne caught up to Peter just as he stepped off the pier. Her breathing was labored but she forced out her words regardless. "Peter!" she exclaimed, perplexed.

"Yes." he replied, sharply. His shirt revealed the dried blood of John Oldham and the slain Indian. She observed his clothing.

"What happened to you?"

He gave her a sharp, biting look, and no reply.

"Are you hurt?" She insisted.

"No, not…"

"Peter," she said, cutting him off. "I haven't seen you in over two weeks and now this!"

"I am not hurt. Others were."

She looked at his shirt again and frowned.

"I am sorry, my love," he said, dropping his tone. He reached out to give her a hug but she pulled away.

"Don't touch me with that mess on you."

Peter's effort to understand her and give her the benefit of the doubt changed sharply again. "Do not press me on this," he said. "I will clean up, directly."

"Yes, you will," she demanded.

Peter looked at her, narrowing his eyes.

"I don't understand how you are not hurt," she said.

"*Woman!* I will not discuss this now."

"Well good. Now then, we have much to discuss about the shoppe."

Anne's attention to him was distracted as she looked out to the river at the bark. She frowned again.

"What happened to the Captain's boat?"

Peter turned and followed her gaze. The ship's bow had some splintered boards and a busted railing on one side. The port hull showed some deep gouges. Peter turned and walked away from her.

"Never mind!" She said. "I don't want to know."

Peter continued to walk forward, head down.

"We have far more important things to do," she added, now with a bit of concern.

As they walked away from the dock, Peter thought to himself that he would do what he had to do to keep the marriage whole. He knew it was his duty, in spite of Anne's demands. Someday, with his love, she might grow tired of her ambition and simply be content with things the way they are. With each step away from the damaged bark, with each memory of the struggle at sea slowly fading, he found himself falling back into another world. It was Anne's world of New London, and now he felt it consume him. He could see her influence was everywhere. Signs had been posted of where things could be found and where people were to go and not go. Corals were built for livestock, a new feature in town. The riverfront was recently groomed for canoes and ships of all sizes to enter and exit, quickly and easily. It was Anne's doing.

"How is your shoppe coming along," he finally asked.

"Our shoppe," she said, correcting him.

"Yes, our shoppe."

"Fine. I've decided we should live there."

"Oh?"

"Yes, we need to be in town now. Mother's old house is just too far away."

Several people waved as they passed by. Peter felt that his short absence seemed like a very long one as he did not recognize some of them. New London was now populated by more than one hundred and fifty people. It had changed dramatically in the two short years since his arrival. Peter dropped his head and wondered where it would all lead. His job had become too big for him to handle alone. He knew he needed to recruit several new deputies and train more soldiers for the militia. This had to be done and done without haste. The territory under his control was far too wide. And Anne was unstoppable. Her shoppe still had some construction left to do but it was already overflowing with goods. She had chosen to trade mostly in fine linens and fabric, organdy and crinoline. Ceramic goods and fine china were also her forte.

"Peter," she said, "I think we should rename the town to 'Fair Haven'."

"That would be hard to do, would it not?"

"I have already started a petition on it."

"You have been busy, little lady," he said cynically.

"Do not call me that."

"I am sorry, Anne."

They walked in silence for a short while. But Anne was never fond of long silences as she felt that it was akin to unproductive time.

"Peter," she said, with a tinge of guilt in her voice, "I have received several letters from my mother."

"Is she well?"

"Yes. Mother responded to my letter about the wedding."

"Oh?"

"She is happy for us; she asked about you."

Peter nodded.

"She is establishing a network of shippers to bring goods here."

"Well that is good news."

"And I also told her that we found father's murderer."

Peter stopped walking. He looked into Anne's determined eyes. But there was nothing more for him to say. She frowned at him and then pulled him along.

"Never mind that," she said. "Let us discuss what we have to do."

She spoke about some improvements she had in mind for the shoppe along with n addition to their living space. Before she could finish, they turned a corner and came within sight of it.

"Anne, who are those men standing at the back door?" Peter asked, with some concern.

"Oh, they are my part-time helpers."

"Helpers?"

"Yes, I have already started the expansion and I needed a few strong men to help ne."

Peter looked over their wilderness clothing and grimy appearance. He frowned. "They do not look like Puritans."

"They are not. They are English, nonetheless."

"Have they been in this country long?"

"Oh yes...a long time. They know the land. They were trappers and now just serve as guides for the new arrivals."

One of the men saw Anne approaching and gave her a warm smile. He was middle aged and tall. His black hair and blue eyes made him instantly handsome in spite of a dirty face. The other man was much younger, and his clothes were filthy.

"I do not like the looks of them," Peter said.

Ignoring what Peter said, Anne waved to the men focusing her eyes on the tall one. They men acknowledged her wave in each their own way. When she was content with the exchange, she replied to her husband, "Don't be silly. They are harmless."

Peter stepped up to the men and greeted them with an air of suspicion. Introductions were exchanged by Anne, and Peter proceeded to question them on their past and future plans. Finally, the dark-haired man, called Edward, grew annoyed and asked, "What sort of inquisition is this? What is your purpose?"

"It is my prerogative."

"What's that?" Edward said, sharply and with a chuckle. "This land is not part of any claim by any king."

"That is not what I meant."

"You're the Sherriff aren't yah?" The shorter man asked.

Peter realized the futility of this line of discussion. He looked at Anne, then back to Edward.

"If you are working for my wife, I will need to know about you."

"She knows all she needs to know about us," the short man chimed in. Then he chuckled.

"This is inappropriate!" Peter exclaimed, leaning into their space. "I shall dismiss you directly." The two men backed off.

Anne stepped over to the tall blue-eyed man and grasped his forearm.

"Now Peter, *you* are inappropriate. I need these men to work on the shoppe. Good workers are hard to find."

Peter cringed when he saw the way she held Edward. He prayed that her heart was not running astray. Since the wedding, he had also noticed that she was falling out of practice with her religion. Hopefully, she hadn't gone too far.

Anne looked up at Edward. She smiled salaciously and swaggered her body in kind to it.

Incensed by her gesture, Peter simply said, "I am very tired."

He took Anne's hand and pulled her away from the Edward. They went into the shoppe; no one was inside. He sat at their modest table and she filled his mug with cold water. After he regained some strength he decided it was time to tell her what he had planned. He began with his ordeal at sea and how the man he had hoped would clear Dekanawida's name was killed. He told her that he would need to see the Governor and make a new case for his innocence. And, lastly, he begged her to retract her accusation. Anne remained silent until he was done.

"How dare you!" she cried out. "How *dare* you continue this ridiculous quest? That savage is guilty!"

Peter boiled inside. All the hard work and trials he had just been through for the sake of justice and peace felt like it was all in vain. Was no one listening?

Anne shouted ever louder at him, "*My father was murdered!*"

"*We know that!*" He exclaimed, trying to counter her intensity.

"That savage is to blame. I have suffered for nearly a year now with this nonsense of yours."

"It is not nonsense," Peter said. "I seek the *truth*."

"Well, it is too late."

"Too late! What do you mean by that?"

"I have written to the Governor, and he is supporting my claim. Mother will do the same. And you ... you were gone for so long."

"Governor Winthrop!?"

"And the Reverend," she added sharply.

"What?"

"That's right, you heard me. They are with me."

Peter's eyes burned red. His heart pounded.

"They are *my* superiors; not yours."

"You were *not* here."

He looked down and swallowed hard. "I have worked so hard...so..."

Anne lashed out again. "So hard at what? Undermining me?"

"Anne ...," Peter said, now in disbelief. He couldn't find a thread of conversation to follow her statements.

"What were you really doing on this last excursion of yours?" Anne persisted. "You continue to go behind my back and make a mockery of me, don't you?"

Peter frowned. Age lines showed in his brow. "What do you infer?"

"*I hate what you've done to me!*"

A rattling at the door distracted them momentarily. It swung open and Edward stepped in.

"Anne! Edward said, anxiously. "Are you all right?"

Peter flashed an icy stare at him. "*Get out!*"

Peter shouted in a voice that he didn't know he had. It sent a shiver through him.

"No, Peter," Anne cried, with forced tears rolling from her eyes. "*You* get out!"

*   *   *

Onasakenrat waited until his canoe was near shore before making his decision. All the while at sea he had kept a sharp eye on the ship that wrecked Oldham's boat and killed the Narragansetts. He figured it would head toward New London – and it had. He instructed his men to follow it. Once Gallop had docked, Onasakenrat beached his canoe several miles downriver and made camp there. He sent scouts through the woods to keep watch on the activities in town. From their vantage point, they could see that a carpenter was already fixing the broken and splintered wood on Gallop's ship. A pot of hot tar was steaming over a fire pit, awaiting the finishing touches. At night fall, Onasakenrat and his men returned to their camp.

By morning's light, Onasakenrat was back on watch. Captain Gallop was spotted walking towards the pier. The Mohegans gathered and continued to monitor the activities of the Captain and his crew. It was clear that he was organizing provisions for another voyage.

"We will go to him now," Onasakenrat said to a comrade.

He and three warriors left the woods and approached the village. At the same time, Peter Wallace stepped out of Will Smith's trading post and headed toward the pier.

"Good morning, Peter!" the Captain said. Then he did a double take. "What happened to you? You look awful."

"I slept in Smith's shoppe last night," Peter said, in a low tone. He removed his hat and brushed himself off. It was the same hat he had brought with him two years ago to Connecticut. Now weather-beaten and faded, it was the first time he realized how bad it looked -- much the way he felt.

"Where is Anne?"

Peter just looked at him.

"This should not be," Gallop said, with a hint of anger. "A man should not be without his wife. I know you have your troubles with her. This needs to be cured."

"My wife..."

"You must go to her now."

"But I was planning on going with you to Boston. I must try to convince the Governor..."

They were suddenly distracted by the advancing Indians. The two men turned in unison and stood with unease as the Indians approached.

"Mohegans?" Peter asked, placing his hat back on his head.

"I believe so. One looks familiar," the Captain responded.

Onasakenrat raised his hand in a sign of peace. The Captain and Peter cknowledged the gesture and returned the same.

In his broken English, Onasakenrat proceeded to tell them that he was on the sland and he saw who attacked Oldham's boat. He conveniently left out any reference to is involvement.

"We believe the attack was carried out by the Narragansetts," Gallop said. He urned toward the pier and called out to one of the men who was loading cargo, then gave hand signal pointing to the ship's hull.

"We captured one of them but he is not talking. My men are bringing him out."

"I will be able to tell if he is Narragansett," Onasakenrat said. "Many of my eople were on the island yesterday. I am certain we will recognize him."

"This is a serious charge," Gallop continued. "John Oldham and his men will be venged."

Within minutes, a warrior with his hands bound was brought up from below deck.

"He is Pequot," Onasakenrat said with conviction.

"This is not possible," Peter said, stunned. "I can tell by his markings that he is ot."

"I tell you this man is Peqout," Onasakenrat insisted. "He was on the island. He vas planning to steal from Oldham. And the people of the island were encouraging him."

"The Manisseans?" Gallop asked.

"Yes, the Manisseans. They have caused us trouble for many generations. They re no good."

"We must be certain," Gallop said. "There are grave consequences to be reckoned vith."

"The Manisseans on the island are allies to the Pequots," Onasakenrat said, irmly. "Both are enemies."

Suddenly Peter saw it. It had been hard to see due to the Indian's body paint and eaded necklace, but there on his neck was an ugly scar. Peter took a step back.

"What is it, Peter?" Captain Gallop asked.

Peter was unable to speak. He kept examining the scar.

"Is your lack of sleep clouding your judgment?" Gallop added.

"Uh...No! No," Peter said, snapping out of his gape. "I think he may be wrong; that prisoner is not a Pequot."

Onasakenrat's face filled with anger when he heard Peter's words. He glared at him and demanded, "Who are you to say I am wrong?"

"The Mohegans have been our allies," Gallop said, intervening quickly. "We have no quarrel with them. Why would this man lie?"

Peter turned his body away from the Indians. He looked deep into Gallop's eyes. "Captain, a word with you...in private."

"Very well. But you must make it quick. I need to sail as the tide is running out. I need to get word of Oldham's demise up to Boston as soon as possible."

Captain Gallop turned to Onasakenrat. "Can you meet my leaders on the next moon, here in New London?"

Onasakenrat nodded. "I will bring them," the young sachem said. "If there is to be war, we would fight alongside the English against our enemies."

"Please understand," Captain Gallop said, "we will try to avoid war at all costs. Our leaders will take a vote on it. I will send word to you upon my return. Many soldiers will be with me."

Peter took him by the arm. "Let us talk!" He demanded. They walked a safe distance away from the others.

"He has the scar!" Peter whispered. "Did you not see it?"

"What do you mean?"

"My Pequot friend who is accused of Jonathan Miller's murder has a scar. But, so does this man."

"I am sorry, Peter, that warrior had many marks on him."

"He may be the one!" Peter insisted.

"This man is a Mohegan. Why would he..."

"I too have seen this man before. I have seen him on Block Island. He is feared out there. What if he is planning to control all the tribes? What if..."

They were cut short by a commotion near the pier. They turned in unison only to see the Indian prisoner drop to his knees with blood flowing from his neck. They rushed over.

"What happened here?" Captain Gallop ordered.

A sailor, who had been knocked to the ground, responded. "These savages started o argue, and before I could do anything, the Mohegan struck our prisoner down."

"What is the meaning of this?" Gallop demanded of Onasakenrat.

The young sachem said nothing; he feigned anger and was very convincing at it as ae paced around the fallen Indian. One of Onasakenrat's warriors spoke.

"The Peqout insulted our sachem. We know this man. He killed one of my prothers. When my leader learned this, his justice was swift."

Gallop said nothing. He simply bowed to the Indians. The Mohegans turned and valked away in silence. Peter addressed Gallop once they were out of range.

"Do you now see what I mean?"

"Indeed. My witness is dead and the key Oldham's death as well," Gallop said, ingrily.

"I must go with you to Boston," Peter declared. "I will tell the Governor what I know of this man and these people. I fear they have ill intent."

Gallop removed his large feathered-hat and ran his hand through his long matted aair. He was still tired from the previous day's battle but knew he had to head back out to sea as soon as possible. He took a few steps while in deep thought about Peter's request. Finally, replacing his hat, he addressed his young friend. "No, Peter, you cannot travel with me. You need to resolve your quarrel with your wife and prepare for our return. It is he most important thing for you now. And more, the Mohegan leaders will be gathering n one month. We will need them, as they may be our only allies, even if they have a sour grape among them.

Peter dropped his head. "Do you know the name of that Mohegan?"

"Yes, he is called 'Onasakenrat'."

CHAPTER 17 – A Princess and a Gentleman

* * *

In the great meeting hall of the Massachusetts Bay Colony, voices were reverberating so loud that some feared the building would fall down on them. Over a hundred men filled the large wooded structure, and many tempers were reaching their crescendo. The heat inside left a haze in the air, and many of the men removed their hats to fan themselves. A musty odor filled the room, and the predominately black and white colors of their outfits produced a monochrome of drabness, save for a few men with the daring to wear a splash of red or blue. The debate had been going for hours.

"First, it was Captain Stone, and now Captain Oldham," John Endicott said in his strong, firm voice. "Who will be next?"

A rumble of voices ensured. On one side, Reverend Cotton and some of the moderates were lobbying for peaceful solutions. On the other, the uncontrollable dark side of revenge and fear ruled.

The Reverend raised his hands and stood. He scanned the crowd looking for John Gallop. Finally, he found him on the far end.

"Captain Gallop, what does our young Sheriff have to say?" he shouted out.

Gallop stood and waited for the clamor to subside. He made his way toward the center of the room.

"In all things, he has done admirably," Gallop began. "For a long time, he maintained order with little help from us. He is for a peaceful solution."

"With whom?" A voice shouted out.

"With many!" Gallop responded. "He is impartial to all the tribes."

A rumble began to swell. Another voice rose.

"Does he not know our people are being slaughtered?"

"He does. He was with me when we attempted to rescue Oldham."

"And who does he think…" John Endicott's voice rose above all but was quickly cut off.

"Peter Wallace, works hard to be fair,' Gallop continued.

Voices rose with words and questions tossed out such as: 'fair', 'justice', 'act
ow'.

Gallop raised his hands for quiet. Slowly the gathering settled down.

"However," he said and paused for a moment before continuing, "The
Connecticut settlements east of Saybrook have grown too big now for just him and his
ew deputies."

Another rumble filled the room. Governor Winthrop rose from his seat and held a
and up high. The crowd grew quiet. He walked over to Gallop.

"We have sent many men to Connecticut," the Governor said," We have trained
many soldiers and built many forts. What more is required?"

"The savages feel the encroachment from our settlements," John Endicott cried
ut. "They claim we don't belong here in the New Land."

"Several tribes are forming allegiances," Gallop added. "While we argue, they
grow stronger." The crowd immediately stirred and chatter ensued among many.

Gallop raised his voice, "They have many more warriors than we do. Should they
and together, we will be doomed."

"They have never been able to do so in the past," the Governor interjected, "and
certainly there is enough land for them too."

Gallop stepped out into the center of the hall, scanning as many pairs of eyes as
e could. He spoke loud enough for all to hear.

"I have sailed many rivers and anchored in many coves and harbors. I have traded
with the Dutch in New Amsterdam. Everywhere I go, I see the restlessness of the Indians.
do not want to end up like Stone and Oldham. The exception is the Mohegan tribe. They
want to join us against the Pequots and the Manisseans. Let us formalize this alliance. If
we prepare now we may avert a greater disaster later on."

"Captain Gallop," Reverend Cotton said, inquiring. "What of the efforts of our
missionaries? What progress has been made in converting these savages?"

"Little to none, I fear."

A wave of voices cried, "*Savages! Devils!*"

The Governor signaled for quiet.

"I am with Gallop," John Endicott cried out. "We must re-double our efforts. Send more soldiers! I will lead them."

"Yes, I recommend this," Gallop said. "The murder of John Oldham was horrific. We must act now!"

"*They must be taught a lesson!*" someone hollered. A roar followed.

Captain Gallop waved his hands to quiet the crowd. "I fear more Puritans will die. We *must* regain control if we are to survive."

The Governor signaled for quiet. It took some time for the men to settle down. Waves of doubt, fear, and second-guessing filled the hall.

"And what of Peter Wallace?" the Governor asked.

It was the heaviness decision they had to make and was evident in their long faces. Only a few seemed content. Eyes darted from one to another and then many looked down to the floor or out a nearby window. A cough. A sniffle. A throat cleared. The short silence felt like an eternity.

"Replace him!" A hardened voice shouted out.

"Let Endicott take charge!" Another voice exclaimed loudly.

The Governor raised his hands. He ignored the last call. Slowly, he called out the names of several of his captains to meet with him privately and then dismissed all the others. Except for the muffled rumble of shoes on wood, the hall was devoid of sound. The merchants and tradesmen left with the knowledge that things would work out. Then, later that day, a decision was made.

* * *

Peter awoke to find himself in bed next to Anne. They were still at her mother's house, a necessity for the time being to alleviate the distractions of town life and to patch up the nasty quarrel they had had a week earlier. Mrs. Smith was instrumental in convincing Anne to apologize to Peter for her behavior. Anne was resistant at first, claiming it was he who should. But in the end, Mrs. Smith reminded her of her duty as a wife and of Peter's status, and that, if she wanted to be successful in town, it would have to start with the apology. Anne eventually took her advice. She and Peter also took the ime to get the farm running again and renovated the rooms in the house with some new urnishings.

A dream still fresh on his mind had taken him far from his home, and for a leeting moment, he thought he was walking over the hills along the Connecticut River. 'eter closed his eyes and tried to keep the dream from evaporating. He was searching for in Indian with a scar. In it, he kept closing in on the elusive native, but the instant he lrew near, the Indian would turn into a butterfly and slip from his grasp. And all the vhile this was happening he heard the voice of an Indian princess calling his name. Peter at up and looked at his wife, and suddenly, the dream was gone.

He had come to grips with his anger over Anne's accusation but his resolve to :hange her mind remained strong. He, of course, had to agree that Anne's two helpers vould stay on in order to maintain peace. Anne had already begun plans to expand the ;hoppe to included larger living quarters. It was far too much a journey from her mother's nouse to town, plus Anne would be able to spend more time on her trade. And now, with he thought that the Mohegan sachem he encountered may be the one who killed her father, he felt he may be closer to the truth - a truth that was not only the answer to a nurder but also part of a plot that could bring war to the land. It was this Mohegan he now planned to bring before Anne.

The morning sunlight streamed into the little bedroom. Peter listened carefully to ;ee if the widow living with them was up. But all was quiet except for a few morning oirds chirping away. The smell of tilled earth from the fields outside filtered in. He stood and looked out a window to find the widow's son tilling the soil. He turned away and looked again upon his beautiful young wife. The soft skin around her face was beginning :o show a few lines of age. Indeed, Anne worked hard and did heavy physical tasks, more so than most women her age. Her raw hands were showing signs of it as well. As he looked at her, his hope for her salvation returned. *Why had she changed so?* He thought. *Or, did she have this unladylike ambition in her the whole time? Could it be something to do with her witnessing her father's murder?*

Though she seldom talked about the events on the day of the murder, Peter recognized that she had seen something so terrifying that she was probably not thinking clearly. Perhaps it would be best for her to get it out in the open, to clear her mind once and for all. She was so convinced that it was Dekanawida, yet so secretive of everything else. He felt if he could get her to see Onasakenrat then maybe she would change her mind.

He looked back down at her. She was indeed beautiful. He eyed her long wavy amber hair and then focused on her full lips, so luscious and moist even as she slept. They continued to haunt him, and he knew she used those lips to manipulate other men.

Peter lowered himself and kissed her. Anne woke with a start.

"What's that?"

"Good morning," Peter said, smiling.

"Oh, Peter, don't do that!"

"What? The kiss?"

"You startled me."

"I beg your forgiveness," Peter said, carefully.

"Is Mrs. Hayes up?"

"I haven't heard her. But, I saw her son working in the field."

Anne sat up and swung her feet to the floor. Her back was to him.

"These days have been good for us," he said.

She didn't turn. The room grew quiet.

"I feel better about … about us," he continued.

She turned her head slightly toward him but said nothing.

"Anne?"

She rose to her feet, brushing her nightgown.

"Anne, I know you do not like to discuss the night your father…"

"I thought we were done with that?"

"But Anne, I…"

"Don't you have to get ready?"

"Well yes, I do need to get going."

"Fort Saybrook again?"

"Yes, I told you that."

Peter got out of the bed and walked around to her side. Anne gathered herself and turned to face him. She reached out and grabbed her husband's arm.

"You are going to see that savage, aren't you?"

"I will visit a Mohegan village first, then yes, I will be going to Saybrook."

"You continue to disobey me."

"No Anne, I do not."

"Yesterday you said you loved me."

"I do, Anne."

"The court will decide his case. You don't need to see him."

"As you say, my wife." He bowed. It was a clumsy gesture at best. "I must be going now."

"Not yet, husband."

Peter looked at her, puzzled.

"We have been married for over a year now and no child has come. Let us try again."

Peter lost his voice. He simply did not know what to say. Confusion took hold and a sharp pain grew in the pit of his stomach.

"Come, Peter, couple with me."

Anne pulled her nightgown up over her head and threw it on the floor. Her round, firm breasts swelled as her breathing quickened. Her body radiated a sensual heat so quickly it was as if a door was open by some powerful hand. Peter couldn't move, it was only on a rare occasion that he saw her naked in full light.

"Come to me," she said, holding her arms out to him.

Anne closed her eyes and pulled him to her. It was at that moment, she pictured what it would be like with Edward. She knew she would always be married to Peter for the rest of her life, but it did not mean she needed to be faithful. The thought of a tryst with Edward sent her mind spinning.

She reached down and stroked Peter's hand in the area between his fingers where the flesh was most sensitive. An uncontrollable shiver ran down his spine. Moving quickly, she sat him down on the bed and grabbed the back of his thick, dark hair. She gently pressed his face to her bosom. The softness and scent of her filled his soul like nothing else on earth. Peter tried to fight off the arousal, but he knew he was losing the battle. Anne pulled his face up and kissed him passionately. She reached down and gently stroked him. It didn't take long for Peter to be ready. Anne lowered him onto his back and climbed on top. She helped him pull up his nightshirt. Reaching down she stroked him until it was what she desired. His confusion ran in chaotic streams of joy and misery. Anne raised herself and slowly slipped him inside of her. She was tumescent - as hot as the summer sun and as wet as the morning dew. She rolled her hips like the waves of the incoming tide. Anne huffed, she moaned, and finally let out a muted gasp when she felt him release. It was over in two minutes.

Anne fell on her back and lay quiet for several minutes. Her hand was busy twisting her long amber hair into silky braids, her mind calculating. Peter, still trying to catch his breath, closed his eyes and tried to understand what had happened. At the moment, he thought he understood it all, but it faded away like a candle's flame at the very end of its wick.

Anne let Peter go to Fort Saybrook. She was content she had set her husband in the right frame of mind. She was no fool, though. He may have told her his trip was to meet the Mohegan elders to prepare them for Captain Gallop's return, but she knew he would see the prisoner as well. However, after her performance that morning, she was sure he would be thinking of her.

Peter left the house and hurried to New London. When he reached the crest of the hill, the one Will Smith had first shown him, he stopped and looked back. He could still picture the line of Pequots crossing in the open as they had done two years prior. He remembered that was the day he first saw Dekanawida. Then he thought of Anne. He thought long and hard about her. He prayed to God that it would work out. A warm breeze suddenly flew all around him. Lifting his face into it, he felt a strange sensation of loss. Like a rogue wave materializing from thin air, a swell of emotion rose from the pit of his stomach and consumed his thoughts. He looked out again over the field below and the path beyond, the one that led to the Miller house. This was the place of his turning point, the place that took him to Anne and Dekanawida, the place that was the nexus to the pain in his heart. Was it too much to ask, he thought, for Anne to simply say that she may have been mistaken? There was so much at stake now. The Pequots were bitter and on the edge, the Mohegans – ready for war, as were his fellow countrymen. What more could he do to help her understand?

He squeezed the damp corners of his eyes and wiped away the biting droplets of despair. The warm breeze faded and disappeared. And, as fast as it had come, the despair left him as well. He stood erect. He thought about his duty and the new deputies he had to meet and bring to Fort Saybrook. Captain Underhill would be waiting for them, and he was not a patient man. He turned back around and headed toward the thriving little town.

* * *

Peter greeted the two deputies near the dock at New London's harbor. They had recently come down from Boston and were both younger than he was. Peter marveled at their naive exuberance. He smiled when it occurred to him that he must have looked just like them when he first arrived. He prayed they would stay that way. They conversed briefly until the pinnace came into view from down river.

It did not take long to secure the ship to the pier. Once all were aboard, along with a good amount of provisions destined for Fort Saybrook, they set off down the Thames River and slipped out into the vast Sound. By late afternoon, they finally arrived at the fort. It was an incredible site to all that approached. Fort Saybrook had become a bustling, growing town, like many along the coast, but more rapidly than any other. Construction of buildings was in full swing on a dozen new dwellings. A Sherriff had been appointed for this town and all settlements up the Connecticut River. Discussions over who would govern the colony was is full debate. It would soon be the largest English settlement in Connecticut.

Peter parted with the deputies after giving them instructions on where they would find Captain Underhill. He then made haste to the prison which was located inside the fortress. The interior consisted of seven buildings: four of which were the barracks for the soldiers and officers and their families; the prison; one structure set apart as the munitions house; and a medical building that had become a necessity as well as a very active place after the last epidemic. One month prior, a doctor had taken up residence at the fort and was currently in charge of expanding the hospital.

Outside the medical house, Peter noticed an Indian woman sitting on a bench and a child playing at her feet. As Peter approached them, the child stopped what she was doing and watched him carefully.

"Good day to you, Peter Wallace," Running-bird said, as she stood to greet him.

"Running-bird! What a surprise!"

"I am glad you are here," she said. A brief smile flashed across her face.

"I too."

Peter glanced down at Little-grey-feather. They locked eyes for a moment. Peter sensed the child knew who he was.

"I did not think you would be back so soon," Peter said.

Running-birds face was filling with despair and anxiety. Peter recalled some of the things she had told him about reading people's feelings and hidden agenda. He was not surprised when she said, "I have word that trouble is about."

"Trouble?"

"War is coming. Is it not?"

"Why no," Peter said, bluntly. Concentrating on controlling his body language, he added, "There is no such thing."

"What of the English alliance with the Mohegans?"

"I know of no new treaty."

Running-bird stepped closer to him. She reached out and touched his arm. She looked into his nervous eyes. Peter felt the guilt.

"Perhaps we should talk about it," he said.

"Yes, we must."

"You are right. There is something afoot, but nothing certain."

He paused and noticed that Little-grey-feather was listening intently.

"I believe I can be honest with you, Running-bird. And I trust you will keep secret what I know."

She nodded in the affirmative. "Peter, I can read it in your eyes. You know more."

Peter looked away. He scanned the walls of the fort and felt they might provide the same protection he needed around his thoughts and knowledge of what was to come to the Naturals of the land. But it was of no use, as he faced this all seeing woman. He looked upon her inquiring eyes.

"I work for peace," he offered.

"I know."

This time it was Running-bird who looked away. She had all the answers she needed and no more words were required about the oncoming war. Knowing that Peter Wallace was a man of his word, she would trust in him to let her know when and where it would start. Running-bird turned her thoughts to the pressing matter at hand.

Peter saw this and asked, "Have you seen Dekanawida?"

"Yes, he is very ill."

"Let us go to him at once."

They walked silently past the guard house and into the confinement area. It consisted of a simple open area with two tables and some chairs. A single guard sat in one of them. At the back end, was a row of three rooms that were built into the rear wall. Each room was enclosed with a heavy oak door fitted with a small barred window in the center. Dekanawida's cell was the one on the far end. Passing a jailor, who nodded when he recognized Peter, they found Dekanawida's cell and peered in. His friend was stretched out on the straw covered floor, lifeless. Peter called out to him but there was no response.

"Jailor!" Peter called out, "Open this cell."

The jailor got up and reluctantly complied. Peter and Running-bird rushed in. Little-grey-feather stood quietly by the door.

"He is ill with fever," the jailor said. "Mark your distance."

"Why is he not in the infirmary?" Peter demanded.

"Savages are not allowed in there."

Peter knelt on one knee and lifted Dekanawida into his arms. He was shocked how light he felt. It had been nearly a month since he had seen him last, and this change was all too sudden.

"What are you doing?" the jailor said, as he nervously reached for his sword.

"Move out of my way," Peter said, rising to his feet. "A precedent is being set. Watch me!"

Peter hurried by the guard and rushed out the door. He crossed the courtyard with Running-bird and her daughter close behind and entered the infirmary. "Stay outside, please," he said to Running-bird. She obeyed, knowing he would have his hands full.

Running-bird waited outside in the sun for what seemed like hours. Finally Peter emerged alone. Running-bird rushed over to him.

"How is he?"

"He has the fever, indeed. The doctor says he needs fluids and rest in a warm place. The doctor was cooperative and will help."

Running-bird smiled for a moment. She reached out and took Peter by his hands. Then she looked up, directly into his eyes. She started to tremble; her smile faded and was replaced by the shadow of fear.

"I do not see his recovery," she managed to say.

"He is a fighter. I am certain he will."

"I do not see it."

Peter was at a loss on pretending any more. She was right, but he had to ask. "What *do* you see?"

"I feel it."

"Your powers?"

Running-bird looked down and away. "Yes, it is a curse," she murmured.

Peter pulled her close and embraced her. He held her tightly for a long minute. Finally, he stepped back to look at her face; they locked eyes. Suddenly, he realized she knew what he was thinking: a short trial, a guilty verdict, and then a hanging. Her eyes watered when she knew that he knew what she saw. This time, she embraced him.

"Only time will tell, Running-bird," Peter said. "The doctor says to return in several days. Dekanawida may recover with proper care."

"I pray my vision is wrong."

"But more, sweet woman, I met a Mohegan named Onasakenrat. Do you know him?"

"Yes. He has an evil heart."

"I believe so," Peter said.

"He has come to my island on several occasions."

"He has a scar similar to Dekanawida's."

Running-bird looked down and away. "I have seen it," she said.

"I will find him, whatever it takes."

196

"Tell me again of the circumstances of Jonathan Miller's death," she asked.

"Why?"

"I am beginning to feel a connection with this Mohegan."

Peter proceeded to tell Running-bird all he knew about the night of the murder. Running-bird asked him to be specific of the date and the weather. As Peter described the event from what Anne and Elizabeth Miller had told him, Running-bird slowly grew sad.

"What is wrong?" Peter stopped to ask.

"It may have been the night my husband was killed."

"Are you certain?"

"Yes. What you have described fits the storm and that evening perfectly. I believe my husband was killed hours before the time of Jonathan Miller's death. The raiders left in a hurry. My husband...," Running-bird paused. An image touched her that she had tried so hard to remove from her mind. She inhaled deeply and continued, "My husband was not scalped. And so, they would have returned empty handed. They would have been angry."

"Do you think Onasakenrat killed both men?"

"I cannot know. But now we can start to ask others about him."

Peter looked around. He thought for a while and then asked, "Were none of the enemy bodies found?"

"No. But we found signs of a great struggle. There was blood on Samuel's weapons."

"Maybe the attackers took the bodies so as not to leave a trace."

Running-bird nodded. "That is what we believe," she said.

"Then, if this Onasakenrat was there, he must have lost someone dear to him. It would account for his need for revenge."

"So now what?"

"Can you stay? For Dekanawida?"

"Yes, but I have no place to go, and I will need food. I had only planned on one day here."

"I will help you," Peter said. "Follow me."

They left the fort and walked down among the structures that made up the growing town. Peter knew of a family that was sure to take care of Running-bird. It was the young couple he had accompanied to New Hartford, as they had since moved closer to the Sound. The wilds of the North had not worked for them. He took Running-bird and Little-grey-feather to their house located just a short walk outside the walled fort. After introductions and conversation on their humble porch, the English couple welcomed their Indian guests with open arms.

CHAPTER 18 – Endicott's Will

* * *

Two weeks after Peter's recent trip to Fort Saybrook, a great commotion arose in the village of New London. Three large ships in full sail appeared moving up river. As they drew near, the sails were skillfully drawn in and secured. Lines were thrown to those waiting on the newly completed pier that reached further out into deeper water. The lead ship was secured there. The other two ships anchored nearby.

A contingent of well-armed soldiers disembarked and headed into town. They were led by Puritan Captain's Endicott and Underhill. Awaiting them, on the center green, were a dozen soldiers under the command of Peter Wallace. Peter was dressed in a metal breast plate and helmet and all the splendor of a man of his rank. Nearby, some thirty Mohegans stood with Onasakenrat. A few elders and warriors from other tribes were mixed in with them.

A separate group of Indians stood well off from the others not far from Will Smith's trading post. Sassacus, sachem of the Pequots from Missituck, commanded this group. The Pequots were invited by Peter, and it was for this reason only that they chose to be on hand. He was the one they could trust to represent their innocence in the matter of John Oldham and Jonathan Miller. Peter had hoped that by having them present it would eliminate any false accusations had they been absent.

Endicott's men approached the Mohegan's first; various conversations erupting and translators trying their best to keep it all accurate. The Pequots walked down to meet them, which only created more chatter and some finger pointing. Within short order, Captain Endicott showed signs of losing his patience. It was impossible for him to determine which tribe was telling the truth and which not. Trying to find a way out of the mess, he turned their attention to a discussion about the Narragansetts and the Manisseans.

"Sassacus," Endicott said, "the Mohegan sachem blames the Manisseans for the death of our countrymen."

"And you trust this one?" Sassacus asked, pointedly.

"Why shouldn't we?"

"The Mohegan is an outcast."

"He is sympathetic to our search for the truth. You are hostile to it."

Sassacus grabbed his long knife and pulled it out of its sheath. Endicott stepped back, several soldiers drew their swords.

"I will cut you down now, English."

"Sachem, please hear me."

Sassacus raised his free hand and looked around. He and his men were clearly outnumbered. Struggling with his temper, he replied, "My words are done here. We remember what white men did to Tatobem."

"You know the Dutch were responsible for that," Endicott lashed back. "We are different, let us talk."

Sassacus sheathed his knife then swept his hand through the air signaling for his men to gather around him. They started to walk away.

"Sassacus," Endicott called out, "what do you know of the Manisseans?"

The leader of the Pequots stopped in his tracks. He turned and glared at Endicott and said but one word, "Dogs!"

Sassacus turned away, his men following in line and they set out at a rapid pace toward the trail that led east into the forest. Peter argued with Endicott claiming he was wrong to let them go so easily. When he realized his words fell on deaf ears, he raced off after the Pequots. His tenuous relationship with Sassacus only existed because of his work to free Dekanawida. Peter knew what was in store and knew he must warn them as delicately as he could. But after going a mile into the trail he realized he wasn't gaining ground. They had broken into a run, leaving Peter hard pressed to keep up. After a while his heavy gear weighed him down. Dejected he headed back to town.

When the Pequots left, Endicott signaled his men to return to their ship at once. As he walked by Onasakenrat, he stopped for a final word.

"Are the warriors of the Wolf Clan with the English?"

Onasakenrat gave him an icy stare. Endicott would not back off until he got an answer. Onasakenrat's chest filled with air; his shoulders stiffened.

"The Wolf Clan will fight with the English only if the English have the same will as we do."

"What is *your* will, sachem?"

"To seek revenge on the Manisseans for the death of our fathers, and to stop the *Pequots and all their treachery."

"You must understand us, Sachem," Endicott said, softening his tone. "We are *Puritan first and foremost. We do not repress others solely for the sake of vengeance. We seek truth first."

"Then explain your armor and your weapons," Onasakenrat said, cynically.

"The devil is at work in this land. It is the will of God that puts us in arms on this day."

"Then your God has the same will as the Mohegan."

Endicott looked away, frustrated at the direction the conversation took. He looked off to where his ships were moored. He thought about what it must have been like for Oldham, Stone, Miller, and so many others in their final moments. There was no end to it. And it was all in his hands now. He had the men, the ships, and the weapons; he had to do something and to do it now. A statement had to be made. He lowered his head for a moment and closed his eyes. He asked God for forgiveness and for the proper answer.

Finally, he faced the young sachem and asked, "What happened to your fathers?"

Onasakenrat squared up and faced Endicott. He spoke loudly so others could hear. As a preacher would give a sermon, he said, "A generation ago, my father and the fathers of my men arrived on the Island-of-little-god, the one you call Block Island, and were all slain but one. It was a trap. Our fathers had plans to talk of trade, but the Manisseans had other ideas. The one who escaped was called Onerahtokha. He was my father. I would not be here but for his strength and will to survive. Then, two years ago, he was killed by a Manissean."

Many had been listening. Onasakenrat paused and stepped back from Endicott. He was pleased his intensions were clear now to all.

"Wait!" Endicott called out. "Will you swear to me that it was the Manisseans that butchered John Oldham?"

"It was. And the Pequots as well."

"We go to the island now, Onasakenrat." Endicott said, firmly. "Does that answer your question about our will?"

"Yes it does, but you cannot fool me. I know the English understand the importance of control over Block Island. It is the guardian to all the land and rivers that touch the Devil's Belt. Is it not?"

Captain Endicott stared at the warrior before him. He knew he could not hide the truth from him. He extended his hand and clasped Onasakenrat's in Indian style. Before he turned and headed to his fleet, he added one important piece of information.

"Captain Underhill will go to meet with Uncas," Endicott said. "We will solidify our alliance with *all* the Mohegan people."

*   *   *

By the time Peter got back to town center, Captain Endicott's ships were in full sail and well out into the Sound on an easterly course. Most of the Indians had dispersed. William Smith toiled on the pier with several other men, gathering up some supplies left by Endicott.

"Will!" Peter called out. "What was the outcome?"

Smith lifted a crate from the pier and said, "Well, yah know I try to keep myself away from these matters. I have to. I trade with everyone."

"Yes, yes, I know, but where are they headed?'

"To Block Island."

"So, they are going there after all," Peter said. "I thought there was a chance they would change their minds. How foolish of me."

"If I were yah," Smith said, struggling to walk with his heavy load. "I wouldn't get involved."

"You know that is impossible."

William Smith set the crate at his feet, stretched his back for a moment, and locked eyes with Peter. "Look, I ain't got nothing against those Indians out there. But I'd say it's time to just think about helping yah wife at the shoppe. That is, if yah want to keep your scalp and all."

Peter gazed out at the ships as they diminished in size.

"I need to stop them!" he said, firmly.

"Peter, look here," Smith said, trying to change the subject. "In these crates are
ilk garments from lands in the Far East."

Peter ignored him - his posture stoic.

Smith continued. "Did you hear me? Silk fabric and clothes, from the other side
)f the world! Don't yah see? The world is getting smaller every day. It's changing. Yah
:an't stop change."

Peter turned and looked him right in the eyes, "I must get out there!"

"Have yah lost yah head?"

"Where can I find a boat?"

"This is simply insane. Those men are off to war!"

Peter grabbed Smith and shook him, *"Get me passage to that island!"*

*   *   *

Running-bird and her daughter were gathering shells on the southeast corner at
.he rocky cove she loved so much. She spoke endearingly to Little-grey-feather as the
;ounds of the waves and seagulls accompanied her tones. The child was watching her
nother carefully and hanging on her every word. She occasionally responded with near
)erfect sentences.

"You feel something don't you, sweet one?" Running-bird asked. "Hold my
iands."

She took Little-grey-feathers hands then looked up over the sand dunes and high
)luffs to where the tree tops could be seen. The wind was brushing against the small oval
.eaves flipping them over and back. The light green side would show in waves much like
:he ripples on the ocean that spread out behind them.

"I do too," Running-bird said. "Close your eyes, little one. There is something,
ndeed in the air today. But we know not what. When this happens I close my eyes. I then
ook out, out from my mind, out from my thoughts, out from what we are thinking about
low, out from the needs in our lives. Can you do that?"

Little-grey-feathers eyes were shut tight. She squeezed them tighter. Then she
nodded.

"Now your mind is free to fly and look out over the world," Running-bird said. "Do you feel that? Are you seeing the world?"

Little-grey-feather nodded again. High above them, an eagle soared in wide circles. It flapped its wings just once to correct itself as a gust of wind disturbed its concentration.

"Tell me; do you sense danger in the air?"

Little-grey-feather immediately popped open her eyes and looked into the blue sky. Running-bird did likewise.

"You saw the eagle with your mind?"

"Yes, mother"

"Good, now watch it carefully."

The eagle dropped lower and caught another glimpse of a fish it was stalking.

"The eagle will not harm us," Running-bird said when she noticed her daughter come unnerved. "Soon it will eat, and there will be enough left over to take back to her nest where her babies wait."

Little-grey-feather could not keep her eyes off the bird. She followed it in its dive and watched its talons strike the surface and pull out a fish.

"A hunter who takes her time," Running-bird continued, "and waits for the right moment, will always win in the end."

Running-bird removed her moccasins and stepped into a crystal clear pool of swirling water. Large boulders, half submerged, helped steady her progress. Once she was knee deep, she extended her hand for Little-grey-feather to join her. The child did not hesitate and entered the water. She had an insatiable need to listen and learn from her teacher. And her teacher was now discussing where the crabs hide. Attached to the boulders, long, slippery strands of amber-brown seaweed swayed with the motion of the current.

"There, my child," Running-bird said, pointing to the gangly weed.

Running-bird showed Little-grey-feather how to carefully lower her hands into the water so as not to make even the slightest ripple. She slowly lowered her body until her knees hit bottom. Now, even more slowly, she inched her way toward the underside of the boulder. Little-grey-feather finally saw a blue-claw stick out from underneath.

Running-bird skillfully moved her hand behind the creature. The child was mesmerized. In a flash, Running-bird snapped up the crab and pulled it out of the water.

At that instant, they heard the echoing boom of cannon fire. Running-bird looked at Little-grey-feather and saw the fear in the young girl's eyes. She knew her child realized it was something man-made, something terrible. She closed her eyes and looked for a vision of what was going on back in her village. Through the darkness, she searched for some sign, anything, and anyone. Then, she saw it. It was a brief flash, but it was enough to tell her of the impending doom falling upon her people.

"We must get back to the village!"

It was all she could say. She picked up her child and ran as fast as she could.

* * *

Peter raced through New London, trying to find anyone with a sea-worthy boat to take him to the island. No one would cooperate. Finally, a fisherman knew of another across the river that was planning on going out for an afternoon excursion. Peter took his armor off. He replaced his helmet with his Puritan hat and paid for passage across the river. He found two men who were preparing to depart for the Sound, and insisted on being taken to Block Island. After much debate, Peter had to use the power of his position and the promise of a handsome fee to get them to accept the job. Once they heard the amount they'd be paid, they set out to sea immediately.

As the mainland fell away behind them, the ever-present glare of the silvery-blue sea lay before them; the reflecting slivers of light in the tiny ripples appeared like the bellies of a million fishes flipping in a playful dance.

While the day was sunny and clear, the sea started to get rough and a challenge to sail upon. The small fishing vessel was tossed about like a cork in rapids. Peter fought off the sickness, but his time on the water helped him through it. He thought about Running-bird and her child. The woman had worked so hard to comfort Dekanawida and to clear him of the murder charge. Peter knew that Captain Endicott had little or no knowledge of the quality of the island people. He prayed that Grey-feather would greet them warmly and find a peaceful solution. Peter was certain that the Indians who killed John Oldham were not from the island. It was just another case of mistaken identity. This was the dilemma of the land. It had haunted Peter from the edge of his conscience to the core of his brain.

Peter knew it would be impossible to overtake the three war ships. He and the fishermen could see them however, and followed their course. Once they got out past a sandy point that marked the beginning of the Narragansett territory, they headed due south. Their new course set, Peter found a moment to look upon his ferrymen and strike a conversation.

"I don't recall meeting either of you before," he said.

The two fishermen were startled at first in the softening of their passenger's disposition. They looked at him and then at each other. One was older with one hand wrapped in a bandage, the other much younger. Finally the older man spoke.

"Nor I, Gov'."

Peter smiled at the man. "I'm just a Sheriff."

"Beggin' pardon, Sir, so yah said."

"Are you not from the Thames?"

The older man handed the tiller to the younger one and moved closer to Peter. "Well, no," he said. "We've only been here 'bout five months."

"Where were you before then?"

"The Narragansett Bay," the old salt said. His cap was tattered as bleached out as much as his face and hands were darkened. His mate was perhaps twenty, shy and homely looking, but on his way to the same fate as the older man. He remained silent and looked upon his master for verbal queues.

"Was the fishing not good there?" Peter asked.

"Aye, it was."

"And..."

"Can't fish when the savages are chasing yah 'bout."

Peter felt discouraged at what the man said. He shook it off and smiled at them.

"The water is so pure and clear here," Peter said, "and I will wager the fish are plentiful."

"Yes Sir, it is. And fewer savages." The old fisherman said and smiled for the first time.

"I am certain there is plenty for all regardless of where one goes," Peter said, carefully.

"Aye, there is. But things change."

Peter looked away and out over the water. The small craft rose and crashed over a series of swells before settling down. Peter looked back upon his ferrymen.

"Do you know why I am in a hurry?" Peter asked.

The old man nodded.

"I aim to prevent what might happen today," Peter added.

"Can't stop it yah know," the old salt said, in a matter of fact tone.

"Oh you are wrong fisherman. I indeed intend to."

"If...if I may Sir," the old salt said, pressing his point, "change is the law of this land."

"As I have said," Peter replied sharply, "I intent...'

"Beggin' pardon again, Sir," the old fisherman interrupted, "My point is this; it seems to me yer living in the past and it is perhaps clouding your judgment of the present."

Annoyed, Peter quickly said, "the past has driven me to where I am now."

"Sir, if you live in the present without a thought to where it leads, you'll miss the future."

Peter looked away, troubled by the man's words.

The old salt persisted. "We left the Narragansett Bay to *not* miss our future."

"I understand."

"I hope you don't miss yours."

Peter thought best to drop the conversation. There was too much on his mind now. But the old salt's words stayed with him for a while longer. *Could he be right about my future?*

It took over two hours for the crossing. Finally, the natural harbor came in to view. As they approached they could hear the cannon thunder and see a dozen or more plumes of dark smoke rising from the village. The three war ships were anchored securely and dominated the scene. The fishermen grew concerned and complained to Peter about getting any closer. He reached into his pocket and extracted some coins. He held them up so they could see them clearly, and they pressed on. Soon the cannons ceased firing, and all grew strangely quiet. As the fishing boat slid into the harbor, they pulled down the sail and crossed behind the first of the large vessels. They quickly passed by the second one, then a head popped out from the stern of the last ship.

"Ahoy there!" an armed sailor shouted.

"Ahoy!" Peter called back. "We are English. I am going ashore."

"No one is allowed on shore!" the guard hollered back. "Take your fishing elsewhere."

"I am Peter Wallace, Sheriff of the colony. I need to speak to Captain Endicott, immediately."

"Not possible."

Peter signaled the fishermen to proceed.

"We have strict orders," the sailor said.

"*This is urgent!*" Peter exclaimed.

The sailor disappeared from the railing and returned a few seconds later with another man.

"You can come aboard, Peter Wallace," the new voice said. "But you cannot go ashore. We will send for the Captain."

"*I have no time for that!*" Peter cried out.

"Then stand off!"

"I cannot."

"Anchor where you are!"

Peter looked out across the water to the beach and saw a number of bodies in blood stained sand. There were eight or nine lying motionless, some Indian, some English. He looked up the hill and could see several Manissean huts burning. A musket fired in the distance, then another, and still another. He heard voices shouting and a dog howl.

Without a second thought, Peter ordered the fishermen to take him onto the beach. They refused. Peter looked at them and then back to the shoreline. He jumped out of the boat and hit the water hard. Struggling to stay afloat, Peter had to undo his sword belt and toss it to the men on board. A guard's voice was heard screaming at him, but no gun was ired. Peter felt he was being dragged down by his clothes. He shed his shoes and stockings. Now, he felt he could swim the distance, but the current was stronger than he anticipated and the tide was on its way out.

Peter thrust his arms forward. He slashed away at the water and kicked with all his life. The distance seemed greater than he had originally thought. His arms ached. He stopped for a moment to get his bearings. It was then that he felt the current pushing him sideways to his left. He went with it. Kicking even harder, he changed his direction to what would amount to a longer swim. It worked. His progress was twice as fast. Finally, with his arms aching to the point of feeling like lead weights, he kicked once more and dropped one leg. He touched bottom. A lick of a wave caught him in the mouth. He swallowed the briny fluid and gagged. Concentrating on his breathing, he fought off fatigue.

Pulling his legs through the water, he finally made land. He ran across the beach, but stumbled once. The sand burned his feet, ignoring this he ran faster. Climbing up the grassy embankment, he came upon the remains of two wigwams. Both were burned to the ground. Three Manisseans lie dead nearby. Two were burned beyond recognition. Peter's stomach turned. In shock, he raced forward. He passed several more wigwams, and a few of these were partially burned. He glanced around them and saw another half dozen Indian bodies scattered about, some were that of children. Gaining his bearings, he finally remembered where Running-bird's wigwam was.

The village consisted of a wide ring of wigwams with a few outlying ones placed at strategic points. Peter now found himself on the edge of the ring. Running-bird's home was on the far side. Smoke was billowing everywhere, but not a single human voice was heard. Peter rushed across the center, covering his mouth. Suddenly the wind picked up and it blew the smoke out toward the cove. It lifted just enough for Peter to see the full horror. There were at least another dozen dead Manisseans and one dead soldier. Peter looked up and spotted Running-bird's wigwam. He took only a few steps before he froze. There, before him, was the body of Grey-feather and another of a woman draped over him. Peter realized it was Grey-feather's wife by the way she was clutching at his fatal wound.

Peter prayed. He could neither understand how it got to this, nor comprehend the magnitude of the English rage. No one was spared, even the dogs were killed.

Forcing himself forward, he found Running-bird's wigwam. No one was inside. Suddenly, he saw something move a short distance behind it. It was her child. She was sitting in a cloud of smoke next to something on the ground.

"Running-bird!" Peter called out.

Little-grey-feather stood up and faced him. Not an ounce of terror or joy showed in her face.

"Child!" he called to her.

She looked at him smartly. Her face was blackened, but her silvery-green eyes showed through like those of a night owl .

"Child, I will not hurt you," Peter blurted out as quickly as he could, not knowing if she understood. "I am a friend."

The smoke blew off again, revealing the body of Running-bird lying face down before him. Her right arm and shoulder were burned badly. The side of her head, bloodied.

Peter dropped down and knelt next to her.

"Oh God! How could they?"

Carefully, he rolled her over. Her chest heaved. She was alive.

"Thank the Lord!" Peter said, unconsciously.

The child was standing next to him. She knelt down and kissed her mother on the forehead. Suddenly, Peter could hear the rattle of soldiers approaching.

"Soldiers," the child said, as clear as a bell.

This startled Peter more than the approaching men. He fell back away from her as if she were a sickness. "What did you say?"

"Go," she said and then pointed to the meadow that was behind her.

Peter gathered himself. He could see that beyond the small meadow was a thick wood less than a quarter mile away. He looked back over his shoulder at a group of heavily armed men returning to the village. He picked Running-bird up and followed the child across the meadow. Little-grey-feather moved at a rapid pace, with her tiny legs nearly in a sprint, she kept ahead of Peter's long strides.

When they reached the edge of the wood, Peter dropped to his knees and placed Running-bird down carefully. Little-grey-feather was finally showing signs of fatigue. Once Peter caught his breath, he motioned to the little girl to climb on top of her mother. He lifted the two of them together and entered the forest.

CHAPTER 19 – The Valor of the Innocent

* * *

Peter was only a few yards into the thick woodland when he stopped in his tracks; he suddenly could not find any trace of the trail. It evaporated in a wall of green, grey, and brown that filled his vision in all directions.

Little-grey-feather made a sound, and then she pointed to her left. Peter took several steps in the direction of her gesture, and then saw the faintest hint of a trail. There were indications of it away and down into a gulley. He followed this for some time until his arms could not carry Running-bird any longer. Finding a clearing in the underbrush, he gently placed her limp body on the cool ground. Little-grey-feather climbed off and raced over to a great oak tree. She stood on one of the raised roots with the agility of a mountain goat. She scanned the woodland, she then turned around and scampered back to Peter. He was still breathing heavily, but managed to talk to her.

"Little-grey-feather, we must rest."

He paused as he watched a frown cover her smoke-darkened face.

"Your mother is alive," Peter said. "I will help her get well again."

"Mother, drink water?" the child asked, in clear English.

"Yes…yes, we will get her water." Peter was amazed at this child. *How was it she knew this?*

He looked down at Running-bird. Examining her wounds more carefully now, he noticed she was still bleeding around her head. He ripped a long section of his shirt tail off and tried to clean the wound as best he could. He found a gash right at the hairline near her temple. Raising her head, he carefully covered the wound with the cloth and secured it.

"Water," Little-grey-feather said, pointing to her right.

Peter followed her line and could make out a narrow path.

"Is there water over there?" Peter asked. "Fresh water?" He wondered if the child knew what he meant.

Little-grey-feather nodded and confirmed with, "Water. Drink."

Peter started to rise, but suddenly couldn't feel his feet. He sat back down and examined them.

One was burned on the crown, and the other was bloodied. He looked at the soles f his feet, and they were raw beyond belief. In all his haste, he never noticed them, nor elt the pain.

"I cannot go much further," he said, more to himself than to the child, but he was nswered.

"Cave," Little-grey-feather said, her eyes aglow with excitement.

"Cave?"

"Cave." She pointed to the south, then spoke several words in her native tongue. 'eter shook his head. She stopped, realizing the communication barrier.

"Yes," Peter said, nodding, "take me to the cave."

Peter rose, lifting Running-bird in the process. He fought off the pain and ollowed the child at a slow but steady pace. With each step, with each rifle of pain, he owed he would do everything in his power to save this kind, lovely woman and her laughter. They passed through the woods in silence.

They climbed out of the gulley and up a slight incline. Not far to one side of the ath, a series of bright sunbeams filtered through. A stand of flowers came to life there. 'urple, blue, and white streaks ran in each petal. A narrow shaft of light lit them up like he flecks of shimmering silver upon the sea. Peter and Little-grey-feather gazed upon hem. Had it been another time, under another circumstance, he would have stopped to gather them.

* * *

"Captain Endicott!" a soldier called out, his blackened face a sharp contrast to his shiny silver helmet. It was late in the day, and the sun was beginning to turn gold. The ea was aglow with colors of early evening.

The Captain was standing in the center of the village with a half-dozen of his men. Most of the smoke had cleared out with just a few lingering whiffs here and there. The bodies of thirty-four Manisseans were laid out not far away, and those of seven of his men lay near his feet. Far down on the beach, but visible to the Captain, another sixty-plus of the inhabitants gathered on the beach, hands bound, waiting to be taken away.

"Here," Endicott called out, raising his arm high above his head.

The soldier approached.

"Captain, Peter Wallace has come ashore."

"What? How?"

"Fishermen brought him here. Our men tried to send him away, but he refused and swam ashore on his own."

"Impetuous!"

"That was some time ago," the soldier said. "They just told me about this now."

"Then, where is he?" Endicott demanded.

"No one has seen him."

"Strange fellow. I'm beginning to understand what they are saying about his persistence."

"Not much of an Englishman I'd say, Captain."

John Endicott looked at his sergeant and raised an eyebrow. "I regret that on this day, none of us were good Englishmen."

"Sir?"

"This carnage appalls me," The Captain said. "And the joke of it is, I was responsible."

The sergeant gaped at him. Endicott looked off, away over to the sea.

"We will search for Wallace," the sergeant finally said. "Perhaps, he lies hurt somewhere."

The sergeant signaled for five other men to follow him. They broke off into two groups and headed out in separate directions.

Captain Endicott elected to stay the night on the island. There was just too much to do. There were a number of Manisseans still scattered about, and he wanted to make it clear to them their choices – surrender or die. He intended to gather up as many as he could and bring them to the mainland. Block Island was to be an English settlement now, and it must be devoid of all Indians. He conducted a funeral service for his men that were killed and he buried them on a hillside overlooking the north end of the island. The intent vas to have their remains rest in peace facing the mainland for all eternity. He also had ill the dead Manisseans buried at their burial ground, which was located a considerable listance away from the village. He felt it would show the survivors that they had respect 'or their dead, and perhaps convince the stragglers to turn themselves in. The night came ind quiet swept across the island, a dead calm quiet like no other.

Peter Wallace woke the next morning with a start. He was dreaming about Anne, ind when he had first met her. It was a happier time, a time of exhilaration. Anne was smiling and laughing in the sun. Her face was radiant. But the dream darkened as a cloud arose behind her image. Her smile disappeared and fear gripped her. A disfigured, giant of a man appeared behind her. Unsure at first, Peter had a dreaded realization that it may nave been her father. He was bloodied and angry. His horrible countenance filled Peter's vision. Then it came to life - the apparition descending on Anne, its clanging jaws chomping wildly. She tried to run, but it was too late; it devoured her completely.

With a start, Peter's eyes opened wide.

"Water!" a child's voice suddenly said.

"Wha...?"

Peter checked his bearings. He looked around him. He was lying at the opening of a small rocky cave in the middle of the woods. The cave was a natural creation in the side of a sloping, wooded incline. It was like an open wound in a deep green setting, and he could hear the ocean in the distance.

Looking inside the cave, he saw Running-bird lying next to him. She had been cleaned up considerably. Green, wet leaves covered her burnt arm. He recalled all that he and Little-grey-feather had done to tend to Running-bird's wounds. Peter remembered how he cradled the young mother and her child during the night and how he attempted to get some rest for himself. But the summer evening was cool and uncomfortable as were his chances of escaping from his brethren who were so bent on conquest, and he only slept in short intervals.

The child was standing with both her hands carefully holding a large quoahog shell. She repeated, "Water!"

"Yes, Little-grey-feather, we need more water," Peter said with a soft smile.

He marveled at the child's maturity. He knew she was just over two years old, but she acted like a child three times her age.

Peter felt content that he had done all he could do to save Running-bird and her daughter. Peter rose to his feet but he stumbled immediately, they were still sore. He remembered cleaning them at a fresh water pond not far from the cave. Then, he heard the warblers singing a playful song - a fine tune to start the day. All around him, bright summer colors of the forest glistened. The pain in his feet were quickly forgotten.

Running-bird had not stirred. In her deep sleep, she remained lost to the world. Peter looked at her and smiled. He remembered dressing her wounds with botanicals of jewelweed and thoroughwort, remedies that Dekanawida had shown him how to use. He remembered how he described these herbs to Little-grey-feather and how she helped him find them. He remembered how he carefully removed the remnants of Running-bird's tattered and burned clothing, and how he had redressed her in his shirt. He remembered cutting what was left of her deerskins and fashioning a piece of them to wrap around her legs. And, he remembered watching Running-bird during the night for as long as he could stay awake. He remembered watching her slow and rhythmic breathing. He remembered her soft skin and the almond shape of her eyes. And, he remembered how beautiful she was in spite of her wounds.

* * *

"Where is my husband?" Anne demanded of William Smith.

Smith was standing behind the long table inside his trading post. He had heard someone come in, but was too busy with some trappers to notice until her words split the air. He saw Anne's red face and fire in her eyes.

"I told you, Miss, he went to the island with the fishermen," Smith said.

"The fishermen returned late last night," Anne said, quickly.

Smith stopped what he was doing and faced her. She was leaning on the table, staring him down. The trappers were invisible to her.

"Well, Miss, he probably stayed on with Captain Endicott."

"I don't believe that was his plan. He told me he'd be back with the fishermen."

"Miss, I told him it wasn't a good idea to go. But, he is the Sheriff and I assume he knows what he's doing."

"What word from this Captain Endicott?"

"No word, Miss."

Anne frowned at him. "You will call me 'Mrs. Wallace'," she said in a huff. She turned and walked out.

"What's with her?" one of the trappers asked.

"Oh, nothing more than her dire need of a husband and a child."

The trappers laughed. "Well she's a fair thing all right. I'd be happy to help her out if her husband doesn't."

Anne walked hard and fast across the street to her shoppe. She was still fuming when she opened the door.

"Edward!" she hollered. Within seconds, the blue-eyed man appeared from a room in the back. His hands and clothes were dirty from installing a stone footing in the earthen floor.

"Yes, Anne?" he asked, shaking the loose dirt from his clothes the best he could.

"My husband is missing," she said, angrily. In an afterthought she added, "And you shouldn't be calling me 'Anne'."

"Yes, my lady," he said and then smiled, broadly.

Anne's demeanor slowly changed. She feigned sadness. She forced a tear to roll down her cheek. She sniffled. Edward stepped over to the door and closed it.

"My husband is missing, and for all I know he could be dead," Anne said.

Edward saw through her calculating heart and knew what to do. He stepped up to her and took hold of her arms. He shook her gently and raised her up on her toes. He bent down slightly, and kissed her lips. Anne pushed him back, with an insincere effort. Then, looking into his eyes, she folded herself into him. He drove her back until they hit the wall. Edward didn't need a second hint; he commenced kissing her hard and long. Anne obliged, willingly. Reaching down, he grabbed her legs, separated them and hoisted her up around his body. Suddenly, Anne felt the rush. Her senses tingled. She marveled at how easy it was for her to open up to him. Her thoughts and body relished this sensation. There was only one other time that she felt this way. But the man that did it to her had a love of the sea and a penchant for trade. It was when she lost her virginity. But that time, it had ended painfully and with someone she feared she would never see again.

Their kissing grew in intensity. She bit his lip and drew blood. Edward reacted by thrusting his pelvis hard on her. She licked his wound and then giggled. He placed his hand over her mouth. A momentary panic swept through her as she struggled for air. Before she knew what hit her, he had dropped his trousers and entered her. The rush was exhilarating. She pressed against him as hard as he was against her. Anne lost all sense of awareness of her surroundings, she wanted more and more. She wanted to scream out to high heaven. Her world was exploding, she felt she had left her body and entered a world of unknown pleasure. Seconds later her body convulsed uncontrollably – she let it all go. And, just as quickly as it had consumed her, she spun down from the euphoria, numb to the world.

Edward slowly backed off, lowering her gently to the floor. Anne giggled through her heavy panting. Edward fixed his trousers and then took a long look at her. He laughed.

Suddenly the door opened wide. Edward's friend entered.

"What in blazes is go…," he started to say, but when he saw Edward's dirt on Anne's clothes and their out-of-breath state, he simply smiled with the grimace of the devil. Anne did not appreciate his gaping gaze. She screamed at him to leave, and then for Edward to do the same. They left obediently, laughing on their way out.

The room grew instantly quiet. Anne looked around. Her head was still spinning and her breathing was heavy. In the sinful quiet she could hear the echo of their passion reverberate in the far corners of the walls. She closed her eyes and prayed for the walls to be silent. As she moved across the room, she felt his seed run down her leg. She smiled. Suddenly, a voice whispered from across the room.

Anne spun around, "Who's there?!"

Nothing.

Worried now, she raced from corner to corner seeking out the source. Still nothing. In her mind the thought of a scandal such as this would ruin her. The voice materialized again, this time from behind her. Anne felt a wave of panic swirl up inside

1er. *Was it the devil?* She wondered. Nothing would interfere with her plans for wealth, 1ot even Edward, nor the devil.

"Who is there!"

The door to the shoppe opened. The light of day flooded the room and illuminated Anne and her dirtied, ruffled clothing. William Smith stood in the threshold. He looked around sensing Anne was not alone then he stared into her eyes. He calculated what might have gone on just moments before he arrived as he had just passed Edward on the outside, and saw the salacious smirk on his face.

"One of Endicott's ships was spotted at the mouth of the river," he said.

Anne was still breathing heavily. She instinctively brushed the dirt and straw from 1er skirt as if it were a routine habit of hers.

"Thank you, Mr. Smith. I will go down to the pier to meet them."

As soon as he left, she grabbed a towel and dampened it in a barrel of water. She lifted her dress and wiped herself clean. Anne stormed out of her shoppe in a huff. In long strides, she made haste for the pier. However, she looked around to see who was watching her. When Smith was out of sight, she caught Edward's gaze. He was standing at a nearby corral. Her demeanor immediately softened. She licked her lower lip filling it with moisture, and then smiled at him.

CHAPTER 20 – Vengeance of Man

* * *

Peter examined Running-bird's arm and shoulder where the burns were and he was sickened by what he saw. In spite of the botanical treatment, he noticed that some sections of her skin were becoming infected. She would need better medicine and clean bandages. If she did not receive proper treatment, the infection could kill her.

Suddenly, out of nowhere, a hard voice erupted.

"*Peter Wallace!*"

The stern cry sent a shiver down Peter's spine. The tone of it was filled with anger and frustration. Peter instinctively looked around for Little-grey-feather. Luckily, she was not far off from the mouth of the cave. She was playing with a pile of shells and some stones. Peter did not need to call to her. She was already up and running to him. He picked her up and slid her behind Running-bird. He raised a finger to his lips, and the child understood without a second warning.

"*Wallace!*" the heavy voice called out again, this time much closer.

Peter was bare-chested, having placed his shirt around Running-bird the day before. He had lost his hat, sword, shoes and stockings, and was left with just his trousers. He knew he looked a sight, and would have trouble explaining his condition to Endicott's men. But, he knew he had to make contact nonetheless.

He gave a signal to Little-grey-feather, and she understood immediately. Their eye contact lingered. She smiled briefly. Peter was amazed and somewhat frightened by her intelligence and instincts. But, he let his concern pass and smiled back.

Leaving the cave, Peter carefully followed the voice as it kept calling his name at broken intervals. He walked on the balls of his feet. His sore feet began to bother him but he persevered as best as he could.

Then, suddenly, there was a second voice – *just two men,* he wondered. The voices crossed behind the cave and headed west. It took only a moment to spot the men. Their metal helmets and breast plates flashed in the sunbeams that filtered through the canopy. Stalking them carefully and moving from tree to tree, he waiting until they were a good half-mile from the cave before exposing his position.

"Here!" Peter shouted. "Here I am!"

The two soldiers instinctively drew their swords and scanned the terrain. Peter tepped out in full view with his hands visible.

"Peter Wallace?" one soldier said, looking rather surprised.

"Yes, it is I."

"What in Hades has happened to you?"

"I was lost … out here, in these woods."

"Indeed, I will say," the soldier said, now laughing.

"I need help," Peter said, as he stepped up to them. He realized he sounded stupid. "What I mean is there are people out here that need help."

"Help!" the second soldier said. "You're under arrest!"

Before Peter could respond, they grabbed his arms, bound his hands, and led him ff.

Twenty minutes later, Peter was standing before Captain Endicott. As soon as the opes were untied from his hands Peter lunged at him.

"*Murderer!*" Peter cried out.

The soldiers pulled him back.

"Settle down, Wallace!" Endicott exclaimed.

"This is an outrage!"

Endicott proceeded to reprimand Peter for disobeying his men who tried to prevent him from coming ashore. The two battled it out verbally for several more minutes until they realized the futility of it all. Peter stepped away, looked around at the sad spectacle and realized that none of it could be undone.

"I need your help," Peter suddenly said, changing his tone.

"Looking at you, that is quite clear," Endicott said.

"I mean for others."

"Others?"

"You know who I mean."

"I cannot help a man who doesn't obey orders."

"I may have been rash, but I had good cause."

Endicott hesitated for a moment and looked upon the young, handsome man before him. In spite of his filthy appearance there was an inner glow projecting through. And this was a man who was in touch with the Indians, a man that he needed.

"I like you, Peter Wallace. If I did not, I would have you in irons."

"No need."

"You can be useful to me."

"I intend to be."

"Then tell me what you need."

Peter proceeded to explain his predicament. He begged the Captain to understand and explained how he followed the retreating Indians into the wilderness and how some needed medical attention. He said it was his duty as sheriff to begin the healing process.

"There are many injured," Peter continued, with a white lie he invented on the spot. He intended on securing more supplies than he needed, just in case. "Two women and two young girls that are hurt badly," he added. "They can bring no harm to you. Provide me with what I need and I swear to you they will not harm our people."

Endicott turned away and took several steps toward the edge of the high ground they stood on. He looked out over the blue sea that stretched out before him. White breakers sent briny sprays into the air around the beach. He watched as seagulls fought over the carcass of a blue crab. Finally, after several minutes of neck twitching and eyes darting around, he turned around and rejoined the group of men.

"Peter," Captain Endicott began, clearly drawn and tired, "Yesterday was a day I care not to remember. I have been in battle before, but I have never experienced anything like what happened here."

"We are responsible, nonetheless." Peter said, carefully.

"Our plan is to place our brethren on this island," Endicott said, increasing his volume, "and make it a colony. Trade and commerce should thrive here. The people that have already volunteered to live in this settlement will be coming in peace. What guarantee do I have that the savages will not strike us again?"

"They trust me, Captain, Isn't that enough?"

Endicott gave him a look of skepticism. "Why are you protecting these people?"

"There is one here, hiding in the woods, that holds the key to a mystery I am trying to solve. Grant me that, Captain. I need this person to stay alive."

Endicott looked out over the charred village. Guilt flowed through him like a warm of angry hornets. The grisly reality of a simple military expedition gone badly was more than he had ever imagined.

"Very well, but I will remain in charge here."

He turned and started to walk away, when Peter hailed him.

"Captain, what have you done with the survivors?"

"We have placed all but a few of the belligerent ones on two of my ships. They will be relocated to where they belong, with the Narragansett's. The ones that continue to resist us will be imprisoned at Fort Saybrook."

"When will you be leaving?" Peter asked.

"Two days, perhaps. I sent one of my ships back to New London this morning."

Peter looked out across the sea in an effort to find it.

"I will leave some of my men behind," Endicott continued. "But I hope you will be with us on the return."

"I intend to be."

"Very well, get what you need from the surgeon, and then have my men get you food and water... and some clothing! You look unbefitting of a Puritan."

Peter gathered up what he needed. He was fitted with a new shirt, socks, and shoes. He was given a large sack with food and a smaller one with medical items. Leaving as quickly as he could he made haste to return to the cave. He checked behind him periodically to make sure he was not followed.

As he crossed over the meadow and entered the woods, he thought about Dekanawida and how the influx of new prisoners might impact his condition. He wondered if Running-bird would ever get to see him again.

At the cave, he found Little-grey-feather sitting near Running-bird. She was keeping the flies off her mother with a flick of her hand. Peter smiled at her and the child returned hers in kind. The girl saw the sack of provisions and knew he had brought them food.

Peter checked Running-bird's breathing. He could not detect any. In panic, he lowered his ear to her mouth. He felt a faint wisp of air. Running-bird felt cold to his touch. Even though it was another warm summer day, the woods and the stones of the cave kept the area where she was very cool.

Peter reached down and lifted her off the ground. He could feel that her back was damp. He sat down and lifted her up and wrapped his arms around her, trying desperately to bring the warmth back to her body. Moving closer, he lifted her bottom off the cold ground and placed her carefully on his lap. He pressed his body against hers even tighter and gently massaged her icy limbs.

"Come on, princess," he whispered.

Little-grey-feather followed suit. She placed herself alongside of them.

"*Come onnn…*"

Peter was rocking her when suddenly Running-bird's eyes opened slowly, dreamily. The first thing she saw was Peter's face and fair eyes. She showed no emotion for a few seconds and then, unexpectedly she smiled.

Peter's heart swelled. He knew, at that moment, she would be all right. He watched as the corners of her eyes turned upward, as if they were smiling, too.

"Brother Peter?" she asked, faintly.

"Yes, I am here. And Little-grey-feather as well."

Running-bird looked around and smiled even brighter. She tried to reach out to her daughter, but suddenly winced in pain.

"My child."

"Mother."

Little-grey-feather squeezed in between them.

"Ah, yes, I remember now. I remember it all," she said, changing her joy to sorrow in an instant. "My people!"

"Running-bird, I am ashamed to tell you what has happened. I tried to stop it, but I have failed. All I can tell you is that most of the Manisseans are now prisoners and are being sent to the mainland."

Running-bird slid back from him and sat on the cool earth. She shivered for a second and then asked…

"Grey-feather?"

Peter looked down, his remorse showing through. She knew the answer.

"I remember seeing some of my people fall before I was struck down," Running-bird said in a cold monotone. "Were many killed?"

"Thirty … or more," Peter replied, reaching out to her in the event she needed his arm for support. "Others are scattered about in the woods."

Running-bird reached out for her daughter with her good arm. She pulled Little-grey-feather to her and hugged her for a long while speaking to her softly in their native tongue. After she released her, she addressed Peter .

"I can see the good you have done for me. And I know you tried to do the same for my people."

Little-grey-feather stood up when Running-bird tried to move her burned arm. Peter, still sitting in front of her, reached out and grabbed an unburned portion of her hand. He helped her move it to where she wanted it to go, to his shoulder. She was in great pain, but tried hard not to show it. Peter was amazed at her courage. Finally, both her arms were around him. She buried her face in his chest and wept.

Little-grey-feather knelt next to her mother and stroked her hair. An odd sort of warmth filled Peter.

Rocking her gently, he said, "I will always protect you."

*　*　*

On the third day, Anne stood on the pier as she had done the previous two days. Endicott's last ship was finally coming into view. She was half filled with anger over Peter. The other half of her was filled with sexual joy over Edward. A joy in which she reveled.

The large ship dropped anchor in the center of the river which was now at low tide. A long boat rowed in, Peter was standing in the bow. He nimbly jumped onto the pier and secured the boat. Anne rushed to him, gave him a quick hug, making sure the others who had gathered about saw her display of affection.

"Home again at last, Husband?" Anne asked, then noticing his drawn face, she added, "You look awful, but do not tell me of your trials. I have heard it all before."

Peter showed no emotion. He was drained, but he put up a good front. He simply kissed her on the forehead and said nothing. They walked off the pier together and up the street. There was a cold calculated space between them. It was noticed by others and whispers began to hiss among the inhabitants of New London.

As they approached Anne's shoppe, she reached out for Peter's hand and pointed to the new construction at the back and side of the building.

"Look how far we've gotten in just a few weeks. Husband, I am glad you are home, but we must talk."

Peter turned to her.

"Are you at all interested in what happened on the Island?"

"Peter, you are always on dangerous missions. I have to live with fear every day. I prefer not to discuss it."

"This was different; like nothing else."

"Hush, it's all the same to me."

Peter let it all slide. He knew he had to get back to the Island and try to help the survivors. He knew the English settlers would be arriving before the end of the month and wanted to maintain what little peace was left out there. He also needed to get to Fort Saybrook to check on Dekanawida's condition. But above all, he remembered how Running-bird urged him to return to his home and his duties to his wife and countrymen. Lastly, he remembered the sweetness of her kiss good-bye.

On the following day Peter needed to purchase some goods that only the Smith's carried. Some items on his list were intended for Block Island. He entered their shoppe and found Will and Mrs. Smith having tea at the large table. The two were engaged in a heated discussion, and after a few seconds of spectating, Peter was invited to join them.

"We have been talking about the night of the great storm," Will said.

"It has been such a long time now," Peter said. "A distant memory for most I fear."

"I was telling the Mrs. what I told you about Sassacus being on the river that night."

Peter turned to Mrs. Smith, "Did you see him?"

"The old fool never mentioned he saw Sassacus and Knoton," she said. "Just that ⁣e saw Indians on the river."

"I was protecting yah," Will said with a tinge of anger coming through.

"Why bring it up now?" Peter asked.

"I don't know," Will said, lowering his head. "Maybe I'm just getting old and ⁣osing my mind."

"I think not," Peter said. "But Mrs. Smith, did you see the Indians?"

"Yes, Peter," she said, "I had gone out to look for Will but couldn't find him right ⁣way. I went over to the river and saw a canoe with two Indians in it, but I didn't ⁣ecognize them. Since Will never told me he saw Sassacus, just Indians, I thought he saw ⁣he same ones I did."

"But you know Sassacus, Mrs. Smith. Did you not recognize him?" Peter asked, ⁣now sitting on edge.

Mrs. Smith suddenly looked sad. "It wasn't Sassacus Peter. And my husband was ⁣nsisting it was until …" She looked away for a minute struggling on what to say next.

"Until what, Mrs. Smith?" Peter asked quickly.

She looked into Peter's eyes, a quiver rolled across her lips. "Oh dear, this would ⁣nave helped you… I'm certain."

"Please continue."

Mrs. Smith composed herself and said, "Will said the Indians he saw were in a ⁣⁣ark canoe. The two I saw were in a maple tree canoe. You know, the sea worthy kind."

Peter's eyes lit up. "There were two canoes. Was it about the same time of night?"

"Yes, right after the main part of the storm came through," she added.

"Those in the maple canoe," Peter asked, "could you tell if they were Pequot?"

Mrs. Smith tried to smile. "They were not. I believe they were Mohegans. And…and I'm certain one was that new sachem of the Wolf Clan."

All fell quiet in the room. They looked at one another. Finally Peter stood.

"I know now," he said, and moved toward the door. "Please excuse me I need to ⁣find passage to Fort Saybrook immediately."

CHAPTER 21 – A Day in Full

* * *

Dekanawida stood before a tribunal of three Englishman, one of which was a Puritan from Massachusetts. He was thin and bony, half the size he once was. He stood facing them with his hands shackled in chains in a hall at Fort Saybrook that was used for trials. The room was filled with nearly twenty people, mostly English settlers and soldiers and a few Mohegans most of whom were seated. There were no women present as they were not allowed at such events.

"Dekanawida of the Pequot Nation," the Puritan judge said. "You have been found guilty of murder by the English court. This is based on Mrs. Anne Wallace's statement. She was the only witness, and no other person has been brought forth. As cleric of Puritan law, I have the authority to grant you one last chance at redemption. Do you understand that I may be able to spare your life under Puritan law?"

Dekanawida's sunken eyes and cracked lips offered no response. He gaped back at the judge but no words came.

"There is no one else who can help you now," the judge continued. "You have stated that you did not kill Jonathan Miller. Anne Wallace's statement says you did. And now *I* ask you, as a man of great faith in the Almighty, did you kill Jonathan Miller?"

"I did not," Dekanawida said, weakly.

"Then what of Anne Wallace's statement?"

Dekanawida looked around the room. He tried to focus on the faces but it was difficult for him to see. He squinted in the hope that he would find Peter or Running-bird in the room. But there was no one there that he knew. Time was slipping away.

"Come now, Pequot," the judge said loudly. "Are you saying that Anne Wallace is a liar?"

"She is not a liar," Dekanawida said, his words barely audible.

"That would make you guilty," an English tribunal said, sharply.

"She is mistaken," Dekanawida replied.

"Pequot," the Puritan judge said, "putting all that aside for the moment. Your life can be spared if you swear allegiance to the English crown and convert to Christianity.

You will remain in prison here and spend the rest of your days working at Fort Saybrook. This is the last offer I can grant to you."

Dekanawida stared blankly at the judge. The room grew dead quiet – not a breath was heard for nearly three minutes.

"*Pequot*," the judge finally cried out, "*respond to me! This is your last chance.*"

All eyes were on Dekanawida. Slowly, his lips parted.

"I do not have the authority to swear allegiance to the English," Dekanawida said. "I will need the approval of my elders. It is Pequot law."

"*He mocks this court*," the English tribunal lashed out.

Without waiting, Dekanawida added, "And, Anne Wallace was mistaken."

"Then you leave me no choice," the judge said. "I sentence you to death by hanging in two days' time."

* * *

Peter stood in shock as he watched the bodies of three men dangle in mid-air, suspended from a makeshift gallows. Their heads were cocked to the side in a grotesque fashion; only the devil could have engineered such an abomination of the human form. A single thick rope running behind each man, stretched up to a large T-shaped framework. The platform they had stood on was narrow, and the front had fallen away by some inferior design. But, all-in-all, the device had worked and killed the men instantly, snapping their necks in the process.

Peter shivered for a moment, but regained control as his anger took over his sadness and disgust. Clenching the hilt of his short sword, he took two steps toward a soldier who stood guard. Feeling threatened, the soldier lowered his pike, blocking his advance. Peter gazed into the eyes of the man, and assessed his ability. He guessed that the guard was twice his age but was broad in the shoulders and appeared strong as an ox. Peter caught himself and relaxed the grip on his sword. He then forced a glance straight up; it was a struggle to lift his head. He could barely make out Dekanawida's face; it was not the one he knew. Instead, in its place, was the face of death. Peter looked back at the guard, his teeth grinding.

"It is done," the soldier said, finally recognizing Peter. "You are the one who defended him, I recall."

Peter frowned, and then nodded in the affirmative.

"The Captain of the guard has been waiting for you."

Peter held his ground.

"I am sorry, Sir," the soldier continued.

Peter looked at him, now with surprise.

"I admire your resolve," the soldier said, removing his weapon from Peter's path. "I have heard of this Indian. He was a good man."

"Yes, he was."

"Go then."

"Your kind words bring me hope," Peter said.

"There are others who think like us."

Dekanawida was dead, and there was nothing more that Peter could do about it. He remembered what Running-bird had said to him about bitterness. So, he simply sought out the fort commander and asked for the body. He claimed that if it was returned to the Pequot's another conflict might be averted. His wish was granted, and he fell silent after he took possession.

Dekanawida's body was covered with salt and then wrapped and tied in a heavy blanket. It was placed on a mule and secured. Peter and a soldier led the beast out of the fort and headed to the sailboat he had arrived on. Along the way, he vowed to learn more about the Mohegan called Onasakenrat. He would put this young sachem to the test. If he could find a way to prove it, Peter would make him pay for killing Jonathan Miller and for the tragic death of Dekanawida.

Night had fallen when Peter returned to New London. He led the mule off the boat and with the help of a sailor re-tied the body to it. As he walked up the street, he began to receive icy stares from the few people still out tending to things. People he knew, people who would typically wave or nod to him, did not this time. He realized the weary image he projected escorting the body and all, must be something to behold. But there was something more, it was as if they knew who the corpse was.

He looked over his shoulder at Dekanawida's body. *Yes, it is quite a sight*, he thought. He regretted not taking it around the edge of town and around the far side. He had hoped the cover of darkness would be enough. As he passed behind Anne's shop, he quickened his pace. But a neighbor's curiosity could not wait and she sought out Anne to ask why and what Peter was doing. Anne was shocked to find out that Peter was back and had not come to her immediately. She raced outside and found him on the far end of town.

"*Peter!*" She shrieked. "*What is that?*"

She gaped at the grotesque body draped over the animal. She ran straight to him, arms flailing. Peter turned just as she collided with him. Anne pounded her fists on his chest. It was a spectacle that would be remembered for a long time by those who saw it. Peter grabbed her wrists tightly and shook her as hard as he could until she stopped. Anne finally broke off, and breathing heavily she screamed at him, "Don't you come back…don't you *ever* come back to me."

Peter held silent and prayed for her, and for his own forgiveness. She turned and stormed off, never once looking back. Finally, without a word, he gathered himself and left quietly, leading the mule with Dekanawida's body draped over its back far away into the forest.

A silent sadness followed him for a long while until a stiff, cold wind rose up and cleared his mind. He vowed to travel all night if need be. He had to make it to Pequot territory as quickly as possible. But his progress slowed as the mule, and he, felt the fatigue of a long, arduous day weigh heavily.

Hours passed and the journey grew difficult in the pitch dark forest. Peter decided it was best to make camp and rest for the remainder of the night. He knew he was walking into great danger and wondered if his life was about to end. No matter, he thought; if it was his destiny to die at the hands of the Pequots he would do it with all the courage Dekanawida and Running-bird had shown. If it were not for the words of the old guard at the gallows, he would have truly thought his mission was a total failure.

As he selected a safe place to bed down, the sounds of nocturnal insects filled the air. He tied the mule to a small tree and took several steps backward. His tired and sore body craved rest. He gazed once more at the odd bundle draped over the mule.

"My friend," he said awkwardly, "I cannot do this anymore. I feel defeated. "

He carefully untied the body and lowered it to the ground. The blanket had bunched up revealing some of the corpse, so Peter straightened it out and made sure it was completely covered.

"My good friend, sleep well tonight."

The crickets muffled his words. Their racket was deafening, but it was still all very beautiful. The night air was electric, the night sky clear and filled with stars. Peter inhaled the warm air and held it for as long as he could before releasing it.

"My God! … My God, we have tried, my brother … we have. Haven't we?"

The cricket's music seemed to shift, circling to his left. They scratched out a riff at one-second intervals, then a two-second pause, then the one riff, and another. In the distance, a reply from their intended mates overlapped with a solid rhythm of echoes. Seconds later, an owl hooted.

"No one can hear us," Peter said aloud with a cynical chuckle. "Even now, the crickets prevent our words from reaching out."

Peter looked straight up. His voice rose in a high pitch as his vocal tubes constricted. "Ohhhhh, heavens. My God, I love thee. But help me now to understand … I may die tomorrow. I can see the Pequots greeting me with arrows and clubs. I can see my body torn and smashed beyond recognition."

The music of the crickets shifted again, this time to his right. Peter slumped down against the base of a mighty oak tree. He looked up and up into its majestic branches. Out and upward they spread, dwarfing him into an ant.

"Oh mighty oak, can *you* tell me my fate?" he spoke aloud. "Have I sinned against my God and my wife? Was I not a good husband? I cannot stop this madness, I cannot."

He fought back his tears and tried to focus, but it was difficult. As tired as he was, he could not put his mind to rest.

Another hour passed. Finally, he sharpened his mind and thought: *So young I am; so strong I am; so venerable I am. But I do have something to offer. I must have a purpose. Does no other man endure what I have endured? Has another man been given uch responsibility? No, no man has…Ah …no, I am nothing so special. What was I hinking I could be, or do?*

Peter rubbed his eyes and then screamed. He screamed so hard he felt his neck onstrict. He stood and walked over to the mule. The beast, startled, pulled itself free and an off in terror. Peter tried to run after it, but stumbled and fell hard to the ground. He elt stupid, like a drunkard.

Then he heard a whisper. It was the voice of Running-bird. She was saying something, but he could not make out the words. He could feel her warmth and enderness, and, for an instant, he saw her smiling face. Then all fell silent. The crickets vere gone. One second of silence, then two, then slowly the crickets came back to life. The cacophony of harmony returned. Then it dawned on him. His efforts on Block Island o save her filled him with a new purpose. Yes, yes, he was good. He *had* good in him, and some had seen it. *Yes, Running-bird and her people will need me, he thought. I need o get back to her.*

Peter slept briefly, but it was a good, restful sleep. He woke at dawn to find the mule standing nearby, looking lost and hungry. He gathered it in, lifted Dekanawida's body over its back and secured the ropes. He proceeded to walk sharply the remaining nine miles to the Pequot village at Missituck. He had two goals in life now. His search for justice would end with Onasakenrat, and his search for love would end on the island.

* * *

Sassacus and Knoton alone walked out of the Pequot fortification to meet Peter in the open field. Villagers had seen him coming and raised the alarm. Had it been anyone else, they would have killed him the instant he entered the field.

Peter exchanged a simple greeting. He explained carefully the death of Dekanawida and the journey he undertook to return him to his own kind. He then handed the ropes tethered to the mule to Knoton. Lastly, he told them that he loved the powwaw like a brother. The two Pequots stepped around the mule and looked over the body.

"Peter Wallace," Sassacus said. "You go in peace. We cannot guarantee the safety of your people and those in the place you call New London. Your wife brought this on, and it is her and others of your kind that we will take revenge upon."

"Why does it always have to be revenge?" Peter asked.

"Your kind and our enemies know nothing else," Sassacus said.

"We must start somewhere," Peter said.

"You cannot stop the forces of nature."

Peter was hesitant to speak further but forced himself to blurt, "Even the forces of nature change."

Sassacus recoiled. "Bah! Dekanawida lies there, a victim of mistaken identity, or was it really someone's revengeful will? We may have questioned Dekanawida's ideas, but he is still a great loss to us. There was a time I could have killed him for trying to take away my squaw, but in the end he was important to our people."

"We *will* make amends," Peter said. "I would give anything to bring Dekanawida back."

"He was a better man than you, Wallace," Knoton interjected. "I was prepared to kill you the minute you set foot in our field, but my sachem wished otherwise."

"I am truly sorry," Peter replied.

"Begone, Peter Wallace," Sassacus said. "For you, we will spare New London as long as you live there. Should you die, or leave, we cannot promise anything."

"Please reconsider your rage," Peter begged them again. "Dekanawida would have wanted you to."

"*Begone!*" Sassacus cried out, "Before I change my mind."

Peter turned and never looked back. His pace quickened with each step and thought of what would happen to the people of New London. The sooner he got back the better. And then, he thought of returning to Running-bird. *What if she was ailing? What of her child?* But how could he leave New London, now knowing that the Pequots might strike?

Peter ran across the open field, the blank-faced Pequots watching him grow smaller and smaller until he was but a speck entering the forest.

By the time he reached New London, the people of the town seemed to already know of their impending doom.

"What word have yah, Peter?" Will Smith asked in front of his shoppe.

Peter paused to catch his breath. "The Pequots promise to leave New London alone," he said.

"I suspect it has something to do with yah friendship..." Smith said.

"I cannot guarantee that they will not strike. However, they promised that as long as I live here, they will leave us alone."

"So stay, young man. You look tired and thirsty. Please, come in and rest a while. The Mrs. will fix you something to eat and drink."

"You must keep this quiet," Peter said. "The people must not know that it is I who may save them. They must prepare for the worst and not count on me."

"I see," Smith said. "A wise decision."

"You must rely on Captain's Endicott and Underhill, and the powers in Massachusetts."

Smith looked down for a moment, then back at Peter. "Will yah tell Anne?"

"I will try to get her to leave New London. I feel once she is gone, you and the rest will have a better chance."

"She'll not go for that."

"Indeed, but I will try."

CHAPTER 22 – Decision

* * *

As the summer ended and fall set in, the people of the land were consumed with the harvest. Like fevered squirrels gathering nuts, the English settlers in Connecticut prepared for winter. Their settlements were expanding north into the highlands and west toward the Dutch settlements.

Anne was busy in her shoppe, organizing fabric by color lots. Edward had built some new shelving for her. He was busy opening wooden boxes that had just been brought up from the pier. One crate contained roles of silk that had come all the way from China. Anne was especially excited about this material. She had already made plans on what to make from it, including a small piece fashioned into a handkerchief for Edward. The fact that Peter was back in town didn't keep her from her lust for the tall, blue-eyed Edward. While she and Peter lived apart, she kept her distance from him, as he did from her. It was for appearances that they pretended to be married. And until she could figure out her next move, she would live with it for a while longer.

On a chilly fall morning Peter felt it was time to talk to Anne about their future. He no longer wanted to live like he was, nor did he want Anne to. When he walked into her shoppe, he had intentions of letting her know about the Pequot threat among other issues. He wasn't surprised to find Edward there. The two men exchanged icy stares until Edward realized he had to leave. He turned away from the shelves he was building and walked out.

"Husband!"Anne said, cheerfully. "Come see what I have." She stroked a fine silky bundle of fabric and pretended she didn't see the tension between the two men. Peter stepped up and touched the silk. For a moment he felt Running-bird's skin, and a shiver ran through him. He cursed his desire for her and knew it to be sinful.

"Anne, I must speak with you," he said, firmly.

"Of course." She held the bundle of silk like a barrier between them. "What is it?"

"I must return to Blocks Island before winter comes."

"Well, well, well, what a surprise," Anne said, disingenuously. It was the first time he'd noticed that she sounded just like her mother.

"It is my job to see that the new colony has everything they need." He stepped round the crate and drew close to her. She stepped back.

"I have forgiven you for bringing that dead savage back here. What new insult will I need to forgive you for this time?"

Peter fell silent, wondering whether to continue this thread or to just get to the point. He watched her eyes carefully. They were darting back and forth, her face grew puffy. Suddenly, she brushed him aside and resumed her fussing with the silk fabric.

Peter grabbed her hand. She turned sharply to him; face darkened.

"You go, Peter Wallace," she blurted out. "Just go and don't return. I will be just fine without you."

"Don't speak to me this way," Peter replied, sharply. "You need to take a long look at what you are doing. It is repulsive to watch the way you throw yourself all over Edward. It will ruin you in the long run. I distain the man. I should have sent him away a long time ago."

"But you didn't. Why? Who is it that you truly long for?"

Peter looked away. He felt time was running out. He had to broach the subject of his departure and the trouble it would bring. Nothing else mattered now.

"There is something else, Anne."

"What else could there possibly be? You just love to leave me alone here all the time."

Peter ignored her sympathy plea and continued. "The death of the Pequot, the one you claimed killed your father has made them angry."

"Too bad! Good riddance to that heathen. And, I have asked you not to discuss him again. The savages should be driven from this land or…or at least be converted. I am so tired of living in fear of them."

"I went to them."

Anne stopped what she was doing and looked up at him, bewildered and angry.

"What do you mean?"

"I went to the village at Missituck, the place we call Mystic. I brought the dead man's body back to Sassacus and his people."

Anne's face reddened. *"You did what?"*

Peter stood his ground. "You heard me!"

"How dare you! You lied to me. You told me he was buried in the woods," Anne said, stomping her foot.

Peter turned away, unable to bear the sight of her.

"I can't believe…" Anne stopped herself. Her demeanor changed to sadness and hurt. When he heard the sniffle, one he came to recognize as contrived, he turned back to her.

"Look Anne," Peter said, carefully. "Look, I had to do it."

He reached out and tried to contain her. She pulled back. At that moment the door opened and Edward walked in.

"Is anything wrong?" Edward asked.

Peter turned and gave him a stare. "No, Edward!"

"I heard a shout."

"Leave us," Peter demanded.

"No!" Anne exclaimed. "He can stay."

Peter turned and looked at her in shock. "Anne, this is for us to resolve."

"Edward gives me comfort."

It was at that instant, and with that expression, that it all became clear to Peter. He walked over to Edward and stood before him. Edward was taller and broader, but Peter would have given him a good fight. Peter had been hardened over the years and was more agile then Edward. Edward felt the challenge. Thinking better of it, he stepped back and reached for the door.

"I will be right outside, Anne. Call if you need me."

He stepped out but left the door ajar.

Peter walked back over to Anne.

"I shall say this just once," he said, flame spewing from his eyes. "And do not speak until I have finished."

His teeth were grinding. Anne withdrew a step back.

"I returned the body of my friend to his people. He was innocent of the crime you claimed. When I was there, the Pequots were planning for war. They said they would spare this settlement as long as I live here. They still respect me."

"Well, I cannot respect you," Anne blurted out sharply. "*I hate you!*"

"*Silence!*" Peter screamed.

Anne recoiled again, sinking into a dark corner. Peter followed.

"Do you understand that if I leave town, they will attack?"

Anne was shaking. She was shaking at his words, and more, for the first time, she felt her own mortality. There was no easy recovery from what he just said. Her body trembled. Her eyes rolled up and saliva slowly formed and ran down in thick strands from the corners of her mouth. Her nose boiled with mucus. Her head grew light and the room began to spin all around her.

Anne fell to the floor in a muffled heap. All sound disappeared as she faded from consciousness. She drifted into her place of safety. In a flash, she was flying, like she had every time she visited this place. She flew and flew ever higher, over a blue landscape. Then she saw the light in the distance. It was the same light, at the same unattainable distance that she flew towards. Trying harder to flap her wings to gain speed and not lose the beacon, she grew frantic. But just as she reached her threshold, the face of the Indian appeared. He had the wound - the red, coagulated gash. His face was hard and clear. Then it came to her: he was still alive!

Peter shook her. "*Anne!*"

Edward entered. He raced over to Anne, brushing Peter aside. Peter let Edward have her. Edward picked Anne up and brought her outside. Peter followed behind, slowly. Edward glared at him to keep his distance. Once outside, Anne came to.

"What happened?" she asked.

"Nothing, my darling," Edward said.

Edward had placed her on the brown, thinning grass of autumn that stretched out in front of the shoppe. Then, he cradled her lovingly. Peter watched and felt sorry for them. Any bitterness that he once had toward them was gone. Now, it was simply a question of their survival.

"Edward," Peter said, sharply, "If I leave this town, the Pequots will come looking for revenge. They will come for Anne."

Edward looked up and snarled at him. "Let them come. We will cut them down in droves. We don't want you here. We don't need you. We can fend for ourselves."

Peter hesitated. He looked at Anne. "Is this true, Anne?"

"Yes," she said, weakly. "We will be fine without you."

"Nonetheless, I will let Captain Endicott know."

"Peter," Anne said. "Leave us."

* * *

Peter returned to Block Island a week later. He and Anne had slept in separate quarters while he waited for passage. The town people knew everything, including Anne's request for a divorce. Much was left unsettled, though. In the few days before his departure, they simply avoided each other at every turn.

Out on the island, the English settlers were busy building homes and harvesting in the fields. Livestock had been brought there, and a pier was erected in the natural cove bringing more commerce at greater speed.

Peter disembarked onto the pier stretching his legs and arms in the process. The sail across the sound took over three hours as the winds were not favorable. He quickly sought the man who was managing the activities at the new colony. He was easy to find as he was tall and lanky, and wore a high Puritan hat that made him look even taller. He had been watching the ship enter the harbor and walked toward Peter without hesitation.

"Peter Wallace," the tall man said. "How was your crossing?"

"It went very well, thank you. I understand you are in charge here."

"Yes. I am James Allen."

They shook hands.

"I have heard great things about you, Peter," Allen said. "You have done well with building good relations with the Naturals."

Peter was pleasantly surprised at the man's words. It was the first time in years that anyone acknowledged what he had done. He momentarily felt that perhaps his efforts had been worthwhile.

"I am honored you say this."

"Well, Captain Endicott and Captain Gallop also feel this way. I had met them ecently and they filled me in on your work and said I should support you as best I can. Come let me show you our progress."

James Allen then led him around the village, showing what was being done. Peter asked about the Manisseans that remained on the island. He was assured that the English settlers where cooperating with them, but had little contact. He said they were still scattered about the island and were in fear of building a new village. "They are like small pands of loners or hermits," Allen said. "They come to us when they have something to rade or if they need help. We seek their knowledge of the sea. So, for the short while we've been here, all is in order."

Peter mentioned he knew some survivors out in woods beyond the meadow that he wanted to look for. He said good-bye to Allen and took off in a jog towards where he ast saw Running-bird.

As he entered the woods, he paused to get his bearings. The foliage was in full autumn color, and the sun-lit day added to the grandeur. However, the terrain looked different, and for a moment, he felt lost. Regaining the trail, he pressed on. Suddenly, alongside the path, he spied a bed of purple and white flowers. He remembered them from the time he and Little-grey-feather took Running-bird to safety. But something was different about these. There were more of them now, and the brush was cleared away and laid out in rows, as if someone had been tending to them. At that instant, he knew Running-bird and her child were alive and well.

Finally, he found the cave. He raced down the incline and around to the front of it as fast as he could. The cave was empty. It showed no sign of anyone having been there at all. Peter froze. His initial elation from seeing the flowers was gone, replaced now with the sinking feeling that the two people he sought were dead.

"Peter!" a soft child-voice said.

He turned around and scanned the woods. Nothing.

"Father!" the voice said louder.

Peter looked up startled, not only by the hidden voice but also by the word choice. He scanned the hillside and there, on top of the cave, stood Little-grey-feather.

"Little-grey-feather! Hello!"

"Hello."

"Where is your mother?"

The child pointed to her left. Peter walked around and up the incline and stood even with the child. She seemed to have grown and matured so much since he had seen her last. He realized she was nearly four-years-old, but she acted like someone twice her age. She raised her hand to his and held it tightly, then she turned and led him deeper into the forest.

After a short while, Peter could see the blue hues of the sea in openings through the greenery. They walked up a rise in the terrain and he abruptly found himself standing near two wigwams. They appeared almost magically, camouflaged by their bark and earth tones.

Peter was relieved when he saw her. She was standing there all the time watching him approach. Holding a wicker basket filled with shells, Running-bird stood as silent as a deer - her countenance bright.

"Running-bird!...It is I... Peter," he called out.

She stood silent for another moment. Peter felt the earth stand still and time evaporate. He feared she would not take well the news of Dekanawida's death, and telling her at all might even be a mistake. She looked good, however, and healthy. He could see some discoloration around her bare arm and a dark shadow along her hairline, but nothing more. He was puzzled by her lack of response. He feared she did not remember. Taking several slow steps towards her, he called to her again.

"Running-bird! Do you not remember me?"

Little-grey-feather let go of his hand and ran to her mother. Running-bird carefully placed her basket on the ground and hugged her child. She stood and walked toward Peter. When they came face-to-face, her distant expression did not change. She appeared confused.

He spoke again, "Running-bi..."

Before he could finish, she placed her hand softly on his cheek, within inches of his mouth.

"You breathe!" she said, softly, and her face lit up.

Peter smiled and released his tension in a short burst of laughter.

"Yes! *Yes!*" he exclaimed. "It is I."

"Brother Peter," she said, letting the elation show. She fell into his arms. "Oh, *eter," she whispered.

Peter's heart was swept away in that instant. His passion for her raced throughout ais entire body. He simply held her as tightly and as long as she did him.

Finally, when she relaxed her grip, and pulled her face away from his chest, he aw the dampness in her eyes.

"I am so happy you are alive," she said in a soft, sweet tone. "I had a premonition hat you were dead. I felt it for a long time. You were in great danger, weren't you?"

"I ... I was not, princess," he said with a struggle.

"I see," she said. "My vision deceived me."

"And you look well," he said, but knew the burned areas of her skin must still aring her pain.

"Yes, my people have nursed me back to health. The English settlers have given as aid, too. But, Peter, you were in danger, no?"

"I went to the Pequot village."

"So, maybe that was it," she said.

Peter wondered if she would ask about Dekanawida. He did not have to wait long. She read his mind.

"Forgive me," she said, suddenly. "I know he is gone."

"Dekanawida?"

"Yes."

"You know?"

"Yes, I felt the hurt all the way to here. And now, I can see it in you. I can see what you saw. How horrible."

"I am sorry," Peter said.

She said, "The news of his death was confirmed by a trader, who had been at Fort Saybrook."

"I am so sorry," he repeated.

Running-bird looked into his eyes. She held onto him again. "I loved him. My time for grieving has past. I know Dekanawida is on his journey to Cautantowwit, our creator—at the place where harmony lies. We cannot speak his name until he reaches heaven. We cannot distract him in his journey, as it would only delay his arrival. He will meet Samuel, and they will have much to talk about. I am certain of this."

"I … I do not know what to say," Peter said, amazed at her inner strength. "It is simply tragic."

"There was always love," she said.

"But you have lost for a second time! How will you survive…without…"

She smiled at him and a gleam rose in her eyes. "Peter," she said, "life is nothing without love. And, I have shared much love."

"You are truly amazing," he said.

"Come, Peter," she said with a sweet smile. "Meet the others. Come see what we have become. You are always welcome among my people."

After meeting the others Peter decided to stay at their settlement rather than return to the English village. He was given a place to sleep in one of the larger dwellings. Evening fell upon them and each member of the small community retired to their quarters. Peter slept better than he had in many a night. In the morning he found Little-grey-feather and two other Indian children playing outside the wigwam he slept in. She had a leather mat on the ground with a dozen or so bundles of foot-long straws spread out on it.

"Hello!" He said. "What are you doing?"

"Playing Pu-in," she said. "Come play with us."

Peter peered over the children to get a better look at the items they were holding. "How does it work?"

"One of these has eleven straws inside, the others have ten."

"May I see them?" He asked. Little-grey-feather gathered them up and handed him the whole bunch. Peter eyed them carefully. "Ah! And you must guess which one it is?"

"Yes, come play."

He sat down and she explained the details of the game. Each one took turns at five guesses. He played with them for an hour. In the end Little-grey-feather won most of the time. Peter excused himself and stood to stretch. He suddenly realized Running-bird was standing behind him.

"She is hard to beat," she said.

"I can see that," he said smiling at her.

"She has an advantage, you know."

"I think I do."

Running-bird took his hand. "Come walk with me," she said. "There are things we could use your help with. But first, let's have something to eat. You must be very hungry."

After a breakfast of dried fish and berries, she took him around the village and showed him some small jobs for which they could use his strength for. There were no fully grown men in the village as they had all been taken away after the raid.

Later in the afternoon, Running-bird invited Peter to take a walk to her favorite place. After an hour they came upon the cliffs that overlooked the ocean. The bluffs rose over nine hundred feet at this point, and the bright blue ocean stretched endlessly to the east. Peter inhaled the cool air that eventually made him lightheaded. Running-bird could see his disorientation and took his hand. She led him into the woods and down a steep ravine until it emerged right at the shoreline. The white foam of the waves breaking on the boulders sprayed a mist into the air. They paused there a while until Peter noticed that she looked uncomfortable.

"Do your wounds still hurt?" He asked.

"Sometimes I do feel the pain, but not today."

"Are you cold?"

"No, dear Peter, I am ... I am simply very happy here with you."

"As I am."

After a while, the chill in the air filled them both. Running-bird sensed it was time to go and led him back into the woods. Peter's heart thumped so loud she could hear it. Once they were out of the wind, they stopped to catch their breath. A quiet calm overcame them. Running-bird turned to him and held him tight, wrapping her arms around him – the way she did when they had met the day before. This time, however, she raised her lips to his. She waited for him to make the first move. His head was spinning out of sheer love for her and out of an incredible chemistry that he had felt ever since they first met. His kissed her softly at first; she responded with equal and endearing sensitivity. And then what followed was a torrent of passion. They slid to the ground. He pulled her on top of him to protect her from the damp ground but she would not have felt it anyway. They moved together, and they felt the other's heat throughout their bodies. Finally, he undressed her and then himself. They made love with all the enthusiasm of two hearts once torn but now on the mend. And in the end, she rested on him and lay in quiet, as their hearts slowly returned to a place of complete harmony.

*   *   *

Fifty well-armed Pequot's entered New London as evening fell. They spread out in a wide arch so that if anyone tried to escape they would be cut down. As the circle tightened several settlers emerged from their dwellings, they were immediately slain in a volley of arrows. Others seeing the attack screamed out a warning, but panic was already in the air.

Knoton met William Smith at the entrance of his shoppe and pushed him back in. Smith fell hard to the floor.

"Do not leave this house," the warrior said. Knoton pulled the door closed and walked quickly to Anne's shoppe. Sporadic musket fire echoed over the village mixed, the percussion of volleys mixing with screams of pain and shouts of anger.

A half dozen Pequots were outside the front of her door slicing away at the bodies of two white men. Edward was one of them - held on the ground while his scalp was being cut off. He groaned as Knoton approached.

"He is the one," a warrior said. "The one who took Peter Wallace's wife."

"Cut out his innards," Knoton said, "and wrap them around that post. Let him lie there where he can watch what we do to his woman."

The warriors carried out the act as Knoton stood at the threshold of Anne's shoppe.

"She is in there," another warrior said.

Knoton signaled for two of his men to follow. They entered the darkened room. Anne had doused the fire and extinguished the candles causing a smoky mist to fill the great room. The Indians spread out and moved slowly forward. The warrior on Knoton's left raised a hand pointing to the back, a split second later a blast erupted from a pistol with a ball hitting him square in the chest. The warrior fell over dead. Knoton and the other Pequot responded by hurling their clubs into the area where the flash was seen.

The room grew quiet. The smoke began to rise and the Indians moved forward again. The light from the opened door was making it easier to see. Suddenly they saw her. Anne stood at the back of the room near the fireplace. She had a hatchet in one hand and a long knife in the other.

"Savages!" she cried out.

They rushed her. Swinging wildly with both hands, she managed to slice Knoton's forearm and bruise the other warrior with her hatchet. Knoton reached out and grabbed her by her long hair. The other Pequot stumbled toward the door and fell to the ground once he was outside. Knoton proceeded to slam Anne's head onto a nearby table. His blood rushed down his arm and into Anne's face. Knoton dragged her off the table and towards the door. On his way out he saw a long hemp rope hanging from the wall and pulled it down.

Once outside he tossed her to the ground next to where Edward was disemboweled. She screamed then followed with a series of unintelligible words.

"Woman," Knoton said. "You are going to die three ways."

With the help of his men, they wrapped the rope around Anne's neck and looped it over the flattened top of the post where Edward lay. Others brought out straw and firewood from her shoppe. Anne was hoisted up but managed to get her hands between the rope and her neck.

"I can pay," Anne managed to say.

Knoton just smiled at her as his men went about the work of busting up the wood, placing it at her feet and covering Edward with it. The rope was hoisted higher, lifting Ann just a few inches off the ground.

"I … have wampum…much," Ann said. She could not free her hands as they pressed tightly against her neck.

A torch was produced. The straw and wood lit. Flames licked quickly around her feet; her dress caught fire in seconds. Knoton stepped forward. He drew out his long knife and drove it into Anne's side.

"For Dekanawida," he said.

CHAPTER 23 – Prelude to War

* * *

Peter remained with Running-bird into December. He explored the island with her, learning where all the main trails began and ended, where all the hidden coves and forest gorges were, where all the best hiding places were, and where all the elusive spirits dwelled. They found where all the other surviving Manisseans were living, or hiding as the case may be. Their love grew unencumbered by anything that had happened to them in the past. The beauty of the island saw to it - the passion and respect they held for one another.

Peter began to wear buckskins and moccasins on a routine basis. However, he put on his European clothes when he went into the English village. He felt he needed to maintain some identity to his position as sheriff. And when he was there, something kept tugging at him to make contact with the outside world. To that end, he wrote many letters to Governor Winthrop with suggestions of defining the Indian territories more clearly. He identified who the peacemakers were and who the troublemakers were among the Mohegans and Pequots, as well as the European settlers. He also sent letters to Will Smith, and one to Anne. But nothing came back from them, though Peter did get a few bits of information from fishermen who occasionally stopped on the island. This news was sketchy and Peter began to sense something was wrong. Finally, just as the new year of 1637 was ushered in, a ship that he recognized appeared in the cove.

It was Gallop's bark, and his men were skillfully furling the sails and lowering the anchor. Peter spied a fanciful hat moving across the deck.

"Ahoy, Captain Gallop," Peter said with a smile and a wave of his own hat. He was standing alongside of James Allen and two others from the English settlement.

The Captain was standing on the deck of his bark, getting ready to descend into the rowboat, when he saw Peter. Not recognizing him, he frowned at first but then smiled once he saw Peter's thick black hair.

The boat had been filled with provisions and four sailors rowed the cargo to shore. Peter and the others rushed down the slope to greet them.

"You are a sight for sore eyes, Captain Gallop," Peter said.

John Gallop got out of the boat and clasped hands with him, and then with Allen.

"You are a welcomed, welcomed guest," Allen said, excitedly. "We have not been faring well. Game has been scarce, and our flour supply is running low."

"Well, all this is yours," Gallop said, sweeping his arm toward the row boat filled with supplies. "All we seek is whatever wampum and fresh water you can spare."

"How go things on the mainland?" Peter asked.

"Not well," Gallop said. "The Pequots have been on the warpath and have raided many a community. Fort Saybrook ..."

Peter cut him off. "What of New London?"

"I have little word from New London," Captain Gallop said. "It is where I am going after this stop."

"You were saying about Fort Saybrook," Allen asked.

"Yes, a large scale raid by Pequots was turned back. But, not without significant loss of life on both sides," Gallop said. "Come walk with me, I need to get my legs back." The three men headed back toward the English village. "The Governor was outraged, naturally, and is forming another expedition. Our scouts along the Connecticut River have reported seeing Pequots as far north as the Wethersfield settlement."

"Are the Mohegans providing this information?" Peter asked.

"Yes, we have allied with them," Gallop said. "Do you know of our new agreement?"

"Be wary of them, Captain," Peter said. "They are not what they seem."

"I know how you feel about them all too well."

"I will wager the Wolf Clan has something to do with this," Peter said. "But right now, I am more concerned with those in New London."

"I take it you have not been home in a while," Gallop asked.

Peter stopped walking, the others did likewise. His face turned a stern color of deep red. "Has something happened?" Peter asked quickly.

"I heard there was some trouble but I have no details. I do know that the Smith's are still actively trading."

Peter looked around to the sea. "May I book passage with you?"

"Certainly, Peter. You have always been welcome on my ship."

"Very well. I will need to say 'good-bye' to someone first, but I shall return before you set sail."

"I sail within the hour."

"That will do."

With a heavy heart, Peter headed back to Running-bird's encampment. He struggled with what he had to say to her, but he knew he had to go back to New London. Not having heard from anyone there in several months was cause for great concern. He would tell Running-bird that it was his duty and that he would return to her loving arms as soon as he could.

When he saw her, he knew by the look on her face that she was already aware that he would be leaving.

"I know you must go, my love," she said. "It saddens me."

Peter moved close to her. "I will return as quickly as I can."

"Do what you need to do. Winter is upon us and we are not well prepared. We will need you here."

"Captain Gallop brought some provisions but I know it is not enough."

He reached out and pulled her close, and kissed her.

"Come back to me soon," she whispered in his ear. "Come back to me."

He struggled for the right words to say, for it hurt too much inside knowing that he might not return for many weeks. He held Running-bird for as long as time allowed. Finally, when their hearts calmed and were beating in unison, he stepped away and did not look back.

* * *

"*Smith! William Smith!*" Peter called out above the grey, barren silence of the ghost town he was gazing over. He stood with Captain Gallop and two of his sailors at the edge of town, dark grey clouds looming, affirming the chill in the air. Not a soul was seen on their way in to shore; not a soul came out to greet them or to assist them in the docking.

"Smith!" Peter called out again. He looked around at the structures and tried to make out Anne's shoppe at the far end of town.

Finally, the door to Smith's dwelling opened. Looking tired and much older than when Peter had left him, William Smith stepped out into the grey light.

"Peter?" the old man called out in a shabby voice. "Peter Wallace!"

He took a step forward and then appeared as if he was about to collapse. Peter and the others raced up to meet him. Smith fell into Peter's outstretched arms.

"Ohhhh," Smith said, with his chin quivering, "my, my, it's so good to see yah."

"And you," Peter said, with a cautious smile. "Come. Let us go in, out of the damp cold."

They entered Smith's shoppe and each found a place to stand near the fireplace. Peter and Captain Gallop warmed their hands against the blazing furnace where Smith's wife had just added more wood.

Without hesitation, Peter asked about Anne.

"Peter...I ...well..." the old man choked on his words.

"Where is she?" Peter asked.

Smith looked down. It appeared that he was crying.

"Where are the town folk?" Captain Gallop asked.

Finally Smith gathered himself. But before he could utter a word his wife raised a hand to him.

"Silly, old fool," she said, wiping away the moisture from her husband's eyes with the hem of her skirt. "He's beginning to lose his nerve. Ever since the Pequots came through..."

"They were here?" Peter asked, sharply. "When? What did...?'

"Mister Wallace," she said, softening her tone. "I'm sorry to say, she is gone."

"Anne?"

"Yes."

"Dead?"

"Yes."

Peter was crushed. He looked away, and then turned from the others. He pulled his hat off and ran his hand into his thick dark hair.

"*God damn them!*" He exclaimed, teeth grinding.

Gallop stirred at Peter's words, so uncharacteristic of the young man yet so appropriate.

"Please understand, Peter," Mrs. Smith said. "Whether you were here or not, this was going to happen. Pequots are never content. But thanks to you, most of us were spared … except for your wife…and Edward."

Peter turned back and faced them. Smith's wife continued. "Seven were killed in all, others wounded. Then, in the days that followed many more packed what they had and headed west, to Fort Saybrook."

A moment of silence filled the room as Peter absorbed this information. He looked down, away, back at them, and lastly looked toward the door. "How did Anne…?" Peter started to ask but then corrected himself, "Was it swift do you know?"

"We don't know," Will Smith quickly reported. He turned to his wife. "Woman, kindly make us some tea."

"Gentlemen, please sit," she said, then stepped away to the storage area. The men sat in chairs near the fire and remained silent, each deep in thought. The only sound heard was the frozen rain tapping an uneven and impassive rhythm on the roof. Mrs. Smith returned promptly with a large kettle that she carefully mounted over the fire.

"They came in the evening" Will Smith began. "Knoton was among them. They forced us back into our homes. From my backroom over there is a small window that faces Anne's shoppe. I saw what looked like Knoton go in with two warriors. Edward's body was already lying outside the front door."

Smith paused. He stood and stepped over to the fireplace, warming his wrinkled, reddened hands. His wife brought out a number of hand-painted tea cups.

"And then what?" Captain Gallop asked.

"Sassacus walked through the town crying out that he completed his vengeance. He said he had no other quarrel with the rest of us New Londoners. He demanded we all stay inside and not travel about the land for at least one moon. He said he will trade with us and us alone."

"*They all died on my account!*" Peter cried out. "And Anne…especially Anne."

Smith's wife spoke out. "She was dead when we found her in the morning. To us, it looked like there was no struggle … or torture. But Peter, as much as we love you, you must know she was not well liked here. And, many blame her for the predicament we are now in."

"She was so young…," Peter said with a heavy heart. His mouth tried to form more words but nothing came.

"Believe what you will," she said. "But you can't change things now."

"Where is … where is she buried?"

"We buried her in the cemetery that afternoon. There is a headstone. We found a good one in her shoppe. A shipment of the stones had arrived a week or so earlier. An omen, you might say. There is no inscription on it. We haven't had the time."

"Very well, I shall go there."

"Now?" Smith asked.

"Yes, I thank you and the others for taking care of things."

"God, bless you, Peter." Smith's wife said.

As Peter walked out to the cemetery, a cold rain fell. The January daylight faded rapidly. A chill rose within him. But it was not from the weather. He thought of all the things he had done wrong with his marriage, of how he should not have traveled so far and wide. He thought of how he might have made her see that she was wrong about Dekanawida, and most of all, he thought of how he should have told her that he loved her more often than he had.

As darkness fell he found the unmarked headstone that Mrs. Smith described. Surrounded by a thin layer of snow and pelted by icy rain, the headstone greeted Peter with an eerie glow. It picked up light from some unknown source, that then reflected it, in an otherwise dim setting. Peter dropped to his knees. They were met with an icy-hard surface that cracked beneath his weight. He dismissed the pain and reflected on his wife.

"You see, Anne," he said aloud. "You still have the light of life in you. You are beautiful even in death."

The rain softened a bit. Peter could hear his own words clearly.

"I should have loved you better. I have heard that you were very happy with Edward. So, I believe you were happy right up until the end. You did what you set out to do. You opened your shoppe at such a young age. You brought commerce here and made the colony grow. Many will remember you in a positive way. I believe this. They will come to recognize your contribution. I will write to your mother, of course. I will not tell her about our undoing. She will know that we were happy and that we were successful."

He stayed for a long while drifting between sorrow and pride, between admiration and hate, between anger and love, between the joy she brought to him and the disappointment that followed.

The icy rain returned. It came down hard and it stung Peter's hands and the exposed areas around his neck and face. Ignoring the harsh weather, Peter rose, confident now and at peace with it all.

"Farewell, my beautiful wife."

* * *

The remaining days of January slipped away, as did all the cold, dark days of February. Captain Gallop was long gone; he had gotten out before the river froze. He sailed south to Virginia and warmer climates. Peter had to stay on; his anger over the Pequots festered against his better judgment. There were letters that Smith had from the Governor saying that Peter needed to remain in New London and prepare for an important event that was left vague by design. Peter spent his days taking care of the shoppe and waiting for news from the Governor. Over time, he grew lonely and frustrated as he realized that he was not needed as much as he thought. He wrote letters to the Governor and to Running-bird but no replies ever came. Not many would venture out on the sea in winter. He regretted not returning to Block Island when he had the chance. Even more, he was hard pressed to find anyone who would take him back. The river would thaw and freeze at unpredictable intervals. No one wanted to go out on the Sound. Yet, all he could think about was Running-bird and Little-grey-feather.

In late February he found a family who offered to buy the shoppe. With some of the proceeds of the sale he had an inscription etched into Anne's head stone. It read:

Anne Wallace

The Youngest & Brightest

of New London

By early March several ships from Fort Saybrook had arrived with over a hundred armed men lead by Captain's Mason and Underhill. The expedition was formed for the sole purpose of bringing war against the Pequots. It would be launched that spring, and secrecy was paramount.

When the weather finally broke and grew warm, Peter found a way to secure passage to the island. Several fishermen agreed to take him over, once their nets were ready for the spring waters.

He was twenty-seven, and after the long dark winter he was beginning to feel as alive as the promise of spring. All he could think about was Running-bird. But on the day he was to leave, Captain Underhill approached him. Peter felt an immediate let down when he saw his stern gaze.

"Peter, you are not going anywhere!" Underhill demanded. "I need you here. You know this land better than anyone."

"Captain, I have booked transport to Blocks Island. I am needed there."

"Your plans have changed."

"Impossible."

"You are under my command now. The Governor has ordered this."

Peter continued to argue with him, but his words fell on deaf ears. Sadly, he walked alone to the pier and watched his opportunity to see Running-bird dissolve. Before the boat left, however, he managed to prepare a crate with some silk fabric, cooking pots, and other provisions from the shoppe, and gave specific instructions on where to deliver them. He wrote the letter to James Allen which would ensure proper delivery. He included a cloth doll for Little-grey-feather and a gift of a set of silverware for Allen and his wife.

In just a few short days, New London became a military camp. April turned into a month of training and scouting. Peter's rage over missing an opportunity to go to Block Island was now channeled into his growing hated of the Pequots. He knew vengeance was a sin but this was a sin that he may need to commit. He finally agreed to support Underhill and began to assist in the planning of the raid.

On the porch of William Smith's shoppe, Peter unfurled a map of the land and pointed to the open field he knew so well. "That," Peter said, his finger tracing a path in the forest, "is a place of their vulnerability. There are a few others as well."

Underhill leaned in and nodded, silent in the company of Peter's expertise.

Many Indians came and stationed themselves all around the outskirts of New London. By early May, a total of seventy Mohegan warriors had arrived, along with Uncas and Onasakenrat. Then a week later, nearly two-hundred Narragansetts joined the force.

CHAPTER 24 – Missituck

*   *   *

In the dead of night, Peter, a Mohegan scout, and Captain Underhill, knelt in tall grass where an open field met the edge of the wood. Dawn was still over an hour away and the sky was dark as pitch. They scanned the fields and the high walled village for signs of life. There was little movement, other than a few small streams of smoke rising from some forgotten fire pit and a random head popping over the top of the wall.

Over one-hundred English soldiers and twice as many Indians lay in hiding just a few hundred yards from the walled village at Missituck. They had marched through the night, being careful not to make a sound. All metal that they carried or wore was covered with wool and other fabric. They traveled on foot, and each step was carefully placed so as not to create even the sound of a twig snapping. When they were within a mile of the village, scouts were sent ahead to find the wind direction. It was imperative that they approach downwind from the village, for fear the Pequot dogs would pick up their scent. The final march took just fifteen minutes to complete and they came into view of the village.

"We are in luck," Underhill said quietly, "we have not been spotted."

The Mohegan scout pointed to the left side of the fortress where one of the openings was visible. The wall was split, with one end continuing out in front of the other, creating an overlap. There was no door. The gap between the walls was filled with thorny brush that was removed every morning and put back in the evening.

When this was explained to Captain Underhill he said, "We will use grappling hooks to pull that out. It will not stop us."

After a while, the Mohegan scout led Underhill and Peter thirty yards to their right. He pointed out a second opening, and then indicated that a third opening was on the far side from that point.

"That's all we need," Underhill said. He was satisfied that his men had enough places to breach the village. He looked at Peter.

"We need so much more, Captain," Peter said, correcting him. "I am here for vengeance as you are, but in the end we will need forgiveness."

"We need God's blessing and some luck."

"There is no luck in this," Peter said angrily.

"Enough!" Underhill demanded. "You have served your purpose; now leave the est to me."

"As you wish, Captain."

Underhill frowned at him and pulled him away from the others. They walked a air distance away to a small, elevated knoll in a stand of trees where a dim outline of the Peqout village could be seen.

"Diplomacy is over," Underhill said, in a raspy whisper. "Action is required!"

"It will not end here," Peter said. "Can't you see?"

"These savages need to be controlled."

"Savages?"

"Yes, the Pequots are driven by the …"

"Captain!" Peter blurted out, his hands extended. "Who are the savages?"

Underhill knew where he was going. He looked away to where the village lay. He urned back and looked into Peter's eyes. "Have you forgotten the innocent men, women, and children that they have slaughtered?"

"Captain, my wife was among them. You know this. Still…"

"Peter, the die is cast. I must carry out my orders."

"You know this will be a day that will brand us," Peter insisted.

"Then we are branded."

Before Underhill could continue, Onasakenrat and Quick-blade appeared behind hem. They had been scouting to the left.

"We have not been seen," Onasakenrat said to Underhill.

"Good! Prepare your men."

"They are ready."

Onasakenrat looked at Peter and smiled. "What say you now of your beloved Pequots?"

Peter said nothing. He glared at the warrior, fighting off his anger. He felt his hands clench. The sachem smiled again, turned, and stepped away into the darkness.

"It is time," Underhill said to his men.

The English officers gathered in a circle and knelt down. They prayed for a swift victory and to ask for forgiveness in the task they were about to execute. Peter was among them. Only once did he look up at Captain Underhill. Underhill had been watching him during the entire prayer.

Finally, Onasakenrat re-appeared. "We *must* go now," he demanded. "Dawn will be upon us soon."

As he spoke, Peter looked at him. The dim light played tricks on his mind, and he swore he could see the outline of a long scar about the sachem's neck.

"Today is our day," Quick-blade said quietly to Onasakenrat. "It will be a day of vengeance. One we have sought since we slew the great Manissean warrior."

Quick-blade then spoke of Onasakenrat's father. But he stopped talking when he noticed Peter's interest in his conversation. They turned away from him.

Peter was stunned. It was all coming together now. It was Onasakenrat who was at the root of the killings. Peter realized that it was these warriors who were on Block Island when Running-bird's husband was killed. And by extension, that was the same night Jonathan Miller was killed. It was clear now that Onasakenrat received the wound in the fight with Samuel and then came to the Miller house for revenge. Anne had stated that the wound on the killer was fresh.

As the men broke off into smaller groups, Peter approached Onasakenrat. He grabbed the sachem's arm and spun him around. He reached out and touched his neck where the scar was.

Onasakenrat shoved him back. Peter stood his ground.

"*Where did you get that?*" Peter demanded.

"Touch me again and I will put my knife to you."

Peter posed his question again, this time louder. Some of the men gathered around. A call went out to fetch Captain Underhill.

Onasakenrat drew his long knife. "You will be the first to die today!" He jabbed his blade straight out.

Peter drew his short sword and deflected the lunging knife just at the last second. He reached out and grabbed Onasakenrat's forearm while he was off-balance and threw him to the ground. In an instant, the warrior was up again and racing headlong toward

Peter. The two collided and rolled to the ground. Fists flew in the air. But it did not last long. Others raced to the scene and pulled them apart. Underhill stepped forward.

"*What is the meaning of this?*" He hissed.

"This is the man who killed Jonathan Miller!" Peter exclaimed, struggling to get free of two men holding him back.

"I do not know of what you speak," Underhill said. "But, this is neither the time, nor place to strike a grievance."

Onasakenrat stepped up to within inches of Peter's face. Underhill put his arm between them. Onasakenrat grinned. "I killed the white man because he was a friend to the Pequots. I am proud that I did. I do not have to justify it to you or anyone."

"This sachem is a traitor!" Peter lashed out.

"This is your last warning, Wallace," Underhill said.

"Captain...I..."

Underhill gave a signal to his men. After a short struggle, Underhill's men bound Peter's hands and made him sit at the base of a tall oak tree.

Once he was satisfied that Peter was secure, Underhill turned away and organized all his men into three attack groups. They were given their orders and sent off in different directions. Underhill remained with two of his men. When all grew quiet again, he approached Peter.

"I will see to it you are finished as sheriff," Underhill said, harshly. "You jeopardized our mission and the lives of our men."

"Nothing is jeopardized," Peter said. "We lost what we could have accomplished years ago."

"I swear to you, Wallace," Underhill now said with an accusing finger pointed within inches of Peter's face, "*you are finished.*"

"I have no qualms about relinquishing my position," Peter said. "I am unable to stop what will unfold on this day. Only now, do I see the root of it all."

"If you mean the Mohegan sachem, there is nothing I can do to him. He is an ally."

"Even if he has masterminded this raid and killed whoever stood in his way?"

"Hold your tongue, Wallace."

261

Underhill reached down and grabbed Peter by his arm, pulling him up.

"He is responsible for the deaths of many innocent people," Peter said, then drove a shoulder into Underhill. A soldier made a move to subdue Peter, but Underhill waved him off.

"He is responsible for the death of my wife and her father," Peter said.

All fell silent. Underhill looked down, his jaw grinding. Then he looked up, right into Peter's eyes; his gaze filled with frustration.

"Are you certain of this?"

"There is no doubt now."

Underhill paused on Peter's words. Peter's clear, wide eyes were all he needed to see to be convinced.

"Unbind him," Underhill ordered.

Peter kept focus on the Captain while the rope was undone. "You need not be concerned with me, Captain," he said.

"You are free to go, Wallace. I will look into the deeds of this sachem when this is over."

"I will stay until this ordeal is over. I will see it to its end."

"As you wish."

"It is my wish."

Underhill's army encircled the walled village – muskets and bows drawn, aimed at the top of the walls for any head that might stand out. Just as the first inkling of light appeared over the wooded horizon, the muskets exploded. First, a single popping sound, then three, then a dull roar like thunder. War cries rose high in the morning air. Screams of pain replaced the howls of warning. Brass, lead, iron, and stone, clanged in sharp, stinging, slivers of anger. Grunts, groans, and gnarled cries of terror filled the Pequot village.

The village was overrun quickly, the wigwams, storage houses, and shelters put to the torch. Peter walked through one of the entrances and immediately found several Pequot women and four children hiding nearby. He led them out and had them sit in the open field. He found a Puritan soldier he could trust and assigned him to look over them. Peter reentered the village but this time the fire and smoke was so thick he had to dodge much of it. He saw bodies in groups; men, women and children – it didn't matter. Underhill's Indians had their shoulders painted white to make them stand out from the Pequot's. He saw dozens of the white-shouldered warriors running in between the burning structures looking for more to kill and for more scalps to put in the belts.

As he was about half way to the center he noticed a familiar figure. It was Knoton, bent over and holding his side. On the ground at his feet were two dead Mohegans. Knoton dropped to his knees as Peter rushed to him. The bloodied Indian fell over onto his back. Peter knelt next to him.

"Knoton, can you speak?"

Knoton's eyes were glazed over. Peter attempted to move him when he saw a huge gash in his side, blood flowing freely. "Do you remember me? Let me help you." He tried to close the wound with his hands. The Indian grimaced and his eyes came into focus.

"Do not," Knoton said; his words filled with pain. "You have come to kill me…"

"Yes," Peter said.

"Then do it."

"I can save you, now. The battle is over."

"No, it is too late."

"Please let me."

A Mohegan raced by them, stopped, and attempted to scalp Knoton. Peter stood and shoved him aside. "He is mine!" Peter cried out. Frightened, the Mohegan left just as quickly as he had come. Peter knelt back down next to Knoton.

"I can get you out of here."

"No, I am dying. Finish me before they scalp me. I …I will not give them the satisfaction … of doing it while I'm alive."

"I cannot," Peter said, aghast.

"If you want to help me, then kill me now. I killed your wife. Complete your revenge."

"I know what you did in New London. And I forgive you for that. Your people have suffered greatly today. There is no need for more killing."

Knoton coughed up blood. Some splattered on Peter's jacket. "She killed the only white man who understood us. I must tell you now."

"What are you saying?"

"Miller."

"Jonathan Miller?"

"Yes, Dekanawida wanted to tell you but … but he knew he would lose you … as a friend. He was in agony over it."

"I do not know of what you speak?"

"We…we were there the night of the great storm. Sassacus and I went out looking … for Dekanawida. They had been fighting for days … over a squaw. We were near the Miller dock when it happened."

"Knoton, you are delirious. I know now that Onasakenrat killed Jonathan Miller."

"He tried to…we saw him … on the riverbank. Onasakenrat drove his knife into Miller, but he was too weak to make it fatal. He couldn't pull it out."

"You saw all this?"

"Yes, we were fifty yards from shore. Sassacus cried out a warning. The Mohegans … they ran off into the woods. Then we saw Anne."

"Yes, I know she was there but she didn't…"

"She was not human. She walked … down to her father like a ghost. She was stiff and unmoved. Miller sat up and called for her to help him. She took the end of the knife and…instead of pulling it out … she thrust it in deeper. It must have pierced his heart. He fell flat and did not move."

Peter's mind was racing. This revelation was astonishing; he had all he could do to keep from screaming. "But…"

"Do it now, kill me. It is my last request."

Three Mohegans raced to where they were. He waved them off at sword point. To his luck another greater prize caught their attention and they left in a hurry. He looked out and saw English soldiers stabbing wounded and dying Pequots. It was only a matter of minutes before they would be upon him.

"Knoton," Peter said. "I cannot believe this. How did Dekanawida know? Did you and Sassacus tell him?"

"No. He was there. He came down the riverbank just as Anne was plunging the knife into her father. He bent down … to revive Miller and Anne walked off…the same way she did before – a ghost. Our canoe beached. Dekanawida looked at us and shook his head. He took the knife and threw it into the river. It was at that point we knew there would be war. And we knew … we knew … we could not tell anyone what happened."

Knoton fell silent. He gazed into Peter's eyes waiting for his request to be carried out. Peter realized that Knoton was right. He was a leader and responsible for the attack on New London. He knew Knoton would most likely be tortured should he survive. And, above all, the events at the riverbank had to be kept a secret.

An English commander was walking toward them with his sword drawn. Peter looked down upon Knoton. He placed his hand over Knoton's nose, pinching his nostrils. Knoton appeared unfazed. With his other hand Peter closed Knoton's mouth. A minute later, the Pequot was dead.

Peter rose and walked out of the inferno slowly, and with great clarity. He found the closure he had been searching for. And no one was left to tell it to that mattered, nor was anyone left that it would help. There was only one person of importance to him now. He removed his Puritan hat and flung it into a burning wigwam. As he came to the walls, he saw that they were being summarily torn down by the Indians, but he did not let that get in his way. He removed his navy blue doublet with the six silver buttons and let it drop to the ground. Entering the open field, he felt his worn shoes were hurting his tired feet. As he walked by a dead Indian, he noticed a moccasin had fallen off the warrior's foot. He sat, removed his shoes and stocking, and placed the Indian moccasins on his feet. They were a tight fit but that didn't matter.

Later that day he learned that over four hundred Peqouts were slaughtered: men, women, and the children. Only a few escaped. Victory appeared to be total. The few survivors that were captured were given to the Narragansetts. The Mohegans took five young boys with the intent of one day making them Mohegan warriors.

Soon, however, it was discovered that Sassacus and one-hundred-and eighty of his warriors were not at the village. They had been in the north, scouting for English targets and Indian villages of English allies. The Narragansetts were appalled that Underhill did not know about this and left without a word. The torched village burned all day. The smell of ash, smoke, and human flesh filled the air for miles around and followed Underhill as he went north with the Mohegans in pursuit of Sassacus.

Over the weeks that followed the remaining twelve Pequot villages were destroyed and burned to the ground. Many were empty when they arrived, but those Peqouts that were captured were handed over to the neighboring tribes. The name 'Pequot' was forbidden to be spoken. The Destroyers were destroyed.

Peter returned to New London and discovered that a fisherman would take him to Block Island that very day. It didn't take long for him to sort out his remaining business with the New Londoners. He left with the fisherman, vowing never to return.

CHAPTER 25 – All in a Name

* * *

The reunion of Peter and Running-bird was one of great surprise, for the young woman was pregnant with their child. And in July the baby came, a boy, who was just like Peter in every way. Peter's life had finally become what he had always wanted. Peter, Running-bird, Little-grey-feather, and the new addition became a recognized family throughout the island. One afternoon Running-bird and Peter were out on a walk through the forest, heading to the shoreline just to be alone.

"Running-bird, there is something I must tell you."

She stopped and turned to him. The forest air was crisp and bright. She looked into his eyes. A moment passed and then she smiled.

"I know what you are thinking."

"I…"

"Peter, you have already told me."

"I have?"

"In your thoughts. And you wear it again now on your face. You know who killed Samuel."

Peter looked down. He felt ashamed.

"Peter, my love, no need to be concerned about hiding it from me anymore."

"I should have known."

"I have come to terms with this long ago. The sachem of the Wolf Clan will meet his match one day. I have seen this too, but I cannot say when or at whose hand."

"I have been remiss in my duties by not pursuing him."

"Yes. And you believe he killed Anne's father as well."

"Yes, I am certain of it."

He was convinced that the Mohegan sachem was the one who killed Anne's father. But none of that seemed important anymore, now that Anne was gone. He knew there would come another day, very soon perhaps, where he would confront his adversary and put the final question to him about Samuel. For now, his new family came first.

"Never leave me again, my love," Running-bird said.

"Never."

"Peter, hold me tight now. I feel something else."

Peter reached out and wrapped his arms around her. He pulled her close. He felt her warmth and she, his. Running-bird closed her eyes and buried her head deep in his chest. Suddenly, she withdrew sharply. An expression of surprise and fear filled her.

"Peter!"

"What is it? What do you see?"

She stared into his eyes for the longest time. Her mouth tried to form words but nothing came.

"My love, tell me," Peter said. "There is nothing that can hurt us now. We have a new life here. No one can hurt us ever again."

"Let us return," she said quickly.

"But we have not reached the cove."

"Peter, I need to be with the children," she said with deep concern in her voice.

"Very well."

They returned to their village in the forest in short order. Their children rushed out to meet them. All was well but Running-bird was still troubled by her false concern.

Over the next several weeks, their son brought stability to their family as he grew. Peter spent many hours with him on the southeast bluffs overlooking the ocean. Peter told his son stories of the lands across the sea, though he was too young to understand. He filled the boy with promises of a voyage on a great white-winged ship to that land far beyond the island.

With his renewed vigor for life, Peter started to work again at maintaining good relations with the English, but stayed on the opposite side of the island and never indicated any need to re-join his own people. A small village grew around him out on the east end, with a mix of every type of person that wanted refuge. One's race, nationality, or faith did not matter. While his efforts were appreciated by most of his countrymen, some felt he was a traitor to his King and to God. These men would occasionally mock him and spit at him. Peter took it in stride and held his head high.

Peter's restless nature continued to tug at him. His Puritan foundation and English heritage, though tainted, would not let his concern over the developments on the nainland wane. Ultimately, he returned to Fort Saybrook late in the year. The English persisted in their effort to eradicate the Pequot name from the land with a law banning it from being spoken. The Treaty of Hartford of 1638, dictated these terms, including forbidding the remaining Pequots from rejoining as a group. Peter felt this was the wrong way to maintain peace and took up a cause to reverse this action. Over the next year, he achieved some modicum of success. He introduced Running-bird to his countrymen in power and she was well received. She too, helped bring the need for Pequot recognition back into society.

Eventually, through Peter's and Running-bird's efforts and those of many others who realized the error, they were able to restore the Pequot name. By this time however, most of the Pequots had assimilated into the surrounding tribes.

The Mohegans were another story. Peter and his followers took great measures to avoid them. His distrust of them and of the sachem with the scar haunted him still.

Safe on their island once again, the days passed quickly; the months turned into years, and his son was running off on his own. Nine years had passed with relative peace in the lands around the great Sound. Nine years in all, and Peter continued his quest to restore the Pequot tribe. He wrote many letters to Governor Winthrop and Reverend Cotton on the subject but never had the time to go to Boston to make the case in person.

* * *

On a hill overlooking the Connecticut River, Onasakenrat spoke to his friend.

"The Englishman is causing trouble again. This Peter Wallace has returned to our lands and is working against what we hope to achieve."

"I thought he was gone from the earth," Quick-blade said.

"He was one of those responsible for restoring the Pequot clan. They have a name again, and I fear they will attack us one day."

"We cannot let that happen," Quick-blade said.

"No, we cannot."

"The Englishman – is he the same one who is out to destroy us?"

"Yes, he lives. And he has a family now."

"You knew this? Why haven't you mentioned it sooner?"

"My agents have brought word that he has married the Manissean princess, the one with the evil-eyed child."

Quick-blade grabbed his sachem's wrist.

"This cannot be!"

"Our scouts have searched the island many times looking for them, but to no avail. We know they have a son," Onasakenrat said, facing his friend, with eyes on fire.

"So, his cup is full," Quick-blade replied, releasing his grip. "And soon he will be upon us."

"I fear this will happen."

"I will end it, once and for all."

"Yes, my friend. But we will do it together."

*   *   *

Little-grey-feather sat on a large boulder overlooking the sea. A young girl of thirteen on the verge of adulthood, she reflected now on many things. She could still sense her mother's wishes and desires from great distances, and she still heard the voices of angry men when they weren't even near. She did not like the way the Mohegans were encroaching on her island. And, she did not like the way they were using the English settlers as allies.

Little-grey-feather had learned to read her mother's thoughts. Of all the people she knew, it was her mother's thoughts that came to her so clear. She learned of her mother's losses and decided that her dear mother had suffered enough, and vowed that she would not lose another. Taking matters into her own hands, she secretly left warnings and taboo symbols on the English doorsteps and in their fields of grain. Often dead things: frogs, snakes, shells laid out in symbols, and fleshy things the English could not identify. She would steal into their village on little cat feet when they were all inside and whisper into their windows, sending chills up their spines. They could not find her and they never saw her. Soon, she became known as Circe, the sorceress.

She had heard that the Mohegan sachem from the Wolf Clan and some of his warriors were in the English village this very day and that they planned to stay for a long time. She, like Peter and Running-bird, had also learned that they were asking about

Island seer and her silver-eyed daughter. Little-grey-feather felt it was time to set out and meet them on her own.

She opened her satchel and extracted several large shells. They had already been packed with clay for added weight. She had filed the edges against stone until they were sharp enough to cut a blade of grass. Then, she heard a voice in her head. He was the one in whom she detected evil. He was the one that in the past had given her shivers on other occasions. He was the one with whom she would carry out her plan of vengeance. Yes, he was the one, and he was on his way to her.

When Quick-blade left the English village in search of Peter Wallace and his Indian wife, he became distracted by an odd feeling that came over him in the open field. He ran his hands across the top of the wild grass, feeling a tickle in the process. He had drawn in the succulent fragrance of the magnificent day that filled the island. Tiny white moths rose like snowflakes and fluttered all around him in their brief moment of life on earth. Suddenly out of nowhere a figure appeared.

Little-grey-feather stood before Quick-blade at a place in the open meadow halfway between the English village and the woods. It was late summer, and the sun was setting on a day that had been brilliant. Now, in the space between the young woman and an aging man, an eerie darkness fell. Time stood still as the hardened warrior could not believe his eyes.

Quick-blade had left the village an hour earlier and was collecting his thoughts on his next move to lead the tribe. But, he was at a loss. Onasakenrat had made many mistakes and let far too many years pass in achieving their goal, but Onasakenrat was still too powerful to overthrow. He had to make Onasakenrat's demise look like it came from battle with an enemy. If only he, the fabled Quick-blade, could find a way. And the way became clear just hours earlier. He would find the seer and the silver-eyed girl, and bring down the remaining seed of Samuel, slayer of the great Onerahtokha. As if by magic, one of them was standing before him.

The girl did not move a muscle; her gaze riveting.

The sun's warmth filled the meadow and stirred the tiny flying insects as they flickered about. The grassy field was neck-high in places, a sprinkling of wild flowers adding radiant color to the field. Filtering through the mysterious landscape was an aura of amber and gold.

Quick-blade watched the girl carefully, waiting for even the slightest of movements. Nothing. He squinted to get a better look at the girl's eyes but they were masked in shadow. He approached her.

"Come no further," the girl demanded.

Quick-blade was not used to being caught by surprise. This girl unnerved him to no end. He stood confused for just a moment; then regained his composure.

"What is the meaning of this?" he demanded, clenching his fist.

"Speak not, but return whence you have come," Little-grey-feather said.

Quick-blade slowly circled to his right, trying to put the dim light of the sun at his back and catch the girl's size. He spoke to distract her.

"And who might you be?" he said, smiling and raising his hands to reveal no mal intent. "A princess of the wood, perhaps? I think that is who you are."

"Never mind who I am," Little-grey-feather said, moving away from him. "I am just one of the others."

"The others?" Quick-blade asked, as he sized up the strength of his opponent. "And, who are the others?"

"The rightful inhabitants of this island."

At this point, Little-grey-feather was in full view. Quick-blade realized he was in no danger from such a young person and stepped toward her. She raised her hand. In it, she held a simple but large seashell. Quick-blade stopped for a moment and laughed. He stepped toward her again. But this time, she stepped backward, cocking back her arm that held the shell. He took another step forward and she launched it towards his head. He raised his arm to deflect it, but the sharpened edge tore at his forearm and cut deep into his flesh. The sting of impact brought him to his senses.

Quick-blade winced in pain, but instinctively drew out his knife. Little-grey-feather ran off toward the woods and disappeared, leaving no indication whether she had entered the forest or ran deeper into the high grass. Quick-blade ran toward where he last saw her. His keen eyes quickly spied her squatting low in the grass within just a few yards of him. He wheeled about, charged forward and grabbed her by the shoulder hrowing her to the ground. But in the process, he lost his balance and stumbled to the ground. Not losing a moment, he scrambled back to his feet. A wildcat met him head on, kicking and scratching as hard as she could. Finally, he wrestled her to the ground and used his body to suppress her. As he was about to strike her, the sun filled her eyes revealing the striking devil's color in them. At that same instant, several drops of his blood landed on her face. Bewildered at the strange countenance gaping up at him, Quick-blade recoiled and lost his grip in the process. Little-grey-feather twisted and pulled her way out from under him. She ran a few steps away then turned to face him.

"Leave us alone," she demanded.

Quick-blade could not tear his eyes away from hers. He sat on the ground, trying to make sense of it. The angry, silvery-green eyes with the bloody face repulsed him. But more, an old image of his battle with Samuel suddenly filled him. The eyes were the same. It was years ago, but he remembered clearly.

"*Leave us alone, Mohegan!*" she exclaimed. "Leave us and our land forever."

Quick-blade feigned defeat. "You have beaten me, young one," he said and gripped his still bleeding arm for effect.

"*Leave us,*" Little-grey-feather screamed again."

"So be it. I will leave. But who shall I say defeated me?"

"No one; we are the phantoms of the woods. That is all you need to know."

"But, I need a name," Quick-blade said, as he got up off the ground. "I believe I do know who you are."

"I am no one," the girl said.

"But, those eyes give you away," Quick-blade said, now circling her again, putting the sun to his back as he did before. "The English call you 'Circe', don't they?"

She followed his movements, and then suddenly another sharpened shell appeared in her hand, as if by magic.

"That is a clever weapon," Quick-blade said, raising his bloodied arm for her to see. "I would not think to challenge you again."

"You are Circe, aren't you?" Quick-blade said, pressing his advantage. "The young sea witch, no?"

He lunged at her with his long knife, aiming it at her heart. She leaped to her right like a fox. He felt the brush of her arm across his face as he missed and fell to the ground. Thinking he had her, he rolled back to his feet. And then he was all alone.

He looked around for movement, and then jumped high to see beyond the tall grass and, nothing. He raced to his left, nothing. And to his right, nothing. He rose up high on his toes and scanned the terrain in all directions – no hint of another human could be seen or felt in the air. Suddenly a flock of birds rose, streaking in all directions and cawing with retched voices. And further away, he could hear the ocean waves crashing upon a distant shore. Then beyond that, nothing.

Quick-blade was not easily fooled, and he was convinced she was still nearby. *The Sorceress of Block Island,* he thought. Yes, he did have this encounter with her...or did he? The blood on his arm convinced him he did. He scanned the field again and again. The eerie darkness was gone. He took several steps in different directions but saw nothing.

After a while, he gave up and tended to his wound. Defeated, he turned and started to walk back towards the English village. But after just a few steps, he heard a whisper. He froze. The sinking sun was now casting an orange and gold stream of light into his face. The whisper was coming from within the rays of light. He could not see in that direction. Knowing his trade as hunter he sunk to the ground, out of the light. He scanned the stem-filled earth for a sign of someone's feet. There, amongst the grasses and the insects, he waited. Nothing. He crawled silently to his right, hoping for a better view. He stood slowly and saw nothing.

The whisper came again. "*Iiiiii...knowwwwww...youuuu,*" it hissed.

For the first time in his life, Quick-blade felt his immortality. Sweat formed on his brow, and insecurity swept through him. His eyes darted around through the long thin stalks of grass. Nothing.

"*Youuuu killed my fatherrrr,*" the voice in the wind hissed, ever louder.

Quick-blade dropped to the ground and crawled in the direction he thought best. The voice called to him again. Anger and frustration filled him; he continued forward on his hands and knees toward where he thought his tormentor was. The voice continued taunting him; relentlessly it echoed. Lying still for a moment, he focused on movement.

He looked around in all directions; then through the tall amber grass he saw a pair of silver eyes gaping at him. These inhuman eyes were ten times their normal size. Quick-blade fell back on his rear. He could not make out a human form behind the evil eyes. Struggling to get away, he cried out his war cry seeking aid. Finally, he rose straight up and ran for his life.

Quick-blade ran long and hard until his lungs burst. He eventually collapsed a good distance away from where he had seen the evil eyes. Panting like a mad dog, his arm started to bleed heavily through his makeshift bandage. He cut a piece cloth from his buckskins and secured it around the wound.

The sky grew purple-dark, but there was enough light on the ground to see the edge of the village. Quick-blade rose again and parted the tall grass. He looked around and saw no one. He listened for the whisper, but heard no words floating on the soft breeze. Feeling he was safe, he drew in a deep breath of air. As he let it out, he heard a hiss above his breath. He froze. Then, he noticed a rustle in the amber grass just to his left. He squared off to face it. Using his patented move, he flipped his knife out in front of him, all the while maintaining his gaze on the spot. He grabbed the knife out of the air and was about to launch it when, suddenly, he heard a strange whooshing sound. Turning quickly around, he caught a glimpse of something spinning towards his face. He tried to duck away, but was too late. The shell caught him across his forehead near his temple, cracking the bone in his skull.

Quick-blade grabbed for his head and tried to hold the loose flesh and bone together. He stumbled toward the village with blood flowing violently. Another shell ripped into the back of his neck sending him to the ground. His head throbbed, but he managed to straighten himself. In the dim light he saw the English houses and, for a moment, thought he'd make it, but a sudden dizziness rendered him immobile. He cried out before falling back to the ground.

Several women heard the shout. One raced through the village, looking for her leader. Within minutes, Onasakenrat, James Allen, and two armed men raced out into the meadow. It didn't take long to find Quick-blade. The odor of human blood filled the evening air. Onasakenrat, dropped to his knees and cradled his life-long friend.

"Who did this?" Onasakenrat asked, with clenched teeth. *"Tell me who did this to you?"*

Quick-blade was barely coherent. But, he managed one word before dying.

"Circe."

CHAPTER 26 – The End

*   *   *

By the time Little-grey-feather returned to her village in the woods, Running-bird knew what had happened. She had sensed it in the evening air. The dark clouds that entered her thoughts came the same way they did on the day that Samuel was taken from her. As her daughter approached, she prayed she was wrong.

Peter was nearby, tending to a repair on one of the wigwams, when he heard the commotion. He instinctively sensed what Running-bird had already known. He also noticed a sudden change in temperature, and saw the storm clouds coming from the southwest. He raced over to where he last saw Running-bird.

Little-grey-feather stood before her mother with her arms folded across her chest. At thirteen, she was not quite as tall as Running-bird, but at that moment, she loomed larger than her and several others that had gathered. Her face exhibited a wild contradiction of fear and excitement.

"What has she done?" Peter asked, catching his breath.

Little-grey-feather remained silent. The wind picked up and a few heavy rain drops fell about them.

"You have killed a man, haven't you?" Running-bird questioned.

Little-grey-feather nodded and offered a cynical smile.

Peter was stunned at the question and even more at the answer.

"What did you do?" he demanded.

Little-grey-feather stood frozen now.

"A man?" Peter asked, "You killed a man?" - His words uneven.

Little-grey-feather unfolded her arms. Her countenance changed to that of a respectful daughter. She simply nodded.

Peter straightened. He looked a Running-bird. He could see she was trying to fight off shock and anger as best she could.

"Did you use those shells?" Peter demanded.

Little-grey-feather looked at her step-father with chiseled eyes, hoping to find a way out. A rift of heavy rain drops splashed on them and then subsided as quickly as it had come.

Peter turned to Running-bird. "Those weapons will give her away."

They both looked at Little-grey-feather, waiting for an answer. She nodded again.

"Was it a white man or a natural?" Peter asked.

"An evil man," Little-grey-feather said. "A Mohegan."

Peter turned again to Running-bird.

"This is tragic. We will…"

Before he could finish, a clamor of approaching men rose above the wind. Peter, Running-bird, and Little-grey-feather instinctively rushed back into their village, alerting all those they could. But the soldiers and Mohegans fell upon the village within seconds in an encircling move. Running-bird found their son and carried him off. Peter grabbed Little-grey-feather by the hand and told her to go to the cave. His final instruction need not have been given; the young girl was off like a flash, racing quietly through the woods. The sky crashed with a deafening roar of thunder. A light rain started to fall.

The people of Running-bird's village gave up without a struggle. They were lined up and put on review. Peter and Running-bird were at the lead end. Peter took their son and held him tightly. Onasakenrat and an English soldier stepped up to Running-bird. All ignored the rain as if it wasn't even falling.

"You are the mother of the she-devil?" Onasakenrat asked.

Running-bird looked away from him. He examined her intently. He noticed her hair was not as bright as he had remembered it; her face was drawn, darkened and scarred on one side. But he knew she was the one.

"*Where is Circe?*" he demanded.

Running-bird remained silent. The soldier stepped forward and pressed his sword against her chest.

"*Leave her,*" Peter cried out. He slapped the sword away. "Speak to me, not her."

"We have no use for a traitor," Onasakenrat said, to the delight of some of the Englishmen.

"I know you," Running-bird said. "*You* are the one!"

Onasakenrat smiled.

"You have the devil in *you*," she said, raising her voice.

"Silence!" he shouted, lifting his hand in a move to strike her.

The rain subsided at his words, but the rumble of thunder echoed in the distance. Peter placed his son down on the ground. A woman standing next to him held the boy close to her. Peter wedged his body between the Mohegan and his wife.

"Leave her be!" Peter exclaimed. "If you have a complaint, then speak to me."

"Peter Wallace," the English sergeant said, as he pulled Onasakenrat back, "we have proof that the she-devil killed a Mohegan earlier today."

"How do you know that?"

"Her name was on the dying man's lips. She is the one called 'Circe'."

"Impossible. She has been with us all day."

"There is no mistake. We know that she hunts with shells."

"Nonsense!"

Onasakenrat stepped up, this time with his knife drawn. "The she-devil killed my friend."

Running-bird pulled Peter aside and confronted the enraged warrior. The wind picked up, the sky grew dark, and the rain could be heard racing toward them.

"There is *no* she-devil in our village," Running-bird said.

"Woman, you are her mother…" Onasakenrat started to say then suddenly felt his throat tighten. Running-bird's eyes spat fire. He gagged then tried to clear his throat. "And …the she-dev … with the eyes…"

His throat burned, the wind made his eyes tighten.

"Look into my eyes," Running-bird demanded. "Open wide, Mohegan."

Onasakenrat was breathing heavily, he tried to talk but nothing came. The others stood and stared, some stepped back in fear.

"How could I conceive a child with silver eyes?" She continued. "Mine are not so."

Onasakenrat stepped back and caught his breath.

"It was her father who had them," he struggled to say. Then suddenly wishing he had not.

"*Her father!*" Running-bird said loud enough for all to hear. She turned to the others. "Did you hear what he said?"

Onasakenrat eyes darted from one to another. Angered faces greeted them.

"You knew him, then?" she continued. "The mighty Samuel!"

Onasakenrat recoiled. Running-bird took a step closer, bringing her face within inches of his.

"Who are you? Who is it that haunts you?" She asked, carefully now. "I see deep into you and I know what you have done."

"*Silence woman!*"

"Do you not want the others to know the truth?"

Onasakenrat lunged at her, but was abruptly restrained by a soldier. Several of the Mohegan braves moved closer to protect their leader; their anger radiating in the air.

"Let her speak," the sergeant said. "I want to hear this."

"I am a seer," Running-bird said. "And so, if the great sachem of the Mohegans were to reveal to us who it is that haunts him and why he cannot breathe now, then I can tell you who *he* really is."

"What is this?" Onasakenrat asked, struggling to clear this throat.

"You have a vendetta against our people, don't you?"

"*Only against you, witch!*"

The sky lite up with fire, a tree was split in two not far away, and huge crack of thunder followed. Many fell to the ground. Onasakenrat shook off the soldier that was restraining him and thrust his knife at Running-bird. Peter saw it coming and pushed her aside, she fell to the ground hard, as Peter filled the space she was occupying. The blade flashed toward him. He tried to deflect it, but the strong hand that held it kept it on its course. The knife penetrated Peter's side.

A cry went out from a villager and several others gasped. Peter clung to Onasakenrat's hand, trying to keep the blade from going deeper. The Mohegan was not deterred, and thrust it in with a strong twist of his large hand. Peter crumbled to the ground, blood flowing freely over him and Onasakenrat.

Onasakenrat withdrew his knife, wiping the blood off on his leathers. Running-bird sat up and crawled over to Peter.

"*Kill them all!*" Onasakenrat cried out. He rushed forward raising his long knife aiming to sink it in Running-bird's back. While his arm was held high, a whooshing sound filled the air as a large clam shell collided with his hand and knife. The blade flew aside. Onasakenrat doubled over grimacing in pain.

Little-grey-feather, dressed as a warrior, was standing on a rocky outcrop above all of them. She had a bow draped over one shoulder, a quiver of arrows on her back, and a long knife in one hand.

"*Onasakenrat!*" She called out. "*The next time I will not miss. I was aiming for your throat.*"

The Mohegans and English soldiers look on in awe.

"*It's the witch,*" Onasakenrat screamed. "*Seize her!*"

The Mohegans and English soldiers raced up the hill to where Little-grey-feather had been. Onasakenrat and the sergeant remained behind.

"It is time to go," the sergeant said. "You have killed a Puritan. That is enough for one day."

"I am not finished with you," Onasakenrat said to Running-bird. With that he turned and left holding his bleeding hand.

Running-bird pulled Peter toward her. Others gathered around and tried to lend support but they quickly realized it was hopeless.

"*Peter!*"

Peter's eyes dimmed. His pain was total. Yet, he did not cry out. He took it as it came. He focused on being strong and he knew that at this moment, in front of his family and friends, it meant everything to be strong.

"Peter... oh my handsome, Peter," Running-bird said.

Peter's son broke free and ran to them. He fell on his father and wrapped his arms around him, crying aloud. Peter reached out fighting through the pain. He closed his eyes. Images flashed about in his mind. He saw his son's face for an instant; then all went black.

Images from his past suddenly flew at him from all sides. His vision was circular – he could see in all directions at the same time. He saw Anne the day he first met her; she was showing her innocent, sweet smile. He saw old Will Smith and heard him speaking in his good-natured slang. Peter then realized that the old man had loved him like a son. And then he saw the foaming blue sea, white winged ships slicing across the briny swells. His days on the water made him feel invincible. It was his escape, and it was a place for being free. Then, he heard Captain Gallop speak to him. Peter replied, *Have I succeeded after all, Captain?* But the Captain disappeared. Running-bird would know. She would tell him. If only he could hear her. Oh, just to hear her sweet voice one more time. Suddenly, the images accelerated. There were too many, and they were obscured in overlap. The pain in his side surged, bringing him back to earth.

"Peter," Running-bird said softly, her lips within a blade of grass to his ear. "You have succeeded. I can see it in the faces that stand now before me."

Peter's eyes opened - glassy but knowing.

"My Love," she whispered, "I will be with you always."

Peter looked upon her. Her beautiful almond shaped eyes were all the heaven he would need. With his last gasp, Peter held her hand tightly.

"They cannot separate us," he managed to say.

"You have saved me," she said - tears rolled down her cheek.

"No... my love...it is you... it is you who saved me."

CHAPTER 27 – The Beginning

*   *   *

The bark slipped quietly toward Fisher Island on a dead calm sea in the heart of the Devil's Belt. It was a grey day, and fog devils drifted all around them. The mud-dark waters showed barely a ripple on its silky surface. An order was given to drop the anchor, t slid into the water with nary a sound. A small boat was lowered with all the care and stealth so as not to be heard for miles. Three armed men boarded the boat with as little noise as possible. One man took the oars at the center, and the other two took positions at either end. The oar mounts were covered with a woolen fabric, and the soldiers wore no armor.

Up on the main deck of the bark, two men of rank watched them depart.

"I don't like this," the navigator said.

"Neither do I," the captain said. "But, Thomas has the best eyes of us all, and Henry is our best fighter. They will be fine."

"It isn't them I am worried about," the navigator said, turning to his captain. The captain showed a sudden look of surprise and concern. In unison they turned slowly around scanning the deck for an intruder.

"Let us prepare to depart then," the captain said, "Just in case."

As the row boat separated from the bark, the oarsman pulled hard in the water with full strokes. He took great care not to make a splash. Thomas sat in the bow and occasionally tapped the oarsman on the shoulder, signaling him to steer to the right or left. The bark rapidly disappeared in the increasing fog. Within minutes, they were all alone. They couldn't see a thing. A grey-white wall encircled them. Thomas stayed true to his heading. After a while, he saw a break in the fog and then spied an outline of black trees and boulders just a short distance before them.

"Stop!" Thomas whispered.

The oarsman steadied both oars in the water and gave a slight pull in the opposite direction.

"What is it?" Henry hissed.

"Rocks, stones - can't land here."

The oarsman didn't need another command and drove the boat back into deeper water.

Once again, they were consumed by the grey-white wall. Thomas directed the oarsman to their left. He changed the heading several times before trying to land. But with each approach, the landing site grew more and more difficult to navigate. Thomas showed his frustration openly.

"Keep trying," Henry ordered.

Thomas thrust this hand out in Henry's direction as if to shut him up. There was no love lost between these two men. They had often come close to a fight over who was the better man on the sea.

They circled back into deeper water.

The next approach proved to be just as futile. There was nothing. The fog-wall suddenly lifted in places, and they could see further out, but there was no island anymore.

"Where are we, now?" the oarsman said, showing signs of tiring.

"The Lord and Thomas only know," Henry said, angrily.

"I will find the way," Thomas said.

"Have you any idea where the bark is?" Henry asked.

Thomas just looked at him. Then he looked at the oarsman and pointed to his right.

"Row there."

"With all due respect, Thomas," the oarsman said, "I could use a break."

"Let me take it," Henry said. They switched positions.

Just as Henry gave his first pull on the oars, Thomas snapped to attention. He leaned over the port side and strained his eyes.

"There!"

The other men looked to where he was pointing.

Through the mist they could make out the shape of a canoe. A lone figure sat in the center. Immediately, they could see that it was a woman who appeared to be naked. Her hair was long and amber in color--it cascaded halfway down her back. Her breasts were firm and pointed. The figure was barely more than a silhouette but it was a shock to their eyes nonetheless.

"It's the witch!" the oarsman said as he scrambled about for his sword.

"Can't be," Thomas said. "This woman looks harmless - quite young and beautiful."

"A goddess, I'd say," Henry added, examining the strange woman. He carefully pulled the oars in.

"Hand me my musket," he said to Thomas.

"What do you plan to do? Your powder is too wet to try a shot."

"Let me worry about that."

"I want to get closer," Thomas said.

The canoe grew dim and the figure aboard seemed to disappear completely.

'Look! She's fading," Henry cried out.

"I did not see her move," Thomas said. "Did either of you see her lift an oar?"

The others didn't answer. Neither of them saw the figure move at all, but they knew she somehow steered the canoe away.

"We all saw it, right?" Thomas asked, nervously.

"Yes, we did," Henry said. "Now stay…"

His words were cut short as something struck him in the back of the head. He lunged forward for a second and then tried to straighten himself.

"What…" the oarsman started to say, but gasped as he saw the blood flow from Henry's head. Henry sat motionless for a second and then collapsed in the center of the boat tipping it slightly. The other two men instinctively drew their swords and looked around. They couldn't see a thing. The boat settled and the silence returned. It was broken by Henry, who moaned disjointedly.

"Let's get out of here," Thomas said, thoroughly unnerved.

The oarsman reached down and grabbed Henry, pulling him away from the center bench. As he stood to change his position, a hissing sound filled the air. An arrow hit him square in the chest. He screamed and fell overboard with a huge splash.

As the oarsman's body disappeared in the murky waters, Thomas was in full panic and prepared himself for the worst. He crouched low in the boat and waited. But nothing came. The minutes seemed like hours as he clung tightly to his sword. With his sharp eyes, he scanned the horizon every which way that he could. He thought to fire a wick and charge one of the muskets, but knew it was hopeless. There was nothing until...

"*English!*"

It was a sweet voice, yet clear in its purpose. Still, it sent a shiver through Thomas's bones. He spun around sharply, but slipped in Henry's blood. His back crashed into the sidewall. He winced in agony but recovered in a flash as his adversary came into view. The canoe floated, as if on a cloud, directly toward the row boat. Still bare-chested and without as much as a movement, she glided forward holding an oar in the water. Just as it was about to collide with his boat, it suddenly turned sharply aside.

The woman was more beautiful than any he had ever seen, a perfect figure with brown silky skin and the face of an angel. She was painted about her face and chest and wore beads in her long amber hair--all done with delicate care adding to her natural beauty. As he looked into her eyes, his momentary delight turned to anger.

"You did this to us!" Thomas exclaimed, his words showing courage.

"There is no danger now," the woman said.

"Look!" he exclaimed, pointing to Henry.

"Fool," she said, looking at Thomas in disgust. "He will die soon." She reached out and grabbed the rail of his boat.

Thomas pinched the corners of his once trusty eyes. He lifted his sword and pointed it at her.

"Don't come any closer!" he exclaimed.

"I do not intend to."

"Was this your work?"

She looked at him, amused at first. Then she saw something in his eyes that piqued her interest. *Could it be?* She was suddenly puzzled. There was only one thing to do with this one.

"Return to your ship," she said.

"I will strike you down first," Thomas said, waving his sword at her.

"I think not."

Circe had concealed a large shell from his view. She waited for him to rise just enough before she spun it into action. The sharpened, spinning disc hit him right on the back of his hand that held the sword. Thomas cried out as his sword flew away, landing with a large splash in the water. He fell backwards and tried to scramble to his feet, but slipped again. He turned toward her then realized that his panic was unnecessary - she made no other move toward him.

As he caught his breath he exclaimed, "You *are* the one!"

"I am whatever you think I am," Circe said. "What I want is for you to go. I want you to take a message to Onasakenrat, sachem of the Wolf Clan. I want you to tell him to stop sending his henchmen to kill me. He is to come alone. Tell him I will give him a fair fight. Tell him that if he does not come, I will destroy his people one by one."

Thomas heard every word, in spite of the pain rifling up his arm. When he felt the blood trickling down into his fingers, he could not look at her any longer. He struggled to stop the bleeding, but to no avail. His breath quickened as the pain continued.

"Let me help you now," Circe said.

Before he could move, she was in the boat with him. She pulled her canoe alongside and secured it. To his surprise, she was virtually naked but for a small breechcloth slung low around her hips. Reaching over into her canoe, she extracted a leather bag. Thomas watched her body move, her breasts dancing around, and for a moment, he thought it was all a dream.

Circe carefully examined his wound. She rinsed it with fresh water that she had in a small hollow gourd. She then placed some green leaves on the gash, then covered it with a piece of silk cloth and secured it with a leather string. Thomas watched her every move. He could smell her body and wanted to touch it in the worst way. He grew dizzy with the paradox of confusion and anticipation. A whiff of her fragrance caused his senses to stir. She felt his reaction, reached out and grabbed his face, placing it against her bosom. She spoke softly to him, but he couldn't understand the words. He felt her warmth and her heart beating rapidly. She lifted his face to hers.

"I...I don't know who you are...or what," Thomas said. "But I have never felt like this."

"I like you," Circe said, smiling. "You remind me of someone."

Thomas frowned.

"Yes, someone who cared for me," she said, "and for my mother. You look like him just a bit. You have his way."

"Is that what saved me?"

"I wasn't going to kill you. Your comrades were the threat. I sensed you were different."

"But…how?"

She fell silent for a long while before continuing.

"I need you to take my message back to the Mohegan sachem called Onasakenrat."

"You *are* the one called Circe."

"Yes."

"But, I was sent to kill you."

"I know."

"Yet, now you care for me."

Circe lowered her face to within inches of his. Thomas gazed upon her silver-green eyes. They weren't so threatening after all, he thought. There was beauty there to behold. Suddenly, she brought her lips to his. When they kissed, he closed his eyes and his pain went away. But as fast as she planted the kiss, she nimbly scampered back into her canoe.

"Woman…I…"

"Deliver my message to the sachem. Tell no one else."

"Yes, I will."

"I like you, Sir."

"But … how can you? I was sent …"

"Be still now, and do what I have told you."

Thomas lifted himself and sat on the center bench. His eyes never left her. She lifted a tiny oar, and before she could strike the water, he grabbed onto the canoe, pulling it close. He lifted Henry's sword and pointed it at her heart.

"I will deliver your message," he said.

Circe looked into his eyes, ignoring the sword. "Why not strike me down? You would be a hero."

Thomas sat motionless, looking back into her eyes, not daring to blink. "I know all about you."

"Is it all evil?"

Thomas paused. He looked her over. "No, I have learned of what has driven you to this."

"Then tell your English brethren to stay away from this island."

"I will. But they will come anyway."

"I am tired of killing. I wish to kill no more. I have just one final task."

Thomas did not want to leave her. His confusion was fading, and all he wanted was just a little more time with her. With confidence he said, "It may take some time to find this sachem."

Circe paused a moment. She examined him carefully. "I know you will succeed."

"For you," he said. "I will … to thank you."

"Do tell your Englishmen to stay away. Tell them that your dead comrades killed me in a fight to the end."

"I cannot guarantee that they will believe me."

"You must try."

"You are not what we thought."

"I am all that you see and know."

"Then count on me to deliver your message."

Circe looked at him deeply. Again, there was something different about this man. Feeling as he felt, she was hard pressed to leave.

"What is your name?" Circe asked, smiling.

"It is Thomas. Thomas Murphy."

"Well, Thomas Murphy, you may come again to my island. I will not kill you."

Thomas smiled broadly. "Thank heavens for that."

"I had no intention of killing you."

"I would like to come back."

"Then do come. I like your kiss."

* * *

One month passes and Circe is anxious. Usually she would have had a visitor, a hunter, someone to come after her in this time frame but none did.

On the next day, she launched her sturdy canoe as evening fell. It was only a forty minute row to the mainland if she struck the water hard and caught the currents correctly. Her face was painted for battle. Her canoe filled with weapons of ruin. Among them, four large shells, sharpened and weighted down with clay.

She made shore just as the moon rose out of the ocean. That was all the light she needed and had planned on. She wore one of the silk garments Peter Wallace had given to Running-bird many years before. He had told her they came from a land called China. They were impractical for Running-bird but Circe wore them with great pleasure. A satchel with a long leather sting draped over her shoulder held the clam shells. A bow slung over the other shoulder and a quiver of arrows on her back. A long knife and hatchet hung from a heavy belt around her waist.

For an hour she made her way through the forest often following the well-known beaten trails. At times she ducked into the brush and ran among the trees when she sensed trouble. Another hour passed and she finally came upon the village of the Wolf Clan. Only a few people milled about. The camp was a shadow of what it once was.

High above an eagle soared in wide circles. It flapped its wings several times to correct its flight. Circe closed her eyes and saw it in her mind.

"Thank you, mother," she whispered.

As she stepped closer to the village she came near a young girl gathering small twigs. She recognized the girl as the daughter of Onasakenrat. Circe extracted her hatchet, stepped lively toward the girl and slammed it into the side of her head.

Circe let out a war cry. The few in the village turned sharply, took one look at her and ran for cover.

"Onasakenrat!" She called out as loud as she could.

Circe grabbed the foot of the slain girl and dragged the body into the center of the village.

A young boy emerged from one of the wigwams. He gaped in awe at what he was seeing. Circe was tall, beautiful, bloodied, and a mystery. Onasakenrat suddenly appeared from another corner and raced to his son. He grabbed the boy and pulled him behind. Circe retrieved her bow and placed an arrow against it. She drew it back pointing it directly at her adversary.

"Why do you show yourself now, witch?" Onasakenrat asked.

"Look at you," she said. "You are nothing."

"I am the grand sachem of the Wolf Clan."

"Your tribe is finished. It is empty. A great leader would not let this come to pass. No one wants to follow you."

"I am…"

Onasakenrat suddenly realized who the dead girl was at Circe's feet. His breathing quickened, his rage flared blood-red.

"I have waited until now," Circe continued, "so that you understand this."

"You've killed my daughter!"

"And I am going to kill your son next. I want you to see this before you die. I want you to know that your line will not continue on this earth."

Onasakenrat drew out his long knife. He stepped toward a cluster of spears and took one, all the while keeping his son behind him. Circe let an arrow fly over his head, but he did not stop. She quickly loaded another one.

"Not my son!" Onasakenrat exclaimed. "You die witch."

He hurled the spear at her as hard as he could throw it. But his momentum took his cover off his son. Circe let fly an arrow striking the boy in the eye. His fragile body spun around and fell to the ground hard. The spear grazed Circe's forearm causing her to drop the bow. Onasakenrat cried out in agony and disgust. He lifted his son hoping for the best but the boy was dead.

"*You are dead, witch!*" he cried out.

They charged toward each other, their long knives held high.

*   *   *

Thomas came to my island a half dozen more times. His first visit was short and direct. He told me about Onasakenrat's death and the dissolving of the Wolf Clan. That was the first and last time he mentioned it. On his second, he stayed a long while. We talked at length about how his wife had died just five years earlier, and we talked about how I came to be. I told him about how my mother took me away to this lonely island to hide me and protect me from harm. I told him how she disappeared one day at her favorite rocky cove on the southeast corner of her island. My half-brother was on the verge of manhood when she went out there. But she never came back and nothing was found of her. However, many have seen her spirit from time to time floating here and there and when you would least expect it.

We walked on the beach many days and talked, and in many sultry evenings until sunset. On his third visit, we made love. Our passion and rhythm were in harmony. It was like nothing either of us had felt before. And mostly, he taught me how to love a man.

Thomas came one last time and took me away with him. With a tear in my eye, I left my wild kingdom island never to return. Before we left New England, we brought the few things I had kept of Peter Wallace and of my mother back to Block Island and buried them near the graves of my people. Their things belonged with them on the island that brought them love and eternal peace. Someday in the future these things may be discovered and their story told once again.

The people of New England believe I am still there, roaming the islands and mainland. I am blamed for all the mysterious deaths and disappearances that still happen there. They claim my mother and I are often seen on Fisher Island and on Block Island, as ghostly apparitions appearing on occasion, to strike fear in their hearts. I have no claim to those places anymore, for I carry a child of my own now. Thomas and I have started anew in a land far to the west. We live in relative peace and with hope for a wonderful future for our children and for their children. My mother, Running-bird, Peter Wallace, Dekanawida, and many others like them have left their mark on the lands around Long Island Sound, and I know it has been for the better.